SILENT DESCENT

Other books by Dick Couch:

SEAL TEAM ONE
PRESSURE POINT

SILENT DESCENT

Dick Couch

G. P. PUTNAM'S SONS
New York

G. P. Putnam's Sons
Publishers Since 1838
200 Madison Avenue
New York, NY 10016

Book design: H. Roberts
Map created by H. Roberts

Published simultaneously in Canada

Library of Congress Cataloging-in-Publication Data
Couch, Dick, date.
Silent descent / by Dick Couch.
p. cm.
ISBN 0-399-13897-8
1. Illegal arms transfers—Russia (Federation)—Kola Peninsula—Fiction. 2. Nuclear submarines—Russia (Federation)—Kola Peninsula—Fiction. 3. Americans—Russia (Federation)—Kola Peninsula—Fiction. 4. Kola Peninsula (Russia)—Fiction.
I. Title.
PS3553.0769S43 1993 93-11038 CIP
813′.54—dc20

Printed in the United States of America
1 2 3 4 5 6 7 8 9 10

In memory of

Sergeant Lee A. Belas, U.S. Army
Private First Class Dustin C. Lamoureux, U.S. Army
Lance Corporal Michael E. Linderman, Jr., USMC
Specialist Fourth Phillip Dean Mobley, U.S. Army

American combat deaths in the Gulf War were surprisingly light considering the scale of operations and number of Americans in theater. But these four young men from Kitsap County, Washington, were among them. I didn't know three of these soldiers, but Dean Mobley was my neighbor. The last time I recall talking to Dean was when I hollered at him to turn down his radio. I can now only hope the four of them are somewhere together around a tall, cool one, and that the volume is up all the way.

ACKNOWLEDGMENTS

I would like to extend my thanks to Mike Beard, Gary Bethke, Jim Bost, Tom Bringlow, Bob Garniss (the real one), Ted Hontz, Dave Ingrum, Pat Kinsey, Bob Ratcliffe, and Scott Richardson, who among others, provided me with geographic data and technical details. They served as my informal mission-planning staff for this effort. As good staff officers, they know that when the information is correct, the staff should get the credit. On the other hand, if there are errors, it's the fault of the commander—in this case, the author.

North Cape
NORWAY
Vardø
FINLAND
RYBAC
PENINS
Seve
MUR
Kol
RUSSIA
N
0
50
100
STATUTE MILES

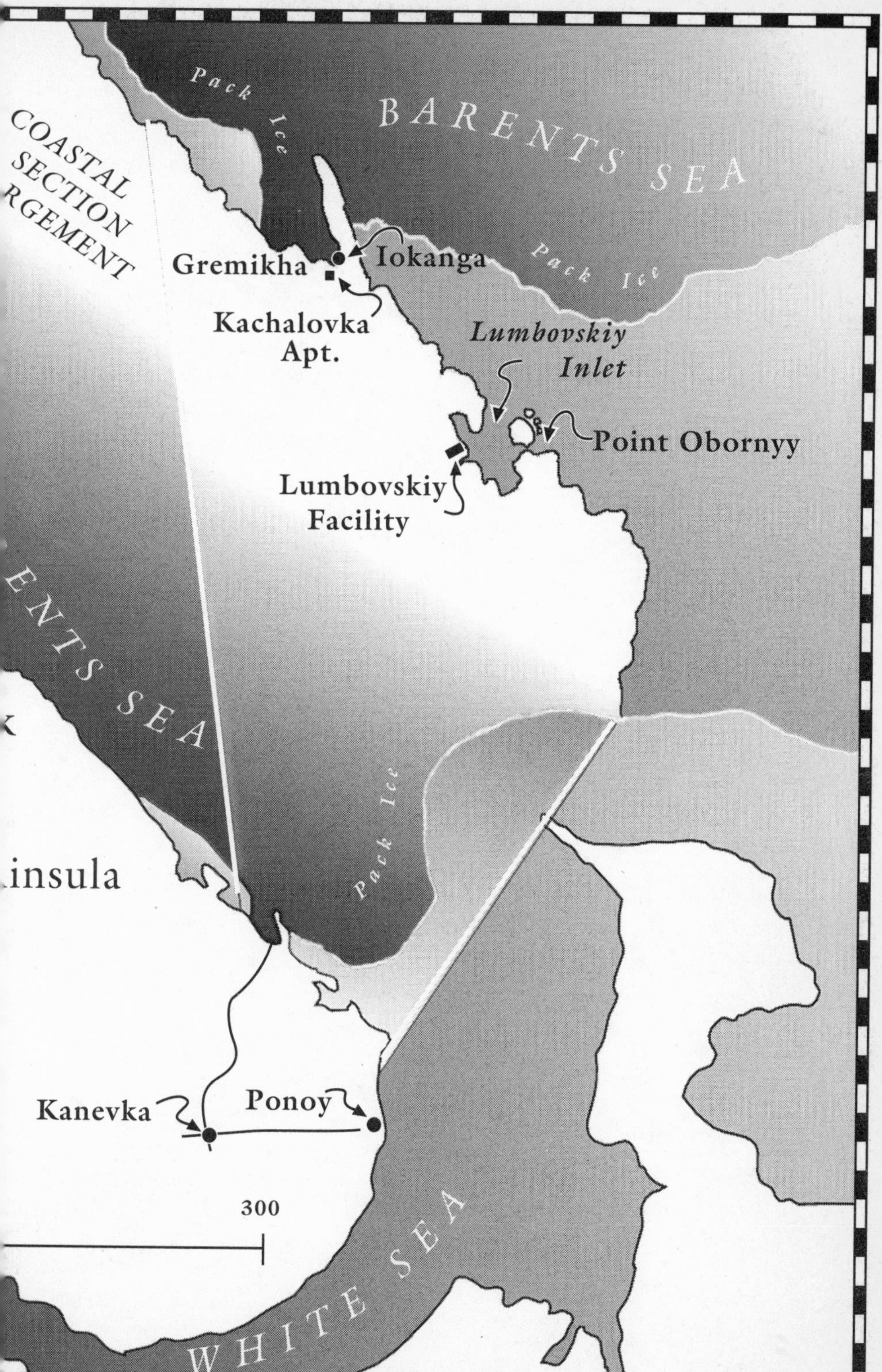

Pack Ice
BARENTS SEA
COASTAL
SECTION
RGEMENT
Gremikha
Iokanga
Pack Ice
Kachalovka
Apt.
Lumbovskiy
Inlet
Point Obornyy
Lumbovskiy
Facility
ENTS SEA
insula
Pack Ice
Kanevka
Ponoy
300
WHITE SEA

When historians finally conduct an autopsy on Soviet communism, they may reach the verdict of death by ecocide. No other great industrial civilization so systematically and so long poisoned its air, land, water and people. None so loudly proclaiming its efforts to improve public health and protect nature so degraded both. And no advanced society faced such a bleak political and economic reckoning with so few resources to invest toward recovery.

Murray Feshbach and Alfred Friendly, Jr.
Ecocide in the U.S.S.R.

It's conceivable that elements of the [former Soviet] military are doing things without instruction.

Gabriel Schoenfeld, Soviet expert,
Center for Strategic and International Studies

PART ONE

Detection

Steve Carter sat on the linoleum of the crowded locker room and laced his sneakers. Actually, sneakers did not accurately describe his new Nike Waffle Racers. Carter was serious about most things, including his running. His T-shirt that proclaimed him a finisher in last year's Boston Marathon was already faded with many washings. The locker room was a utilitarian, Spartan affair, with cold tile floors and the smell of disinfectant. None of that mattered—suburban health-club frills such as carpeted floors and saunas and massage tables would be lost on him. He was there to get in his miles and get back to his desk, though he knew his daily run was an integral and productive part of his day. It was when he did his best thinking.

Carter had a classic runner's build—smooth, tight, long-muscled legs and a small upper torso. His hairline was beginning to recede, and that added prominence to the aggressive hook of his nose, which was in sharp contrast to his soft brown eyes. There was a slight stoop to his shoulders, an indication that the years and the miles were beginning to take a toll on him.

He wound his way up two flights of stairs and down a brightly lit corridor to the heavy glass double doors. A uniformed guard checked the laminated badge he wore on a chain around his neck and waved him past. Aside from a color photo and his employee number, the badge carried several ciphers that permitted Carter access to sensitive information and admission to restricted portions of the building. He was again checked at the traffic gate before he proceeded along the access road to Dolly Madison Parkway. Five minutes later he was on the jogging trail between the George Washington Parkway and the Potomac. He brought his speed up to a comfortable six-and-a-half-minute-mile pace. On familiar terrain like the Parkway trail, he could run mile after mile and not vary more than a second either way.

Carter was a Senior Analyst with the DDI, or Deputy Directorate for Intelligence, at the CIA's Langley headquarters. He was not a spy in the classical sense, nor was he even considered an agent. He stole no enemy secrets, he didn't run agents into denied areas, and he didn't deal with the massive array of technical collection apparatus or satellite imagery that had become such a large part of the national intelligence effort. He hadn't George Smiley's talent for intellectual manipulation or the dash of a James Bond. In fact, he was one of a dying breed of analysts who focused exclusively on the military capabilities of the republics of the former Soviet Union. Ninety-five percent of his time was spent on the Russian Republic, which alone now had the strategic nuclear weapons and delivery systems to threaten the West. The numbers of warheads and missiles were shrinking, but they were still counted in the thousands. The exact number of active warheads and launchers was of specific concern to Carter. And just because the Russian nukes were largely confined to a single warhead per missile, they were still incredibly large and dirty thermonuclear warheads.

The Agency, along with the U.S. military, was in a state of flux. Assets and talent were shifting to anticipated threats in the Third World and to the Mideast. Many of the cold warriors had retired, and the paramilitary and covert activities had been handed off to the military. Those who had once worked to develop an extensive intelligence product on the Warsaw Pact nations were gone. Many analysts of the Directorate of Intelligence were being shifted to economic intelligence, a business Carter considered boring after all these years of working against the threat of nuclear annihilation. In the words of the new Director, they were becoming a kinder and gentler intelligence service. The DDI's Soviet Division—the official title was now the Russian and Federated Republics Division, but the old name still stuck—was still very active, although it was less than half the size it was five years ago.

Carter was with the Intentions Branch of the Soviet Division. The Branch's most recent charter was a fifty-page document that detailed their responsibilities for monitoring the decline of Soviet military power. Carter had reduced the bureaucratic text to three questions that were now printed on a single computer sheet in dot-matrix script and tacked to the wall over his desk.

1. *What can they do?*
2. *If they can't do it now, how long will it take them to regain the capability to do it?*
3. *Who are those guys?*

It was analysts like Carter and the Directorate's superb computer-modeling capability that had generated accurate and highly significant data in answer to the second question. Their projections showed that if the hard-liners took control of Russia with the intent of reviving the Soviet Union as a superpower, it would take them fifteen years to regain the conventional military infrastructure they possessed in 1990. Senior U.S. military officers had passionately and unsuccessfully challenged these findings. The facts were there: it was clearly more cost-effective for America to drastically reduce force levels and rearm in the unlikely event of a resurgent Russian military threat. Strategically, Russia was still dangerous and would be for several years, but their economy had made them incapable of sustained conventional military action.

Carter pounded smoothly along the scenic trail toward Key Bridge, off in his own world of computer projections and weapons-degradation estimates. Intelligence analysts were a curious lot. They drank tea rather than coffee, listened to National Public Radio, and carefully read *The New York Times.* They drove Volvos and were active in the PTA, and they were invariably good at crossword puzzles and Trivial Pursuit. Carter had been recruited by the Agency fifteen years ago during his senior year at Brigham Young. After a year at Stanford to pick up a master's in economics, he had quietly settled his family in the Virginia suburbs and worked diligently to predict the political, military, and economic intentions of the Soviet Union. He often referred to intelligence analysts like himself as nerds with a strategic mission.

During the past few months, he had begun to focus on some trends that simply didn't make sense. In the late 1980s, Soviet military forces had been organized into regional commands for combined-arms, theater-specific operations. These designated Theater of Military Operations, or TMOs, united army, naval, and air assets under single unified commands, much like the organization of the U.S. armed forces under the theater CINCs, or commander in chiefs. Both nations had prepared in much the same way for the conduct of joint-service military operations in a particular theater. With the dissolution of the Soviet Union, the Russian military had abandoned the TMO concept, along with their plans for offensive military operations, and organized their forces into regional military districts. Carter had developed a computer model that reflected the individual military readiness of the Western, Southwestern, Southern, Far Eastern, and Northern Military Districts. The model tracked the material condition of equipment, combat readiness of personnel, logistic sustainability, and command-and-control capabilities of each district. The program was specifically designed around those forces retained by the Russian Republic, but had been modified to reflect the combat capabilities of forces in Ukraine, Belarus, and Kazakhstan. Since confederation, Carter had been able to track and document an exponential decline in the overall level of combat readiness in the Russian military. Each district, faced with lack of funds and spare parts and a disintegrating economic infrastructure, had experienced a uniform deterioration in military effectiveness.

All of them but the Northern Military District. This district, with its headquarters on the strategic Kola Peninsula and its naval units sequestered in the White Sea or berthed in the port of Murmansk, had become more resistant to the decay commonly found in other military districts. For several years, the Northern District had declined in accordance with the computer projections, but the decadence had ceased to follow the trend about six months ago. The decline, at least in some of the northern forces, had ceased altogether. *There's a pattern developing that should explain this,* thought Carter. *There has to be a pattern, and I have to find out what it is.* Within sight of Georgetown, he turned back north, allowing the endorphins to massage his thoughts as he once more reviewed the data.

It was in the shower after his run that an idea had come to him. He quickly dressed and hurried to his computer terminal. After a phone call to Lloyd's of London, he hurried upstairs to see a colleague in the Domestic Collection Branch. Then, for several days, he pored over data and made a general pest of himself with the satellite-imaging people.

"Got a minute, Charles?"

"By all means, Steve, come on in. Dolly, hold my calls," which meant don't interrupt me unless it's someone more important than Steve Carter. He motioned Carter to follow him into his office, which was adorned with several pictures of its occupant with past DCIs. "Have a seat. How're Sharon and the kids?"

Carter had a sheaf of papers under one arm and a spiral notebook in his free hand. He almost set the papers on a corner of the desk near the chair, but didn't want to commingle them with the loosely arranged piles of intelligence summaries, bulletins, and Agency directives that covered the top of his branch chief's desk. "They're just fine, and thanks for asking. I wanted to talk to you about . . ."

"How many kids you have now, four?"

"Five—look, I've been talking with the verification guys over at NSA and—"

"Five! Good Lord, man, you can't feed that many mouths on a staff salary. I'll bet you must be run by one of the more generous case officers at Moscow Center." Grey chuckled at his own joke and dropped his voice to a whisper, "Just don't let them pay you in rubles." Charles Grey III was a portly, foppish man and an Amherst graduate who occasionally wore white socks and loafers with his three-piece Brooks Brothers suits. Like many career agency staffers, he was independently wealthy and not about to allow the Cold War to fade quietly away.

Grey was born about ten years too late to be an OSS hand, but as he approached retirement, he liked to think of himself as one of Wild Bill Donovan's original recruits to the Office of Strategic Services, the forerunner of the CIA. He was a veteran anti-Communist and shared an old-school skepticism of the Russians. It was a legacy of his generation of spies, but it was not without basis. The espionage business had supplied him with vivid examples of the KGB's talent for duplicity and brutality—lessons taught in terms of agents' lives. The KGB might no longer exist, but how much had really changed? For him, communism was not dead—just in remission, or worse yet, inside a Trojan horse.

He began to inquire about the ages of the kids when Carter cut him off. "Look, Charles—Sharon's fine, the kids are fine, and I don't think Moscow Center has the budget to support a mole in the DDI these days. I need to run something past you—Ivan's not doing what he should be doing. It may be nothing, or it could be something rather significant."

Grey often played the role of a pompous academician, but he was also a solid intelligence professional. He understood that a good FI analyst had to be very smart and have good instincts as well. Grey knew Carter had both. He rocked back in the leather swivel and hung one leg on the corner of the desk as he waved for Carter to continue.

"You know that our projections on the degradation of Russian military capabilities have been pretty accurate." Grey nodded. Indeed, it had been a feather in his cap that the work of his branch had provided such a strong input to the national intelligence estimate. The administration had based its disarmament program largely on this product. "Within the Russian military districts, the allocation of diminishing resources would sometimes favor one branch of the service or another, but most of the time, the Russian Army has fared better than the Navy or Air Force. You also know we've recently documented that the Northern District has somehow been able to dramatically retard the rate of military decline."

"The Northern District?" Grey was not a detail person.

"The Northern Military District—the army units on the Kola Peninsula and what's left of the Northern Banner Fleet in the White Sea. There are also some naval air and air force squadrons up there. And it's where the Russians store the greatest number of their tactical nuclear weapons. The resurgence in military capability on the Kola started to show up in our program about six months ago. Coinciding with these anomalies, the Lloyd's Register began to show a significant increase in deliveries of grain to Murmansk. The grain is from Argentina and the ships of Liberian registration, but they're owned or can be traced to Brazilian shipping companies or Brazilian shell corporations. We've also identified unusual quantities of machine tools and electronic components that are manifested for delivery to Murmansk. I just checked with Domestic Collection. Western travelers and businessmen have repeatedly been denied all access to the Kola and Murmansk, and it's been increasingly difficult for them to get into Archangel. Our British liaison with MI-5 confirms this."

The Domestic Collection Branch was responsible for the information-gathering activities of American citizens who traveled abroad or conducted business overseas. It was a program that carefully debriefed travelers and corporate employees who had access to areas of special interest around the world.

"Just what are you hinting at, Steve?"

Christ, thought Carter. *Do I have to draw him a picture?* "First of all, whoever's in charge up there has found some way to motivate his military forces, which means he's able to feed and perhaps even pay his troops. He's also been able to maintain at least some of his hardware. Access to the Kola and the surrounding area has been severely restricted. Grain is being delivered with some sort of a Brazilian connection, and Brazil, as we know . . ."

"Has one of the more progressive international arms operations." Grey was now seated squarely at his desk, elbows resting on his blotter.

"Exactly. And we know that neither the Brazilians nor the Argentineans are in a position to extend credit unless there's a good reason for it, or a third party is guaranteeing payment. Charles, I think there's a real possibility that the Ruskies are going into the business of selling nukes, if they haven't done so already. That guy in the Northern District needs hard currency to keep his forces intact—at least to feed them and maintain a stable level of combat readiness." Carter had used the term "Ruskies" on purpose. It was a favorite of the old guard.

"Really? Couldn't they just be trading conventional arms for grain?"

"Maybe some of their good stuff, like the newer SA-14 shoulder-fired missiles, but the Brazilians don't really want to handle Russian conventional hardware—they have their own arms industry to protect and promote. If the Red Army on the Kola is selling conventional arms, it would be easy enough for the Third World to buy direct. No, I think there's nuclear weapons involved."

"Can we verify this?"

"Perhaps. I need your help with some specific tasking at the National Reconnaissance Office." It was no small request, for the NRO was an independent, supersecret, and very turfy component of the national collection effort.

"I don't know about that," replied Grey. Access to the NRO meant going up through the Director, and he was clearly reluctant to put himself in a position to step on some important toes.

"Then get me a liaison contact," said Carter smoothly. "If I'm right, they'll need our help on the assessment side, and they're sure to be grateful if we call it to their attention. Hey, Charles—everybody's looking for work these days."

Grey pondered this a moment, then reached for the telephone.

* * *

General Dmitri Borzov arrived at the headquarters complex at exactly 6:30 A.M. on Monday morning, November 22. The single guard at the entrance saluted and jumped to open the door as he mounted the steps. He walked the mile and a half from his quarters each morning, allowing twenty-five minutes to cover the distance. In the old days, Zil limousines could be seen lined up at the headquarters between 7:30 and 8:00 depositing senior officers. As the commander of the Northern Military District, he still rated a limo, but his walking to work sent a message to other senior officers on the District headquarters staff. The headquarters was located in Severomorsk, fifteen miles north of Murmansk and twenty miles from the Barents Sea. For most of the year it was either cold or wet or dark, or a combination of the three. Since Borzov's arrival, it was not an uncommon sight to see senior colonels and generals trudging through the snow or riding the bus.

Borzov collected the overnight message traffic from the communications center and made his way to his office on the fifth floor of the headquarters complex. There was a small elevator reserved for the private use of general officers. Borzov made it a point to use the stairs, and now no one rode the elevator.

"Good morning, General."

"Good morning, Major Likhvonin. Quiet evening?" Borzov took the morning report from Likhvonin and walked briskly into his office with the staff duty officer in his wake.

"Yes, sir. A backfire bomber from the Naval Air Command was on routine patrol and made an emergency landing at Umbozero South. It turns out there was a malfunction in a fire-warning indicator. The aircraft is now on its way back to its home field."

"Very well." Borzov shrugged off his greatcoat and draped it around a sturdy wooden hanger fixed to a peg on the wall. He carefully placed his gloves in the round combination cap and set them on the shelf over the coat. The District Commander stood just over six feet. His broad shoulders and the uniform saved him from a lean appearance, for he was uncharacteristically thin for a Russian. His short blond hair, which was remarkably thick, and wide-set clear blue eyes afforded him something of a Nordic appearance. A jagged scar on his cheek did little to diminish his handsome features. He wore a hearing aid in his left ear, an impairment resulting from a *mujahidin* grenade whose shrapnel had also been responsible for the scar. He laid the report on his desk top and sat down.

"Stand at ease, Major, and continue." Borzov would read the overnight report and forces-status summary carefully, but he liked a short personal briefing before he did. He also knew it kept his duty officers sharp and allowed him a few moments on a rotating basis with the more junior members of his staff. Occasionally he would ask that his morning briefing be given by one of the senior enlisted men in the duty section.

"There are three combatants and two auxiliary vessels underway at this time. Two Udeloy-class destroyers are conducting sonar calibration and training with an Akula-class submarine northeast of Kaldin Island, and the fleet oiler *Kushva* is underway for Archangel for scheduled repairs. She is following the icebreaker *Kapitan Danilkin,* which is escorting two merchant ships into the White Sea. There's also a buoy tender conducting routine maintenance of the sonobuoy barrier off the Rybachiy Peninsula. Two battalions of infantry from the 122nd Motor Rifle Division are still in the field under arctic survival conditions at the central Kola training area. There are also three companies of heavy artillery exercising on the range south of Camp Zukov. Five naval air and three air force sorties are planned for today, all reconnaissance aircraft on training and air-crew familiarization missions. And Admiral Zaitsev would like to see you today at your earliest convenience."

"Understood. What is the nature of the artillery exercise?"

"They will be firing 152mm self-propelled artillery with minimum rounds per tube for sighting and calibration checks. Stocks are being drawn at random storage facilities to verify ammunition suitability. As the General is aware, there have been some quality-control problems with existing artillery stocks."

Borzov nodded—he was painfully aware of it. Two weeks ago a faulty artillery round had exploded and killed an entire gun crew. Borzov considered the Major's report a moment in thoughtful silence. "How is the new boy?"

"Sir?"

"Your new baby. I understand your wife presented you with a son last week."

"Why—uh yes, sir, she did," stammered Likhvonin. "Both Yelena and the baby are doing well, thank you, sir."

"Excellent. Take good care of them, Major. These are difficult times for all of us, but sometimes it is most difficult for our families, eh?" Borzov got to his feet. "Good report. Tell the Admiral that I will see him at 7:10. That will be all."

The Major came to attention and saluted. He executed a precise about-face and marched out of the office. Borzov smiled grimly as he watched him leave. *The young officers! How will they cope with the mess we've handed them? They've taken the oath—sworn to protect the motherland, but what have we left them to protect? The Union is gone and the Republic is on her knees—tired, sick, and old.*

Borzov sat down behind the desk and looked around the rich, mahogany-walled office. The ornate cornices and superbly crafted molding somehow managed to resist the contamination of the worn, contemporary furnishings. Since the building predated electricity, there was no central fixture in the ceiling, and the room was lighted by several floor and table lamps scattered about. Unlike the walls in the office of a Western general officer, the room was not littered by plaques and photos from previous duty stations. His eyes found the only trophy he permitted himself, a present from his SPETSNAZ regiment in Afghanistan. It was an American Stinger-missile launcher mounted on a hand-carved plank. One of his platoons had scaled what the *mujahidin* had thought an unclimbable rock face and surprised the rebels in their base camp. The commando assault from above followed by a coordinated attack in battalion strength had wiped out two hundred of the devils, and captured several crates of the deadly missiles. *God damn the Americans and their technology!* He remembered that first day when they lost six Mi-8 helicopters to the Stingers—he knew then that it was over. There had been a chance if the government had moved quickly and massively to attack the rebel supply bases in Turkey and Pakistan through which the missiles were delivered. But they lacked the political will, and so the men in the field endured five years of bitter, bloody frustration. Before Afghanistan, he had often wondered how the Americans, their forces so well trained and equipped, could have been routed in Southeast Asia by such an inferior enemy. Now he knew.

"General Borzov . . ." The intercom issued a guttural hiss that squelched the rest of the transmission. Borzov smacked the side of the speaker as a drill instructor might slap a draftee for a parade-ground infraction. *Another technical marvel from the great socialist experiment!* He punched the transmit button.

"Would you please repeat that, Sergeant."

"Yes, sir. Admiral Zaitsev is here to see you."

"Understood. Ask him to have a seat—I'll be with him in a moment."

The Sergeant acknowledged and Borzov scanned through the classified message traffic on his desk, scribbling a directive on one and a question on another. He then placed them in his out-box, from which they would be routed to his chief staff officer. Borzov rose from the desk and began to quietly pace the room. Zaitsev had been an unexpected ally in his goal to preserve the integrity of their forces and to serve the *Rodina* in these terrible times. Since the fall of the Union, Borzov had found that senior members of the officer corps acted in two ways—either they used their position and power in an attempt to guarantee their privileged status, or they accepted the new order and worked for the good of their service. Many of the sycophants and politicos had immediately scurried off to Moscow to salvage what they could of their spoils. Borzov mercilessly purged from his command the bootlickers who remained. The task had been easier than expected. Those senior officers who owed their position to political connections in Moscow had those ties swept aside by the democratic movement. In the old days, such officers would have been untouchable, but not now. For the most part, Borzov had been proud of the armed forces. They had stood with the people, which was the place of the Red Army. And in his command, the officers suffered along with their men. *The changes had to come—we all knew that,* he thought, *but would we have allowed the change if we had known how painful it would be?*

"Sergeant, show the Admiral in and bring us a pot of tea."

The Admiral stepped into the office and stood at attention, hat in the crook of his arm. Zaitsev was smaller than Borzov, shorter and more finely featured. He was an aristocrat with a proud white Russian lineage, which Borzov would have found tedious except that the man was a patriot and extremely competent. The Admiral had the spare, hard look of a seagoing man, although it had been a decade since he had commanded a man-of-war. He was a submariner and a survivor of the fierce political struggles within the Soviet Navy. Before becoming commander of the Northern Red Banner Fleet he had commanded the Soviet Pacific submarine force. Zaitsev was something of an organizational genius, and it had been he who had worked out the details of selective equipment maintenance and rotational readiness training. He was older than Borzov, and for a brief time before Borzov's appointment, had served as District Commander. Zaitsev was religious when it came to military courtesy, and if he resented serving under a younger man who now held his former position, it did not show.

"Alexandr Ivanovich, please be at ease and come sit down." Borzov led him to two straight-backed conference chairs that bracketed a small, unfinished wooden table. An orderly set the tray on the table and retired. An pungent aroma filled the room as Borzov poured the sweet, steaming liquid into two porcelain mugs from a tarnished metal pot. Zaitsev sipped the tea out of courtesy. It was a brew that was more suited to the harsh mountains of the Hindu Kush than a naval mess. "Tell me, my friend," continued Borzov, "how are things at fleet headquarters?"

"Difficult, but we do what we can. I've had to take another submarine out of service. It was either a Yankee or a Sierra. I prefer not to give up another Oscar unless it's unavoidable, so the Yankee is being deactivated. I've given instructions for the missiles and torpedoes to be offloaded and transferred to the central naval storage facility. Naturally, it will be done at night under the standard clandestine procedures." Zaitsev's voice was strained, and it was as close to a show of emotion as Borzov had ever seen in him. He looked at the old seaman carefully. As if sensing Borzov's concern, he continued, "The captain of the Yankee was the son of an old family friend. It was not pleasant having to relieve him of his command."

"If I recall, we have two Yankee-class ballistic submarines still operational, do we not?"

"We do," replied the Admiral, "but the other boat is ably commanded and is a newer construction."

Borzov nodded his approval. For Zaitsev, as for them all, it had been a long season of difficult choices—one that showed no signs of coming to an end.

Funding for the Russian military was now less than forty percent of what it had been before the dissolution of the Soviet Union. Some military districts cut personnel or tried to run their men and machines on reduced stocks of food and spare parts. With Zaitsev's help, as the navy had the highest equipment-to-manpower costs, they had deactivated or mothballed seventy-five percent of their ships, aircraft, tanks, BTRs, and other equipment. Personnel cuts had run no deeper than fifteen percent, and military pay was sharply reduced, with officers, especially senior officers, the most severely affected. As a result, the Northern Military District had two fully operational squadrons of aircraft, one naval air reconnaissance squadron and one tactical fighter squadron. The navy maintained one surface-action group with support vessels and six nuclear attack submarines. He could, in time, put a large army in the field, but only one motor-rifle division was kept at operational readiness. Several military security detachments were also kept at pre-federation strength, as well as one SPETSNAZ brigade.

When practical, personnel were rotated through the operational components, but this policy of rotation was not allowed to affect the combat readiness of the units. Those selected forces that remained operational were as capable—or more capable—as ever. The large number of military personnel that were without training funds or equipment were not allowed to be idle. Civil affairs programs and local assistance projects in the areas surrounding Murmansk and Archangel were developed to absorb this manpower glut. So far the strategy seemed to be working. The reduced forces remained at a high state of readiness, and at least from the Northern District, there were no large numbers of soldiers and sailors being released into a faltering economy with too few jobs. So long as he tended to his own, Borzov calculated there would be no serious objection from Moscow.

"I wish it were not this way," continued Borzov, "or I had more resources to allocate to the support of your naval units, but that is not the case."

Zaitsev nodded solemnly. "Do you see any relief in the foreseeable future?"

"Not from Moscow or the general staff. I'm afraid their problems go far deeper than ours."

"And the special project?" Zaitsev did not meet his eye, for it was a business of which he only partially approved.

"It is going well," replied Borzov, "but realistically it can only sustain us at these levels."

"I see." Zaitsev sighed imperceptibly and rose to leave. "Thank you for your time, General. We'll continue to do the best we can with what is available."

"Tell me, Alexandr," Borzov said as he walked him to the door, "what would our fathers have done in this situation?" Both of their fathers had served in Red Army during the Great Patriotic War and both had risen to senior field-command rank. And both were exiled and eventually killed by Stalin in the purges that followed the war. They had been a part of the victorious march across the eastern front that crushed the Nazis, but they had also seen the prosperity and freedom of the West. Most were not allowed to return home to speak of what they had seen.

"I'd like to think they would be doing what we are doing now."

"So do I." The two men shook hands and Borzov beckoned to his chief staff officer, who was waiting in the outer office.

Armand Grummell stood beside an easel that held a map of northwestern Russia and the Baltics. He had estimated he would need about seven minutes, and he finished within a few seconds of the allotted time. He had not once looked at his notes, and the briefing followed the classified sheets of stapled text lying on the table almost verbatim. Very quickly and succinctly, the Director of Central Intelligence had built a compelling, but circumstantial, case that the Russians were selling modified tactical nuclear weapons to the Third World. A great deal of his case was the result of Steve Carter's work. Grummell snapped his telescoping pointer closed, signaling that his brief was concluded. His White House briefings were legendary, and this one was no exception.

"Any questions?"

"You gotta be shitting me, Armand. Hell, I thought we had a deal with those people." The speaker wiped his tired face with both hands and looked down the table to a man wearing a charcoal-gray suit and an inscrutable expression. "That right, Dick?"

"That's correct, Mr. President, but if what Armand and his people at CIA are saying is true, they're violating our agreement."

Secretary of State Richard Noffsinger was something of a novelty in his position—a career professional. President Bennett had broken with tradition and appointed a seasoned and highly respected Foreign Service Officer to the top post. As a result the State Department ran like a top.

If Noffsinger was concerned over the new turn of events in Russia, he didn't show it. Years ago, the notion that the Russians had violated an arms accord would have caused a major scramble in the Department, but statecraft as it had developed with the republics of the former Soviet Union was now a series of fluid arrangements. The Russian Bear still had his big claws, but it was generally accepted that he was less inclined to use them.

"Any confirmation on this?" President Bennett swept the table with his eyes. An urbane man sitting next to the President cleared his throat. He had the polished look of a man who took a manicure with his weekly haircut and always dressed for dinner. He met Grummell's eye and nodded. Bennett noted this, and it made him uneasy. He was never comfortable when his National Security Advisor and CIA Director were polite to each other.

"We repositioned a KH-19 reconnaissance satellite to more closely monitor the Kola Peninsula and the approaches to the White Sea. Our information confirms increased activity of sailings into Murmansk of vessels whose registry can be traced to holding companies of Brazilian origin. We know they're delivering grain and some quantities of manufactured goods, but we don't know what, if anything, they're taking away." Morton Keeney straightened his floral silk tie that had no need of adjustment and continued.

"We've concentrated our coverage on the various known nuclear storage sites in the district. This has been no small task, since there are several major depots in the greater Murmansk area and across the Kola. They've decentralized their magazine storage since the accident near Severomorsk in mid-May of 1984 effectively destroyed the entire cruise-missile inventory of the Northern Red Banner Fleet. It's very cold up there, so the satellite IR imagery is quite good. Most facilities show activity slightly above normal, but that's not surprising given the stand-down of some of their strategic rocket forces and the repatriation of warheads from Eastern Europe. The only real inconsistency we've found is at the Lumbovskiy weapons facility located on the coast some two hundred miles southeast of Murmansk. This is a known high-security storage area, but it's quite remote and the activity there is way above normal."

"There's been a lot of talk about unrest in the Russian military," said the President. "Maybe they're just putting the bombs a little farther from the reach of some ambitious colonel."

"Possibly," added Armand Grummell before Keeney could reply. "We've been able to detect concentrations of acid being dumped into the Barents Sea, which would indicate they're converting some of their plutonium weapons into nuclear-reactor fuel. But in spite of all this activity at this facility, we've seen few of the large canisters normally associated with strategic weapons. We think they're handling only tactical nuclear weapons, and repackaging or rebuilding some of them for different applications."

"You have a team working on this?" asked the President, looking down the table to Keeney. In situations like this, Keeney would normally organize a small, ad hoc committee from his national security staff. They would usually hole up in the Executive Office Building, meeting daily in person, or electronically if one or more of them were out of town. They would have no other duties but to work the problem until it was resolved. Though these NSA staffers would have at least some technical background, their primary task was political advice and to serve as a sounding board and validation body for any administration response to the crisis.

"Yes, sir. I've got three of my best people on it. They've only had the information for a day now, but it's apparent the math is all wrong, and that a lot of surplus tactical warheads are finding their way to the Kola for storage or dismantling. Until we can get some additional information, the seaborne pollution Armand talked about seems to be as serious as the imbalance in the warhead count. They're also aware that several scientific exchanges scheduled in Murmansk to deal with industrial-pollution problems and to assist the Russians with the dismantling of their excess nuclear weapons have been canceled. The Kola Peninsula itself has always been a high-security area, but a few military and industrial exchange visits did take place after the democratic movement took hold in 1991. There's been nothing for over a year."

The President rubbed his hands together and frowned, wishing there were more facts available, but he knew it would take time. He had already had to answer congressional allegations that he was fabricating latent Russian military capabilities to delay scheduled defense cuts. *Congress is all for curbing military spending,* thought Bennett, *until the cuts call for the closure of a base or a defense plant in their home district.* He turned back to the men at the table. "Anything else?"

"Yes, sir," replied the man to the President's left. James Garza, Bennett's Secretary of Defense, had a Ross Perot haircut and a direct, matter-of-fact way about him. He seemed to lack the poise and refinement of the others around the table—more like the President himself. "The increased satellite coverage has revealed some subtle changes in their fleet operations. Over the past few months, there has been the usual low level of naval activity, which would normally indicate their ships were putting to sea on a rotating basis to conduct engineering tests in the White Sea. This was our assumption, since sorties made by ships of the same class had different hull numbers. The resolution capabilities of the KH-19 have allowed us to determine that only a small number of their vessels are active, and those that are active are spending almost half their time at sea. From this we've concluded that those few surface combatants that are actively steaming are in a very high state of readiness. What we've not been able to determine is why these warships have been ordered to paint different numbers on their hulls. It seems they want us to think more ships are seaworthy but that fewer are in a high state of combat readiness.

"We always keep an attack submarine in the Barents Sea to track their subs into Murmansk and the White Sea. As you know, submarines have individual signatures, so each Russian boat can be positively identified by the sound it puts into the water. Over the past six months, we have established that there are only seven active Russian boats—three Akulas, two Sierras, and two Yankees. Only the Akulas and the Sierras, both attack submarines, have gone out into the Barents Sea and ventured into the North Atlantic. We haven't seen the rest of the submarine fleet for some time, and since there's an unusually low level of activity in their repair facilities, I have to conclude that only a few boats are combat-ready and that the majority of their undersea fleet is becoming increasingly less capable of open-ocean operations. We're also seeing indications that selected portions of their air force are maintaining a routine training schedule while most of their squadrons are standing down completely."

"Any reason why they'd be doing this?"

"It's a guess on my part, sir, but I'd say this new tempo of operations is being driven by their resources. Unlike our armed forces where sixty percent of our budget is tied to personnel costs, the Russians put most of their money into equipment and upkeep. Someone, probably someone with operational experience, has elected to keep a small percentage of the forces fully combat-ready rather than submit to an overall degradation of the entire command. And the Northern District seems to be doing a better job of it than the rest of the military.

"Thanks, Jim." Bennett again turned to his CIA Director. "So, what's the bottom line?"

"Something very different is going on in the Northern Military District," said Grummell. "The other districts continue to show a steady decline in training and combat capability. The Northern District seems to have chosen to keep selected military units at a preconfederation condition of readiness, and let the bulk of their equipment and personnel stagnate. They are feeding and paying their troops, which is no small feat in Russia today. They also seem to have developed a line of credit that allows them to purchase grain and other staples. And from all indications, it would appear they are modifying and selling tactical nuclear weapons to pay for what they need."

"Can we confirm this?"

"We're trying. As you know, we still have an active port-callers program—seamen embarked on merchant ships who call on port cities of interest and report what they see. Those aboard ships putting into Murmansk and even into Archangel say that the crews are either confined to the ship or their movements ashore are restricted to the wharf area. We've also had some reports that the OMVD security forces, the ones garrisoned in the Baltics prior to their independence, are now visible in both cities. Movement of civilians in the Kola has always been restricted. Things loosened up after the breakup of the Union, but now the lid is back down on security."

"Who's in charge up there?" asked the President. This time Grummell looked at his notes.

"Colonel General Dmitri Borzov, fifty-three years old—quite young for a Russian general of senior rank. Good Russian family—his cousin, Valeriy Borzov, was the one-hundred- and two-hundred-meter sprint champ at the '72 Olympics. He was the ranking SPETSNAZ officer during much of the fighting in Afghanistan, and was promoted to the rank of brigadier general at the end of the conflict. He earned political favor and a promotion when, as a unit commander, he refused an order to move his motor-rifle division closer to Moscow during the coup attempt against Gorbachev. He was promoted to colonel general a little over a year ago and appointed commander of the Northern Military District. As a matter of some interest, he relieved Admiral Alexandr Zaitsev, who was serving as interim District Commander, and then retained the Admiral on his staff as his naval-component commander."

"I'd like to see one of our admirals get relieved by an Army four-star and stay on to work for him." The President laughed. "So he's a politician as well as a soldier—anything else?"

"Not much. A check of the files at DIA indicates a superb operational record and a flair for special operations. The two contact reports filed by U.S. Army officers who have met him socially paint him as aloof, competitive, and very cool to Westerners."

"And I assume that we have no human intelligence assets in the area?"

"Yes and no," replied Grummell as he detached the wire-rimmed glasses one ear at a time. "As you know, our best HUMINT source on Soviet and Russian weapons technology is the agent MUSTANG. He's provided us with a few reports since the breakup of the Union, but we know he was transferred on short notice to the Kola some six months ago. Since then he hasn't reported in, and we have no way to initiate contact with him."

"Well, see what you can do. If the Russians are selling nukes, we're going to need hard, reliable information, right, Dick?"

Noffsinger nodded. "If we're thinking of going public or taking it to the U.N., we'll need irrefutable proof."

"I don't suppose we can look for any help from Stozharov?"

"I don't think so," replied Noffsinger. "Any direct confrontation that exposed his control, or lack of it, over the military could be embarrassing. I recommend that we let them know we've noted an increase in merchant traffic from South America into Murmansk. Maybe bring up the nuclear-proliferation issue in a broader sense—ask them if they know anything about nukes in the Third World. Ambassador Simpson is pretty sharp, and I think we can trust him to get the message across in general terms. We also have to consider that Stozharov may not know anything about it. Sometimes our information is better than his."

"Sound reasonable?" President Bennett looked from Noffsinger to Grummell and Keeney. Both shrugged. It sounded reasonable, but if it proved to be the wrong approach, neither wanted to be on record as having endorsed it. "Fair enough," concluded Bennett. "Dick, have Simpson call on Stozharov and see if he can learn something. Mort, I want you to take the lead on this. Keep me informed. It's Tuesday, so let's talk about this again at the end of the week. Thursday's Thanksgiving, so make it Friday."

Keeney remained behind as the others filed out of the Oval Office. Noffsinger glanced at his watch and strode off down the hall. Outside the door, Grummell caught Garza's sleeve.

"Jim, we have no other tested reporting assets in the Kola, and I sense the President will want more than we can deliver through technical collection. MUSTANG is a proven and highly reliable agent, and is probably in a position to provide the exact information we need. I hate to hit you with this cold, but could your people in Florida get a team in there to make contact with him if there's no other way?"

Garza thought for a moment and then spoke cautiously. "I'm sure the problem has been worked by the planners, but more in the context of a conventional war scenario. The Russians have let most things slip, but their security forces are still relatively intact." He looked at Grummell carefully. Both men knew that placing a special operations team on Russian soil would be a most serious undertaking, with the gravest consequences if it went badly. Garza also knew that the CIA Director would not have asked if he had any other way of reestablishing contact with his agent. "Let me check with our people down there and get back to you before our next meeting."

Grummell nodded, and they followed Noffsinger down the hall to the elevator that would take them to the side entrance.

Colonel Viktor Makarov sat in the passenger's seat of the LAZ-469 and observed the guards at the gate as they checked the documents of those entering the grounds of the Lumbovskiy complex. The complex, situated on the Lumbovskiy Inlet, was just over two hundred miles southeast of Murmansk. Makarov was a thick man with heavy, Slavic features and dark eyebrows that stretched almost unbroken across his broad forehead. He had a veined, weathered complexion and a mole that rested unapologetically on his left cheek. The temperature was nearly minus ten degrees, but he wore a black beret instead of the normal fur-lined winter hat of the Russian army. Occasionally, he drew a small flask from within his greatcoat and tipped it to his lips, ignoring the man at the wheel.

It was very dark, and that would change little. Between 10:30 A.M. and 1:30 P.M. there would be a glow from the south and a period of twilight to remind everyone that most of the world would have some sunshine in their day. From mid-November to mid-January, the sun would not break the horizon. The jeep had pulled off the road onto the frozen tundra about fifty meters from the gate. Alongside Makarov sat a nervous Major Alksnis, whose men were responsible for the physical security of the Lumbovskiy complex. It seemed ludicrous to the Major that these elaborate security measures were required at such a remote site; however, Makarov was not a man whose instructions were questioned. Nor was this the first time he had arrived unannounced for one of his surprise inspections of the installation's security.

The Lumbovskiy complex was a series of two-story slab buildings surrounded by two concentric rings of ten-foot chainlink fencing. Between the two layers of chainlink were antipersonnel mines. The sprawl of dirty concrete boxes was bathed in yellow-white, stadium-type lights, and the cold silence was broken only by the distant whine of gas turbines that powered the facility. The buildings were served by a single road and a pair of railroad tracks that connected the facility to the village of Gremikha some thirty miles to the northwest. From there, the tracks wound their way along the coast and finally to Severomorsk, Murmansk, and the Norwegian border. A guard stood in the road and carefully checked the occasional car that approached the gate. A large German shepherd sitting by the guard shack alertly watched the proceedings and huffed clouds of steam into the cold glare of the lights. A bus pulled up to the gate and one of the guards boarded it to inspect the passengers.

"Your guards seem to be rather proficient today, Major. You must have heard that I was coming." The bus pulled away from the gate, leaving a blue diesel cloud in its wake.

"Your visits are always a pleasant surprise, Colonel." Alksnis in fact had been tipped off by a fellow garrison security commander in Olenegorsk that Makarov was in the area. He usually arrived unexpectedly midweek, and the Major had correctly guessed he would show early on Wednesday.

"Really?" said Makarov evenly. "When I was a major in charge of installation security, I used to hate it when the Colonel turned up unannounced. By the way, one of my men was aboard that bus, and I can assure you that his papers were not in order."

"Colonel, I'm quite sure that—"

"Enough, Major. The purpose of my visit is to instruct as well as inspect. I realize this is a remote site and that these hostile conditions would tend to discourage an intruder, but we still have a job to do, eh? Now, I know this is not exactly a Black Sea recreation facility, but there are worse postings than the Kola."

The thought of a security detail at one of the labor camps in eastern Siberia flashed across Alksnis' mind as he sought the proper response. "I understand, Colonel," he said meekly. "Perhaps I should insist on more careful inspection of documents by my guards." It was the proper response, for Makarov had no tolerance for officers who did not take responsibility for the performance of their men.

"Very well," replied Makarov, and Alksnis breathed an inward sigh of relief. The bus had stopped a short distance from the gate and discharged a single passenger, who was now trudging back toward the gate. "Now let's properly introduce your guards to my intruder, and see if we can find out what went wrong."

Major Alksnis started the LAZ and eased along the icy road to the guard post.

The door to Dr. Leonid Zhdanov's office indicated that he was the senior civilian scientist at the Lumbovskiy site. Although this was true, he was also in charge of all operations conducted at the complex. The title of the facility was the Northern Military District Munitions Disposal Site Number Three at Lumbovskiy, and Zhdanov presided over a staff of two hundred, sixty of whom were military personnel. Since it was a military installation, an army officer would normally have been placed in command. Instead, General Borzov had determined that the man who had once so ably managed much of the Soviet Union's nuclear-weapons production would be in charge at Lumbovskiy, even though he was a civilian.

Zhdanov had the disheveled, careless look of a laboratory scientist. But his close-set, pale-blue eyes were both clever and cunning. He was a gifted scientist who discovered early in his academic career that he had a passion and considerable ability for organization and management. He had responded to the challenge at Site Three by assembling the best available talent from the atomic-weapons factories of the former Soviet Union, and had very effectively gone about the task of dismantling nuclear warheads. Under his direction they had also set up a pilot processing facility to convert plutonium into reactor fuel—fuel for domestic consumption and to feed hungry French and Japanese reactors in exchange for hard currency. He had just as efficiently set up a small and highly secure laboratory within the complex that reconfigured some of these warheads into small, serviceable tactical nuclear weapons for use by forces less sophisticated than the Red Army. Zhdanov was going over production schedules with the director of what he called the "special-weapons facility," when the intercom on his desk hissed.

"Doctor, there's a Colonel Makarov here to see you."

Zhdanov slumped back in his chair. *I don't have time for this gorilla,* he thought. The General had made it clear that his authority as director at Lumbovskiy was indisputable—except in the area of security. This was the exclusive domain of Colonel Viktor Makarov and his OMVD thugs. Zhdanov sighed and reached for the intercom.

"Very well, Ludmilla Makutinovna. Tell the Colonel I will be with him in a moment." Zhdanov had just turned back to his scheduling when the door flew open and Makarov filled the entrance. Zhdanov felt a pang of fear. There was something about the OMVD uniform and that dreaded black beret that projected terror and cruelty.

"How nice to see you again, Colonel," he said in an exaggerated show of warmth. "How long has it been—at least two or three days?"

Makarov's eyes twinkled. "I was here exactly ten days ago, Doctor, but I agree with you—it seems like only yesterday. Sorry to barge in like this, but I have other duties to attend to, and I didn't want to leave without paying my respects to the director of the facility." He was talking to Zhdanov, but he was not looking at him.

"I assume, Colonel, that you have met my assistant, Doctor Shebanin?" Katrina Shebanin was a tall, angular woman in her late thirties, with straight brown hair and wide-set, dark eyes. The high cheekbones and a slight gap in her front teeth hinted of her Tartar ancestry. The long white lab coat was open to reveal a colored cotton blouse and pleated tan slacks, but she wore sturdy, white, rubber-soled lab shoes. She was a little too rawboned to be considered pretty by Western standards, but a handsome woman nonetheless. Makarov leered at her.

"Why, yes, Doctor Katrina and I have met before. And how are you this morning, *Doctor?*"

"Very busy," she said coldly. "I have a great deal of work to do—work which Dr. Zhdanov and I were reviewing before we were interrupted."

"I see." Makarov smiled. "With so many of our scientists out looking for employment, it must be reassuring to have such an important and demanding position. Before I leave, I'd like to inspect the physical security of your laboratory, Doctor, and since I can do so only with your authorization, perhaps you could make time in your crowded schedule to accompany me. It shouldn't take more than a half hour."

Shebanin frowned. The prospect of spending even a short while with Makarov was grim. She could have him admitted to the lab in the company of a subordinate, but she knew her presence might keep him from finding a reason to come back. "If the Colonel would be kind enough to wait a few minutes while I conclude my morning meeting with Doctor Zhdanov, I will join you for the inspection."

"Excellent. Doctors." Makarov smiled as he touched his crop to the flared tip of his beret and retreated to the outer office.

"What a pig," spat Shebanin. "I thought his kind were banned when they pulled down the statues of Lenin."

"There's no reason for him to question the security of your project is there?"

"Of course not! The security at my laboratory has been properly implemented and documented, and he knows it."

"I'm sure you're right. You want to go with him now and come back later to work on these figures?"

"No, I don't. This is a good time, and the Colonel can wait until we're finished."

Twenty minutes later, Shebanin swept through the outer office and motioned for Makarov to follow. He rose and smiled cordially, but inside he was seething.

Makarov and Major Alksnis completed their inspection of the special-weapons facility in less than an hour. Since they were not allowed to enter the actual working spaces where the weapons were modified and assembled, they confined their inspection to examining the access lists, personnel check-in/check-out procedures, and the classified nuclear-materials custody records. Everything was in order. Shebanin escorted them from the building to their vehicle.

"You know, Doctor," said Makarov as he hefted himself into the passenger seat, "you might be a little more civil to me. One never knows when a ranking officer in the OMVD might be of service."

She leaned close enough to smell the musty-rancid odor of borscht and vodka on his breath. "Look, Colonel, we both have a job to do here, and I prefer to do mine with as little contact with you as possible, is that understood?"

Makarov hesitated a moment before answering. "Yes, Doctor, that's quite clear." His head snapped around and he nodded sharply to Alksnis. The LAZ's wheels spun as it pulled away from the laboratory building, crabbing sideways in the loose snow before straightening onto the frozen roadway.

Major Brisco read the intelligence report and frowned, occasionally looking up at the Army captain who stood at a relaxed parade rest in front of the desk.

"I believe the Major will find everything is in order, along with a projection of the enhanced rebel capabilities we can reasonably expect from the introduction of the new weapons." Brisco stared at the Captain for a long moment. *Kelly, you are such a prick! You're an arrogant bastard and your work sucks. Now you're in here at 4:00 P.M. with this piece of shit, trying to get me to buy off on it.*

"How many times do I have to tell you?" said Brisco evenly. "You're a reporter, not an analyst. The General doesn't care and the Colonel doesn't care and I sure as hell don't care what you *think* the FNLA are going to do with this shipment of Chinese arms. Just the facts, Kelly, just the facts—number, type, caliber, condition, port of entry, destination, and end user. Let the analysts work up the scenarios and the absorption factors. They may have other information than just this report and can draw better conclusions." *And they're probably a lot smarter than you.* "Now, I want this redone, and this time, I want it done right."

"You mean now? Major, it's the day before Thanksgiving and this is a four-day weekend. I can get on it first thing Monday morning, and have it ready for the nine A.M. staff meeting."

"You've had this information since Monday morning. You could've had a draft report for me yesterday, or this morning at the latest. Now you think I'll roll over because it's quitting time. You're trying to hustle me, Kelly, and I don't like it. Your weekend starts when that report's done, and done to my satisfaction, understood?"

"Jawohl, Fräulein Sturmbannführer." Kelly clicked his heels together and took a step toward the door. There was a strange smirk on his face.

"As you were, Captain!" Brisco got up and walked around the desk past Kelly and closed the door. She was a tall woman, just over five feet ten inches. She then sat on the edge of the desk in front of him with her arms folded. "Captain Kelly, I think it's time you and I had a little chat," she began softly. "And during our chat, I'll be doing the talking and you'll be doing the listening—while you're standing at attention, of course . . . NOW!" Kelly came to a rigid position. Brisco began to pace the room.

"Captain, since you came down here from Fort Bragg last month, your work's been marginal at best, your attitude's shitty, and you have a difficult time taking directions. You seem to think staff work is beneath you. Just because you're an airborne, devil-warrior from the sky doesn't mean you can sit around on your butt all morning drinking coffee, take two hours at the gym over lunch, and start to clean out your in-basket midafternoon. Now, I understand you're here to get your joint-service ticket punched. I also know that you're a fast-track West Pointer and that you play golf with the Colonel every other Wednesday afternoon. Well, you may allow the Colonel two-foot gimmes out on the links, but I run the Colonel's intelligence-production effort. I'm the one who makes him look good to the General. He knows he can get in eighteen holes on a Wednesday afternoon because I'm here taking care of business. You getting all this, Captain?"

"Yes, ma'am, but I just—"

"And so we further understand each other, they say the only way you can hurt a junior combat-arms officer with a staff-tour fitness evaluation is to roll it up and poke him in the eye with it. Don't believe it, Kelly. I write your evaluation, and if you don't get with the program, I'll burn you. You'll have to wear asbestos gloves just to hold it while you read it."

"Major, I don't think that—"

"I don't care what you think." She stopped in front of him, standing closer than would have made him comfortable if she were a man. "Furthermore, I don't care that you're sexist and probably a racist, and that your personal hygiene could be a whole lot better. I only care that your work is accurate and timely, and that your reporting is properly formatted. You starting to get the drift of this conversation, Kelly?"

"Yes, *ma'am!*"

"Excellent—maybe there's hope for you. Now, get your butt out of here, and do your job. I'll expect that report back on my desk within the hour." He stood rooted to the floor, purple with rage. They stared at each other for ten seconds. "Well?"

"Yes, *MA'AM!*" Kelly saluted, and Brisco let him hang there for a moment before she returned it. He did a smart about-face and made for the door.

"And remember," she called after him, "just the facts."

After he was gone, Major Janet Brisco took a pack of Camel straights from her bottom drawer and shook one onto the blotter. She had developed a raspy voice, and the cigarettes probably didn't help. They weren't supposed to smoke in the building, but the Colonel looked the other way, at least in her case. She lit one and brushed an imaginary ash from her uniform blouse, shaking her head wearily. *The boys just keep coming at me,* she thought. When she was a second lieutenant, it was the sergeants. As a captain, it was the lieutenants. Now she had to occasionally put the boots to a captain. It happened less frequently, but it still happened. Kelly really wasn't a bad officer; he just assumed that because she was a woman, she'd clean up the report for him, like she was his secretary or something. Brisco tilted her head back as a perfect smoke ring expanded out over the desk. *I had scholarships to Stanford and Harvard, but oh no, I had to take on the system and go to the Air Force Academy. Talk about one of your basic white, male, military strongholds!*

Brisco had grown up in a subsidized tenement in East St. Louis, but a feisty Granny Brisco had told her she could have anything she wanted if, in Granny B.'s words, she "busted her sweet ass." Janet believed her. And as a black, female national merit scholarship finalist, all the service academies wanted her, but Colorado Springs was the closest to home. It hadn't been easy for her at the Academy or in the service, and the sexism was far more institutionalized than the racism. But times were changing, and on balance, the Air Force had treated her fairly—just so long as she staked out her turf and was prepared to defend it. Her paycheck was the same as her white male counterparts', but she was still a woman in a man's world.

Early on, Brisco had learned the key to success in the military, and it cut through the black-white, man-woman crap. If you're good, really good, at your job—people notice. Once they found she could do the job, they piled on the work and the responsibility. The Air Force, like most big organizations, had its rumor mill, and the word was out that Major Janet Brisco was sharp—that she could cut it. On her last evaluation she was ranked number one of the seven majors working in Special Operations Plans. "A highly intelligent, dedicated, and resourceful field-grade officer," the Colonel had written. ". . . is most highly recommended for accelerated promotion to the rank of lieutenant colonel and for positions of increased responsibility and for command." The evaluation had been signed by the Commanding General. *Command,* Brisco thought, *that's what I really want. I'm the best damned operational planner they've got here, and now I want my own command.*

She stubbed out her cigarette and looked at her watch—4:30. She had an early dinner date with a Tampa physician that evening and tickets to a concert. *Well, I'm not going to miss my date because junior can't get his work done on time.* Brisco carefully placed the garrison cap on her head and checked herself in the mirror on the back of the office door. She ran her thumbs along the inside of her belt to smooth the wrinkles from her slim waist—hat with a slight tilt, gig line straight. There were three rows of decorations above the left pocket of her light-blue service blouse. Among them were two Meritorious Service Medals and several Air Force Commendations medals.

"Captain Kelly," she called as she walked from her office to a series of partitions that formed office cubicles for the junior officers and the senior enlisted men.

"Major?"

"I have to leave now, but I'll be coming in on Friday morning. Put that report on my desk along with a number where you can be reached. You'll be coming in, too, if there's a serious problem with the report. I'll be at my quarters for about forty minutes if you have any questions."

"Yes, *MA'AM.*" Brisco didn't like his tone, but let it pass.

She signed out on the daybook and showed her badge to the enlisted security guard, who knew her by sight.

"G'night, Billy."

"G'night, Major. Y'all have a good weekend." Billy was a tall, redheaded Army PFC, and he missed very little that went on in the office. The boy grinned from ear to ear and pressed the electronic buzzer that allowed Brisco to open the metal cipher-lock door. She returned his smile and allowed it to linger as she heard Captain Kelly furiously pounding the keys of his word processor.

It was Friday morning, and winter had the Russian capital firmly in its grip. The novelty of the first snow was well behind them, and dirty white mounds now choked the city. Sour-faced Muscovites trudged past shops with expensive goods to jobs that paid little. President Mikhail Stozharov sat in his office contemplating his meeting with the American ambassador. These meetings were never comfortable for Stozharov, for the Americans usually asked something of him he could not give. They were scrupulously polite and meticulous in their adherence to protocol, but they knew he played the game with very few strong cards. It's not that they didn't try to understand or empathize with his difficulties, but nothing in the American experience could have prepared them for the kind of problems he dealt with on a daily basis. Even an intelligent and perceptive man like Joseph Simpson failed to entirely understand what was taking place in Russia. The vast economic and political structure in the United States was taken for granted by them, yet it had taken them two centuries to develop it. The Russians had been in the business of political and economic freedom for two years, plagued by the remains of communism hiding like pockets of cancer in the fabric of their society. It would take decades to root out the last vestiges of the old bureaucracy, teach initiative, and to develop a functional market economy. And as President of the Republic, he had very little means at his disposal to advance this process. His secretary opened the door and looked in.

"Sir, the Ambassador is here."

"Very well, Tanya Pavelovna. Please show him in." There was probably some tactical advantage in making him wait a short while, but Stozharov wanted to get it over with.

"Mr. President, good morning. Thank you for seeing me on such short notice." Joe Simpson was the epitome of an American—tall, urbane, successful, and with a practiced courtesy and refined manner that seemed at odds with his rags-to-riches success in the meat-packing business. It was the presence of a man like Simpson, born with little or nothing but born in America, that spoke more clearly about the virtues of a market economy than the mountains of consumer goods turned out by Asian factories for the American shopping malls. Simpson's Russian was passable, but Stozharov preferred English, which he understood and spoke far better than he allowed people to think.

"You are quite welcome. Please, be seated. Would you like tea—coffee perhaps? I think you know my Foreign Minister, Vladimir Solovyov."

"I do, and thank you, but I think I will pass on the tea this morning." His refusal of tea meant he wanted to get right to business. Simpson had hoped to speak with Stozharov alone, but Solovyov's presence had not been unexpected. The Foreign Minister nodded cordially to Simpson while the President retreated behind his desk and seated himself. The President of the Russian Republic was a short, energetic man, of considerable girth with pudgy, busy hands, but he was remarkably nimble for a man of his dimensions. His survival and rise to power following the breakup of the Soviet Union was proof that he was also politically quite agile.

"Please convey to President Bennett my personal regards, Ambassador. Now, how can I be of service?" Stozharov knew Simpson would not have asked for a meeting like this unless there was something of immediate concern to Bennett or that smug bastard, Morton Keeney. Usually Simpson called or met with Solovyov in advance of such a meeting, but he had done neither.

"Mister President, as you know, there is a growing concern on the part of the American people about the environment, and our Congress is calling for a strong resolution that specifically addresses pollution in the Arctic Ocean. In response to this concern President Bennett has taken a special interest in this vital area. Some of our remaining indigenous populations live near Arctic waters. At the request of the scientific community, several of our military satellites were shifted into a polar orbit to study the Arctic Ocean and those bodies of water contiguous to the Arctic Ocean."

"Which bodies of water?" said Stozharov, raising his hand for clarification.

"Those that are adjacent or next to the Arctic Ocean—the Barents Sea, the Kara Sea, and the Laptev Sea."

"I understand," replied Stozharov, motioning for the Ambassador to continue. He was a student of geography and noted that Simpson had neglected to mention American Arctic waters like the Bering Sea and the Beaufort Sea.

"With this increased coverage, we are building a database with which to monitor the effects of pollution in the Arctic Ocean. Mr. President, our satellite coverage has also surfaced an increased level of grain and bulk cargo shipments to Murmansk. Further study by our intelligence community has traced these shipments to Brazilian holding companies with close connections to their arms industry." Simpson paused for effect, adding a measure of gravity and contrition to his voice. He was good at this sort of thing. "My government is concerned that there may be an arms-for-grain exchange taking place, and if that is the case, it is counterproductive to our mutual goals."

There was a moment of silence before it was broken by the Foreign Minister. "Should this arms-for-grain be something of an embarrassment for either of us, like Mr. Reagan's arms-for-hostages arrangement?"

There was a hint of a twinkle in Solovyov's eye. He and Simpson had spent more than a few evenings over vodka or Kentucky bourbon talking politics and world events. Both of their presidents relied considerably on their understanding of the opposition, and the two men formed an important, informal line of communication. In the case of Solovyov, he had served as Foreign Minister since Stozharov came to power and was known to be a close confidant of the President.

"Normally it would not," said Simpson carefully. "However, our intelligence and information services focus on certain groups that traffic in international arms, and in some cases, we have penetrated those groups. Our evidence is circumstantial, but we believe someone is selling nuclear arms. Sir, I am here on behalf of my government to seek assurances that nuclear arms are not being sold by the Russian Republic."

Both Stozharov and Solovyov stared at Simpson. Their faces revealed nothing, but their silence spoke loudly. Solovyov recovered first. "Are you saying that nuclear arms are being shipped out of Murmansk in exchange for grain?"

"Sir, I am suggesting that there has been some unusual activity in the Murmansk area, and we have indications that several heretofore nonnuclear countries may be receiving nuclear weapons. President Bennett has directed me to place this information before you and ask for your assurance that the Russian Republic is not contributing to the proliferation of nuclear weapons."

Stozharov held Simpson's gaze for a moment and then glanced at Solovyov. The Foreign Minister responded with a serious, puzzled look and an imperceptible shrug. Normally, Simpson would have come to him before making such an accusation, but he had clearly acted on specific instructions from his government to go directly to Stozharov. The Russian President sighed and pursed his lips.

"Mr. Ambassador, please convey my concern to your Mr. Bennett regarding these developments. You may also assure him that it is not the policy of this government to distribute, sell, or share nuclear weapons or nuclear-weapons technology under any circumstances. We will continue to abide by our stated goals to reduce our stockpiles of nuclear weapons and to properly and safely dispose of these weapons in accordance with our bilateral agreements."

Stozharov and Simpson again stared at each other across the desk without speaking. The meeting was clearly over, and Stozharov rose, allowing the American ambassador to take his leave.

"I will convey this information at once, and thank you for seeing me on such short notice." Stozharov did not offer his hand or make any attempt to walk Simpson to the door, which had the effect of adding a measure of indignation to his words.

"Mr. President, Mr. Foreign Minister." Simpson inclined his head politely and left without another word.

Stozharov sat down, placing his hands flat on the desk, and exhaled forcefully. "I don't like this, Vladimir.

"Could there be some mistake?"

"Possibly, but it's hard to believe the Americans would make such an accusation unless there was some basis for it. It is not in their interest to do so. We know they have a good intelligence service, and those spy satellites of theirs can count the bricks in the pavement."

"Perhaps," replied Solovyov thoughtfully, "but they must have no real proof of these nuclear weapons' coming from Russia. Otherwise, they would not have sent their ambassador here with such a weak indictment. Kazakhstan would be a more likely source."

"I hope you're right," said Stozharov. "But we have no proof that these weapons are not coming from Russian soil. Colonel General Borzov is a loyal and capable commander, and we know he has brought order and discipline to the Northern Military District. It is hard to conceive of nuclear weapons leaving the port of Murmansk without his knowledge. Let's hope the good General has not stepped over the line. I want you on the next flight to Murmansk to speak with him. Tell Borzov the Americans suspect us—specifically him—of violating an international accord and selling nuclear weapons. Let's see where he stands on this."

Stozharov reached over and pressed the intercom. "Tanya Pavelovna, ask General Rakipov if he would do me the honor of a visit this morning—on a matter of some urgency."

"The KGB?" asked Solovyov. It was no longer called the KGB, but old habits were hard to break.

"The KGB. I want to know why I have to be informed by the Americans of something that may be happening within my own country. Report to me immediately on your return from Murmansk."

John Moody woke up in pain. His head felt like it was in a vise, and he was so thirsty that his whole body cried out for water. He sat upright in bed, which took the pain up another order of magnitude, but he had to get a drink. Only after walking into the closet did he find the door to the hall and finally to the bathroom, where he jammed his mouth to the faucet and spun open the tap. With his thirst problem solved, Moody made his way back to the bedroom. He carefully sat on the edge of the mattress.

"How yuh doin', hon?" Moody jumped, which sent another lance of agony through his forehead. "Sorry—didn't mean to startle you." She had the blankets pulled up around her chin, or chins as Moody noticed, and the teased blond hair partially covered her rounded shoulders.

"What's your name?"

She laughed deeply, and it shook the whole bed. "It's Trina, but last night you insisted on calling me Cuddles. A real charmer you were, last night." She laughed again, but it was kindly.

"Uh, Trina, just where the hell are we?"

"We're at my place in Virginia Beach. Actually it's my folks' place, but they only use it in the summertime." Moody glanced around. It had the look of a summer place—light cream wood-grain paneling, acoustical tile ceiling, and plank flooring. Light gauze curtains fought to hold off the gray dawn. The windows were opaque with frost.

"Aren't you cold, darlin'?" Moody realized that he was nude and that his clothes were strewn over one side of the room along with Trina's. But he wasn't cold.

"How'd we get here?"

"Well, I drove, and you followed," she said, nodding toward the window. He walked over and parted the curtains with one hand and rubbed a peephole in the frosted glass with the other. There in the front yard at the end of two ten-foot skid marks, leaning up against a tree, was his 1965 Norton Atlas 650. It was a clean bike, and the chrome gleamed in the glare of the front-porch light. It was one of the few material possessions he truly valued. He stared at it for a moment before bowing his head. *This shit's gotta cease,* he told himself. *I do enough crazy things on the job without carrying on like this off duty.* He walked back around the foot of the bed and sat down.

"Uh, Tracy, I hate—"

"It's Trina, darlin'."

"Sorry, Trina. Look, I hate to rush off, but it's a Monday. I gotta get dressed an' go to work."

She smiled warmly at him as he crawled around the floor sorting through the clothes. "John-boy, I kinda thought we were just two ships passing in the night, but you can tie up here anytime you're in the neighborhood."

"Now, that's real nice of you, Trina, an' I might do just that." Moody wriggled into his jeans and prudently dropped to the floor to pull on his boots—hopping around on one leg would be courting disaster.

"It's awful cold out there, hon. You sure you gotta go just yet?" It was inviting—Trina was a big, warm woman.

"You're a sweetheart, but I can't stay. You can hoot with the owls, but . . ."

"Yeah, I know, yuh still gotta scream with the eagles."

"You got it," said Moody as he pulled a wool sweater over his bare chest and tucked the leather flight jacket under his arm. He hesitated, then leaned over and kissed her full on the mouth. "Don't get up—I'll let myself out." Trina didn't move.

Moody found two more closets before he found the front door. He kicked the motorcycle to life and headed toward the Lynnhaven Bridge, en route to the Naval Amphibious Base at Little Creek. It was five minutes to eight when he rolled into the SEAL Team Two parking lot. Moody jumped off the bike and headed for the locker room at a dead run.

John Moody was one of the few men in the last decade of the twentieth century that could legitimately call themselves cowboys. He grew up on a small ranch in Wyoming and attended the University of Montana at Missoula. He earned money during the summers on the professional rodeo circuit and moonlighted as a dirt-track motorcycle racer—county-fair, flat-track stuff where the top three finishers split a one-hundred-dollar purse. He was not a large man—under six feet and a hundred eighty pounds, but he had a compact, useful build. Moody had been All Big Sky Conference at wide receiver, and a low NFL draft pick. He had adequate speed and superb moves—a pattern receiver, but he couldn't pass the physical. "Your skeleton looks like a junkyard," the football doctors told him, "too many broken bones and torn ligaments." So he joined the Navy after graduation and qualified for Officer Candidate School. The Navy doctor who examined him when he applied for SEAL training also had a problem with his condition.

"I don't know, Mr. Moody, the SEALS are pretty tough on their people. It's plain that you've been ridden hard and put away wet on more than one occasion."

Moody picked up on the flat west-Texas drawl of the medical officer sitting behind the desk. "I been throwed a few times, Doc," he said in his best aw-shucks, down-home cant, "but I keep gettin' up an' comin' back. An' I got a few all-around trophies to show for it. Don't you reckon that's what the SEALs are lookin' for—a guy that don't have any quit in him?" He pushed the Underwater Demolition/SEAL screening-exam results across the desk to the doctor.

"Let's see," the doctor said, slipping on his reading glasses, "you ran the mile and a half in seven minutes, thirty-five seconds. You managed one hundred and fifteen push-ups in two minutes and one hundred and twenty-seven sit-ups in two minutes. Pull-ups—twenty nine." It was the strongest performance of the fifteen OCS candidates who had taken the exam. There were only two billets for SEAL training in his OCS class. "Moody, in my best medical judgment, you just barely qualify for sea duty, but something tells me you might make a good Navy SEAL."

"Thanks, Doc—I won't prove you wrong." Moody got up to leave.

"One thing, Mr. Moody, you've had some vicious fractures and that's a pretty good-sized plate in your arm. And I know you have some bone fragments under your left kneecap. Aren't you in pain?"

"Sometimes, but it's no big deal." He gave the doctor a broad grin. "I can always tell when it's going to rain, though."

"Okay, son, but I guess you know, the SEALs spend a lot of time in the water."

"No problem, Doc. That's what they taught us during the first two weeks here at OCS."

"I don't get it—taught you what?"

"Why, they taught me how to swim, of course," and he was out the door.

"Mornin', sir, the platoon is formed. All present or accounted for." Moody glanced behind him to the thirteen men paraded on the grinder in two ranks. Like Moody and the chief, they were dressed in light canvas UDT trunks, double-sided blue-and-gold T-shirts, running shoes, and rigidly starched fatigue caps. Platoons normally had two officers assigned to them, but his assistant platoon commander was away at Army Ranger school.

"Thanks, Master Chief," he replied as he returned the salute. "Stand easy." The chief nodded as he shifted his plug and moved to a relaxed parade rest. Moody executed a wobbly about-face as a whistle sounded from a distant loud-speaker, calling the whole world to attention. Moody saluted, along with the other operating platoon commanders and department heads, as the national anthem boomed across the base. Moody dropped his hand as the three "carry on" whistles sounded.

"Team Two, parade rest! Morning, men, I hope everyone had a good Thanksgiving. The Commanding Officer will be holding mast in the conference room at ten hundred hours—the bloodmobile will be in the compound at eleven hundred—the master-at-arms will kick off the combined federal campaign . . ." The Executive Officer of SEAL Team Two droned on for another five minutes while the assembled platoons and support elements endured.

SEAL Team Two is one of three East Coast SEAL teams and one of the two original SEAL Teams commissioned in 1962 when President Kennedy ordered all services to develop a special-warfare capability. It was SEAL Team Two, along with its West Coast counterpart, SEAL Team One, who fought in Vietnam for ten years. Since the old Underwater Demolition Teams were converted to SEAL Teams, there are now a total of eight teams, three SEAL teams and one SDV (swimmer delivery vehicle) team per coast. Years ago, the teams had been assigned specialties—jungle warfare, desert warfare, and cold-weather operations. SEAL Team Two is the East Coast cold-weather operations team.

Team Two had basked in the glory of Vietnam through the seventies and into the eighties. It was not unusual to see a SEAL in the team area with a Silver Star medal and several Purple Hearts atop his rows of campaign ribbons and unit commendations. But Vietnam had faded and was finally extinguished by the Gulf War. Now, SEAL Team Two was struggling with its assignment as winter-warfare specialists—all the assignments seemed to pass them by. Team Four had participated in Panama and Grenada, and it was Team Eight from the East Coast that saw most of the combat in the Persian Gulf during *Desert Storm.* For the SEALs in Team Two, it seemed as if the action was always someplace where it was warm.

The Executive Officer concluded morning quarters with an appeal for contributions to the Navy Relief Society.

"Team, atten-HUT! Platoon commanders and department heads, take charge and carry out the plan of the day."

Moody again saluted and turned back to his men. "Stand at rest." The platoon SEALs began to mill about in place. Some folded their arms for warmth, while others blew steamy clouds into clenched fists. Moody took a small spiral notebook from the pocket of his trunks and began flipping pages. "Okay, guys, after PT we're due in admin for service jacket review." The platoon issued a collective groan. "Then we have a Draeger compass swim in Desert Cove at eleven hundred. Have your rigs set up and ready by ten forty-five. Unless the winds come up, the jump is still on for fourteen-thirty. We got a CH-46 scheduled, so if we hustle, we can get in five jumps. I want everyone making at least two free-falls." He cast a critical eye skyward at the gray canopy. "I'll try to talk the pilot up to eleven thousand feet, but no promises. Master Chief?"

The chief stepped out to one side with an identical notebook and began a short litany of administrative detail, making individual assignments for the dive and the jump. Master Chief Earl Tolliver was a medium-built man, fortyish with gray hair and eyes to match. He had a measured, plodding manner that many wrote off to his rural Georgia background. But he was a patient man and a very intense one. This careful approach to life had served him well during two decades as a Navy SEAL.

"Be on time and have your equipment ready," he concluded as he put the notebook away, "or I'll have your ass. Lieutenant?"

"That's it, guys. Garniss, you lead PT and the run today." Another collective groan. "Platoon, ten-HUT! Fall out." The platoon reluctantly expanded into a circle as a rangy SEAL with a leer on his face drifted to the center.

"You sure you want this, sir?" said the chief, who had joined the circle next to Moody. "You open your eyes wide enough an' you'll bleed to death."

"I'm sick, Master Chief, and I'm counting on Garniss to make me well." The chief shrugged and began to stretch.

"Okay, girls, let's start with neck rotations." Garniss knew his business. He started slow, working different parts of the body. Twenty-five minutes later, Moody and the rest of the platoon were doing two-hundred-count flutter kicks while their stomach muscles screamed in protest. Garniss moved them from exercise to exercise, calling for fifty push-ups between each one. Twenty minutes later, Garniss assembled them in a column of twos and led them out of the team area at a brisk trot.

"You sure you're gonna be okay, sir? Y'all look like you'd have to get better to die." Master Chief Tolliver was fifteen years older than Moody. He was breathing hard, but easily keeping up with the others.

"You want to be the one to tell Garniss to slack off?" They exchanged a grimace and plowed ahead. Garniss led them off the road to a trail that wound its way toward the beach and into the sand dunes. Another groan from the platoon.

Morton Keeney sat calmly near the head of the table and watched as his two staffers helped themselves to the coffee service at the far end of the room. They shared a laugh and talked about the prospect of the Redskins repeating as Super Bowl champs. Keeney had little interest in sports, and he was always amazed how those in government with dramatically different political agendas could invariably unite in their support of the capital's football team. Keeney was a man who liked to control the agenda and the players, and to sit on the sidelines and await the outcome was, for him, a pointless exercise and a waste of time. He picked a speck of lint from the lapel of his suit and glanced up at the wall clock. The meeting had been scheduled for Monday at 10:10, and they were already two minutes late.

One of the NSA staffers was Dr. Anne Bunting, Ph.D. Bunting had once held the chair at the Harvard Kennedy School of Government, and rumor was that it could again be hers if she chose to return to Cambridge. She was a formidable woman in her mid-fifties—attractive and confident, and from a very good New England family. Keeney had mixed feelings about her. For one thing, he found her abrasive, and she could be incredibly gullible when it came to dealing with the former Soviet republics, but when it came to domestic policy and public-opinion issues, she had few peers. It was whispered that she was near psychic when it came to predicting public reaction to administrative policy. Some even claimed that George Bush drew his famous line in the sand before the Gulf War only after consulting with Anne Bunting. Many had been surprised that she had been invited to serve in the Bennett White House. Keeney didn't particularly feel there was a place in government for women or liberals, but Bunting's experience and intelligence were too valuable to overlook.

While Keeney had personally hired Anne Bunting, she was not oblivious to his opinion of her. She also knew he was a gentleman from the old school, scrupulously fair, and would never allow his personal opinion to color his judgment in matters of statecraft. Oddly enough, she liked working for him. Most men with a sexual bias could not help but allow it to affect their opinion of her expertise in her field. She knew Keeney did not like her, but he trusted her, and she found that strangely comfortable and a little intriguing.

Bunting was talking with a man who was ten years her junior but who looked much younger. Although he was well dressed, his tie was slightly askew, and his thick, curly hair needed attention. Albert Patterson had spent most of his bureaucratic life with the Department of Energy, and was an expert on civilian nuclear power and the management of nuclear fuels and nuclear waste. His academic credentials were solid, but he had a tendency to be critical of DOE's loose domestic oversight of the nation's military nuclear-weapons sites. It was probably this tendency that prompted the Secretary of the Energy to make him available to the NSA. Morton Keeney, however, would not have taken him unless he felt he could be useful on the NSA staff.

Keeney again looked at the clock and cleared his throat. "Why don't we get started. I'm sure the good Colonel will join us presently."

As Bunting and Patterson made their way to the table, in walked a man who looked just a little too old for the uniform he wore. Richard Geist was one of the military's leading authorities on nuclear weapons. He was a caustic, thirty-five-year Air Force veteran, and a disciple of Curtis LeMay. Geist's tardiness had been borderline rude, but that was not unusual—he had little tolerance for polite conventions such as punctuality. Neither Bunting nor Patterson particularly liked Geist—few people did. But in their case it was partly because he was a lot smarter than they were. Bunting and Patterson took their seats at the small conference table on either side of Keeney. Geist slumped into a chair, leaving an empty seat between himself and Patterson so he could maintain a certain distance from the group.

Keeney smiled to himself; he could handle the Geists of the world. *Intelligence, my good Colonel,* he thought, *is no substitute for low animal cunning.* "In your packet in front of you," Keeney began, "you will find some rather startling photographs of the nuclear storage facility near the village of Gremikha." There was a rustling as they removed a series of color eight-by-ten photographs from a folder that had TOP SECRET—EYES ONLY blazed in a red diagonal stripe across the front cover. Keeney had had a struggle with the National Reconnaissance Office over the release of the photos to his staff, more for the highly classified resolution capability of the satellite than the content of the pictures. Like many top-secret bureaucratic organizations, the NRO often felt the intelligence product they generated was too sensitive to be shown to anyone but their own staffers.

"Just what are we looking at?" Anne Bunting turned one of the photographs bottom side up. She was not a technician, and often became impatient when confronted with technology.

"A good question, Anne." Keeney smiled. "That's why I've asked Gary Adams from the NRO to join us. Gary's an expert in photoreconnaissance interpretation. He's also personally responsible for each of these photographs. I'm counting on him to tell us what all these wonderful colors mean."

Adams was dressed in a dated wool sports coat, poorly matched knit tie, and earth shoes, but he wore them as a badge of honor so others would know he was not a politician or a political appointee.

"What you have in your folders is a spread of thermal-imaging photos taken along the coast of the Kola Peninsula from Murmansk to the White Sea. These photos were developed to highlight certain specific ranges of temperatures which can tell us something of the contaminants present in seawater, especially along the littoral areas where the concentrations are greatest. Now, on the large-scale photo—that's right, ma'am, the one on top—you can see the rainbow of color that's coming from the Kolskiy Inlet and Murmansk, possibly the densest concentration of industrial pollution per cubic meter of seawater in the world. There's absolutely nothing living in that body of water, or for miles out into the Barents Sea. The same can be said for the approaches to Archangel in the White Sea at the bottom right of the photo. Those two ports are contenders for the shitty-city award." A stern look from Keeney broke off Adams's attempt at humor. "Sorry—midway down the Kola coast, you can see the pronounced yellow feathering coming from the Lumbovskiy Inlet. That's a new feature we began to notice about four months ago.

"The next photo is a medium-resolution take of the Gremikha-Lumbovskiy area. Again, note the bloom of color just off Lumbovskiy."

"The color seems to originate offshore," said Patterson. "Is the effluent being taken offshore by some kind of outfall?"

"It would seem so from these photographs," replied Adams, "but for the most part, the Russians aren't nearly so sophisticated in their dumping practices. We think they're pumping to just beyond the shoreline and what you see are the chemicals as they clear the band of coastal pack ice and bloom into the open water."

"And just what are the chemicals?" asked Dr. Bunting.

"Just what you would expect from the processing of plutonium. Making fuel from U239 is an acid-wash process, and the by-products are hydrofluoric acid, nitric acid, carbon tetrachloride, and sodium hydroxide. Together, they form the basic components of Drāno. It's hard to find a more toxic combination of chemicals to release into the environment."

"So what are we looking for here—proof for some sort of censure by the United Nations for environmental pollution?" said Bunting.

Adams shrugged. "That's not really my area—I'm a photo guy."

"Russia and the other former Soviet republics are a massive open sore of toxins and contaminants," said Patterson. "This may be a serious incident, but it's just one more. If we complain to the U.N. about it, the Russians could just as well point to some of our own problems. I'm sure some colorful photos could be taken of the Chesapeake Bay or San Diego Bay."

"Look, we know the Russians are trashing their country and their coastline," said Geist with a measure of irritation. "They've been doing that since 1917. What's this have to do with selling nuclear weapons to the Third World?"

"That's a good point, Colonel," said Keeney, addressing all of them. "As you know from the material you received from CIA, the Northern Military District appears to be a possible point of origin for the sale of nuclear weapons. Since the Lumbovskiy facility is processing smaller, tactical nuclear weapons, we feel there is a strong possibility that it's also a rework facility where they're preparing some of these smaller weapons for sale. Our own people at Los Alamos tell us the tactical weapons are the least cost-effective in converting weapons-grade plutonium to fuel. In other words, the processing of plutonium for reactor fuel may well be a front for the more serious business of converting nukes for export."

"What have we done to confront Moscow about this?" Again it was Bunting.

Keeney gave the group a synopsis of Ambassador Simpson's meeting with Stozharov and the Russian President's denial of any wrongdoing. He made it clear that Stozharov had been confronted directly about the Russian military in the Kola selling nuclear weapons.

"This just seems all wrong," Dr. Bunting began slowly. "I find it hard to comprehend in these times of unprecedented international cooperation and openness that this kind of thing can take place. Quite frankly, I find it hard to believe any members of their scientific community would be so irresponsible as to cooperate in the preparation of nuclear weapons for sale in the Third World. These are good people, by and large, and they've had enough of that sort of thing. I don't want to seem too naive or paranoid, but I hope this isn't some CIA scheme or an attempt by the military to stir the pot a bit to rekindle the Cold War."

Keeney stared at her a moment. *How can someone as smart as Bunting not see how desperate even scientists can become when they're out of a job? I guess that's what happens when you fall off the turnip truck in Marblehead. To her, going hungry means the lobsters are out of season.* "Anne, I understand what you're saying. I find it hard to believe and most disturbing, but the facts indicate otherwise. There are a lot of very capable people over there without work, and they still have families to feed.

Most of us have never been in that position or had to make those difficult decisions."

"Well, what input do you want form us?" she replied, trying not to sound too defensive.

"Perhaps you can tell me. Now that you know the facts to date, I'm asking for your help in seeking a suitable course of action. What can we do? What are the policy issues at stake if we take action or we do nothing?"

"All right," Bunting said, warming to the subject, "we *suspect* the Russians of selling nuclear weapons, but the evidence is still circumstantial. We *know* they're polluting the environment with the reprocessing of plutonium. Tell me, Mr. Adams, is there any way that our satellite coverage can confirm the sale of nuclear weapons or even if they're operating some sort of a conversion plant for nuclear bombs?"

Adams thought for a moment. "No, ma'am. We can count warhead and missile containers, and monitor the movement of certain raw materials. To a certain degree we can optically and thermally sort through their garbage and chemical by-products, but nothing in the way of actual confirmation unless they're really careless."

"I see. I think Morton's concerns are certainly worthy of further study, but without proof and in the face of Stozharov's denial, what can we do?" There was silence around the table. "Let's get back to the environmental problems. Mr. Adams, is this discharge at the nuclear plant really something new and important?"

"Well, ma'am, I'm not really an environmental expert, but the concentrations at the point of discharge are quite strong, and that's pretty bad stuff they're putting out. Is it in itself worse than the huge volume of effluent from the pulp mills in Archangel? I'm not sure I can answer that."

"But it is a new source of pollution and it is serious?"

"Yes, ma'am."

"I was doing some reading on that region this afternoon," Bunting continued thoughtfully, "and the Norwegians do a lot of fishing up in that area. They operate the largest fishing fleet in the Barents Sea and they're quite active on the Skolpen Bank. They've also been most vocal on Arctic environmental issues. I would think they would have serious concern about this new form of pollution."

"Possibly," Keeney conceded, wondering where this was going.

"The Alaskan Congressional delegation along with the environmental lobbies are asking for strong legislation that will hold Russia accountable for pollution in Arctic waters. I think we have enough here to call the Russians to task for this new and highly toxic source of Arctic pollution. Maybe if we lean on them with this evidence, it might force their hand, so to speak, or put them on the environmental defensive until a stronger case can be made on the proliferation issue. So far, the Norwegians have made any foreign aid contingent on Russian efforts to curb pollution in the Baltic Sea." She tapped her pencil point on the table for emphasis. "Perhaps a well-documented charge of environmental irresponsibility in handling nuclear materials will cause them to rethink their stance on selling weapons."

"In other words," said Keeney, "let's publicly try to make the Russians respond to our evidence of pollution while we seek to verify our suspicions about their selling nuclear weapons."

"We could file an official complaint through the U.N.," Patterson offered, "and see what kind of reaction we get from that. The Marine Environmental Protection Committee of the U.N.'s International Monitoring Organization is the body charged with that responsibility. I think that, based on the evidence, we could even demand that a U.N. monitoring team from the IMO be sent to make an on-sight inspection of the facility."

Keeney twisted his gold Cross pen thoughtfully in his fingers. *It's not much, but it's about all we have.* He glanced down the table to Geist. "Colonel, we didn't hear much from you today. Any opinions on the subject?"

"Hey, look, the Russians are going to continue to pollute, just like the clans in Somalia are going to continue to kill each other while the rest of the people starve. It's just another tragic and unavoidable part of our new world order. As for the nuclear weapons, I don't doubt that they're selling them. If not in the Kola, then probably in the Southwest Military District or Kazakhstan. Hell, I'll lay odds the rocket forces out in Kamchatka are swapping the nukes with the Japs for Toyotas. Either we take strong action now or there'll be no stopping it, and we all know this government lost its stomach for strong action a long time ago."

"So what do you recommend, Dick," Bunting said caustically, "launch a few Tomahawk missiles?"

"Or some form of covert strike," snapped Geist. "I know, let's get Greenpeace to take the *Rainbow Warrior* into the Barents Sea and they can launch hippies in Zodiacs—that'll show 'em."

"You don't get it, do you, Colonel," she flared. "Public opinion won't sanction any kind of military response—the Russians are our friends. But there's a lot of support for environmental issues. We make this an international pollution issue and we may get some help from the EC and the Japanese."

"Christ, you really think the Russians give a shit what anyone thinks about pollution in the Barents Sea, a piece of water they feel they own? Get real. Unless we can prove they're making *and* selling nukes on a cash-and-carry basis, they'll just ignore us."

"Anne, Dick, let's settle down," said Keeney. "This is all very interesting, but I'd like to take something to the President in the form of a recommendation."

"In my opinion," replied Bunting, "we have to go with the pollution issue until the intelligence agencies come up with something more concrete. And even then, the environmental issue is the one that people will connect with."

"And by then," said Geist dryly, "it'll be too late."

"Albert?" said Keeney.

"I'm with Anne. The Colonel may be right, but the country is more interested in the environment than confronting Russia about nuclear arms."

"Thank you for your time," Keeney concluded. "I want you all to stay on this thing. If you have any additional thoughts, you all know how to get in touch with me."

Keeney sat in the back of the Chevrolet Caprice as the driver skirted traffic around the Lincoln Memorial and toiled across the Arlington Memorial Bridge. He would be a few minutes late for his meeting at the Pentagon, but they would not start without him. Keeney missed the stretch limousines that used to escort senior administration officials about town, but that was no longer fashionable. He was a man of considerable means, and for a while he hired a limo and driver himself, but had been advised by the White House Chief of Staff to cease the practice. Even if it cost the taxpayer nothing, it was still bad form.

The meeting had been interesting although inconclusive. He knew Colonel Geist would take a hard line and, unlike Anne Bunting, would ignore the domestic consequence of taking strong action. Geist had been borderline insubordinate, but that was not unusual. He certainly didn't mince words, and perhaps that was also why the President placed a great deal of importance on his opinion. Keeney smiled as he thought ahead to his meeting in the Oval Office later that day. He could just picture the President leaning forward in his chair asking, "Now, what did that hard-boiled sonovabitch Dick Geist have to say?"

PART TWO

Options

President Bennett leaned back precariously in his leather swivel with his feet crossed on top of the blotter. A number of presidents had conducted business from the antique, superbly crafted cherry-wood desk, but none had probably used it so cavalierly as William Bennett. His sleeves were rolled up and his tie loosened so the knot hung below the second button of his shirt. He took a final drag on his cigarette and crushed it out on the lip of the wastebasket. It was a habit of his, and the enameled metal on the inside of the can looked like scrap iron.

"What do you think, Mort?"

Keeney sat upright in one of the padded office chairs in front of the desk. He balanced a saucer on the knee of his crossed leg and frowned. The creases of his light-charcoal suit trousers were crisp and straight, and the paisley handkerchief that peaked from his breast pocket matched his tie. When he took a measured sip from the teacup, the motion of his arm revealed monogrammed initials on his starched white cuff. Morton Keeney looked like a cover of *Gentlemen's Quarterly.* He was the President's closest adviser, and the White House staff often likened them to Oscar Madison and Felix Unger.

"I think we may have a problem. I agree with Armand that everything points to the fact that the Russians are selling nukes—probably reconfiguring them to the needs of Third World users." Armand Grummell, seated next to him, nodded imperceptibly in agreement. "And I agree with Simpson's assessment that Stozharov probably doesn't know or doesn't know for sure what is happening on the Kola. Until this thing came up, we thought for sure it would be warheads from Kazakhstan or Ukraine filtering south."

"Christ," fumed Bennett, "I know things are bad over there, but how could a major theater commander take it on himself to do something like this, and furthermore, how can he continue to do it if Moscow knows and disapproves of it?"

"As the fabric of Russian society continues to implode, regional power bases are bound to arise and fill the vacuum left by the old Soviet system," said Grummell in his measured, bookish fashion. "Sometimes these enclaves are controlled by bona fide, reform-minded leaders and sometimes by reactionary, Mafia-style rulers. It's not unreasonable for the military to fill such a void. The fact remains that there are certain ethnic regions in Russia, including entire military districts, under local control—regions that have come to feel they simply do not have to respond to direction from the central government."

"What do you think this guy Borzov is up to? Is he trying to establish a power base and wait for things to become further undone so he can make a move on Moscow?"

"That would be very unlikely," continued Grummell. "In spite of the turbulent nature of Russian history, there has never been an instance where the military took control of the government. Even during the aborted coup attempt in 1990, only a few senior military leaders sided with the rebellious faction. The Russian military cadre is a remarkably professional and patriotic lot, much like our own officer corps, and the average Russian soldier is very close to the land and the people. The coup against Gorbachev was doomed from the start because the Red Army, while it may take to the streets, would never fire on their own people without serious provocation.

"We've assembled a rather complete dossier on Colonel General Dmitri Borzov, and there is nothing to suggest that he is anything but a loyal Russian and a highly capable military commander. At this time we can only conclude that he is making the best of a difficult situation with the resources at hand."

"And selling nukes," retorted the President. "When do you think we will hear back from Stozharov on this?"

Keeney cleared his throat. "I think we should give him a week, perhaps two. One thing we have to think about is that he may elect to just look the other way." Bennett shot his National Security Advisor an incredulous look. "Consider it from Stozharov's perspective. He's up to his eyeballs in political, economic, and ethnic problems. Now, here's one of his key military district commanders who's doing a reasonable job of maintaining a reduced but effective force and still manages to feed his troops. Russia really doesn't need the men it has in uniform, but then, it certainly doesn't have jobs in the civilian economy for them either. He can't be happy about Borzov selling nukes, but there's not much he can do about it. He may *ask* him to stop, or he may just ask him to be more careful. He may not want to embarrass himself by giving him an order and risk that Borzov would simply choose to ignore it."

President Bennett slipped another cigarette into the side of his mouth and lit it in a practiced motion. He swung his feet to the floor and pulled himself up to the desk, resting his elbows on the blotter. After a long draw, he carefully tapped the ash into the brass artillery-shell-casing ashtray on the corner of the desk and looked sharply at Armand Grummell.

"Tell me about your agent on the Kola."

"MUSTANG has been a reporting asset for almost eight years, and his product has been graded with the highest degree of quality and reliability. He has held positions within the old Soviet Defense Ministry that have dealt directly with the development and production of strategic as well as tactical nuclear weapons. He was also actively involved in working with the warheads repatriated from the non-Russian republics."

"In other words, he'll probably know what's going on with the nukes on the Kola Peninsula."

"Yes, sir. I believe that's a fair assumption."

"And right now, this MUSTANG is out of contact?"

"Yes, sir."

Bennett took another pull on his cigarette and stared at the ceiling for a long moment. Then he looked at Grummell.

"Okay, I want you to make every reasonable attempt to recontact your agent and find out what's going on. That means let's explore all the options. Prepare an agenda that details what might be required in the way of proof to expose this thing in a U.N.–type forum. We just can't sit by while they give nuclear weapons to every Third World tinhorn who wants them. Mort," he said, turning to Keeney, "let's give Stozharov a week on this, then find a pretext to send Noffsinger to Moscow—maybe to discuss that last request for technology to deal with their aging nuclear reactors—whatever works that will attract the least attention. I want him to confront that fat little SOB and ask him directly just what he's going to do about this."

"Yes, sir, but I don't think his position will be any different than what he discussed with Ambassador Simpson."

"Maybe not, but if he's going to stonewall us on this thing, I want it on record that he did it personally with the Secretary of State on an official mission. Keep me posted."

Bennett ground out his cigarette while Grummell and Keeney both nodded and rose to leave.

General William Tecumseh Thon, or Billie T. as he was called behind his back, sat at his desk on the second floor of the U.S. Special Operations Command (SOCOM) headquarters building. He was wearing gym shorts, an Airborne Ranger T-shirt, and paratrooper boots. Thon had just come back from his five-mile run and was working his way through a stack of paperwork while he cooled down. He scanned each page and occasionally scrawled an illegible signature. Standing in front of the desk was his Command Sergeant Major, a ramrod-straight NCO dressed in an immaculate Class-B uniform. He was delivering a carefully prepared brief on the general morale and concerns of the enlisted personnel at a battalion of the Fifth Special Forces Group he had recently visited. Occasionally, Thon looked up from his desk to the sergeant or to the TV screen behind the Sergeant, which was tuned to CNN. The Command Sergeant Major continued as though he had Thon's undivided attention. He had learned, as had other members of the headquarters staff, that Billie T. could watch TV, read, and listen to a briefing officer at the same time. Most who served in senior staff billets on the SOCOM staff had their pet story of Thon's finding and questioning an insignificant error in a position paper or during a briefing, a detail that should have been well beneath the broad concern or expertise of the Commanding General. Opinion was divided at Special Operations Command as to whether he was a meddlesome micromanager or just sending a signal to his staff that it was hard to slip one past the old man. All agreed, however, that Billie T. was the smartest general officer in uniform.

"Excellent report, Command Sergeant Major. Is First Sergeant Morales still assigned to 3rd Company?

"Yes, sir, to the best of my knowledge." With Thon, it was always best to add a disclaimer.

"He's been there a while. It might do well for him to come here for a staff tour. He'll squawk about being sent to a headquarters, but I think he has the makings of a good Sergeant Major—what d'you think?"

"I agree with the General—he's a damn fine NCO."

"I know how much you fire-breathers like this staff duty," said Thon, forcing a smile from the Command Sergeant Major, "but it's part of the penance if you want to make E-9. Give him a call, and then have the G-1 see if they can find a good spot for him in operations." He stood up and groaned as he bent at the waist in a trunk rotation. Thon was not a tall man, just under five feet eight, with a compact, muscular build. He had a youthful face and light-brown hair, cut short enough to hide any gray that might be lurking about.

"Yes, sir. Anything else, sir?"

"Yeah, get the quartermaster to issue me a new body—one that's young and strong."

The Sergeant chuckled. "Y'all do all right out there, sir. We old men just have to learn to compensate."

Thon grinned back at him. None of the general or flag officers at SOCOM could keep up with Thon; in fact, few of the field-grade officers could run with him. Periodically, he would take one of his senior colonels out over the lunch hour and punish him. Running with the Commanding

General this time of year was an unpleasant chore, but in the summer when temperature and humidity soared over ninety, it was life threatening. Thon took the towel from around his neck and wiped his face as he headed for the private shower that adjoined his office. The Command Sergeant Major made a crisp facing movement and made for the entryway.

Twenty minutes later, Thon was back at his desk, reviewing budget figures for his far-flung and diverse command. The Special Operations Command was in all respects, with the exception of the uniforms they wore, a fifth service. Thon commanded the Army's Rangers and Special Forces, the Navy SEAL Teams and Special Boat Units, and the Air Force's Special Operations Squadrons. Only the Marine Corps and their Force Reconnaissance Battalions had escaped the special operations consolidation at SOCOM. He was also responsible for the training of the reserve components that supported these forces. It was the only sector of the military that had escaped the dramatic cuts that came with the end of the Cold War. Yet, as Thon liked to point out, the whole outfit cost the same as a fully loaded Trident submarine or two B-2 bombers. "A bargain at twice the price," he had boasted to the generals and admirals of the other services. Most took issue with this, but so far, Congress had agreed with him.

Thon was, in many ways, the first of his kind. He was a four-star general officer who had begun his career as a Special Forces officer and had remained in Special Forces his entire career. One of the wood-paneled walls featured an enlarged black-and-white glossy of a young SF second lieutenant clad in jungle cammies with his band of Montagnards in the central highlands of Vietnam. It was clearly the same man as the one behind the desk. For years Thon had been regarded as one of the brightest officers in the U.S. Army, but he was a "snake eater," or Special Forces man—a capable West Pointer who had squandered his chances for senior command opportunity by staying with the "Green Beanies" too long. Then the Soviet Union threw in the towel, and the Army began to understand what Thon knew all along—special operations was going to be the focus of action for the U.S. military in the nineties and beyond.

"General, I have the Chairman of the Joint Chiefs on the scrambler."

"Thank you, Sergeant. I'll take it here." Thon released the intercom and snatched the handset of the STU-3 on the credenza behind him. "Hello, Scotty, you there?"

There was a short hiss and a chirp as the secure connection was made. "Billie, how are you? Staying in shape?"

"Always, Scotty, always. Just takes a little longer—the other side of the hill is steeper on the way down. What can I do for you?"

"Can you come up here tomorrow morning—I need to talk to you."

General Winston Scott was an old friend and classmate, but it was still an order from the Chairman. "That means you want me to fly up tonight. Of course I'll be there, but can you give me some idea of the subject?"

"It probably won't develop into anything, but we may want you to start serious planning for an action. Say about nine A.M.?"

"Nine A.M. sharp, General."

"Thanks, Billie." Scott chuckled. "See you then."

Thon hung up and thought for a moment. The STU-3 could handle secret-level material, and the Chairman could easily have patched through to him at the comm center on a top-secret line. But Scott clearly wanted to talk about it in person and in a secure space. Thon punched the intercom.

"Yes, General?"

"Book me on the red-eye to Washington International and get me a room at the Army-Navy Club."

"Aye, aye, sir."

It was the first of December and General Winston Scott, Chairman of the Joint Chiefs of Staff, had been in his Pentagon office since 6:00 A.M., long before the sun rose over the marble government buildings across the Potomac to the east. On this cold Wednesday morning, the sun would not actually rise, but serve to provide a dull lighted background for the heavy gray clouds that rolled down the eastern seaboard over the capital. While the General had an intense work ethic, he made very efficient use of his staff, so he was usually not bothered in the early-morning hours except for an eight o'clock briefing by his deputy and an occasional phone call from the Hill. It was approaching 9:00 A.M. and the snake of vehicles that slowly wound their way up the George Washington Parkway still had their lights on. Weather patterns changed swiftly this time of year, and there was talk of snow, that filled military and civilian employees alike with a kind of festive apprehension. If it came quickly, there was no escape. The bureaucracy had a knack for holding the government employees at their desks just long enough for the snow to cover the roadways, then releasing them in time to obstruct any meaningful work by the snowplows.

General Winston Scott, West Point Class of 1964, was one of four black cadets to graduate with his class. He was a large, deliberate man with close-cropped salt-and-pepper hair and kind, dark eyes. He had a polite but imperial bearing, and a direct manner in dealing with subordinates. The loyalty of those who served on his staff was ferocious. Scott was an infantry officer and, like so many of the Army's top brass, had his roots in Vietnam. His contemporaries pegged him as a solid professional but something of a plodder. Few thought he would ascend to the Chairmanship of the Joint Chiefs, and even fewer thought he would be as good at the job as he was.

Scott pushed aside a huge bound volume that represented yet another revised military budget. It seemed that most of his working day was devoted to budgetary considerations and less with the employment of his forces. And when he wasn't fighting with congressional staffers over details in the budget, he was refereeing food fights within the services over allocation of the diminishing defense appropriations. It was partially for that reason that he looked forward to meeting with Billy Thon. The U.S. Special Operations Command was the only domestic unified command and had no specific assigned theater of operations, but it still reported directly to JCS. SOCOM was tasked with the training and preparation of all special operations forces located in the continental United States. Military operations were normally conducted by the other unified commands, or the war-fighting CINCs, such as the Commander in Chief, Pacific, or Commander in Chief, Europe. Each of these war-fighting CINCs had their own staff component for managing special operations in their theater of responsibility. For all its flash and notoriety, SOCOM was just a large training command that prepared special operations components for deployment to the out-CONUS CINCs. They were the end users who would ultimately send them into battle.

At 9:00 A.M., Scott observed his midmorning ritual by brewing himself a pot of stiff, black Starbucks coffee made from freshly ground beans from Kenya. This time he poured two cups. He knew without checking that Thon would be waiting in the outer office for their scheduled appointment. He opened the door and found irrepressible Billy T. relaxing comfortably as he paged through the morning's edition of *The Early Bird.*

"Billy, good to see you. Come on in."

Thon jumped to attention. "Morning, General. It's good to see you again."

"Jack, see that we're not disturbed."

"Yes, sir," replied Scott's executive assistant.

Thon followed Scott into the office. It was a semiformal, comfortable ritual they played out. Thon and Scott had been classmates at West Point. Thon had stood at the top of the class, Scott in the middle, and both now had four stars. But Scott was senior by virtue of his promotion number and his office, and publicly, Thon would always defer to him. In private they would be less formal, but both understood who was the boss.

"Coffee?"

"Thanks, Scotty. How's your boy doing?"

"Great. He's carrying a solid two-five grade-point and running second-team halfback. We're gonna kill Navy this year."

"That's terrific. We owe those squids a good thrashing. Got any cream and sugar?"

"It's in the cupboard, wimp." Thon laughed and took liberal amounts of both. It was not the first time he'd come up against the Chairman's coffee. He took the leather armchair across the desk from Scott and sat back, patiently stirring his cup. He knew he had not been called up to talk Army football, and Scott's buoyant mood seemed to preclude any negative news, usually in the area of force reductions. When Congress was in session, it was open season on the military budget.

"Bill, what I'm going to be telling you is classified Top Secret, Code BEARCAT." It was the highest security classification within the Department of Defense. If the Chairman's office wasn't a Class Three security area, which meant it was periodically swept for listening devices, BEARCAT information couldn't be discussed there. "There's a situation developing in Russia that may require the insertion of a special operations team," Scott continued. "The boys at Langley have some pretty compelling information that the Russians are building special nuclear weapons for sale in the international arms market. Right now, both State and CIA are trying to bring this thing to the surface. Diplomatic efforts may not do the job, and the Kola Peninsula has once again become a very highly restricted area. The spooks have a well-placed agent on the inside, but they have no way to contact him. I want you and your planners to develop a mission concept for placing a team into the Kola with secure uplink communications and the ability to support agent operations for a period of up to two weeks. Think you can handle that?"

Thon cautiously sipped his coffee. "Hell, why don't we just have a team parachute into the Kremlin and snatch Stozharov. We could conduct a field interrogation and wring the truth out of him." They both laughed. "Seriously, times have changed, but that's a pretty well-fortified piece of real estate. I'll have to talk to my planners. Getting in there will be hard, but it can probably be done. Making contact with an agent and then making an extraction without raising the alarm may be another matter altogether."

"Haven't you done any planning in this area?" asked Scott smoothly. He had the ability to ask hard questions without making them sound like an indictment.

"Only what SOCEUR may have worked up associated with the general war plans for defense of Europe in a conventional war scenario—plans that are out of date with all the changes that have taken place. In broad terms, special operations support for conventional war on the continent would call for dropping platoon-sized units and SF "A" Teams across the Kola for demolition- and interdiction-type raids."

"What do the plans call for in the way of extraction?"

Thon snorted. "In a general war scenario, I believe both the planners and the troops know these would be one-way missions. Either they make their way east to Norway or hole up and wait for repatriation. Can't this agent be contacted by any other means?"

"Would we be having this discussion if they could?" Thon started to reply, but Scott held up his hand. "Like most special operations, it's a contingency only, but these things have a way of being dropped on our doorstep on short notice. It's my understanding that a military option is the last resort, but if they do turn to us, I want to be ready."

Thon felt a cold stab of fear. "Wait a minute, Scotty—we're a supporting command. You don't mean that . . ."

"I do, Billy. I want you to take this for action—if it happens, it'll be a SOCOM operation. Naturally, I'll want a level estimate about the probability for success along with your concept of operation. CIA and DIA have been alerted through BEARCAT channels and will cooperate fully with any and all intelligence requirements. And," Scott added gravely, "CINCEUR has been told that he is the *supporting* CINC on this operation. He wasn't happy about it, but his staff and his assets are at your disposal. It's your ball game, Billy. Don't let me down."

Thon registered what Scott was saying, and he was stunned. No wonder Scott had brought him up to D.C. for a face-to-face. Normally, this operation would be directed by the Special Operations Command, Europe. SOCEUR was the special operations staff element for the Commander in Chief, European Theater, but totally under CINCEUR's command. It was his turf and he had the assets in place. Asking SOCOM to take action violated the theater CINC's authority—the whole reason for having a theater CINC forward deployed.

"Why, Scotty?" Thon said quietly.

"Part of it is security. Many of our special operations teams there are training with allies, and it could be difficult to stand them up without sounding an alarm. You have a closed shop down there and can draw on domestic assets across the special operations community. Staging assets and downloading intelligence here in CONUS will create less of a stir than over in Frankfurt. And part of it is the risk to CINCEUR's position if something goes wrong. The Europeans are getting a little frisky as the EC becomes a reality. They want a U.S. military presence, but we're always the focal point for the politicians when it comes to a little U.S.A.–bashing. With the exception of the Brits, our allies have their own agenda, and their security is a joke. I want this to clearly be a unilateral operation, with no overt connection to our deployed forces in Europe."

"And?" asked Thon pointedly.

Scott got up and began to pace. "Billy, remember when we were company commanders in Vietnam? Remember when battalion had a nasty job to do, one that could put a few of our boys in body bags if things turned to shit?" Thon nodded. "When it was a tight-ass, hairy operation, which platoon did you call on to do the job?"

"Third Platoon," said Thon without thinking.

"Why?"

Thon smiled. "Remember Stoddard, the shavetail lieutenant from Arkansas?"

"The one who threw up on the dance floor at the Presidio and then rubbed some major's nose in it when he laughed at him? As I recall, they drove him from the stockade to the battalion airlift at Travis. You had to sign for him at the gate and promise that he would board the plane for Vietnam." They both laughed.

"That's the one. He was a fuckup as a stateside officer, but a helluva platoon leader."

"And you trusted him," offered Scott.

"Yeah, I trusted him."

"Well, there you have it—I trust you. Brad Hollingsworth has done a good job with the European Command, but I want you on this. I hope to God that State or CIA or somebody sorts this thing out and we don't have to get involved. But if we do have to take the action, it'll be damned important for all of us in the military, and the special operations community in particular, that it be done right."

Thon was silent a moment and shrugged. "It seems that when we're playing for marbles at this level, it should be different than when we were captains—I mean, commanding the armed forces of the United States is a little different than commanding an infantry company."

"Yes and no. I still need someone I can trust to do the job, if it can be done, and to level with me on the probabilities for success and compromise. It may be the President who gives the final order, but it's our budgetary ass that Congress will set their teeth into if it turns bad."

"Sounds like a lose-lose situation, Scotty."

"When has it ever been different for a peacetime army?"

"What's our time line on this?"

"Yesterday. I need you to move as soon as possible, but six weeks at the outside and probably a lot sooner. Better figure on a month. I'll need a mission concept and probability factors by the middle of next week."

Thon whistled soundlessly and rose to leave. "Scotty, I'll give it my best shot. Now, if the General will excuse me, I've got a lot of work to do."

Scott walked him to the door. The two men shook hands, and Thon strode quickly from the office.

Thon booked himself on the next flight back to Tampa, but before he left the Pentagon, he found a secure telephone and placed a call to the SOCOM J-5, his senior staff plans officer.

* * *

Steve Carter was lost. Twice he had stopped to ask directions, listened carefully, and set off with new determination, only to find himself wandering in circles. *I'm a reasonably intelligent guy,* he told himself, *I should be able to do this.* The walls of the SOCOM headquarters building were punctuated with large color glossies of green-faced men parachuting, helicopters landing, Green Berets training foreign irregulars, and soldiers firing every imaginable weapon. Certain photos had become landmarks as he wandered the corridors, and when he came to the AC-130 gunship for the third time, he was ready to give up.

"Y'all look lost—can I help?"

"I sincerely hope so. I'm trying to locate the Special Plans Section of the J-5 shop. I'm afraid I'm going to grow old trying to find it."

"Y'all in luck—that's near where I work. Man, you really are lost. It's a-way over on yonder side of th' building. I'm just over here 'cause our Coke machine is broke."

"Lucky me," replied Carter. They set out at a pace that Carter would have found slow at a funeral procession, but then, he had spent little time in the South.

"By th' way, I'm Tech Sergeant Davis, J-3." She seemed to know and greet everyone they passed in the hallway.

"Pleased to meet you, Ms. Davis. I'm Steve Carter, civilian."

"Well, you must be awful important. You got a lot of hash marks on your badge."

"I'm into computers," said Carter in a conspiratorial tone. Davis nodded as if she totally understood. Carter followed her to a completely uncharted section of corridors amid a running dialogue about the "good eatin' " in Tampa. They arrived at a large steel door with a cipher lock. Davis pressed a button on the intercom station.

"May I help you?"

"Yeah, got a Mr. Carter here. I found him out roamin' the halls looking' for y'all."

"Be right there," said the speaker.

"An' if y'all go to the Fish Grotto," Davis said as she continued down the hall, "order the boiled shrimp—an' make sure to tell 'em to go heavy on the hush puppies."

"I'll do just that, Sergeant," replied Carter, "and thanks for the help." He waited a few moments and the vault door was pulled back.

"Mr. Carter?"

"That's right. I'm here to see a Colonel Noreen."

"Right this way, sir." He followed another Army sergeant through the door. This one had the clear look of a guard. "We have your clearances on file. Now I just need to check your IDs and special-access codes, so I'll have to borrow your badge for a few minutes. While you're in the SCIF, you'll have to be escorted at all times."

"Skiff?"

"SCIF. This is a Special Compartmented Information Facility. It's protected against electronic penetrations, and is cleared for top-secret codeword material and secure data processing. If you'll sign in right here, sir, someone will be along in a few minutes to collect you." Carter handed the man his ID badge and then took a seat along the wall of the narrow office. This was all familiar to Carter. In his line of work, he often waited in reception areas to be "collected." The sergeant sat behind a bank of TV screens that seemed to monitor a series of hallways and doors. Carter was always intrigued by the way the military handled security—it was more obvious and formal on military bases, where there seemed to be an abundance of guards and cipher locks and TV cameras. At Langley, security was taken no less seriously, but handling classified material was a significant part of everyone's job, and it was less conspicuous.

On the table beside Carter were neat stacks of defense- and service-related journals. He picked up one and began to leaf through it, keeping his briefcase flat across his knees.

"Mr. Carter."

"Uh . . . why, uh yes." He rose and took the offered hand of a tall and absolutely stunning black woman in an Air Force uniform.

"I'm Major Brisco. We thought you might have gotten lost." She signed something on the security desk, then motioned to Carter. "Please follow me." She led him on another corridor expedition. The hallways were shorter this time, but just as many turns.

"The plane was late due to the storm in D.C.," offered Carter, "and when I got here, I did get lost."

"If it's any consolation," she smiled, "I always get lost at Langley."

She led him into a small, well-appointed briefing room. When they entered, an Army colonel and a lieutenant colonel rose from the small, mahogany-veneer table. The carpet was several grades better than Carter would have expected and the walls were shrouded in blue drapes, designed to mask briefing materials when not in use. Brisco stepped to one side while the Colonel came forward and offered his hand.

"Carter, I'm Colonel Bill Noreen, Chief of the SOCOM J-5 Special Plans Section. This is Colonel Jack Ostermann, and you've already met Janet. Both Major Brisco and Jack have been cleared for this project." He motioned Carter to a seat. "Well, it looks like you people up there at spook central have really cooked up a good one this time," Noreen continued, "but the boss says we're to give this thing top priority." His smile was broad and affable, but his eyes were wary. "Going into the Kola any time of year is a pretty tall order, and as you know, it's pretty cold up there right now. We haven't been told exactly why you want to put a team in there, but I hope it's damned important." He glanced at Ostermann and Brisco, still smiling.

"Well," Carter said, clearing his throat, "the policymakers seem to feel it is. We all hope the required information can be brought out of the area by other means, but if it can't, a clandestine military option may be considered."

"I see." Noreen was a plump man, with gray hair and outrageous dark eyebrows. He had several rows of ribbons on his left breast, and a host of pins and patches that meant nothing to Carter. Were it not for the uniform, Noreen would look more like the senior partner of a law firm than a colonel in the Army. He pursed his lips as he rocked back in the chair and toyed with his pencil on the table.

"Look, Carter, putting a team into Ivan's backyard to do a little snooping is no easy matter. Now, I understand you folks at Langley probably filter across borders and slip into denied areas all the time, and I'm sure you're very good at this sneaky-pete stuff, but we're military. We have prescribed capabilities and limitations, and we sometimes get uncomfortable when we get drawn into this spy business. And we get real irritable when someone from the outside tells us how to do our job. I'm sure you can understand that."

Carter stared at him for a long moment. He was not a military man, but he had learned that sometimes the best defense was a good offense. "Just what are the exact duties of Major Brisco and Colonel Ostermann?"

"I beg your pardon," said Noreen, sitting up in his chair.

"Major Brisco and the Lieutenant Colonel, what are their duties? I've been directed to brief you personally on this matter, but I was told nothing about them."

"Well, uh, Colonel Ostermann is my senior security officer and security manager, and Major Brisco is one of my senior planners—she'll be the focal-point officer and planner for this operation. Listen, what's this all about?"

"Colonel, this proposed operation and any information concerning it is classified Top Secret BEARCAT. That means no one, except for yourself, is to have full access to this information unless they are directly involved with the planning and execution of the operation. If Major Brisco is your action officer, then she will have to be a part of this briefing. Your security officer can do his job without full knowledge of the details—at least at this stage of the planning.

"Yes, but he's—"

"Mr. Carter's right, sir. It's strictly based on the need to know—BEARCAT classification guidelines are quite specific. I probably shouldn't be here." In deference to his senior, Ostermann made no move to leave.

"Very well, Jack, we'll do it his way, but stay in the building until we're finished." Noreen waved and Ostermann let himself out.

"Okay, Carter, it's your show."

Carter again paused for a moment to collect his thoughts. "Colonel, perhaps we ought to get a few things straight before I begin. I have the impression that you think that I, or someone else at the CIA, has hatched some wild scheme that's going to compromise your people or get some of them killed. Or maybe you feel that I've come down here to give orders." Carter looked sharply at Noreen—the man's jaw muscles were working furiously. Brisco, he noticed, was watching him closely, but her face was unreadable. "First of all, I'm an intelligence analyst. I was one of the people responsible for uncovering some rather distressing developments that appear to be taking place in Russia on the Kola Peninsula. I'm here to work *with* you in formulating a plan to use a military special operations team to obtain proof of these developments. I am not from the Directorate of Operations, nor do I have any operational experience. If, and I do mean if, there is no other way to document what I believe is happening over there, the policymakers may elect to attempt a military penetration of the area to get the information. Any use of the military will be based on your planning agenda, and I'm sure the final decision to commit to the operation will be made well above our pay grades. Are you with me so far?"

He looked from Noreen to Brisco, and both nodded. The Colonel seemed to relax a bit. "Now, I've been sent here to brief you on what we're after, and why some of your people may be asked to go there. I will serve as liaison officer to Langley and grade the final product when it comes in. An operations officer from the DDO was specifically not included to avoid conflicts. As you know, we're pretty much out of the paramilitary business. So, Colonel, it's *your* show—or our show if you like. Your job is to develop a workable plan, and mine is to help you—are we clear on that?"

Noreen glanced across to Brisco, who looked passively at him. He turned back to Carter. "Mr. Carter, I sincerely appreciate what you've said, perhaps more than you can imagine. You're right—I've been directed by General Thon to develop a feasible operational scenario. But all too often, there's an agreement at the CINC level, and then we here at the planning and operational end get jerked around. Now that we're on the same sheet of music, perhaps can you tell us what is so important up on the Kola, and we'll tell you if we can do the job for you."

Carter took a standard, unmarked Hydrographic Office Chart 3180 from his briefcase. It detailed the Kola Peninsula from the North Cape to the approaches to the White Sea. "You've been given the general coordinates of the target area?" Both nodded. "We think the Russians are selling nuclear weapons specifically for Third World end users, and we feel they are preparing the weapons at this location." Carter tapped the chart near a shallow inlet on the northeast coast of the peninsula.

"Lumbovskiy?"

Carter nodded.

"That's supposed to be an intermediate maintenance and storage facility," said Noreen. The missile and munitions storage sites across the Kola Peninsula were all well-known.

"It is," replied Carter, "but we also feel it's where they're reconfiguring tactical warheads for export. Lumbovskiy appears to be an ideal facility for this kind of clandestine venture. It's very remote, and the facility is served by a ten-thousand-foot landing strip here at Kachalovka. The port of Gremikha, some thirty miles up the coast, is a protected, ice-free anchorage."

"Are these weapons being made available to terrorists?" asked Brisco.

"Possibly," said Carter. "The Brazilians would seem to be brokers here, which means they could end up anywhere."

Carter briefed Noreen and Brisco for the better part of an hour, emphasizing that proof of the preparation of nuclear warheads for export or actual sales on the weapons could only come from their agent at the facility. The only things omitted were the resolution capabilities of the KH-19 satellite and the increased satellite coverage of the Barents Sea and the White Sea. They were cleared for that information, but had no need to know.

"And the President just can't go to Stozharov and ask him to stop it?" asked Noreen when Carter had finished.

"It may not be that easy," said Carter. "We're making inquiries in that direction, but it hasn't been productive. If Stozharov knows what's going on, he may not be able to do anything about it. The infrastructure that distributed power for the leaders of the Soviet Union is not available to the President of the Russian Republic." Carter pulled his notes together. "Now that you know what's at stake and why it's critical for us to recontact our agent in the Kola, do you have any ideas how that might be accomplished?" Noreen looked to Brisco.

"I was given this tasking twenty-four hours ago, so there will be a number of changes and revisions to the operational scenario as we fully define the mission profile and support requirements." There was no hint of apology in her tone, nor was she making excuses—she was all business. "You're sure your man is at this facility?"

Carter nodded. "I'm given to understand that if nukes are being reconfigured at this site, he'll be there."

"On a mission like this," Brisco continued, "we normally set the parameters and task the operational component to develop the mission concept and operational scenario. Given the lead time and the unique nature of this operation, we've taken on that responsibility here at the mission-tasking level. By the end of the week, I hope to have all the operational components in isolation." She flipped the cover sheet on the briefing easel parked in front of the table to reveal a blow up of the Kola Peninsula. "Naturally, getting in will be a lot easier than getting out."

Brisco went on to describe the terrain and weather features of the Kola around the Lumbovskiy facility. Carter was amazed at the varying weather patterns on different parts of the Kola Peninsula and how quickly they could change. The meteorological forecast could be critical. Then she outlined the general operational plan. He was also impressed with how much Major Brisco had accomplished in so short a time. He had almost no operational experience, but it seemed to be a logical and well-conceived plan.

"The Russians couldn't have picked a more difficult and inaccessible location, which was probably by design on their part. But we can use that to our advantage as well. It will stretch our capabilities to the fullest, and I'll have to consult with the operational elements before I can give you any realistic odds for success. Computer simulation can also help us with the probabilities. It won't be as accurate as with battalion- or regimental-size units, but it'll give us some idea of our chances. Currently, I have only two programmers cleared for BEARCAT material, and I may have to ask for interim clearances on two more so we can go round the clock on this thing. On the surface it looks doable, but it'll be dangerous and there are a lot of unknowns involved, both in the planning and during the conduct of an actual operation." She glanced at Noreen. "Mr. Carter, we're not in business here to turn away work, but if there's another way, I'd just as soon not have to put my team in there, at least not with the lead time you've given us."

"I understand, Major. Please be assured that I will honestly relay your reservations to the people at Langley and up the line, but I'm sure the final decision will be made at the national command level." Brisco and Noreen exchanged a knowing look as Noreen rose, signaling an end to the meeting.

"Flying back today?"

"That's right, Colonel. I'll be on the late flight back to Washington. The Director will want a briefing early Friday morning."

"Thanks for your candor and your understanding of our position on this thing, Carter," said Noreen, shaking his hand. "I'm sure we'll be seeing more of each other as planning for this thing unfolds. Now if you'll excuse me, General Thon will want to speak to me before he leaves for the day." Noreen glanced nervously at his watch and hurried out the door.

"What time is your flight, Mr. Carter?" asked Brisco.

"Eight-thirty, and please, call me Steve."

"Well, Steve, then you have a few hours to kill."

"I do, but I've brought along enough work to keep me busy."

"Tell you what, let me check my messages and whip through my in-box. Then why don't I show you a place where they serve an absolutely sinful lobster bisque. Your lunch on the flight down couldn't have been that good."

Carter laughed. "That sounds terrific. You know, it seems like everyone down here is either eating or else they're talking about food."

"Let's just say that we haven't discovered many alternatives to grease and butter. I hope you don't have a thing about low-cholesterol cooking."

"Nothing that I can't put on hold for one meal."

"Then I'll be back for you in about fifteen minutes. You're welcome to stay here, but you'll need an escort if you have to leave the room. There's a phone in the corner for unclassified calls." She smiled and left. He sat down at the conference table and began making cryptic notes on a yellow legal pad.

Commander Jim Griffin sat in the small control room of the USS *Archerfish* with the petty officer of the watch. On any other submarine in the U.S. Navy, the commanding officer wouldn't stand a steaming watch, but *Archerfish* was anything but just another submarine. In fact, only a handful of people in the U.S. Navy knew about her existence. The unlit cigar clamped between his teeth was about half its original length, marking the midpoint of the watch. Smoking was not permitted due to the small size of the boat and the capacity of the atmospheric scrubbers. Griffin didn't like snuff, so he consumed one cigar per watch without lighting it. He was a big, unkempt man with thinning red hair and a florid, perpetually angry-looking face. The planesmen joked that they always wanted to know where the skipper was so they could trim the boat accordingly. Griffin was meticulous, demanding, feared, and respected. He was also recognized by those in the submarine community as the best attack-boat driver in the Atlantic submarine fleet.

"Depth, speed, and course as before, Captain. Inertial navigation holds us fifty yards left of track. All other conditions normal."

"Very well, Bodine."

The *Archerfish* was like a modern airliner. She "flew by wire," usually on autopilot. The boat would automatically correct course and speed, and could be programmed to hold a prescribed depth or temperature gradient. Computers controlled virtually all life-support and shipboard systems, which allowed a complement of only four officers and seven enlisted personnel to manage the vessel. She was not a large boat, barely eighteen hundred tons, but that was still a very small crew. Griffin's last command, the *Atlanta,* a sixty-nine-hundred-ton Los Angeles–class boat, had a complement of one hundred fifteen.

When he had received orders to the boat eight months ago, he had been furious. "What the fuck do I want with a toy submarine," he screamed to the submarine detailer at BUPERS. "Does it come with its own bathtub? They make submarines at Electric Boat; who makes this one—Mattel?" When the detailer said that it was a German-built boat, Griffin replied, "I don't want a fucking BMW, I want a submarine—a real submarine."

But that was eight months ago. Jim Griffin had come to love the *Archerfish* like a truck driver loves his new Porsche convertible. On *Atlanta,* he had occasionally slipped into Soviet waters and played sneak-and-peak games in the Sea of Okhotsk with the diminishing number of Russian submarines that now put to sea. But even the quietest nuclear attack submarine rattled like a bucket of bolts compared to the *Archerfish.* She was a black hole in the water, a passing shadow—much like an F-117A stealth fighter in comparison to conventional aircraft. Griffin had once taken her around the North Cape and into the approaches to Murmansk—something he would never have done with the *Honolulu.* Air Force F-16 pilots talked of "strapping the airplane on their back," as opposed to climbing into the cockpit. It was the way Griffin felt about the *Archerfish*—he strapped it on.

She was an advanced A-212-type boat built in Bremerhaven with an advanced Sterling engine and AIP (air independent propulsion) capability. This extended her range tremendously and allowed her to operate under the ice. The *Archerfish* was a well-guarded secret, and she was kept in an underground berthing complex near Karlskrona, a facility once used by German U-boats. Since the embarrassing grounding of a Soviet Whiskey-class submarine off their coast in 1978, the Swedes had allowed the U.S. Navy to maintain a small, secret sub base near their own naval port of Karlskrona. Griffin's mission was more one of test and evaluation than open-water operations. The surface Navy saw the project primarily as a means of studying conventional submarine technology. With the new emphasis on power projection in littoral areas, the admirals hoped to develop new tactics to protect their carrier-battle groups against these small, silent boats in restricted waters. The submariners, whose nuclear fleet was being scuttled with the shrinking defense budget, were looking for a new threat and being forced to consider cheaper boats. As a community, the submariners hated the thought of "regressing" to non-nuclear propulsion, but it was better than sitting in port.

"Captain, request permission to stream the radio wire. We're due to copy traffic in ten minutes."

I know that! thought Griffin. Lieutenant Commander Graham Smith was the executive officer, and Griffin didn't like him. He wasn't quite sure why, but that mattered little. Maybe it had to do with commitment. Smith was an Annapolis man who went into submarines out of the Academy. He had received top marks at nuclear power and submarine school, and outstanding fitness reports as the weapons officer on *Atlanta.* He had qualified on the boat in near-record time. Then he left submarines for SEAL training, making him the only man in the Navy who wore dolphins *and* that ridiculous SEAL pin, the one they called a "budweiser." He was certainly competent, admitted Griffin, and he probably knew the boat better than anyone. *But why would a young man with his potential leave subs to be a SEAL? And why,* noted Griffin with a grim look, *does he persist in wearing both pins on his khaki shirt with that goddamn SEAL pin over the submarine pin!*

"Okay, Graham," said Griffin, "stream the wire." Then to the watch team he called, "Mr. Smith has the con." The sailors in the control room answered up, indicating they were ready to take new orders.

Smith went about the business of bringing the boat to periscope depth and streaming the communications wire, which was stored in a reel housed in the sail. The wire was positively buoyant, and it floated as it was towed slowly at shallow depth, allowing the boat to communicate without surfacing. *Archerfish* was also equipped to use the ELF, or extremely low frequency, communications system. It was a highly secure system that didn't require them to come to shallow depth, but it was very slow.

Graham Smith *looked* like an officer on a recruiting poster—handsome, square-shouldered, and with an easy smile that suggested a hint of smugness. And, for reasons Griffin could not understand, Smith never quite acquired that white, semi-chalky complexion that was common to most submariners. The Captain also resented his being back on submarines after leaving the service to play boy commando. Smith was smart and he knew the boat, but a good submariner had to be more than smart. It took dedication, patience, and long periods underwater to develop a sense of awareness and perspective needed to fight a submarine in the silent, three-dimensional darkness of their undersea world. He had to learn to *think* like a blind fish, and the Graham Smiths never seemed to do that, no matter how smart they were.

"Captain."

"Yes, Graham." Griffin was in the middle of an engineering casualty drill and resented the interruption.

"Priority from COMSUBLANT. We've been ordered back to port ASAP."

Unusual, but not unheard of, thought Griffin as he read the computer printout. "Very well, set a course for home at best speed. We'll acknowledge and give them an ETA next time we snorkel."

"Aye, aye, sir." As executive officer, Smith was also the navigator. On a nuclear boat, he would have laid down a track on a nautical chart, and then given the helmsman a course to steer, but the *Archerfish* was a different kind of submarine. Instead, he nodded to the quartermaster of the watch, who sat at a PC-type computer console in the corner of the cramped control room. The sailor punched in the latitude and longitude of Karlskrona, a shaft revolution count for "ahead full," and their normal running depth of three hundred feet. The computer chirped twice and issued a short, quiet series of clicks before signaling its readiness with a long buzz.

"Ready, sir."

"Engage," replied Smith.

"E.T., go home," the quartermaster said with a grin as he punched the "enter" key. The watch section carefully monitored their dials and gauges while *Archerfish* came about and went to the ordered depth and speed. "Steady on course two-five-seven. We're making turns for eighteen knots—depth, three hundred feet. She says she'll have us at the Karlskrona Point Breakwater tomorrow morning at 10:07. Plenty of time for some Sunday-afternoon liberty, huh, Captain?"

"We'll see," said Griffin. "Mr. Smith, take the deck and continue with the engineering drills. I'll be in my quarters."

"Aye, aye, sir."

John Moody sat cross-legged in the middle of the family room surrounded by an assortment of gaskets, parts, and tools. It was a dark, cheaply furnished room. Several acoustic tiles in the ceiling were missing. Extension cords crisscrossed the room to two floor lamps with dented shades that projected yellow cones of light down on him. Across the room, a cracked wooden door led out to the carport. In the corner, an old console TV with a defective vertical hold flipped through scenes from the Redskins game. Moody wore an old pair of blue jeans and an olive-drab, Army-issue T-shirt. His arms and hands were smeared with a dull, black layer of grease that made his fingernails appear like white disks on top of his fingers. He wore an old red bandanna around his head like a sweatband, a habit from days when his thick brown hair was much longer and had to be tied back out of his work. Before him, with its kickstand on a two-by-four wooden block to hold it upright, was a Suzuki VS-1400 Intruder minus its engine housing and a host of vital components. An old canvas shelter half protected the worn, indoor-outdoor carpet from most of the damage. There seemed to be no pattern or apparent method to what Moody was doing, but his hands found the proper tool or part while his eyes never left the engine. He moved like a surgeon hurrying through an intricate but routine procedure.

"Sir, I sure 'preciate your taking th' time to fix my scooter. The dealer wanted four hundred bucks to do th' job." Moody mumbled something and kept working. "You know, she'd been making that sound for a couple of weeks, but I never thought it'd be somethin' serious. I mean, hell, I take purdy good care of her. Now what's that thing called again?" The tall, wheat-haired young man seated on the sofa stared intently at Moody. "Sir?"

"Wha . . . huh?"

"I said, what's that thing called again?"

"It's the timing chain, Walker, the timing chain." Moody found his beer and took a long pull before turning back to the bike.

"Yeah, right—guess that's different from th' chain that drives the back tar." Moody shot him an incredulous look as he snatched a ratchet and adroitly swapped a twelve-millimeter socket for a fifteen. "Anyway, sir," Walker continued as he lifted two more beers from the six-pack seated beside him and set one on the floor next to Moody, "I'm real grateful." Walker was a rangy, long-muscled kid from Arkansas. He was sharp featured and his face had a kind of permanent sunburned look that accented his soft blue eyes. Although he was no more than twenty-four, there were already permanent squint lines at the corners of his eyes, giving him an affable, innocent quality. He took the can of Strohs from his mouth and slurped a line of foam from his mustache.

"Hand me that torque wrench, will you?"

"The what?"

"That barlike thing over there—the one with the little gauge on the end of it."

"You got it, sir."

Moody quickly finished buttoning up the engine and slowly got to his feet. His knees popped audibly and he bent carefully to one side, then the other, to relieve kinks in his back. Then he walked around the motorcycle, inspecting it carefully as he wiped his hands on an oily rag. There was a smudge on his cheek, which seemed to mock his fine, almost delicate features and serious green eyes. He nodded to himself and swung a leg over the bike. He kicked it over twice and the machine boomed to life. He revved it several times while Walker held his head in his hands in an attempt to escape the deafening noise. Moody let the machine settle to an idle and leaned over the gas tank to listen. After several minutes of a dull throbbing punctuated by the crashes of thunder as he opened the throttle, he looked up through the blue exhaust haze to Walker and smiled. Finally, he hit the kill switch and a welcome silence settled over the smoky room.

"She fixed?"

"She's fixed," replied Moody, "but you gotta quit lugging it. The engine's designed to be wound up."

"Yeah, Ah know, but it feels like it's gonna fly apart when Ah do that—kinda scary."

"Walker, this is a pretty hot bike. You might want to think about trading down to a Yamaha vertical twin or something a little less spirited."

"Yer probably right—she's somethin' of a crotch rocket, all right, but I kinda like her. An' damn if she won't straighten out yer arms when you get on it."

Moody just shrugged. Motorcycles were right up there with diving accidents and parachuting mishaps as a leading cause of broken Navy SEALs, but he knew Walker was a reasonably good rider. He just had a lot more bike than he needed.

"Hey, John, telephone. I think it's the quarterdeck."

"Be right there," he called back up the stairwell. Moody shared the beach house with two other team officers. They rented it for eight months of the year, and moved out from May through August when the rent tripled during the tourist season. It was a shabby, two-story beach bungalow, and it had the reputation as one of the more active bachelor snake ranches on the beach. Fortunately, the SEALs were on pretty good terms with the Virginia Beach Police, many of whom were ex–Navy SEALs, and most complaints about the noise were easily handled. Moody climbed the stairs to a dated kitchen that was segregated from the living room by a Formica breakfast bar. His two housemates and three girls were watching the football game on a color portable. He ripped a paper towel from the dispenser and used it to handle the phone.

"This is Moody."

"Mr. Moody, this is Petty Officer Rufo on the quarterdeck. This is a phone tree contact exercise for Bravo Platoon. I've got you down for a contact time of two-fifteen." Moody was silent for a moment. "You got that, sir?"

"Yeah, I got it. Is the duty officer there?"

There was a chuckle at the other end of the phone. "He said you'd ask to speak with him, and that I was to tell you he was busy. He also said to tell you fuck off—his words, sir, not mine."

"You talked with Master Chief Tolliver?"

"Yes, sir. He's been contacted."

"Okay, Rufo. Don't bother with Walker—he's here with me."

"Understood, sir."

Moody hung up the phone and thought for a moment. *A phone tree exercise was the code phrase for an immediate recall of his platoon. Now why would some asshole be holding a recall drill in the middle of the Skins game—unless it's not a recall drill.*

"What's up, John-boy?"

"Fun and games," he replied. The two SEALs looked up from the game and gave him a knowing look.

"You gotta go in?"

"Yep," Moody replied. "If I'm not back by supper, don't forget to feed Tom." Tom, a black Labrador with a gray muzzle, briefly lifted his head from the carpet at the mention of his name, and then went back to sleep. He was Moody's dog, but one of the girls was rubbing his ear and he had no intention of moving.

"Take it easy, man."

"Later, Johnny."

Moody waved unconsciously and made his way back down the stairs. *Now, what could they be up to?* He shrugged. *Nothing to do but go in and find out.*

"Problem, Boss?" Walker was wheeling the motorcycle toward the door. He sensed something was different.

"We're recalled."

"No foolin'?"

"No foolin'," replied Moody.

"Think it's a drill?"

"Probably—we got to saddle up and head for the base."

Up in the living room the two SEALs looked up as the two motorcycles tore out of the driveway. The girls were too into the game to notice.

For Major Dan Black, Sunday was family time. He was also watching the football game, hoping that by some miracle the Tampa Bay Buccaneers would upset the hated Redskins. It didn't help that his two sons, seated on either side of him, were both wearing feathered headdresses and brandishing foam tomahawks. They let out a whoop as Rypien hit Art Monk with a TD pass that effectively put the miracle out of reach.

"Another beer, hon?"

"No, thanks. After this is over, I'm going to take these two braves out in the yard for some touch football and teach them some respect."

"Uh-uh, Dad!"

"No way, José. We'll crush you like the hogs are crushin' your Bucs."

"We'll see about that." Black grabbed each in a headlock and began to gently bump their heads together.

"No fair!"

"Dad's a bully—Dad's a bully!" They struggled, but Dan Black was a powerful man with huge arms.

"Hey, you guys—how many times I have to say this, huh? Not in my family room." Black looked appropriately chastised and turned them loose, taking a few punches on the break. He had a heavy build with strong features and dark, flashing eyes. His mustache was so thick that it took on a sculpted look and helped frame a perfect, even smile. His bald head, though edged on the sides and back by rich brown hair, saved him from looking like Tom Selleck.

Black had been passed over for lieutenant colonel several times and would probably retire as a major. Too many of his performance evaluations said he lacked command and leadership potential. That was okay with Black. He had made it perfectly clear that he had no interest in flying a desk or commanding anything but an aircraft, and if they took him out of the cockpit, he'd quit. His performance evaluations also reflected what was common knowledge around the 8th Special Operations Squadron as well as the rest of the Air Force special operations community—Dan Black was the best special operations pilot in the U.S. Air Force.

Occasionally he would take one of his fighter-jock friends on an insertion-profile training mission, which called for flying a four-engined MC-130 at three hundred fifty knots, one hundred feet off the deck over hilly terrain. Usually they couldn't wait to get back to the relative safety and comfort of their F-15 or F-16. Black was rated in all Air Force strategic and tactical support aircraft, but the 130 was his weapon of choice. He no longer competed in the annual C-130 "rodeo" competition, which determined the best 130 pilot in the Air Force. He had won it so many times that he was considered in a class by himself.

The Extend-a-Phone on the coffee table rang and Black grabbed it, snapping up the aerial.

"Hello."

"Major Black?"

"Speaking."

"Sir, this is Sergeant McWilliams at the squadron. We have a Code Three for you, sir."

Black glanced at his two boys and sighed. "Understood, Sergeant, thank you." He reluctantly telescoped the antenna back into the phone and pushed himself to his feet.

"Where you going, Dad? Can't stand to see your team getting slaughtered?"

"Sorry, guys. Got a call from the office, and I have to go in for a little while."

"You be back for dinner, Dad?"

"I sure hope so, guys."

He looked at his wife, who was standing in the kitchen doorway. She was as good at reading the look on his face as he was at flying airplanes. She also knew he wouldn't be home for dinner.

Katrina Shebanin sat near the front and stared ahead as the headlights picked up a succession of ice-encrusted craters. She swayed gently from side to side as the driver adeptly wove the bus around and between them. It was like driving on a World War I battlefield, and she admired his skill. More than one vehicle had broken an axle or lost an oil pan along this stretch of road. Occasionally a vehicle would have the misfortune of breaking down when one of the unpredictable winter storms swept in from the Barents Sea. When that happened, a heavy-duty wrecker had to be sent to recover the vehicle and sometimes a smaller truck to bring back the frozen bodies.

Each Saturday morning, the bus made its way for thirty tortuous miles along the coastal road from the village of Gremikha to the facility at Lumbovskiy and back. And each week, production schedules allowing, senior members of the staff were allowed two days off site for rest and relaxation. In Gremikha, apartment accommodations were available for them, which told the local population of the importance of these weekend visitors. The village offered reasonable shopping, several small restaurants, a single nightclub, and a surprisingly good library. Gremikha Harbor and Svyatonosskiy Inlet offered shelter for the small fishing fleet and a factory ship that put to sea from there. The town was also an occasional port of call for one of the coastal freighters of the Murmansk Shipping Company, which provided the community with an assortment of consumer goods that were quite exceptional given the remote location. It was the westernmost port in the Barents Sea that remained free of pack ice year round. About half of the time, Katrina stayed at the facility and enjoyed a few quiet days off, reading or listening to music. But Gremikha offered a change of pace and a change of menu. It was an oppressive and drab fishing village, sprawled on the rocky Kola coast, but it represented the only civilization between the facility and the Murmansk area some two hundred miles to the northwest.

The trip took just over an hour each way unless there was an unusual amount of snow or the bus stopped by the airfield at Kachalovka to meet an incoming flight. Due to the workload, Katrina had not been away from the facility for three weeks, and she actually found herself looking forward to a few days at Gremikha. The realization of that thought sent a shiver through her. *Good Lord,* she thought, *eight months ago I was in Murmansk looking forward to an occasional visit to St. Petersburg. Well, things change, I suppose, and not always for the better.* Challenging work for scientists that paid a decent salary was another commodity in short supply since the passing of the Soviet Union.

"What do you have planned this trip, Katya?"

"Oh, I don't know. I've heard the steamer was in a few days ago, so I thought I'd prowl the shops. Eat, sleep, read—the usual." Dr. Zhdanov seldom took time away from the facility, and there was a festive air about him. He was like a sixth-grader on a school outing.

"I hear the club has a new singer and that she's quite good. Why don't I buy you a nice dinner and we'll go listen to her."

"Komrad Doktor, is this official business?"

They both laughed. Zhdanov had a reputation at the facility as a bit of a stuffy bureaucrat, but he was a gentleman and a kind, harmless one at that. He had been one of the last to drop the salutation of "comrade" in addressing his staff. He might have gone on indefinitely had not Katrina and several of the others started clicking their heels in Gestapo-like fashion and formally addressing him as "Komrad Doktor."

"Let's just say that your part of the project is ahead of schedule and you deserve an adequate reward."

"In that case, I accept. But you know, I love expensive food and lots of it."

Zhdanov rolled his eyes. "That is a well-documented fact, comrade—I mean Katya." He blushed, which again made her toss her head in laughter. "Nonetheless," he continued, "I'll call for you at six P.M. sharp."

Shebanin and Zhdanov arrived at the nightclub about 8:30 P.M. They had taken a chance on a small bistro down near the wharf area and were rewarded with fresh sole and a passable bottle of wine. After a hot cup of strong tea, they donned their parkas and trudged back up the hill to the only nightspot in Gremikha called, in irreverence to the former Soviet government, The Gulag. They found a table in the corner, ordered vodka, and settled down to listen to the lilting melodies spun by a young Crimean folksinger. Between sets, a rather amateurish four-man combo played Western music for dancing. Katrina found herself starting to relax, and she could see that Zhdanov was enjoying himself immensely. He tapped his foot to the music and smiled as he sipped the chilled vodka. *It must be something genetically common to those of us in the scientific community,* she thought. *We seem to find ourselves drawn to places of amusement, but our entertainment comes from watching other people have fun. We seldom participate, but we like to be close to those who do.* The effects of the vodka were beginning to tell on Zhdanov as he alternated telling amusing anecdotes about his graduate work in Helsinki with borderline maudlin stories of his wife and two sons in St. Petersburg, whom he missed terribly. On balance, Katrina was having a good time—up to that particular point of the evening.

"Good evening, Doctors. May I join you?" Colonel Makarov jammed a cigarette into the corner of his mouth as he pulled a chair from the table and sat down.

"Why, ah yes, Comrade, please do," stammered Zhdanov—he was suddenly nervous and ill at ease in the presence of the security man. Somehow the universal greeting of the old Communist state seemed to fit, but Makarov failed to notice—he was staring intently across the table at Katrina.

"Thank you, Doctor Zhdanov, but I already have. It's nice to see the distinguished members of our scientific community out enjoying themselves." He signaled to the waitress, who brought his drink from another table and set it in front of him. He downed it quickly and called for another.

"May I buy you a drink?" Zhdanov shrugged indecisively while Katrina shook her head. "Another round. Perhaps the lady will change her mind when it arrives." The waitress smiled self-consciously and retreated.

Makarov's nondescript sports jacket fit him poorly. He was a man who would never look quite right unless he was wearing a uniform. Katrina knew the type well. The KGB had sent their goons in civilian clothes to lurk about at the university looking for dissident students. They stood out there just as Makarov did here. The club was a hangout for the local fishermen and merchant seamen. In the old days, there would have been careful, furtive glances at a man obviously connected with state security. Now there was indifference or an occasional hostile stare.

Makarov was an oppressive and menacing man, and the absence of his uniform did little to make him appear less so. He had heavy jowls that were darker than the rest of his face, and he always seemed to be in need of a shave. At first glance, Makarov could have been written off by his appearance as a low-level, physical-security type, but his shrewd and highly intelligent eyes, which now roamed over Katrina, indicated otherwise. The scrutiny made her skin crawl, and she reached nervously for a cigarette. His hand shot across the table and snapped open the lighter. She inhaled and nodded curtly.

"We don't often see you in town, Doctor Zhdanov," Makarov said, reluctantly looking away from Katrina.

"The work at the site is going well," he said defensively, "and even scientists need some time off."

Why is it, Katrina thought, *that we still fear these people—is there something imprinted in the Russian psyche that forces us to continue to grovel before these animals?*

"I'm sure it is, and I'm sure General Borzov is most happy with the work you carry forward for the new Republic."

The band broke into a scarcely recognizable version of "Pennsylvania Six Five Thousand." Makarov quickly crushed his cigarette and reached across the table, pulling Katrina to her feet. She was almost as tall as he, but not nearly so heavy. His eyes were alive with anticipation.

"You don't mind if I dance with the lady?" he said to Zhdanov. The Director looked bewildered and spread his hands in acceptance.

"Well, *I* mind," Katrina said, loud enough for those at the adjoining tables to hear. A cloud of anger passed across Makarov's face as he glanced quickly about the room. She tried to sit down, but he levered her forearm, forcing her to remain on her feet.

"No need to cause a scene, Doctor—it's just one dance." The smile became a leer as he continued to pull her toward the dance floor.

She snatched a drink from the table and threw it in his face. His head snapped back in surprise, and she nearly tore free from his grip. Makarov issued a low, barely audible snarl and grabbed her reluctant arm with both hands. He was beginning to win the tug-of-war when she jammed her lighted cigarette into the back of his hand.

"You bitch!" He clutched at her, but this time she broke free and stepped back against the wall out of reach. He started for her, but was held back by the scraping sound of chairs hastily being pushed from nearby tables. Several rough-cut men closed ranks behind him, and one man took a bottle from the table by its neck.

"Is this what you *chekist* bastards do for a living now?" said one particularly large man dressed in a pea jacket. "Harass women in night-clubs?"

"The lady said she don't want to dance, mate," said another. "Maybe you best shove off."

Makarov surveyed the ugly mood of the men that now ringed the table. Out of habit, his hand moved for his jacket pocket to retrieve his credential, then he froze. That would no longer work, and he knew he had but one option. He shot a murderous look at Katrina and grabbed his drink from the table. He threw a greasy five-thousand-ruble note on the table and parted the crowd as he made his way back to the bar.

Zhdanov found himself on his feet next to the table. His mouth moved but nothing came out. "Good Lord," he finally managed. "What could have gotten into the man? I mean he simply . . ." He was badly shaken and totally unprepared for the cold look of hatred on Katrina's face.

"You do something about that bastard, you hear me!"

"Why yes, of course, but what can I do, I mean if he—"

"God damn you! You're the facility director—I work for you! Either you do something about him or find yourself another physicist!"

Again Zhdanov's mouth opened and closed silently. For a moment he thought she was actually going to strike him, and he took a step back. Instead, she grabbed her parka from the back of the chair and hurried for the door. From the bar, Makarov watched her go and calmly sipped his drink. A dozen pairs of eyes watched him and prayed he would get up and try to follow her.

Late Sunday afternoon they began the tortuous journey back to Lumbov-skiy. Katrina had kept to herself for the remainder of the time in Gre-mikha. She had thought of seeking out Zhdanov to apologize, for she knew he wasn't a bad man, just a weak one. But each time she looked at the bruises on her arm, she began to tremble with rage. *All the reforms and change will be worth nothing,* she thought, *unless we can rid ourselves of beasts like Makarov.* She desperately wanted to be back at the facility and the privacy of her quarters, so she was somewhat irritated when the bus turned off for the airfield at Kachalovka. It was fifteen minutes from the main road to the airstrip, but would delay their arrival at the Lumbovskiy by over an hour. Kachalovka was a remote, snow-covered strip that handled a limited volume of military and civilian traffic.

When they arrived, Zhdanov left the bus and hurried into the small terminal building. He returned with two men, both wearing the greatcoats of the Russian Army. Both of them carried small grips and flat attaché-type cases. Katrina watched them approach as Zhdanov and one of the soldiers deferred to a taller man between them. General Borzov boarded first, nodded politely to the others in the bus, and took the first seat by the door.

When the bus finally crawled through the main gate at Lumbovskiy, Katrina was physically and emotionally exhausted. She had slept very little the night before, and all she wanted to do was to get to her room and take a hot shower. As she stepped from the bus, a large form appeared at her elbow.

"Doctor Shebanin?" Katrina had seen Colonel General Borzov briefly on two occasions when he had addressed the staff on visits to the facility, but he had never spoken to her in person. There was firmness to his voice, authoritative but not harsh.

"Yes."

"May I please have a word with you in private?"

"Right now, General? I mean, it's been rather a long trip." She was surprised to find herself balking at the request of a Russian general officer, but she was near the end of her patience with those who controlled her life.

"I understand." His tone was apologetic but still firm. "But if you would please indulge me, I have work to do this evening and must leave very early in the morning."

She shrugged. "Very well."

"Thank you. Shall we say in ten minutes in Doctor Zhdanov's office?"

He touched his hand to the brim of his cap and joined Zhdanov and the other officer who waited at a distance. She collected her bag and began to trudge off toward her quarters, too weary to focus on why the District Commander would want to speak to her in private. Fifteen minutes later she was at Zhdanov's office. Doctor Zhdanov admitted her without a word and then left, closing the door behind him.

"Thank you again for coming." He motioned her to one of the two padded chairs by a coffee table in the corner. "Tea?"

"No, thank you, General."

He took a cup and saucer from the desk and joined her. His brown army uniform was devoid of decorations or piping except for the three silver-backed stars of a Russian colonel general, and a single ribbon signifying he had won the Order of Lenin, the Soviet Union's highest award for valor. Borzov was a man who seemed to lend power to a uniform. The teacup looked almost ridiculous in his weathered hand. He sipped carefully and returned it to the saucer on the table.

"Let me come to the point, Doctor. I understand you had some difficulty with my chief of security."

Her mind raced—*so this was it!* "Yes, General," she replied carefully. "The man nearly attacked me in the club in Gremikha. He forced his company on Doctor Zhdanov and myself, and then when I refused to dance with him—well, this is the result." She pulled up her sleeve to reveal the blue-green splotches on her forearm. The outline of a man's grip was clearly visible.

A look of pure anger flicked across Borzov's stern features. "He did this to you?"

She nodded, almost afraid to speak. When she found her voice, it poured out. "General, why are men like Makarov allowed to be in uniform now—why is the OMVD still around? They weren't necessary in the Union, and they certainly aren't necessary now." She bit her lip and fought back the tears, ashamed that she was becoming emotional in the presence of the District Commander. "Isn't the cold and the isolation enough? Why do we need them here to guard us?" She folded her arms and raised her chin, forcing herself to meet his eyes.

Borzov again sipped his tea and measured her. It was a critical appraisal that somehow did not make her uncomfortable.

"Doctor, just how much do you know of the work here at Site Three?"

The question was totally unexpected, but the topic was on more familiar ground. "As with Site One, where I worked before coming here, we are dismantling the nuclear components of various air- and ground-launched tactical nuclear weapons to recover the plutonium and U235, and then sanitizing the delivery vehicles and detonation materials." It was the approved response.

"And of your particular project?" He leaned forward with his forearms across his knees.

"Well, we're not told the exact nature or purpose of our work in the special-weapons facility, but it's plain to see we're reconstructing nuclear weapons. The specifications vary, but in general we're modifying or reconfiguring some of the smaller tactical weapons to conform to different launching and delivery platforms." She hesitated, but the look on the General's face invited her to continue. "A few of them look like they could be adapted for intermediate-range ballistic missiles, but most appear to be destined for artillery shells or air-launched weapons. It also seems they are being designed with a less rigorous arming sequence and with fewer safety interlocks."

Borzov nodded appreciatively. "And could you speculate where the weapons are going when they leave here?"

Katrina was beginning to relax. She felt comfortable talking with him about her work, and the General was an intense listener. "I just assumed that our weaponry was being tailored to the requirements of the Russian Republic, rather than the old Soviet Union. And perhaps," she said tentatively, "modified to circumvent restrictions imposed by arms-limitation accords with the United States."

Borzov stared at her a long moment and seemed to reach some sort of a decision. He rose, went to the side table, and returned with a cup of tea. "I think you should have some tea." It was polite, but a command nonetheless. He handed her the saucer as he took his seat, and again leaned forward on his forearms.

"The weapons you have been assembling with such care are being constructed and sold to other countries—countries that do not have nuclear weapons, but have the cash or foreign credits to pay for them." Katrina stiffened, the cup frozen halfway to her mouth. Borzov made a patient, reassuring motion with his hand and continued. "Now, let me tell you why I have chosen to share this nuclear madness with other nations who have not yet developed the technology. Our homeland is on the brink of economic collapse, and the next year or two will be critical to this great free-market experiment on which we have embarked. There is no turning back, and we face chaos and anarchy if we fail. I feel the Red Army has a vital role to play in this transition. First of all, it must remain strong if it is to oppose the graft and corruption that threaten our distribution systems and our new commercial enterprises. Inefficiency and corruption brought down the Communist system—that and military pressures from the West. We cannot allow the old *nomenklatura* and the bureaucracy to sabotage our new democracy. Currently, the Army is without sufficient funds to maintain itself and its equipment. We can barely feed ourselves. The sale of these weapons is bringing in food and enough hard currency to keep the Northern District forces intact and to keep a portion of those forces combat-ready."

"But . . . the weapons. Every second-rate nation in the world will have them—the next war in the Middle East, or Yugoslavia for that matter, will be a nuclear one." Her voice trailed off at the horror of the thought. "We can't do this!" she added softly.

He regarded her thoughtfully. "Are you willing to risk revolution here at home to guarantee that the next foreign war will not be a nuclear one? And who will stand to lose if such an event takes place—us or the United States?" Borzov smiled ruefully and shook his head. "The Americans have won what they called the Cold War, and they did it without firing a shot. They simply built a huge war machine and forced us to bankrupt our economy trying to keep pace. It was military or economic defeat—we chose economic, but it was a defeat just as surely as if we had been beaten on the battlefield. Now we're supposed to destroy what's left of our military might—the Americans even make shipments of food and aid contingent on this." The General paused and looked down at his hands. "It's . . . it's too much to ask of a proud nation. The Union had to go, but our motherland and the people should not have been made to suffer so much. If the weapons I have asked you and Doctor Zhdanov to build should be used by others against the United States or her allies, then so be it. I do not relish the prospect, but I have an army to feed and a nation to serve."

He gave her a sad smile. "When you chose to be a scientist and I chose to be a soldier, we did not think it would be like this, eh?"

There were a thousand questions racing through her head. *How could this be allowed to happen!? The Americans are bound to find out and do something—or will they?* But there was no denying the sincerity of the man sitting across the table from her, or cause to think of him as anything but a patriot.

"As for our friend Colonel Makarov, he will never again bother you. He will hear it from me, personally, that he signs his own death warrant if he does." For the first time, she saw a hard look come to his face, and with it a touch of savagery. "He will remain as head of security for our nuclear bases because he is quite good at this difficult and thankless job. If the old Union did nothing else, it produced an abundance of efficient security officers." Borzov again looked directly at her. "And so, Doctor Katrina Shebanin, will you continue to serve as director of the special-weapons project?"

Katrina hesitated, but there was only one acceptable answer.

"Yes, General, I will."

They were both silent for a long moment before Borzov spoke. "Come, let me see you to your quarters."

"Thank you, General, but that's not necessary."

"I understand, but perhaps it will help you to see that not all men in uniform are brutes."

"See you a quarter and bump a quarter."

"And a quarter."

"Okay, shit-for-brains, I call you."

He turned over a queen. "Two pair, whores and fours. I'm bettin' you didn't get that other john, sir."

Moody sat there looking at his hole card, an ace, which did nothing for the two jacks he had showing."

"Crap!"

"Come to Papa," Garniss crooned as he raked in the pot. They sat on the steel deck around an equipment box with a camouflage nylon poncho liner draped over it. Moody and two other SEALs tossed crumpled bank notes onto the green surface. Garniss made change and palmed the bills. Occasionally a pocket of turbulence caused the players to grip the edge of the makeshift card table. They had finally left Oceana Naval Air Station at 8:00 P.M. Sunday evening, eastern standard time. That was five hours ago. The plane lifted off well after dark to avoid any satellite coverage from one of the NATO RHORSATs as well as anything that might still be operational from the former Soviet Union. The SEALs, dressed in an assortment of sweat clothes, running shoes, and uniform parts, were surrounded by a scattering of white box lunches, most of which had been cannibalized to one degree or another.

One of the uniformed flight crew made his way back from the forward part of the aircraft, working his way among the equipment boxes strapped to the floor and against the sides of the fuselage.

"You know, you guys shouldn't be gambling on a government airplane." He had tech-sergeant stripes on his hooded parka.

"Shouldn't or can't, Sarge," said one of the SEALs. The sergeant laughed and sat down to watch.

"Okay, ante up." When the pot was right, the SEAL to Moody's right began dealing.

"Anything wild?"

"Yeah," said the dealer, "red deuces, treys, one-eyed jacks, an' the man with the ax."

"Aw, for Christ's sake," said Moody.

"Hey, sir, it's dealer's choice. I play your silly games—you play mine."

"Not this time, O'Keefe. You and Garniss got all my money anyway." He looked up at the sergeant. "You want in?" The Air Force man nodded as Moody rose to make a place for him at the table.

He moved forward stiffly, careful not to step on any sleeping members of his platoon. He took a paper cup from the dispenser and poured himself a cup of warm black coffee from the urn lashed to the bulkhead. Then he sat down on the canvas bench-seat next to one of his SEALs who was still in his BDU utility uniform. He was quietly smoking a cigarette and staring patiently into space. They sat together in silence for several minutes.

"Whatta you think, Master Chief?"

"Don't really know, sir. This one has a different feel to it."

"Know what you mean. They don't usually send a Blackbird out for milk runs." Blackbird was the nickname the SEALs used for the special-mission MC-130H Combat Talon II, a modified C-130 Hercules that was equipped with precision navigation equipment and terrain-following radar. It also had a highly sophisticated electronic countermeasures suite and a variety of sensors that allowed it to find holes in enemy radar coverage to insert special operations teams into denied areas. Regular 130s cost about twenty-five million, but the Blackbirds, with their special equipment, cost over four times that amount.

"Think it'll be a go?"

"Well, there's the old risk-reward theory," replied Tolliver. "The greater the risk, the more important the target. And usually, the greater the risk, the less likely we'll get a green light." Moody nodded. Both he and the Master Chief had responded to emergency recalls before, and occasionally they had been flown out to preposition for a mission. Only once had it been for real, and that was a tense but uneventful embassy evacuation. "Somehow, this one's just got a heavy feel to it. Chances are it's just a contingency, but with this kind of security, it'll be very secret or very hairy—or both."

"Roger that, Master Chief." They talked for a few minutes, and finally the Chief tipped his hat over his eyes and fell off to sleep. Moody sat staring at the padded gray bulkhead across the body of the plane.

An emergency recall with a flyaway was always no-nonsense business. When Moody and Walker had arrived at SEAL Team Two, they were met at the door and herded into the conference room. The Team Two Operations Officer put them in isolation and gave them a warning order. Isolation meant just that—no contact with anyone outside the team area and no phone calls. Other SEALs with soothing voices would call the wives and say their husbands were on a confidential training mission. They were told their men might be away for several weeks. The wives would thank them for the call and say they understood, and for the most part they did, but that didn't make the waiting any easier.

The warning order was a short equipment briefing that told the platoon in isolation just what apparatus and weapons they needed to load out for the mission—nothing more. Canvas-covered six-by-six trucks pulled into the compound and waited for them to manifest and stage their gear. It was a broad warning order and specified most of their standard operational deployment inventory—extreme-cold-weather gear, weapons, LAR-V scubas, static line and free-fall parachutes, drysuits, and all their personal winter-warfare survival equipment. Someone wanted them quickly, and that someone either didn't know or wouldn't tell them exactly what they were going to be doing. The few items the platoon left behind led Moody to believe they would stage from a friendly base with some support available. *We're obviously going north,* Moody had thought, *but why doesn't a platoon in Machrihanish take the action—*

they're on call and probably closer to the action. It had taken Bravo Platoon four hours to stage and load the equipment. After the gear was checked, rechecked, manifested, and loaded, Moody just had time for a few words with Master Chief Tolliver before the Commanding Officer of SEAL Team Two called him into his office.

Commander Dan Stuckey was a tall, lean man in his late thirties who looked barely twenty-five. He was one of the element commanders with Team Eight during Desert Storm, and had a reputation as a good operator as well as a good CO. Moody liked and respected him. In the office with Stuckey was Lieutenant Commander George Oliver, the Team Executive Officer. Oliver was what was known in the teams as a ticket-puncher. Ticket-punchers remained in the operational platoons for as little time as possible—usually just long enough to get a platoon-commander qualification entered in their service jackets. Then they sought out staff-duty assignments, returning to the teams only for their department-head tour and XO tour, doing whatever they could to mold their career for quick advancement. Operational assignments and serving extended tours as platoon officers were coveted by officers like Moody, but did not usually lead to fast promotion. There was a natural animosity between the ticket-punchers and the operators.

"Mr. Moody," the CO began as he closed the door to his office, "they didn't tell me much about this one, so I don't really know anything more than you do. But reading between the lines, I'd say something big might be going down, and it's probably very sensitive. I don't know why they didn't pull Mike or Romeo Platoon in on this thing. Both are training with allies in Europe. Maybe they don't want them in on this. Anyway, my orders were to get my best C-1 cold-weather platoon saddled up and into isolation. They specified an Alpha Seven load-out, which you guys just completed. There'll be a 130 at Oceana in a half hour, and only the pilot knows where you're going.

"John, as you know, this could be nothing, or it could turn into a real sonovabitch." Stuckey got up and walked around the desk. He was dressed in blue jeans, a rugby shirt, and deck shoes with no socks. He looked at his platoon commander straight on. "The XO wanted to swap you for Delta Platoon, but I overruled him." Moody and Oliver exchanged a quick "fuck you too" look. "You're my best winter-warfare operator, but the XO has a good point—you have a reputation for getting a little crazy every so often. This has come up before with you, and there's no room for that shit in this business." Moody adopted his best sincere-and-responsible look. "Now, I know you can do the job, just don't do something stupid and hang us both out to dry, okay?"

"Yes, sir."

" 'Cause if you do, I'll kick your ass." Stuckey wasn't just using a figure of speech, and Moody understood that he wasn't. Sometimes it was like that in the Teams.

"Understood, sir."

"I tried to send the XO along in case you needed someone to fight with the staffers, but SOCOM turned me down. I guess this thing is being pretty tightly held, so you're on your own. That's just about it—is there anything else you need?"

"Yes, sir. Can I have Warrant Officer Ligon?"

"Is he available?" said Stuckey, looking at Oliver.

"Yes, sir," replied Moody before the XO could speak. "Master Chief Tolliver called him just after the recall and told him to stand by. We're probably going to stage from a friendly base, and I'd feel a lot better having Ligon there to help us. If it doesn't look right, I'll send him back with the plane."

Stuckey rubbed his jaw. "How does he feel about it?"

"The Master Chief says he's ready. He knows the deal, sir—he'll be all right." It was a touchy subject. Some or all of Moody's platoon would be called on to make up the action element if the mission was a go, but it probably wouldn't include Ligon. He was black, and in a Nordic or winter environment, a black man was a conspicuous advertisement for the presence of the U.S. military. There were all too few blacks in the Teams, and they were usually assigned to SEAL Team Four or Eight, which had responsibilities in the Caribbean and Africa. Moody wanted Ligon for his equipment-maintenance skills, for the man was about as handy as a pair of pants. He was a superb technician and could fix anything. Once the nature and type of the mission was known, the SEALs often had to reconfigure or modify their equipment and weapons for the specific task. Ligon would be invaluable when it came time to stage their gear for the mission. The Navy had mandated that *all* its units be integrated, and that direction took precedence over operational considerations. But the SEALs usually found ways to get their best people to the right places. Ligon was Team Two's lone black SEAL.

"Any problem, George?" Oliver raised his eyebrows in a neutral gesture. "Okay, John, you got him. Tell him to get ready, but we can't hold that plane for him."

"No sweat, sir. The Master Chief has him loaded out and standing by."

Stuckey gave him a sideways look—he knew he had just been hustled, but he let it pass. He glanced at his watch. "I guess that's about it. Good luck, John. Take care of your men, and do us proud."

"Thanks, skipper. I won't let you down."

"Take care, Moody," said Oliver evenly.

Moody shook hands with both and left to board the trucks with his men.

"Sir . . . sir . . ."

"Yeah, hey what, Master Chief?" Moody jumped awake.

"We're about fifteen minutes out. I just told the men to get into uniform—thought you might want to do the same."

Moody got up from the seat and worked through a quick routine of neck rotations and trunk twisters. Then he pulled his torso forward and rested his forehead on his knees for a full minute. Sleeping on a canvas bench-seat passed the time, but it usually trashed his body. Moody walked back to the tail section of the aircraft and took his uniform from a hanger clipped to a cable run on the side of the fuselage. He dressed quickly and stuffed his sweat clothes into a kit bag. When he returned to his seat, the rest of the platoon was busy strapping themselves in for landing. Moody smiled to himself as he detected a slightly different whistling noise from the landing gear. The Blackbird had skis fitted to its landing-gear wheels. Then he buckled up, joining the others as they bumped and swayed in unison while the aircraft extended its flaps and searched for the ground. Had there been a window in the Blackbird and had there been a moon, he could have watched as the aircraft settled onto a white, barren, unlighted strip on the west coast of Greenland.

President Mikhail Stozharov sat at his desk smoking and drumming his fingers on the polished wooden desk. He had no clear idea of the developments that might be taking place on the Kola Peninsula or within the Northern Military District, and he certainly knew that he had no room, politically or economically, to maneuver if the allegations made by the Americans were true. Being President of the Russian Republic was like riding a unicycle, and it would take little in the way of a domestic or international crisis to tip him over. *Sometimes I wonder if it's all worth it,* he thought to himself. The Swiss bankers had been most eager and helpful in providing him with a discreet account where he had put aside some funds for the day when an unpredictable turn of events, or his own frustration, would force him from public life. He would not be a wealthy man, but reasonably comfortable, even by European standards. *Perhaps,* he thought, *I'll travel on the lecture circuit, like Gorbachev, and demand huge sums of American dollars to speak at rich dinner gatherings of retired military officers and politicians. Gorbachev was a fool in many ways, but he was not stupid.*

"Mr. President," came the voice over the intercom, "the Foreign Minister is here to see you."

Stozharov leaped to the button. "Send him in at once!" He came around the desk to meet Solovyov at the door, relieved that he was here and slightly annoyed that he had not been sent straight in. "Vladimir Igorovich, welcome back! I wasn't sure that you were going to be here in time." He led the Foreign Minister to a small conference table set in an alcove at the side of the office. One end of it was buried with stacks of economic reports and manufacturing projections that, if a third of what they reported were true, indicated that Russia would soon be awash in a surplus of manufactured goods and agriculture products. Bureaucratic optimism had not died with the Soviet Union.

"I'm sorry to be so late in getting back, but there was a whiteout at the Severomorsk and we had to bus down to Malyavr to get a flight out. I spent most of Monday afternoon with Borzov and another hour with him this morning. He is a shrewd one, our Colonel General Borzov. After we exchanged pleasantries, I showed him the letter that was prepared under your signature." Stozharov had sent an official letter with his Foreign Minister indicating that he was on a special fact-finding mission to selected military districts to assess the material conditions of equipment and the readiness of the armed forces. Solovyov was to take up the matter of nuclear weapons at a time of his own choosing. "He then gave me quite an extensive briefing on the status of the Northern District forces. I must say, for whatever else he is up to, he is running a first-class military organization. He described in detail the process by which he has placed most of the ships and aircraft squadrons in a stand-down status or restricted availability, allocating just enough resources to keep them from further deterioration, while he maintains selected surface combatants, submarines, and aircraft in a high state of readiness. I'm no military expert, but he seems to be doing just that. And he's not one to whine about the shortages like some of our district commanders. He stated rather bluntly that he was critically short on a number of items—especially spare parts—but he would make do with what they had if nothing could be done about it.

"I really had no choice under the circumstances but to accompany him on a brief tour of the port facilities at Severomorsk and the military air installation. Most of the ships and planes were sealed up or in a mothballed condition—clearly out of service, but those vessels and aircraft that were operational seemed to be in excellent repair. And the soldiers and sailors had that old pride we used to see back in the seventies and early eighties—like they had a purpose. We dined at a regimental mess, and it was a fare of boiled potatoes, bread, field rations, and Red Army–issue vodka. I was most impressed with the young officers. They had a spirit and élan that is now rare in our armed forces."

"The nuclear weapons, Vladimir," the President said, glancing at this watch, "what about the weapons."

"I asked him about compliance with directives to dismantle nuclear weapons, and he assured me they were on schedule. When I questioned him about any irregularities or missing weapons, he became somewhat distant, and said that all deactivation activity and storage of nuclear materials was being conducted in strict accord with military directives.

"This morning before I left, I pressed him on the issue. Per your instructions, I said we were being urged by the West to account for all our nuclear warheads and to document the destruction of those rendered safe. I told him the Americans had even gone so far as to suggest that we may be guilty of allowing nuclear weapons to fall into the wrong hands. He looked me right in the eye and said that I had the word of a Russian general officer that he was properly managing the men and materials under his command. And then," Solovyov continued, "he told me that we could expect no problems with the Northern Military District, civilian or military, so long as the administration of the armed forces in the District were left to his discretion. He then added that he felt he could, at least in the near term, maintain his forces under current conditions and at current troop strengths."

Stozharov pondered this a moment. "What he is saying is 'leave me alone and I won't release a half-million hungry, unskilled ex-soldiers onto your economy.' "

"Exactly."

Stozharov smiled in resignation. "Ever think we'd see the day when a senior Russian military commander would openly defy the government?"

"Never. I just hope this is the only one."

The intercom hissed, "Mr. President, the Ameri—"

"I will be with him in a moment," Stozharov interrupted. Then, turning to Solovyov, "You may want to remain for this. It might be interesting."

When Secretary of State Richard Noffsinger was shown into the office, President Stozharov stood behind the desk and greeted him formally. After the customary pleasantries, Noffsinger got to the reason for his visit.

"Mr. President, have you been able to determine if there has been any unauthorized shipments of nuclear weapons or nuclear materials from the Murmansk area or your Northern Military District?"

"No, Mr. Secretary. We have investigated it thoroughly, and I have been given every assurance that your suspicions are totally unfounded."

Noffsinger asked the same question another way, using different words, carefully and with great tact, but he received the same answer. He quickly extended the best wishes of the President of the United States and, as protocol dictates, allowed the President of the Russian Republic to terminate the meeting.

PART THREE

Decision

The big C-141C Starlifter gently raised her rounded snout at the last moment and squatted smoothly onto the end of the runway. As soon as the nosewheel touched the ground, the pilot reversed the engines and slowed the aircraft to taxi speed before selecting one of the concrete ramps from the main strip. A blue pickup truck with a lighted Follow Me sign raced out to meet the plane and preceded the big droop-winged transport across the tarmac like an Asian child leading a water buffalo.

Inside the aircraft, Major Dan Black and his detachment waited patiently while the aircraft seemed to taxi forever. Black headed a contingent of twenty-two men, half officers and half senior enlisted. The officers were an assortment of pilots, navigators, electronic-warfare experts, and mission-planning specialists. Among the enlisted men were some of the most talented mechanics, riggers, and technicians in the U.S. Air Force. The men sat toward the front of the aircraft, just forward of a small mountain of equipment boxes strapped to the aluminum deck. They were all wearing cotton flight suits that bore only rank insignia and a Velcro name patch on their left breast. There was nothing that identified the detachment members as a component of the 8th Special Operations Squadron. As the Starlifter finally rolled to a stop, only Black unstrapped himself and joined the flight crew chief at the forward door. He cocked his head and smiled to himself as the two port engines were shut down. *So they're going to dump us here,* he thought. Black knew they would be stopping at Ramstein—he just didn't know whether it was a fueling stop or a staging area.

"Nice touchdown," he said to the pilot who just stepped down from the flight deck. He was a reserve Air Force captain—a weekend warrior who drove 737s for United Airlines—and had almost as many flight hours as Black.

"Why, thank you, sir," he replied casually, in spite of the fact that a compliment from Major Dan Black was no small thing. "Looks like you have a reception committee."

Black donned his blue garrison cap and descended onto the tarmac. It was 4:30 A.M. local time and bitterly cold. The area was unlighted except for the rotating beacons of the aircraft and fluorescent glare that escaped from the small gap in the doors of a single, isolated hangar. The Starlifter's two J-79 turbofans wailed mournfully into the darkness. A small herd of forklifts congregated off to one side. A single officer waited by the hood of his staff car while his driver sat at the wheel with the motor running. There was enough light for Black to catch the reflection of the eagles on the epaulets of his trench coat.

"Morning, sir," he said as he saluted. "I'm Major Black with the 8th SOS out of Hurlburt.

"Major, I'm Colonel Bost, Deputy Base Commander." He returned the salute with an impatient motion. "We were just notified of your arrival a short while ago, and quite frankly, we're a little unprepared for a special operations contingent."

This kind of a reception was all too familiar to Black. The Special Operations Squadrons had always been well down on the budgetary food chain, with Tactical Air Command, Strategic Air Command, and even the Military Airlift Command having priority. That had all changed with the collapse of the Soviet Union. Congress had built a fence around the Air Force's special operations components, while they decimated the regular Air Force. The change in funding priority had generated a lot of resentment. Four years ago, Dan Black would have had to grovel to secure a staging area and some reasonable accommodations for his men, but not now.

"Does that mean we can't stay here, sir?"

Colonel Bost eyed him coldly. "Of course not, Major, it's just that we've had to scramble a few people to take care of you." *That's interesting,* thought Black. He said nothing and simply stared at Bost. "My instructions are to see that you have a segregated, secure area and that your aircraft is out of here by first light." *So,* mused Black, *the 141 can't stay, which means they'll have to fly up to Rhineholm to refuel before heading back to the States. It also means something important is up and they want our presence to remain secret.*

"Understood, sir. Is that our hangar bay over there?"

"That's correct. Lieutenant Johnson and his people will see to your equipment." A young second lieutenant standing off to the side, dressed in khaki fatigues and a fur-hooded parka, came to attention.

"With the Colonel's permission, my master sergeant will supervise the offloading of our equipment, and my detachment security officer would like to inspect your hangar and office spaces before we do. And my second-in-command, Major Lusk, would like to talk with the head of your physical security team. I'm sure you have separate messing and berthing arranged for us. My supply sergeant can work that out with your facilities manager."

Bost clasped his hands behind his back and rocked forward on the balls of his feet. He took a deep breath and shrugged. "Very well, Major, you may proceed. The captain in charge of my air police is inside the hangar along with my transient billeting manager."

Black looked back to the door of the Starlifter, flipped a thumbs-up to the sergeant in the doorway, and followed it by pumping his fist to signal "on the double." The sergeant disappeared from view. There was a flurry of controlled activity in and about the aircraft. Two officers and a first sergeant burst from the doorway and made for the hangar at a brisk trot. A master sergeant appeared and signaled to the forklifts as electric motors aboard the aircraft began to grind open the rear clamshell doors and lower the loading ramp. Several other members of the detachment began making their way to the hangar carrying oversized attaché-type cases, while the rest of the detachment, officers and enlisted alike, began wrestling equipment boxes to the rear of the plane. Black watched impassively alongside the Colonel.

"Another thing, Major." Bost paused as he rolled his lower lip forward in a frown. "I understand some of you special operations types get a little frisky when you're away from home. I want you to know that none of that will be tolerated while you're on my base."

Black turned to face Bost. "Colonel, when my men and I are 'away from home,' as you put it, we're usually on very serious business. We're not here for the fräuleins and the beer gardens, and I can assure you that I hold the men of this detachment to a standard that's far stricter than any you impose on your base personnel. They know what's expected of them, and they'll conduct themselves accordingly."

The Colonel eyed Black carefully. He had the look of a man who tolerated no foolishness from his subordinates. His stern look also said, *You fool around with my men and you'll have me to deal with.* Bost had a general dislike for what he politely referred to as the nontraditional elements of the Air Force, and a thinly veiled loathing of special operations jockeys like Black. But the tasking had come directly from the commanding general through a special "eyes only" message directly from Joint Chiefs of Staff. The commanding general at Ramstein didn't get too many "eyes only" communications from JCS. There was no way these unwanted guests were not going to get whatever they asked for.

"Okay, Black. Is there anything else you require?"

"Why don't the two of us find some place where it's warm, sir, and I'll tell you about our support requirements. We just came from Dixie, and it's cold as a witch's tit out here."

* * *

The MC-130H landed at Camp Melville Greenland just before 5:00 A.M. on Wednesday morning. Melville was a curious installation with a curious mission. The camp was actually several miles inland from Melville Bay, a relatively protected piece of water fronting Baffin Bay on the west coast of Greenland. It was a satellite of Thule Air Force Base, and operated under the broad U.S.-Danish basing agreements that governed Thule. Located some three hundred miles east of the town of Thule, the small installation was ostensibly a weather station, oceanographic facility, and extreme-cold-weather-survival training base. It had the look and feel of a snow-covered military base, with prefabricated buildings and modular working spaces. There was even a small cinder-block administration building with two flagpoles out front—one flew the Stars and Stripes, the other a white Danish cross on a red field. There were no fences and few locks on the doors, except for those areas where classified material was kept. The camp looked much like one of the early oil-exploration bases on the North Slope of Alaska.

The base itself was run by a civilian contractor that provided housekeeping and food services. It was a small corporate enterprise that legitimately managed a few other remote facilities, but it was actually a proprietary company owned and operated by the Central Intelligence Agency. Most of the permanent personnel were either retired CIA or military personnel who stayed on a few years to augment their retirement checks. The camp's only link to the outside was a four-thousand-foot snow-covered strip with a TACAN navigation beacon and limited ground-controlled-approach, or GCA, capability. The navigation aids were of no small consequence to the resupply effort, since the camp was just a few hundred miles from the geomagnetic North Pole, making a compass almost worthless. Twice each week, a ski-equipped DeHavilland Twin Otter made the run from Thule, weather permitting, with mail and spare parts, and each month, a C-130 arrived with fuel and other consumables. Even in the worst weather, the arrival of an aircraft drew as many as a dozen curious inmates from the security and warmth of the buildings.

Moody and his platoon had been at the camp for just over thirty-six hours. Navy SEALs are adaptable creatures, and they quickly settled into the Spartan berthing area. They had been assigned an insulated Butler building as a barracks, with a central oil convection furnace that heated the entire building. On Moody's instructions, Master Chief Tolliver had set the temperature for fifty degrees and promised a broken arm to anyone who changed it. In order to keep the platoon segregated from the rest of the camp, an Army field kitchen unit from Fort Bragg had been flown in a few hours ahead of them and was now serving hot, tasteless, institutional-style meals. A second Butler building with mesh equipment bays and shop facilities was allocated for their equipment. A few of the

SEALs bitched about the conditions and the chow, but they were careful not to complain within earshot of Tolliver.

Early that morning, Moody had taken them out on a fifteen-mile forced march on cross-country skis near the Haffner Glacier. The SEALs were like a herd of young thoroughbreds, much more content and manageable after a brisk workout. While they were out, an unscheduled Twin Otter had delivered a small quantity of supplies and some additional people to the camp. After the noon meal, the civilian in charge of the facility notified Moody that he was to muster his platoon at 3:00 P.M. in a central building that served as a briefing room. The camp operated three hours ahead of Greenwich Mean Time and observed such conventions as morning, noon, and evening, but Melville had not seen the sun since late September and would not see it again until late February.

A few minutes before the hour, the platoon filed into the conference-like facility, a prefabricated one-room rectangular building with an arched roof. The front wall contained a large white board and a battered pull-down screen. There was an unfinished plywood podium and an electronic component rack stocked with a large TV monitor and several VCRs. Two dozen or more gray metal folding chairs lined the polished green linoleum. The room smelled of fresh wax and fuel oil. An air of expectation gripped the SEALs of Bravo Platoon as they milled about quietly and joked among themselves. About half held Styrofoam coffee cups, and a few of them smoked. Moody sensed this might be their initial operational briefing, and the men were dressed in their camouflage battle-dress utility uniforms with starched caps. They all now wore Danner boots, and most had blue wool watch sweaters under their BDUs.

"Well, while I don't normally fraternize with officers, I'd sure make an exception for her."

Moody and Master Chief Tolliver turned as a tall, black female Air Force officer led three Army men, two officers and a first sergeant, and two civilians in by the side door. The new arrivals took a moment to stomp the snow from their boots and hang their parkas on the hooks along the wall. They gathered in the front of the room, carefully eyeing the SEALs. Several of them busied themselves with briefing materials, but it was clear the lady was giving directions.

"Relax, Ligon, you're a married man," said Moody.

"Thanks for reminding me, sir. I almost forgot."

"Great ass, though," said one of the SEALs.

"Can the chatter," growled Tolliver, and the platoon fell silent.

The woman set an attaché case next to the podium and strode confidently to the back of the room where the Navymen were gathered.

"Afternoon, men. Any coffee left?"

"Yes, ma'am," responded Ligon as he jumped for a cup. "Allow me."

She swung her eyes across the group and stopped when she found the black collar bars. The SEALs wore nothing but rank insignia when deployed on a special assignment—no name tags or service designations.

"You must be the O-in-C." She nodded a curt thanks to Ligon and took the coffee. "Moody, right?"

"Yes, ma'am. Lieutenant John Moody, SEAL Team Two." He extended his hand. "And this is Bravo Platoon."

"Lieutenant—gentlemen." She took his hand and shook it firmly. Janet Brisco was dressed in tailored utilities with subdued-brown oak-leaf patch sewn onto her collar points. The blue-lettered, brown patches over her breast pockets said "U.S. Air Force" and "Brisco." Her smile was guarded and professional. "I'm Major Brisco, SOCOM J-5—pleased to meet you. Now, Lieutenant, if you'd like to get your men seated, we'll get started with your operational briefing."

Moody hesitated, just for a second. "Okay, guys, find a chair."

The SEALs shuffled forward and began filling the back rows first. One of the Army officers was busy with the VCR while the others sat in the first row of chairs. Moody held back and turned to Brisco.

"Uh, Major, the ops briefing is normally given by the operations controller. Is he going to be along soon?"

Brisco gave him a long, cool look. "I beg your pardon, Lieutenant?"

"The ops controller, ma'am. Is he coming or not?"

"Mr. Moody, *I'm* your controller and I'll be giving the operational briefing." Moody looked at her in disbelief.

"With respect, ma'am, the operations controller is the task unit commander, and he's usually someone with special operations training and experience—you know, a SEAL or a Special Forces officer, or maybe a Ranger. And usually it's at least a light colonel."

"Well, not this time, Lieutenant. You'll be working for me." He started to say something, but held back. "You have a problem with that, Lieutenant?" A long moment of silence passed between them. "Well?"

"Hell, yes, I have a problem with that! Unless this is some kind of logistic exercise or a training evolution, I want an experienced guy looking out for us."

"And you think I don't have that experience?"

"Look, lady, I mean Major, I *know* you don't have that kind of experience. Jesus, you gotta . . ." Moody glanced past Brisco and saw that everyone had turned in their seats to watch them. The Army captain had stopped tuning the TV monitor and stared blankly. "Look, could we step outside and talk about this."

"Absolutely!"

Moody held the door for her. "You might want your parka—this could take a few minutes."

"Not as long as you might think, Lieutenant, and I'm *plenty* warm, thank you!" She brushed past him, and he followed her out.

There was a loud silence left in their wake.

"I got five bucks says the cowboy can handle her," said one of the SEALs.

"You're covered," said another, "but I want some odds."

"She looks mean, aw-right, but the cowboy ain't never been throwed. I'll give you ten, but it's gotta be even money."

The swarthy, capable-looking Army man with first sergeant chevrons on his collar points and a broad, knowing smile turned to the men behind him. "Can I have some of that action?"

Outside, Moody stood with his arms folded while Brisco paced, trampling a troughlike pattern in the loose snow. "First of all," began Moody, "why isn't someone here from the European or Atlantic Special Operations Command?"

"Because SOCEUR and SOCLANT are not in on this thing. US SOCOM at MacDill was given the action on this, and I'm the action officer."

Moody's eyes widened. "You mean this op is being run by the SOCOM headquarters staff?"

"That's right. I suppose you have a problem with that too?"

"Hey look, Major, no offense, but when we're out there doing our thing, we've got two bad guys to deal with. There's the bad-guy who shoots at us and our own bad guys—the senior planners and staff types who think we can march fifty miles a day and fight battalion-sized engagements when we get there. Our lives depend on a controller who knows who we are and what we can do. We need someone with experience, and that means someone who's been on my end of the stick—not some . . . some . . ."

"Some female staff puke who's not a member of the club—that what you mean, Lieutenant?" There was a hard edge to her voice.

"Hey look, Major, this total-force-integration, 'girls-can-do-the-job' crap is okay for the admin inspections and congressional visits. And it may be okay for the peacetime military, but that crap stops when we put live rounds in the magazines. Those men in there will do just about anything I ask them to do, and they count on me not to get them killed if it's at all possible. I have to depend on my operational controller not to hang us out to dry when some asshole up the line thinks we should do a scene from *Mission Impossible.* This ain't flip charts and staff meetings or some TQL seminar, sweetheart—it's life and death."

Brisco glared at Moody. It would give her almost a sexual gratification to tear him up one side and down the other. She could do it and she was very good at it, but what would that solve? She turned away from him and gazed across the compound at the low, snow-packed buildings. A single quartz-iodide pole lamp on the corner of the building made it a surrealistic world of dull white-and-gray shadows. She huffed a few clouds into the cold dry air and turned back to him.

"Now you listen to me, Lieutenant." Her voice was low and serious. "Right now, the mission we have is a contingency—an option that may be taken only if there's no other way to resolve this matter. I have specifically asked that we not have to put you in the field, but ultimately, that decision will be made by JCS and the President. This mission will take you to a SOCEUR area of responsibility, but he's not a player because it's a very sensitive issue and this is to be a unilateral action. And if the mission is approved, it *will* be a SOCOM action. It has to be set up quickly and done quickly—neither of us has time for this male-female bullshit." She paused and took a deep breath. "I know my job, Moody, both as a planner and as an ops controller. I also know I have a duty—more than that, a sacred trust—to take care of my team in the field." She folded her arms across her midsection for warmth and again began to pace. "Tell me something, Moody, how come you're here? I'm sure there's some SEAL commander who's been around a little longer than you—someone with more experience. Why you?"

Moody shrugged. "I've got a platoon that's been together a while and is pretty well qualified in winter-warfare operations. We're consistently graded outstanding on our cold-weather ORIs—those are operational readiness inspections, Major."

"I know what they are, Lieutenant." She again stopped and faced him. "When SOCOM got the tasking on this, they assigned their best action officer, and here I am. I ask for the best cold-weather-capable SEAL unit, and they sent you. That's where we stand. Now here's what's going to happen. I'm going to brief this mission, and if you like, you can pretend I'm John Wayne and I'm wearing a green beret. Then, when I'm finished, a number of things can happen. You can get on the scrambler and call your CO—tell him you're an unhappy camper and that you want to come home. But you damn well better have some reason other than the fact that I don't use a urinal. And *I* may go back to SOCOM and say I want another action element—that you have a serious gender problem and can't focus on the job. I can do that, no questions asked—I'm the operational controller. Or we can both go to work and get the job done. As you're going to find out, this is one dangerous mission with huge implications for national security, and we don't have a shitload of time to get ready for it."

Moody looked straight at her and saw nothing but determination. He knew he'd have to hear her out. "After you, ma'am." He smiled stiffly and reached for the door.

* * *

Major Brisco shifted the podium a few feet toward the center of the room, trying not to let on that her hands were so cold she could barely grip the top of the lectern. "Good morning, gentlemen," she began, commanding her voice to be measured and very steady. "Once again, my name is Major Brisco, and I will be your operations controller for this action. This will begin a series of briefings that will read you into the mission and the planning that has been accomplished to date. From this time forward, you will be confined to Camp Melville until the mission is authorized, canceled, or passed to another action element. Before I get into the mission concept and operational scenarios, Mr. William Buskirk from the National Security Agency will give us a briefing on communications security and operational security. Needless to say, strict OPSEC and COMSEC will be observed during the planning, rehearsal, and operational phases of the mission. Bill?"

An affable-looking man in his mid-forties, looking more like a weekend hiker than a security officer, walked carefully up to the podium. He adjusted his glasses as he opened his brief.

"This mission and anything associated with it is classified Top Secret BEARCAT. We will cover the COMSEC aspects of the operation during the briefing segment that deals with the communications plan. My remarks for now will address the operational and physical-security issues."

Buskirk went into a short litany of national security regulations and the stringent rules that govern the sensitive information associated with this level of security classification. The final portion of the briefing applied to their conduct if they were captured—what they could divulge immediately when questioned, and what they should resist disclosing unless the brutality of interrogation became life threatening. He talked about the consequence of capture and torture with the same level of emotion as he did the penalties for failing to properly lock up classified material at Camp Melville. For the most part, the text of his remarks was boilerplate, more applicable within the scope of an ongoing general military conflict, but it had a terribly sobering effect on the men. When Major Brisco called on Steve Carter to brief them on the political and military scenarios that necessitated the mission, he had their undivided attention.

Carter referred to a chart of the Barents Sea and the northeast coast of the Kola Peninsula, and he repeated the same basic information he had presented to Brisco and Colonel Noreen at SOCOM headquarters three days earlier. Quite often, special operations teams were allowed only that information essential to complete their mission, and denied any nonoperational or non-mission-specific information for security reasons. It was also highly unusual for an intelligence analyst to brief an operational component, but this was not a normal operation. Brisco felt it would help the team to focus on their preparation if they knew the full background and reason for the mission. They were, after all, invading a friendly country—the sovereign territory of a former adversary. Carter proved to be a capable and highly effective briefer. Brisco also felt that if nothing were held back and the team members knew what was at stake, they would be more accepting of the difficult and dangerous mission profile she had developed.

"There it is, gentlemen," concluded Carter, "and now you know about as much about this problem as we do on the surveillance and intelligence side. The fact that we have a well-placed agent in the Kola is extremely sensitive information, and the agent's life depends on the confidentiality of that knowledge. You are being told of this only because it is information essential to the planning and execution of your mission."

Carter rubbed his hands together and paced quietly before the group in the way of an academician. "Nuclear proliferation and regional nuclear conflict have largely replaced the Cold War and the threat of a superpower thermonuclear exchange. And while we have been expecting something of this nature for several years, even predicting it, it's no less disturbing when it happens. So far as we know, this is the first and only incident of the wholesale proliferation of nuclear weapons. It may, therefore, be the ultimate decision of the policymakers to take action to put a stop to it. Right now, we desperately need to confirm our suspicions. Currently, the State Department and the intelligence community are doing what they can to surface our agent in place, but if those efforts are not successful, you may be assigned the task." He started to say something else, but stopped short. "Thank you for your attention. Major Brisco?"

Brisco rose and stepped to the front of the room. "Thank you, Steve. Now that you know where you're going and why you may be asked to go there, I'll proceed with the operational portion of the briefing. Normally, those of us on the mission-tasking end of things assign targets, and we leave it to you at the task-element level to develop a concept of operations. And as you know, the workup of your mission concept would include infil and exfil plans, time on target, action on target, contingency planning, and support requirements. Due to the specific nature of this mission and the short lead time we've been given, I've developed a general operations scenario, which I'll address later in the briefing. Naturally, if there's a better way to do the job, or any portion of it, I'm prepared to listen.

"The mission concept is to place a team of five to seven of you right here," she pointed to the chart, "about six to eight miles inland from the Lumbovskiy facility. It's an uninhabited wilderness area and should allow a team to lay up for an indefinite period of time. Once there, you will go to ground and establish a base camp with SATCOM capability while an attempt is made to contact the agent. You'll be jumping in and coming out by sea, which is why a SEAL element was chosen for the mission." Brisco didn't say it, but had it not been for the extraction by sea, which would obviously have to be made by submarine, a Special Forces A Team would have been a better choice than a SEAL platoon. Long-range reconnaissance and lay-up were a primary mission specialty of the SF teams. "You have a question, Lieutenant Moody?"

"Yes, ma'am. I was wondering just how we're supposed to make contact with this agent."

"Good question, and the answer is that you're not. Your job is infiltrate the area, make camp, and communicate. Sergeant Valclav will be accompanying you, and it will be his job to contact the agent. Perhaps this is a good time to make introductions." She motioned for a burly man in front of her to stand. "Gentlemen, this is First Sergeant Sergei Valclav of the 20th Special Forces Group."

He was short and stocky, with a weathered complexion and thick black hair that curled about his ears in a nonmilitary fashion. He had a grin that would have been cruel were it isolated from the twinkle in his dark eyes. Valclav faced them with feet apart, hands on his hips. His eyes swept the group and he nodded politely.

"I've met a few of the SEALs, Major," he said with an easy smile. His English was clipped and very precise. "Some of them owe me money."

"And the reason the sergeant will be joining us?" persisted Moody.

"Sergeant Valclav is a former Estonian national, born in St. Petersburg and raised in Tallinn until he and his family emigrated to the United States. He is fluent in a number of languages, including Russian. Since he can pass for a local, it will be his job to make contact with our agent and task him with validation requirements concerning the sale of nuclear weapons." Valclav again flashed them a smile and sat down. "And now I'd like to get on with the operational briefing."

For the next two and a half hours, Brisco worked herself through the mechanics of the operational planning and target analysis she and the SOCOM J-5 staff had put together—weather, topography, military air and maritime activity, indigenous population, and border-guard movements. Occasionally during the briefing, Moody would catch Master Chief Tolliver's attention and they would lift a cautious eyebrow to each other.

Later that evening Moody, Tolliver, and Sergeant Valclav were sitting around a card table in one of the modular huts that served as a recreation area for teams in isolation. There was a battered Ping-Pong table at one end of the room and a full-size pool table with smooth, threadbare green felt nearby. Garniss was trying to decide whether to hustle some of his platoon mates in a game of eight-ball, or join the card game underway in the corner. It was a business decision, not a matter of recreation.

Right after Major Brisco's briefing, Tolliver had made a beeline for Sergeant Valclav while Ligon had sought out one of the Army officers, a Ranger who was a specialist in special airborne delivery. It hadn't taken Tolliver long to determine that the SF first sergeant was a seasoned special operator as well as a language specialist. Ligon reported, almost reverently, that the Ranger, even though he was an officer, was one of the best in the business, and had extensive experience in covert airborne delivery. Moody and his Master Chief had managed a few moments together alone in the barracks to talk about the operation. They quickly agreed that it was a dangerous piece of business, but it was doable. They also agreed that the mission profile and operational scenario, as briefed by Major Brisco, were well thought out and afforded the least chance of compromise given the mission requirements.

If all went according to plan, the success of the mission depended on Valclav. It was their job to get him on the ground and in close proximity to the agent. His task was to contact the agent, and he would be taking most of the risk. But special operations often did not go as planned.

Tolliver took a tin of snuff from the side blouse pocket of his BDUs. He rolled off the lid in a practiced, one-handed motion and offered some first to Moody and then to Valclav. The platoon officer declined, but the sergeant took a pinch.

"Master Chief, I'm still trying to think of a reason to tell that bitch to pound sand, but I can't come up with one, can you?"

"No, sir. She seems to know her stuff. I've sat through a few operational briefings in my time, and that was one of the best." The tone of his voice was almost one of disappointment. "I still can't believe we're talkin' 'bout putting a team onto Soviet soil."

"It's Russian soil," said Valclav.

"Whatever," replied Tolliver gruffly. The two senior enlisted men eyed each other with a curious kind of affection. They were from different services and completely different backgrounds, but they were cut from the same piece of cloth.

"I just wish," continued Moody, "that she was a little more senior—at least a light colonel." All three nodded solemnly. When the team was in the field, and plans changed or new orders came down from above, it was the operations controller who had to do a reality check on them. Ultimately, it was the controller who had to balance operational requirements with the safety of the team, and stand up for the guys in the field. It was a delicate job that required intelligence and experience—and often, courage.

"Well, speak of the devil," muttered Tolliver. Moody and Valclav turned to see Major Brisco come through the door, followed by the CIA man, Carter. It was like a western movie when the bad guy walks into the saloon. The platoon went about their business, but there was a noticeable change in the air. Moody motioned them to the table. The three of them rose as Carter held a chair for her.

"Evening, gentlemen. Please, sit down." Brisco glanced around the room. "So this is how SEALS relax in isolation."

"Pretty much," replied Moody, "only don't play cards or shoot pool with them unless you've got money to lose. They're a bunch of sharks, and they conspire against officers."

"Does that include you?"

"Especially me. I think I made O'Keefe's house payment for him last month." It was an open invitation for Brisco to question Moody on the propriety of gambling with his men, a practice specifically forbidden by military regulations.

"Tell me something," she said, "now that you and the Master Chief have had time to think about the mission, how do you feel about it?" Moody had sensed this wasn't a social visit, but he was surprised by how little time she wasted coming to the point.

"It's a pretty dangerous piece of work, but you've got a reasonable plan." Moody paused to take a swig of Coke. He tapped a pencil on the yellow legal pad in front of him and continued. "The three of us have been working on some training and rehearsal schedules. We'd like to get at least two training jumps in, but most of the work will be conditioning, communications drills, and water work. I'm a little concerned about the extraction. Everything else is a part of our ORI training, but this is a new wrinkle."

"I know," said Brisco. "Can you think of a better way to get out of there?"

Moody considered this. "Not really. We'd talked about going cross country to the west, but it's three hundred miles to the Norwegian border. A lot can happen in three hundred miles. Besides, that's the way they'd expect us to go."

Brisco nodded. "How long will it take you to get ready?"

"We'll know more after we've spent some time in the water and see whether or not this Estonian can swim as well as he claims. I think we can do it in two weeks or so—twenty days max unless we have problems. What's our response time on additional equipment?"

"If you want it, you get it—twenty-four hours maximum delay. We have dedicated support aircraft in Thule and at Fort Bragg. If the weather's socked in, they'll air-drop it to us."

"Great," replied Moody as he pulled a frayed piece of notebook paper from his shirt pocket. "Here's a preliminary list the Master Chief drew up. Will you be here the whole time?"

Brisco shook her head. "Mr. Carter and I will be leaving tomorrow morning to brief the support elements. We'll be back in three days. Then I'd like to see some rehearsal component training." When there wasn't time or the facilities to do a complete mission rehearsal, training was focused around certain key components of the mission profile, and short-duration "mini-rehearsals" called component training were executed. "Any problem with that?"

"None, Major, In fact, I insist. I want you to see some of the things you're asking us to do." Moody's tone was not insubordinate, but indicated that he wanted her involved and to know that she was responsible. She met his eyes and nodded her agreement. "And now I think it's appropriate that we observe a little SEAL preoperational custom."

Moody caught Garniss's eye, who, somehow, always seemed to be nearby when he was needed. The lanky SEAL nodded and slipped out the door. There was a clumsy silence around the table while they waited for his return. Seconds later, he burst back through the door carrying a box, which he brought over and set on the card table in front of Moody. The rest of the platoon had quietly drifted over and now stood in a circle about them. Moody slid the top from the box to reveal a forest of glass necks. He set one of the Heinekens in front of Carter and another before Brisco before passing one to each of the members of the platoon and to Sergeant Valclav.

"Excuse me, ma'am," said Garniss as he reached over Brisco's shoulder with an opener and deftly popped the cap off her beer. Several other tops bounced onto the linoleum and rolled across the room. There were restrained murmurs of "aw-right" and "go for it" as a few of the SEALs pried the caps off with their teeth.

"I thought the isolation area was supposed to be dry," said Brisco as she and Carter followed Moody's lead and got to their feet.

"It is and it will be again in a few minutes, but traditions have to be observed," he smiled warmly, "even by those in the Air Force and the CIA." Moody raised his bottle. "Gentlemen—and lady—to the mission."

"To the mission!" The SEALs and Sergeant Valclav upended their bottles. like so many small, green-tinted water coolers, bubbles filled the bottles as the beer was greedily consumed.

"I, uh, don't drink," whispered Carter.

"Oh, yes you do," said Brisco out of the corner of her mouth, and she began to chug the beer.

One of the SEALs produced a metal garbage can and set it next to the table. There was a cinder block in the bottom of it. First Moody, then each of the others in turn, crashed their empty bottles in the bottom of the can. Brisco took her turn, and Carter, smiling self-consciously and stifling a belch, followed suit. Brisco noticed that Garniss quietly slipped the three remaining unopened beers into the can.

"That a standing tradition with the SEALs?" Brisco asked after they were seated. The can was removed to its place by the icebox, and the SEALs were back playing pool and cards.

"It is at Team Two. Some platoons knock down a bottle of scotch—we're beer drinkers."

"I was kind of hoping my new snake-eater friend here would break out some vodka. Maybe after the postoperation briefing, eh?"

"You can count on it, Master Chief," replied Valclav.

"Major," said Moody, leaning across the table on his elbows, "where will you be running the operation from?"

"The SOCOM Crisis Management Center at MacDill. It's got the SATCOM relay capability as well as the command-and-control facilities. There's a special CAT team—crisis action team—in place for special operations with twenty-four-hour watch-keeping capabilities."

"I see. Then I'd like to ask you for a favor."

"Ask away."

"Once we've finished here, I want Master Chief Tolliver to be there with you for the duration of the operation. During those times when we're not in communication, he'll know what we're thinking and probably how we'll react in any given situation. He'll also be valuable as an adviser should we have to deviate from the plan."

"And he'll also be able to serve as kind of my SEAL conscience." Brisco smiled, but her eyes were wary and serious.

"That too," replied Moody evenly. He looked at Tolliver, who nodded imperceptibly in agreement. This was new to him, but it made sense, both from an operational standpoint and for the morale of the men in the field. Tolliver would make a royal pain of himself if his men were being used poorly or needlessly endangered. He was also, for the most part, able to hide his disappointment. He assumed that Moody would lead, and that he would be left behind in some kind of support roll. But it was never easy for a SEAL to be told he would not make the "traveling team," as they called it, no matter what the circumstance or how dangerous the mission.

Brisco looked from Moody to Tolliver and back. "You got it." She hesitated, then added, "And since you want him in this role, why doesn't he accompany Mr. Carter and myself as we brief the support components. You do have some civilian clothes, Master Chief?"

"Yes, ma'am," Tolliver replied, but he was looking at his platoon officer. Moody raised his eyebrows, asking for the Master Chief's decision, and Tolliver again nodded.

"My Master Chief will be happy to accompany you," Moody said.

The five of them sat and talked for another hour and a half. Pocket notebooks came out onto the table and the conversation became animated. Occasionally someone would preface a remark with "if we go" or "it's still a contingency," but the discussion was deadly serious. When the meeting finally broke up, both the planners and the operators were feeling better. The mission had become no less dangerous, but there was now agreement on the direction of their preparation.

There was no such thing as dawn at Camp Melville, but Bravo Platoon was up well before reveille preparing for a conditioning march. Now that something of the mission was known, they had a goal to train for and a specific equipment load-out to prepare. The men were paired up with one *akio* between them. These were small, low boxlike equipment sleds on flat wooden runners towed by a man on snowshoes or skis. In rough terrain, one man would pull the *akio* while the other pushed. They would start out that morning wearing Sorrell arctic boots, with cross-country skis and snowshoes in the loaded sleds. Valclav had his own personal arctic gear, but most of the operational equipment was standard among the special operations components. As the platoon filed out of the compound, Moody remained behind with Tolliver. Major platoon decisions and assignments were always talked over between them before final directions were given to the men. Moody had felt somewhat awkward and even a little guilty about taking Tolliver out of the platoon workup and assigning him to Brisco. His unilateral decision also meant that he, and not Tolliver, would lead the ground element.

"Master Chief, I felt a little bad about giving you up to the Major—I mean, without talking it over with you first. Probably only five of us are going to make the jump, and one of the two of us needs to be with the controller."

"And y'all weren't going to be the one to stay back, right, sir?"

Moody tried to frame a better answer, but finally shrugged. "That's about it, Master Chief."

"Well, seeing as how this is probably a one-way trip," deadpanned Tolliver, "I guess I'll let you an' some of the younger guys go on ahead." He grinned and rubbed the back of his neck. "But I never though I'd see the day when I'd have to play nursemaid to a black split-tail Zoomie—an' I done some time in this man's Navy."

Moody smiled. "Just between you an' me, Master Chief, I think I'd rather tangle with a SPETSNAZ brigade than go a round with that lady. Looks like we both may have drawn combat assignments."

Tolliver nodded grimly. "Who else you figure to take along—if we go?"

"I pretty much know who I want—same guys you'd probably take. I want all of them but Ligon going through the mission workup—see who's looking good out on the glacier. We'll sort 'em out when you get back from the support briefings. Speaking of Ligon, shouldn't he be going with you, at least to the air-crew briefing?"

Tolliver frowned. "I think I can handle it, although I'll probably recommend that he go out on the final lift. We already talked about it, and I want him here supervising your practice jumps." There was a moment of silence between them. There was enough moonlight for them to see the file of men and their *akios* working their way across the snowfield toward the glacier. Suddenly, Tolliver felt a lot older than his forty-one years. "Reckon you better be catching up with the men. You ain't gettin' any younger yourself, sir, an' since none of them wants to be left back if this thing goes down, they're all gonna be bustin' ass."

Normally, Moody would have risen to the chief's gibe, but he sensed Tolliver's mood and let it pass. "Guess you're right on that score. Take care, Master Chief, and keep an eye on that wench."

"Aye, aye, sir."

Commander Jim Griffin sat in his small office in Karlskrona and smoked. *This is so very typical,* he told himself. *Hurry up and wait!* They had ordered him back to port at best speed, and now he'd been forced to sit around for four days. When he'd asked SUBLANT about the nature of their recall, he'd been told tersely to "stand by." The four days hadn't been wasted, however. *Archerfish* was a submarine, and there was plenty to keep them busy with standard upkeep and routine maintenance. Griffin had found that German-built submarines were a lot like German-built cars. They were high-performance machines and could operate flawlessly between scheduled maintenance, but if you cheated on repairs or replacement parts, whole systems could shut down.

The message traffic had ordered him to prepare his boat for extended seagoing operations, but there was no hint of what that might mean. So Griffin had set his small crew and group of shore-based technicians about the task of making *Archerfish* ready for sea and replenishing her stores. On balance, Griffin was forced to admit that the German boat had very few problems coming from the yards—far less than he had experienced on a new construction from Electric Boat, the builder of America's nuclear undersea fleet. *Archerfish* was the second new construction that Griffin had put to sea.

Griffin loved being underway, but the in-port periods in the cavelike berthing space were the pits. When a nuclear fast-attack sub was back at its base, the crew came to aboard the boat each day. The duty section slept aboard each night and, workload permitting, watched a movie. The officers and crew took their meals aboard, eating in shifts. It was cramped, but it was home. The small crew of the *Archerfish* ate and slept ashore, and much of the work was done in shop spaces surrounding the berth. Even the simulator, where they accomplished much of their in-port training, was ashore. The *Archerfish* was more of an aircraft in a hangar than a ship at the pier. The berth itself was a small floating dry dock, so the sub could be protected from the corrosive effects of salt water while in port, as well as from the extensive tidal changes along the southern Swedish coast. It was like pulling your speedboat up on the trailer after a weekend of cruising.

Griffin shared an office ashore with Graham Smith, although there was a partition that allowed the commanding officer some privacy. The two men couldn't be more different. Griffin's desk was a mound of reports, messages, computer printouts, and schedules. Smith often accused him of cleaning his desk with a hand grenade, but Griffin could repeatedly thrust his hand into the pile and retrieve a specific document. At one side of the desk was a large ashtray piled with used butts. On the partition behind the desk, next to a large color photograph of the *Atlanta,* was a picture of two little girls in one-piece Speedo swimsuits sitting on the diving board of a backyard pool. Several years ago his wife had demanded that he choose between her and that "goddamn boat," and he had, but he missed his daughters terribly.

Graham Smith sat at his desk on the other side of the partition. There was very little paper on his desk. When he needed to reference some detail about the boat or lay his hands on a specific report, he deftly stroked the keyboard of his PC and brought the document up on the screen. When they went to sea, Griffin packed his paperwork in a bulging leather briefcase and a stack of manila file folders, while Smith downloaded the data from his desktop machine to the hard drive of his portable notebook computer. In addition to the PC humming on Smith's desk there were two electric charcoal-activated filter fans, busily vacuuming particles of smoke that wafted around and over the barrier that separated Smith from his commanding officer. Also propped on the desk in a silver frame was a leggy Miss America type leaning against a late-model Corvette. "All my love, Candy" was scribbled across the sky above the car and girl.

The stuff that kept these two professionals from severely chaffing each other, aside from their commitment to *Archerfish,* was handball. Three times a week they took to the court, where youth and speed was challenged in sweaty combat by skill and cunning. The games, no matter who won, were bitterly contested, and the frustration of their different personalities was exorcised. The crew would rather miss mail call than have the skipper miss his handball game with the XO.

Today the game had been canceled, but any tension created as a result was absorbed by anticipated arrival of a briefing team from the U.S. Special Operations Command. The message that contained their security clearances indicated the briefing would be conducted by an Air Force officer, a civilian, and a chief petty officer, and that it would be a highly classified briefing for the commanding officer and selected key personnel only. With the small crew of the *Archerfish,* there were few non–key personnel, but Griffin had decided to include only his executive officer and the Chief of the Boat, or COB, until he could learn more about what was being planned for them. The COB, pronounced "cob," was a senior chief electronics technician with a master's degree in computer systems and who, in Griffin's opinion, was the smartest man on the boat. He valued the Cob's opinion, and more important, he trusted him.

A third-class petty officer, dressed in dungarees with a .45 hanging from a khaki canteen belt that identified him as the Petty Officer of the Watch, knocked once and opened the door to the office. The weight of the automatic caused the leather holster to sag to his midthigh, giving him a Clint Eastwood look.

"XO, they're here. I took them to the conference room, and I passed the word for the Cob."

"Thanks, Prout. By the way, you ought to strap that hog-leg down in case you have to draw on somebody."

"I would, sir, but then it'd slow me down in case I need to whip my pecker out."

"Good point, Prout—I didn't think of that." The sailor grinned and closed the door behind him. "You hear that, Skipper?"

"Yeah. You go on ahead—I'll be along as soon as I finish this memo."

"Aye, aye, sir." Smith shook his head as he grabbed his ball cap from the hook on the door. The Captain still scribbled his correspondence on a yellow legal pad for the yeoman to type. Smith and the other officers did all their work on computers that were tied to the ship's office and shop spaces by the LAN, or local area network. Smith suspected his captain had more of a control problem than a computer-literacy one. Griffin often complained that computers were like power steering and automatic transmissions on cars—they took the feel out of driving. Smith considered this a strange comment from a man who commanded a submarine with more data processors on board than crewmen.

Major Brisco, Steve Carter, and Master Chief Tolliver waited patiently, looking at the large map of the North Sea, which hung at one end of the conference room. The other three walls displayed color sketches of ironclads and sailing ships hung at neatly spaced intervals—the same cheap prints that adorned offices and hallways of U.S. naval facilities around the world. Graham Smith met Senior Chief Cornelius Dawgs at the door and preceded him into the conference room. Brisco and the others, still in civilian clothes, rose to meet them.

"Afternoon, ma'am—gentlemen. I'm Lieutenant Commander Smith, Executive Officer of the *Archerfish,* and this is the Chief of the Boat, Senior Chief Dawgs." He smiled brilliantly and held his hand out to the lady. "The Captain will be along in a few minutes."

"Commander, I'm Major Brisco, U.S. Special Operations Command, and this is Mr. Steve Carter of the CIA." Both of them presented their identification badges. "I think you know the Master Chief."

Smith had been so taken with Brisco, he had failed to notice the other two. He was shaking Carter's hand before he really saw Tolliver. "Well, I'll be damned. I never expected to see you here, Instructor."

"I could probably say the same for you, sir." A trace of guilt passed across Smith's face, for he had left the SEALs for duty back on submarines. Tolliver noted this and continued. "But I can't say I'm not glad you're here, given the mission that's being planned."

"Instructor?" interrupted Brisco.

"That's right, Major," said Smith. "Master Chief Tolliver was an instructor in basic UDT/SEAL training in Coronado, and he put me through training a few years back. SEALs always have fond memories of their instructors." The two SEALs smiled carefully at each other. Smith had been a strong trainee, but there was an arrogance about him that had attracted a great deal of extra attention from the instructor staff.

"Attention on deck!" said the Cob. Griffin never really entered a room—he barged into it.

"Carry on, please," he said, but no one moved. A glance told him that Brisco was in charge of the briefing team, and he stepped toward her. "Welcome to Karlskrona. I'm Commander Jim Griffin, captain of the *Archerfish.* I assume you've met my XO and the Cob."

"We have, Captain. I'm Major Brisco from Special Operations Command, and I've been assigned as controller for a contingent operation we're here to brief you on."

"I assume this *contingent* operation involves my boat?"

"Yes, sir, it does."

"Well, let's get to it, then. We're busy folks here, and it sounds like we're going to get a lot busier." Griffin slumped unceremoniously into his chair at the head of the table and waved for Brisco to begin. The others shuffled about to find chairs while Brisco remained standing. She was not unnerved by Griffin's abruptness, but she did find it interesting. Men often did that to test her or shake her confidence, but she sensed that Griffin couldn't care less if she was black or a woman—or a general or a private, for that matter. This was business that involved his boat, and he was anxious to know about it.

"Captain, we may be directed by national command authority to place a special operations team on the Kola Peninsula. The mission concept calls for them to be parachuted into the area and extracted by submarine—your submarine. Before I outline the mission scenario and the details of the extraction, Steve Carter will provide you with some background information and an overview of just why we are being asked to plan for such a mission. Steve?"

Carter rose and began his briefing. Brisco saw a look of concern on Griffin's pinched red face. He would have preferred to learn immediately of his part in the scheme, but forced himself to be patient. He was a big man, with an ample roll pressing against the buttons of his rumpled wash khaki uniform shirt. He focused totally on Carter, scarcely seeming to breathe and only occasionally blinking his watery blue eyes. The rest of them may as well have not been in the room. *I'll bet they're a charming pair to work for,* she mused as she looked from Griffin to Smith. The younger man was a little too good-looking, almost pretty. His uniform was freshly pressed, and his hair well cut and precisely combed. He had the same arrogant-but-competent look about him as did Moody, but he was more of a smooth article. The two enlisted men sat next to each other, like a pair of aging spinsters at a singles bar. And just like a pair of senior noncoms in the Army or Air Force, they would probably disappear together at the first opportunity to talk about the mission and compare notes. *Men,* she thought to herself with a slight smile. *Like most gals in the military, I knew I was entering a man's world when I went into this business, but I never thought much about having to work exclusively with them on a daily basis. What a bunch of characters! Is it the system that attracts them or the system that makes them this way?* After Carter finished, she rose and took his place at the end of the conference table. Griffin took this as an opportunity to light up. He inhaled deeply and expelled a blue cloud over the other conferees. Brisco paused and stared at him.

"Is there a problem, Major?" Griffin took another drag and looked unapologetically from the cigarette in his hand to Brisco.

"Not unless you don't have another one of those, Captain."

A look of understanding—possibly acceptance—flicked across Griffin's large face as he fished into his shirt pocket. She walked around to his chair at the head of the table as he shook the pack. She took a cigarette and neatly broke off the filter, depositing it in the ashtray. Griffin tossed the pack on the table and offered her a light.

"Thanks, Captain," she exhaled, "I was fresh out." On her way back to the front of the room, she picked a piece of tobacco from the end of her tongue. For the next hour and a half Brisco talked about the operation and the role of the *Archerfish* in retrieving the special operations team from the Kola Peninsula. The other four men listened and endured as the ventilation system struggled to stay ahead of the two smokers' combined output.

"And there you have it, Captain," she concluded. "Now you know why we may be asked to put a team in there, and how we would like to bring them out. The MCS [Mission Capabilities Statement] for the *Archerfish* says you can do it. Now, you have to tell me whether or not it can actually be done, and more important—can you do it?"

Griffin did not move for a full minute, and Brisco was about to repeat herself when he rose from the chair and strode to the other end of the table where she had laid out a map of the Barents Sea and the Kola Peninsula.

"So you want me to take my boat from here and make an underwater transit some two thousand miles to a position off the Lumbovskiy Inlet, clandestinely take aboard six Navy SEALs, and bring them home?"

"Yes, sir."

"Uh, Skipper." It was Senior Chief Dawgs.

"Yeah, Cob, what is it?"

"Sir, as I recall, there's going to be several miles of pack ice there—maybe as much as five or ten miles of it."

"The Senior's right," said Griffin. "Can the SEALs cross it?"

"That's the plan," said Tolliver, looking at Smith, "or go through it. I assume you don't want to surface that close to the Russian coast unless you have to."

"That's an interesting thought, Instructor—I mean Master Chief. We'll have to take a look at it."

Griffin studied his executive officer for a moment before turning back to the chart. *Just maybe,* thought Griffin, *having a SEAL officer as my exec may not be such a bad thing after all.* He stared at the chart for several minutes and straightened up.

"Major, what you want is feasible, but it's going to be a pretty tight fit. I won't make any commitments for my boat without seeing current meteorological and hydrographic data, as well as an updated threat profile for the Russian attack boats and destroyers out of Murmansk and Archangel. I'll also need an overlay of their satellite-coverage capability along our projected track and the latest plot of their active hydrophone arrays—and that's just for starters. Naturally, I'll want detailed rules of engagement in writing. I'll not take my boat that far into Russian territorial waters without a clear understanding of my range of options. We can be awfully quiet out there, but if the Bear comes looking for us, I want to know exactly what I can and cannot do."

As if on cue, Steve Carter fingered the cipher locks on his leather briefcase and began disgorging folders marked TOP SECRET—NOFORN/EYES ONLY and accordioned stacks of computer printouts. "I think you'll find it all here. Your rules of engagement are being drafted and will be delivered by courier prior to your sailing."

Griffin snorted as he began to sort through the material. "How much time we got to prepare for this little caper?"

"I need you to be on station in about three weeks."

"Lady, you got to be shitting me!"

"I wish I were, *Captain,*" she said evenly, "but that's all the time they've given us."

Major Dan Black sat at his desk at Ramstein AFB drumming his fingers on the blotter. Adjacent to the hangar was a small administration facility with office, conference, and communication facilities. By military standards, it was a well-appointed office—almost elegant—but since the furnishings had to pass muster at the GAO, it lacked the corporate feel of a private-sector executive suite. Directly behind this complex were transient quarters that could house the entire detachment in private rooms. Just a few years ago, a Special Operations Detachment would have been billeted at the end of a secondary strip in tent barracks and been glad to get it, but funding and operational priorities had changed all that. These comfortable facilities and the large hangar complex had been built to accommodate the now obsolete SR-71 reconnaissance planes and their crews. Ironically, the SR-71s were also nicknamed "Blackbirds," just like his MC-130s. *Now,* he mused, *the only Blackbirds that venture over enemy airspace are my MC-130s—ugly ducklings that go where eagles no longer dare to fly. And now we have the use of these wonderful facilities. Who says there's no God and that the meek won't inherit the earth.*

Black had just walked Major Brisco and the others back to their extended-range Gulfstream IV executive jet. He had been mildly surprised to learn that the mission controller was only a major, and shocked to find she was a black female. The briefing had done much to dispel the apprehension he had felt. She was a pro and that was really all he required, but it was still an eye-opener. Dan Black was raised and schooled in a time when blacks who went to college or became Air Force officers were looked on in two ways—they were either very good athletes or very smart, and they all were male. They were also a bit of a novelty, and too few in number to be threatening to the white, male world of pilots. A black female, in special operations no less, was very different. After the briefing, he found himself hoping she had an able mentor in the form of a senior colonel to run interference up the chain of command if needed. This one was obviously no shrinking violet that would knuckle under to a superior, but competence went only so far—then you needed rank.

Major Brisco had asked to brief Black alone, since they were not in a strict isolation facility. She had emphasized security and need-to-know constraints on the information, but left it to his discretion as to how to handle it. Black had flown special operations sorties where the controller had insisted the details of the mission be withheld from the air crew until they were airborne. Security that tight was not good for efficiency in the preparation phases, and even worse for morale.

"Okay, boss, what's going down?" Major Jim Lusk strolled into the office and heaved himself into one of the chairs attending the desk, hooking one leg over the chair arm. Lusk was Black's deputy detachment commander and a superb special operations pilot. He was also as irreverent as he was capable.

"Can't tell you, Jim. If I tell you, I'll have to kill you."

Lusk accepted that, nodding his head philosophically. "In that case, you might as well kill us all. That Navy chief had a few minutes with the master sergeant before he boarded the Gulfstream, and if you don't tell me what's going on this very minute, I'll be the last man in the detachment to know—and the last to die, of course."

"That's what I like about you, Jim." Black smiled. "It's your sense of propriety and adherence to the chain of command."

Lusk leaned forward across the desk, unable to contain himself. "C'mon, Skipper, what's up?"

"We got a tough one, Jim." Lusk had worked with Black for almost two years, and knew him well. As Black's face turned serious, Lusk sat up and dropped his leg, knowing the kidding was over.

"I want to keep the details of the mission and the targeting between the two of us for right now, but we have a modified KC-10 penetration and we have to be ready to fly it in about three weeks."

Lusk whistled softly. "Sensor pass?"

"Airborne delivery—six to eight personnel."

"Personnel—no shit?"

"No shit." Then Black gave his number two a quick overview of the mission profile.

Lusk whistled again and was silent, mentally thinking of work schedules and rigging time. "When do we get the bird?"

"Tomorrow. I told them we'd pick it up ourselves. There'll also be a practice bird at Rhineholm Mainside if we need to do some crew training."

Lusk again nodded. "And the other equipment?"

"Whatever we want and whenever we need it. I got the impression the whole fucking Air Force supply system is at our beck and call."

It was normal procedure for both Black and Lusk to train for the mission as command pilots, but Lusk would not fly unless, for some reason, Black couldn't. As detachment executive officer, he would be in charge of preparing the mission aircraft and serve as a backup crew leader. Finally, he broke into a broad grin.

"Once again, Cinderella gets to go to the ball."

Black smiled. Lusk, too, had been in special operations for his entire Air Force career and, like Black, was a major-for-life. And after years of "sucking hind tit" in his service, both he and Black enjoyed having the whole U.S. Air Force cater to their every support request as they prepared for a mission.

"Any problems?"

"No sweat, Dan—we got plenty of time. Let me get with the Master Sergeant and I'll have a rough workup plan to you by the end of the day. We'll be ready."

* * *

Dr. Leonid Zhdanov sat at his desk finishing the end-of-the-week plutonium-processing reports. One thing that had not changed with the passing of the Soviet Union was the requirement for frequent progress reports and output figures. Of course, the reports now seldom went further than the military headquarters at Severomorsk and the format had been greatly shortened, but there were still numerous documents to file in order to satisfy the Russian craving for paperwork to process. Zhdanov was more than a little excited, because tomorrow he would take this report to headquarters and deliver it in person. Then, following a series of facility manager meetings, he would be able to spend Saturday evening and part of the next day with his family in Murmansk. For him, it would be Christmas two weeks early. It had been almost four months since he'd seen them. Several times that afternoon he'd left his desk to go the window down the hall to look outside. He could see very little, but the occasional glimpse of a star through the curtain of mist that swirled in from the Barents Sea filled him with optimism. The courier flights that came from Murmansk were often canceled due to weather, and nearly as often for mechanical reasons. The marine forecast from Tromsø, which he could occasionally get on the short-wave, had predicted no major storm activity. But the Barents was a most unpredictable piece of water.

"Dr. Zhdanov," said Ludmilla from the doorway. "There's a call for you from District Headquarters. Can you take it?"

"Of course, I'll be right there." He hurried out of the office and down the hall to the communications facility. They had an adequate internal telephone system at the Lumbovskiy complex, but they had yet to install a reliable switching system that would allow for the transfer of calls from the one dedicated land line to Severomorsk. Zhdanov had lost count of the number of times he had been cut off or had to shout to be heard when calls went through the exchange in Gremikha.

"Zhdanov speaking."

"Will you please hold, Dr. Zhdanov? The District Commander would like to speak to you."

"Of course." A stab of fear went through him. Was something wrong? Something with Irina and the children? Could there be some problem with the work at the facility—something damaging to him? *And why would General Borzov call for me when he must have been told I will be there in less than twenty-four hours?* Zhdanov wiped the moisture from his palms on his trousers and shifted the receiver to the other ear. *Or could they have found out about the other things I have been doing?*

"Dr. Zhdanov?"

He jumped as the phone crackled in his ear. "Yes, Comrade General."

"*General* will do fine, Doctor," said Borzov evenly. "I understand that you are scheduled for a visit here tomorrow."

"Yes, sir."

"I was wondering if you would—I mean, since you are the facility director, I thought it proper to speak first with you to authorize a visit to headquarters for Dr. Shebanin. It is my understanding that the courier aircraft has plenty of seats. If her duties permit, and if she would like to get to the city for a short break, why don't you ask her to accompany you on your trip?"

"Why, uh, General, I see no reason why not." Zhdanov felt a flood of relief. "I'm sure she would welcome the opportunity for some time away from the facility and from Gremikha as well."

"Very well. We'll expect you both tomorrow, then. Good-bye, Doctor."

"Good-bye, General."

Back at his desk, Zhdanov sat deep in thought, trying to find some motive or reason for Borzov's action. *Could there be a problem with the Special Assembly Area and Borzov wanted to talk personally with Katya about it? Was there to be a change in their assignments?* A hint of panic began to tug at him. *Was Dr. Shebanin about to be named to replace him as head of the facility?* Zhdanov reached for the telephone and stopped. *Perhaps it would be better to speak to her in person.* He pulled his parka from its hanger on the wall and bolted through the door.

"Goodness, Doctor, you startled me," Ludmilla said. "Is something the matter?"

Zhdanov dismissed her question with an impatient gesture. "Of course not. I'll be over at the Special Weapons Facility if you should need me."

"Very well, Doctor," Ludmilla replied, registering a wounded look, and returned to her typewriter.

Five minutes later he was stomping the snow from his shoes in the security access area that screened those who entered the Special Weapons building. Even though he was the facility director, there was a two-person rule for any visitor allowed inside the building. But since he *was* the director, one of the security men jumped to accompany him to Dr. Shebanin's office. The guard led him into a changing room, where they both pulled on cotton, lint-free coveralls and slipped booties made of the same material over their shoes. From there, Zhdanov followed him into the assembly area.

Reconfiguring old Soviet warheads was nearly the equivalent task of building new ones from scratch. Making a nuclear device was one thing, but making a stable, effective weapon that was small enough to hang on the belly of a jet fighter or fired from a large artillery piece, together with safe, reliable arming and firing sequences, required a level of technology that few nations possessed. The building was a series of laboratories that took plutonium, or U239, from the existing weapons and carefully recast, formed, shaped, milled, and assembled the material into new weapons. Then came the delicate arming and triggering mechanisms. It was a time-consuming and exacting process. The new warheads were to be small, compact devices. They were simple and effective nuclear weapons, but they resembled no other weapon in the current Russian atomic inventory. The plant was a relatively modest facility, nothing approaching the size and complexity of the larger factories that had built over twelve thousand nuclear bombs for the Soviet Union. Here, there were about thirty scientists and technicians at work, all dressed and gowned like operating-room personnel. Most of them, like Zhdanov and Shebanin, counted themselves fortunate in finding work in the new order. The guard delivered Zhdanov to an office built into an interior corner of the building. They waited at the entrance until Dr. Shebanin opened the special, airtight door.

"Thank you, Igor. I'll look after the Director."

"Very well, Miss Shebanin." He turned and headed back to the entrance.

"Why, Dr. Zhdanov," Katrina smiled, "what a pleasant surprise. What brings you down here to the factory floor? You haven't been reading those Western management-technique books again, have you—the ones that tell you to get out and walk around?"

"Hardly," he replied. "I spoke with General Borzov a few minutes ago. I have to fly to headquarters for some meetings, and he suggested that you accompany me." Zhdanov felt a little self-conscious—it was hard to be businesslike wearing a gown and cotton booties. "Don't get me wrong, I'm happy for the company, but is there some reason for your going? There's no problem with your work here, is there? He said you might enjoy some time in Murmansk," he added lamely.

Katrina Shebanin watched Zhdanov fidget and slowly shook her head. *This is another legacy of the Soviet system—the absolute paranoia of those in positions of authority within the bureaucracy.*

"Look, Leonid," she began patiently, "he knows I didn't have a particularly easy time of it in Gremikha last weekend. When I met with him in your office we talked about that, and we also talked about my work and its relevance to his goals for maintaining the Army and the stability of the region. It was my impression that he just felt comfortable talking with me—I'm not in the military and I'm not one of his direct civilian subordinates like you. My sense is that General Borzov is a pretty straightforward man, and I wouldn't read too much into this." Zhdanov looked a little more at ease. "And who knows, he may even want to just buy me a drink."

A look of pure amazement spread across his face. That possibility hadn't even crossed his mind—until now. "You think that he might—I mean, would he . . . of course, there's no reason why he shouldn't do that, I mean . . ."

Katrina laughed out loud. "God, Leonid, but you're priceless." Zhdanov flushed and gave her an embarrassed smile. "We had a nice talk, and he may just want to see me again—and he may not. Don't go around the bend on me. One thing the General's right about—I could use a few days in Murmansk."

She walked him to the door of the facility. He tried again to apologize, which caused Katrina to again break out in laughter that only added to his embarrassment. Later that afternoon she received a personal call from General Borzov. On learning that she would be making the trip to Severomorsk with Dr. Zhdanov, he politely asked if she would join him for dinner Saturday evening. She was able to accept before the phone connection dissolved into a drone of static.

"Will that be all, Dr. Shebanin?" The bellman had placed her overnight bag on the luggage rack at the foot of the bed and made a show of turning on the lights and opening the bath and closet doors.

"That will do nicely," she replied and handed him a five-hundred-ruble note. He smiled his thanks and backed out the door. It was a simple room, clean and with a touch of faded elegance. The few Westerners who were allowed into Murmansk usually stayed here at the Rossiya, so it was better tended than most lodgings in the Murmansk-Severomorsk area, and the service was surprisingly good for a former state-run hotel. Katrina realized just how Spartan the conditions were at the Lumbovskiy site and even at the weekend accommodations in Gremikha. She sat on the bed and tested its spring. *What to do—should I go shopping or take a nice warm bath?* Ten minutes later, with her hair tied up, she slid beneath a warm ocean of bubbles, leaving only her head and shoulders exposed. *God, do I miss this. Not every night, but at least once a month.* With a touch of sadness, she tried to remember the last time she experienced such a bath.

The weather was marginal, but the Ilyushin Il-114 had taken off without delay. That suited Katrina, for she had spotted Colonel Makarov in the terminal. He had given her a long, murderous look, then turned abruptly and hurried from the building. They landed at the Severomorsk Airport, which was midway between the district headquarters complex and the center of Murmansk. The Severomorsk area, located some fifteen miles northeast of Murmansk on the Kolskiy Inlet, and the regions to the north and east of Severomorsk were dotted with military installations. There was an official car waiting to take Dr. Zhdanov to headquarters, so she had taken a cab to the hotel. The immediate area around the Rossiya was something of an international district, as much as was permitted in Murmansk, and there were several shops with foreign goods. It was a small oasis of color in an otherwise drab and dirty city. A light snow had fallen the night before, but already the smokestacks of factories and steel mills were blanketing the streets and roofs with a yellow-gray layer of grit. There was no escape from the heavy, putrid, sulfurous odor of the pulp mills south of the city.

Katrina lay back, surrendering to the perfumed warmth of her bath. The water had begun to cool slightly, and as she had twisted open the hot tap with her foot, a fresh warmth began making its way from her feet up toward her hips. She'd had little time to think about her dinner companion until now. Her unscheduled absence required that she work late the night before to catch up on paperwork and to brief her production manager on what was to be accomplished in her absence. The flight had been rough and the interior of the aircraft bitterly cold. But now, with the preparation and the flight behind her, she was filled with a mixture of apprehension and anticipation as she contemplated an evening with him. *What would it be like to have dinner with the commander of the Northern Military District?*

Katrina knew she was no longer a young woman, but thirty-eight was not old—certainly not too old to look forward to a nice dinner with an attentive man. Her academic career had prospered where her romantic life had not. She was married two years out of the university, full of love and optimism, but they had quarreled often and, of course, there was her work. Then one day she told him she was leaving, fully expecting him to cause a scene. Instead, he shrugged and a look of relief had spread across his handsome face. Such divorces were common in Russia, made easier by the fact that there was usually very little communal property. There had been a number of affairs since then, some with long-term possibilities, but any permanent relationship always required that she compromise her work. *Russian men seem incapable of understanding that my work is as important to me as their work is to them.* She knew Borzov had been divorced once and widowed once—that too, happened all too often in Russia.

During that first meeting with him last week, she had been too tired and upset from her confrontation with Makarov to focus on him—she recalled only her perception of the General and very little of the man. She did remember that he was an intense listener, and that his eyes were a soft blue, almost paternal, until they discussed the business of Makarov's actions. Then his eyes flashed, and she had become aware of his capacity for anger. When she described what his security chief had done to her, it seemed to kindle something vicious inside him—a strong, primitive feeling that he had easily controlled but could not entirely hide. To have the favor and protection of a powerful man like Borzov was flattering and reassuring, but it was also dangerous. A man didn't rise to become a colonel general in the Russian Army by being a kind and gentle man. It was said that Borzov owed his position to the reputation he earned as a leader of the SPETSNAZ brigades in Afghanistan rather than any family connections, but he also had to be politically savvy as well as a good soldier to become a military district commander. *Ah, but those eyes! No man could be totally bad with eyes like that.* She reached for the wristwatch that she'd discarded on the tiled lip of the tub. *Here I am dreaming like a schoolgirl, and I'm going to be late for dinner.* With that, she leaned forward to find the chain to the drain stopper and yanked it. Then she stood up and turned on the shower to wet her hair.

The Metropol Café was a small restaurant just a block from the hotel, and about half filled with early diners. The maître d' clearly expected her and escorted her to a quiet table in an alcove off the main dinning area and away from the door.

"Madam, the General telephoned to say that he would be a few minutes late. May I offer you something to drink while you wait?"

She ordered a glass of red wine. Things were changing so rapidly in Russia. She wasn't certain if her host's European-like demeanor was driven by market forces or local deference to a ranking military officer. From her seat she could see some of the other diners as well as a view of the street in front of the restaurant. The soft glow of a streetlamp softened the jagged piles of snow that had been plowed to either side of the road and that now lined the curb. Nearly all the whiteness had been trampled and graded away, leaving dirty slush in the roadway and a rumpled, gray snowpack on the sidewalks. A few progressive shops had scraped their walks, leaving a patchwork of cobblestones that looked as if they were embedded in wet, off-white cement. The wine, which arrived in a heavy stemmed glass, was excellent. The anxiety of seeing General Borzov again was somewhat diminished by the wine and the warm buzz of friendly conversation that now floated above the diners. She was beginning to relax, almost grateful for the time alone.

In the hotel room, she'd taken particular care in getting ready. The black knit dress was graceful, simple, and well-tailored. She had bought it in Paris almost ten years ago while attending a symposium on quantum physics, and had occasion to wear it only once or twice a year. Her trim figure had changed little in that time. She wore her hair off her neck and tied up on the back of her head, which emphasized her height and gave her a regal presence. A single strand of imitation pearls lay just above the swell of her ample breasts. She appeared oblivious to the heads that turned when she crossed the dining area, but she was quietly pleased with the stir she had caused.

"My apologies for having kept you waiting."

She startled, almost spilling her wine, and checked herself as she started to rise. *Those eyes,* she thought, *they're so blue and alive—like a cold flame.* He smiled easily, brushing her shoulder as he slid into the seat beside her.

"It's not a problem, General. Actually, I rather enjoyed the time to myself—I mean," she stammered, "it's quite comfortable here." His smile broadened and he raised his hand in a gentle acknowledgment.

"I understand completely," he said. "It is pleasant here. Like you, I work long hours and take little time for myself. Sometimes I come here, to this very table, and just relax by myself over a glass of wine. By the way, you look stunning."

"Thank you, General." She looked away, trying not to blush.

"And perhaps this evening, Dr. Katrina Alexandrovna, it would be less cumbersome if you were to call me call me Dmitri."

Katrina looked at him carefully. He had a way of being relaxed and open without surrendering his importance. Both his words and his manner invited her to consider him a man and not a soldier—perhaps not tomorrow or in some future official capacity, but for now. The waiter brought him a glass of wine and quietly laid two menus on the corner of the table.

"In that case," she replied, "please call me Katya."

"Very good, Katya. Here's to you and your day in the big city." They touched glasses and drank. There was a twinkle in his eye as he spoke. He knew that she, too, had spent a great deal of time in St. Petersburg, and Murmansk paled by comparison in every category except industrial output and military dependency. "Perhaps I need to mention this," he continued in a more formal tone. "I hoped to see you again, but I felt I had to speak first with Dr. Zhdanov. It was not his approval or his—uh—support I was seeking, but he is your superior and I must observe protocol."

"I can understand the general's concern for observing the proper chain of command and adherence to protocol. And now, Dmitri, I'm starving."

He looked at her sharply for an instant, then laughed. It was a warm, good-natured laugh, and the blue eyes became slits, punctuated by the creases in his weathered face. Borzov was in his early fifties, but he could shed decades when he laughed. He handed her one of the menus and began to study the other.

She perused the bill of fare, occasionally stealing a look at him over the top of her menu. He wore a black turtleneck and a simple Western-cut light-gray sports jacket with charcoal slacks—a solemn ensemble except that his tanned face and blond hair prevented him from looking cold. He wore no jewelry, but a dark-red silk handkerchief peeked from his breast pocket. There was a faint odor about him, and Katrina couldn't decide if it was the smell of a well-scrubbed man or some subtle Western cologne.

He surrendered none of his authority without the uniform, but he did seem to acquire a gentleness and a measure of grace in civilian attire. Katrina laid the menu on the table and a waiter appeared.

"Madam?"

"I'll have the sturgeon." The waiter politely nodded his approval, and Katrina instantly knew he could not be Russian.

"The same." Borzov smiled, indicating they would both care for more wine. The waiter retrieved the menus and slipped away, returning a moment later to top off their glasses.

The meal was excellent. They shifted to tea with dessert and talked. She was delighted to learn that his interests ranged from ballet to Western literature. The Vladimir Chamber Choir was scheduled to perform in Murmansk the following week, and he was excited at the prospect of seeing them again. He had studied voice as a boy before going off to military school. His prize possessions were a Japanese stereo component sound system and a collection of Pavarotti albums. The conversation drifted to current events in the Republic and the economy. There, he spoke freely, even critically, of the events since confederation, but she could sense he was more comfortable away from politics. Finally, they talked quietly, almost nostalgically, about their marriages, as if the time for commitment and dreams, like the days of czarist Russia, belonged in a different era from their own. Suddenly they looked around and the restaurant was empty. The maître d' stood patiently by the door, making no move to intrude.

"I suppose we should leave," he said, "since they're too polite to ask us to go."

They're probably only this polite because you are the District Commander, she thought, *but it's considerate of him to view it that way.* He graciously thanked the entire staff, including the chef, who seemed to materialize at the door as they departed.

She nervously fumbled with her room key and finally dropped it before she could get it into the lock. He quickly retrieved it and opened the door.

"It has been a lovely evening, Katya." He was not that much taller than she, but he seemed to tower over her as he moved a step closer.

My God, those eyes! Even in the dim light of the hotel corridor, she could see they were an inferno. Impulsively, she leaned forward and kissed him on the mouth. As she started to draw away, he placed a hand around her waist, the other under her chin. He stared into her eyes for a long moment, then kissed her gently. She started to speak, but he touched his index finger to her lips.

"I would like to stay," he said in a strained voice as he dropped his hands to his sides, "but only if you want me to . . . and if you feel it is right."

She smiled softly, amused and totally charmed. This warrior, this man who had cheated death many times—holder of the Order of Lenin—was trapped between passion and duty. There was no doubt that if she declined, he would leave without word and bear her no ill feelings. But that was the last thing she wanted.

"You may come in, General," she said in a husky voice as she kissed him hard, running her tongue across his lower lip, "but if you do, you will have to adhere to my rules of protocol."

"Agreed," he said as he put both arms around her and gazed at her fondly.

Katrina blinked and looked again to be sure, but it was so—he was actually blushing. That and his tender smile made him look even younger than when he laughed. Suddenly he swept her into his arms and carried her inside, roughly kicking the door closed behind him.

The taxi deposited her at the airport just before 11:00 A.M. She was relaxed and totally at peace. He had been tender, passionate, and a little clumsy, but very strong. They made love far longer than she would have thought possible. Neither of them was particularly young, nor had either had sex for some time. It was like the arrival of a late spring, long awaited and beautiful.

"So how was the shopping in Murmansk?" asked Dr. Zhdanov, who was waiting for her at the boarding stairs.

"Terrible," she replied as she walked past him. "There was nothing on the shelves worth buying and the prices were outrageous." But there was a delicious smile on her face. This puzzled Zhdanov, but he shrugged and followed her up the stairs. He had a whole new set of photos of his children, and he couldn't wait to show her.

Morton Keeney sat quietly with Steve Carter in one of the small conference rooms in the basement of the White House. Keeney sat in his usual place at the head of the table, while Carter waited in one of the chairs along the wall. NSC meetings, even working groups, didn't often take place at the White House, since any prolonged or recurring gatherings were a sure tip to the press that something was afoot. The Washington press corps looked for two things in anticipating a crisis—National Security Council staff activity and a surge in the deliveries of Domino's pizzas to the White House. Either one could be the prelude to an air strike on Baghdad or a show of force in the Adriatic. Dr. Bunting had called this meeting, and done so with some urgency, claiming she had new information that related directly to the issue of proliferation. Keeney decided on the White House for his convenience. He had asked for a knowledgeable CIA representative to be present, and found Carter waiting for him in the room when he arrived. He had seen Carter's name on the intelligence reports, but this was the first time he'd met him.

Albert Patterson arrived first, followed by Bunting, and finally, Colonel Geist. Geist paused at the door and made straight for Carter.

"What in the hell is a good intelligence analyst doing here with a bunch of political hacks?"

"Colonel Geist," replied Carter, rising to shake his hand. "It's nice to see a familiar face. Surely you don't fit into that category?" Geist had been detailed to the Agency several years ago for a tour, and was well remembered there. The Deputy Director of Intelligence himself had asked for an extension of Geist's tour. When that was denied by the Air Force, he had let Geist know there would always be a place for him at Langley if he ever left the service.

"Thanks for the compliment, Steve," he replied lowering his voice, "but with things as slow as they are at the Pentagon, I'll take anything that's available, even a dreary NSA staff job." Geist nodded to the assembled group. "They're so politically correct, they make you want to throw up. I'm surprised to see you here. Nobody available from the DDO?" The reference to someone from the Directorate of Operations was his way of asking if the CIA had any operations planned to deal with the problem on the Kola Peninsula.

"We're still just gathering facts, and I guess they thought I might be of some help."

"Rog, Steve, and I'm here as a liberal counterbalance to the rest of these hawks." Carter started to say something, but stopped as Keeney cleared his throat, clearly impatient to start the meeting. Geist smiled and held out his hand. "Nice to see you again, Steve." He winked and wandered off to find his seat at the table.

Keeney nodded with a slightly exaggerated show of patience as Geist took his seat. "Okay, let's get started. This session has been convened at the request of Dr. Bunting. It seems she has some information that bears directly on the matter of the Russians and their nuclear weapons. Anne?"

"Thank you, Morton," she began. "I have some contacts within the French government, and as Al and I have discussed over the past several days, the French are always looking for a cheaper source of nuclear fuels. And as most of you know, they've also been known to exchange technology and modern conventional weapons for uranium." Keeney nodded grimly. That's why South Africa has an air force composed of Mirage fighter-bombers and a mobile police force well mounted on French armored cars. "Russia has been forced to divert existing stocks of their nuclear fuel for export to gain hard currency, while their conventional arms sales have fallen off due to their industrial and economic problems, not to mention that it's a very competitive business. In the meantime, the French, seizing an opportunity, have stepped up their efforts to sell arms to the Third World. In many respects, they have attained the same shameless mercenary posture in this regard as our own country."

Keeney gave here a tolerant smile and inclined his head politely. "We all know where you stand on conventional arms sales, Anne," he said not unkindly, "but I understand you have some information about nuclear proliferation."

"I do," Bunting continued. "It seems that for the last several months, those with money to spend in the international arms bazaars have been noticeably penurious. My French colleague, who shares my feeling that both France and the United States are selling far too many weapons abroad, at first welcomed this flat trend in the arms market as a positive sign. But he contacted me just yesterday and reported that the reduction in arms traffic is in fact due to the expected release of, as he puts it, a 'new class of weapons' that will soon be available. The way he tells it, 'the guys with the shekels are saving up to buy the big firecrackers.' And," she continued, looking at Keeney, "he tells me that the dealers lining up all the big money seem to be Middle Easterners with Brazilian connections."

"Tell me, Anne," said Keeney smoothly, "does your friend in the French government have any idea when the big firecrackers are going to be in the stores?"

"He does," she replied with an equal measure of triumph and smugness. "Sometime very soon after the first of the year. I pressed him on this and he said it could be as soon as the first week in January."

Al Patterson fairly bubbled with excitement, while Geist looked bored. As Keeney considered his next move, Steve Carter caught his eye, indicating that he wanted to speak. Carter was there to serve as a technical expert and to address any specific question should Keeney require assistance. Normally, the National Security Advisor would not want his agenda cluttered by the thoughts of some minor functionary, but this Carter fellow was a sharp one, even if he did dress like a graduate student.

"Anne, Al, this is Steve Carter from CIA. I'm going to ask him to comment on what Anne has just told us. Mr. Carter is with the Intelligence Directorate and an expert on our problems in the Northern Military District. He's the analyst who has compiled most of evidence to support a theory that the Russians are either selling nuclear weapons or getting ready to." He waved casually in Carter's direction.

"Your information is particularly interesting, Dr. Bunting," Carter began. He remained seated, crossing his legs and leaning forward in his best academic stoop. "Particularly the time frame for delivery of the weapons that you've indicated—that's new to us, and quite frankly, it's a real breakthrough." Bunting tipped her head to acknowledge the compliment and listened carefully as Carter continued. "As you're probably aware, we've been monitoring the accelerated delivery of foodstuffs and machine parts to Murmansk and Archangel, and we're quite certain that the Russians have been unable to ship enough timber and crude oil to pay for it. Are you saying that the Russians are being paid in advance against the future delivery of nuclear weapons?" Carter's tone was respectful, almost deferential, which was not lost on Bunting.

"That's a good question, Steve." Keeney raised an eyebrow at Bunting's use of Carter's first name. He really had her going. "Again, I pressed my contact on that very issue, and the answer is yes—the promised delivery of battlefield nuclear weapons seems to have stimulus enough for a number of confidential letters of credit to be placed on account within the international banking community for use by the Russians."

"Thank you. What you've told us corroborates a great deal of information we've been able to gather on the technical side. And, if what you say is correct—that no weapons have yet left Russia or the Northern Military District—then we seem to be working toward some kind of deadline if we're going to prevent it." Keeney watched in admiration as Carter handled Bunting, but what Carter did next made him seriously consider trying to pirate the analyst away from the CIA and getting him assigned to his own staff. "Dr. Bunting, this is a difficult topic to broach, but I hope you'll indulge me. This information is fascinating, and since it may impose a deadline on our work, it's important that it be accurate. At Langley, all information is graded for its accuracy, by way of corroborating data and by a subjective determination on the reliability of the source. I fully understand that you are in no way bound by our constraints in the intelligence community, but it would be of tremendous help if there was some way to verify your source." Carter paused, as if in thought, while Dr. Anne Bunting had the strange feeling this mild-looking CIA man was subtly crowding her into a corner. He continued in the same reasonable tone. "Perhaps not here, of course, but . . . if you could share with me the identity of the individual who told you this information—in strict confidence, naturally—then we could check it out and lend some additional credence to your source."

"I'm not in the spy business, Mr. Carter," Bunting replied as if Carter had somehow been indecent with her, "and I am certainly not going to name names to the CIA!"

"I totally understand, ma'am," said Carter evenly, raising a hand in a conciliatory gesture. "But please understand that your information, while I personally believe that it is most important, will have to be verified or in some way corroborated, don't you agree?"

"You don't have to believe me," she said as she resolutely folded her arms. "But I can assure you the person's access to this kind of information is impeccable."

"I'm sure it is," said Keeney, smoothly intervening, "but Mr. Carter does have a point. Any advice or recommendation I take to the President will have more weight if the information is based on facts that can be verified." Dr. Bunting started to respond, but Keeney was too quick for her. "I understand that our protest in the U.N. about the pollution from plutonium reprocessing has been sidetracked."

"That's correct," replied Patterson. "Ambassador Kirkland's presentation before the General Assembly caused quite a stir, especially among the Scandinavian and Baltic delegates, but there's not a lot of sympathy from the assembly at large, especially from the Third World. The matter has been referred to committee. Something may come of it, but only if we offer to pay for it, and even then, it'll not happen anytime soon."

"Thanks, Al." Keeney lifted his notes and tapped them into a neat pile on the table. "If Anne's information is correct—and like Mr. Carter, I have no basis to doubt that it isn't—then in about a month, Russia will start shipping nuclear weapons by sea from the Kola Peninsula. Any suggestions?" There was a silence around the table. *Wonderful!* thought Keeney. *I need information on which to base policy, and all we have is some secondhand information from a liberal, left-bank friend of Anne Bunting.* He pushed his luck a bit as he allowed the pause following his question to linger to the point of becoming pregnant.

"Before I continue, I'd like to remind all of you that information placed before this group is of the highest classification, and," he paused for emphasis, "would have serious consequences if it were to fall into the wrong hands. The CIA has an agent in the Kola, a well-tested informant in a senior position within the scientific and bureaucratic establishment. This informant is probably in an excellent position to confirm and document that the Russians in the Kola are preparing to sell nuclear weapons. Now, Dr. Bunting has presented us information that indicates it may happen very soon. Unfortunately, we have no means of contacting this agent-in-place at the present time. The Kola Peninsula, as we all know, is becoming an increasingly restrictive area. Efforts are underway to establish contact with the agent, but so far they've been unsuccessful."

"If I may?"

"By all means, Anne."

"Are you saying that if we can get in contact with this agent in the Kola, he's in a position to confirm and even document what we've been talking about?" Keeney nodded. "Well, then, we better do what we can to find this gentleman. I think it may take a consensus of world opinion, as opposed to unilateral action on the part of the United States, to force the Russians to give up this dangerous course of action. But to do that, we need concrete proof. It seems to me that with all the various means at our disposal, we should somehow be able to accomplish this."

Keeney considered this as he looked to Geist. "Colonel?"

Geist tossed his pen on the table in a show of resignation. "Look, it'll help if we can put a smoking gun in the Russian's hands and have the world point to them as the bad guys—once again. But don't think they'll respond to any kind of condemnation from the United Nations. Those people over there are hurting, I mean *really* hurting. And when you talk about action from the U.N., you're really talking about the EC, the Japanese, and us. The Europeans looked the other way during the genocide in Yugoslavia, and the Japanese are busy stockpiling plutonium, supposedly for peaceful purposes. If we do prove the Russians up there are making and selling nukes, who's going to do anything? The U.N.? Give me a break! The only way to effectively stop it is a naval blockade. We can do that, but it's an act of war. It's like I said before, Mort, unless this country's ready to take strong, unilateral action, we're not going to stop it. I think we're just pissing in the wind on this one."

"Don't sugarcoat it, Colonel," Keeney said sarcastically, "I want to know exactly how you feel about this." Patterson and Bunting smiled.

There was heavy silence about the table until Dr. Bunting shifted in her chair. "This is about money, right? I mean, the Russians are desperate for hard currency, so they're willing to do just about anything to get it, correct?" There was a grudging agreement around the table. "Well, if we can prove the Russians are getting ready to sell nuclear weapons, then perhaps we can use this to support a domestic program of increased aid to Russia as well as more financial help from the NATO allies—so long as they refrain from selling the nuclear weapons."

"Kind of like the way we beat up the Gulf War allies to pay for the cost of the war," said Geist.

"Something like that," Bunting replied, "but it may be the only way we can keep them from putting their nuclear inventories on the market."

President William Bennett sat in the Oval Office scowling at the editorial page of the *Washington Post.* Mike Kinsley had thoroughly toasted him again, and Doonesbury was still lampooning a sexual indiscretion on the part of one of his cabinet members. He turned to the sports page and it got worse. His Missouri Tigers had been thrashed by Colorado, knocking them out of contention for a bowl bid. "Crap!" he said aloud as he pushed himself to his feet. He began to pace, stopping at a bay window that overlooked the Rose Garden. It was a dirty, gray-clad day that promised rain and looked cold enough for sleet. He turned from the window and continued his circuit of the office.

Bennett was troubled. The special operations option was becoming more of a viable alternative. Of course, there could still be a breakthrough on the diplomatic front, or this elusive agent could surface within some existing intelligence network. But William Bennett, a man with a rural background and modest education, had scratched his way to the top rung of the political ladder by always preparing for the worst-case scenario. The initial probability assessments indicated the mission had a fifty-percent chance of success and a seventy-percent chance of avoiding compromise. That's what the computers said. Bennett was nearly computer illiterate, a condition he jealously guarded for fear it would degrade the people skills he considered the most essential tools of his trade. But he did understand the principle of GIGO—garbage in, garbage out. Computers could be fooled and lied to, and they could do the same thing to their masters. If there was chance a for something to go wrong, Bennett always planned for it—even counted on it. A great deal of his success in the presidency had been his ability to ignore things that went right and totally focus on the possibility of things turning sour.

The news that the Russians had yet to ship nuclear weapons was a mixed blessing. Anne Bunting's piece of information had yet to be verified, but it hadn't taken long to confirm that several substantial letters of credit had been placed on deposit in favor of the Murmansk Shipping Company. Perhaps the only positive aspect of the banking mess was that the CIA now had some very quiet and highly placed sources within the international banking community. It now seemed that quick action could prevent what appeared to be a massive hemorrhaging of nuclear weapons into the Third World. But rushing ahead with the insertion of a special team without adequate preparation could only jeopardize their chance for success.

"Mr. President?"

Bennett walked over and tapped the intercom. "Yes?"

"Sir, they're here."

"Very well. I'll be with them in a moment." He crossed the large circular Oriental rug to the closet and traded his sweater for a tweed sports jacket. Although he had specified that this was to be an informal meeting, it was clear that the subject under discussion was deadly serious.

Morton Keeney led Armand Grummell, James Garza, and Richard Noffsinger into the room, with two Army officers bringing up the rear. Keeney, Grummell, Noffsinger, and Garza were all dressed in conservative sports jackets, dark slacks, and striped ties. This was as casual as these close advisers could permit themselves. Anything less formal, if observed by the Washington press corps, would signal something unusual. Winston Scott and another general officer were both paraded in Class A uniform. Bennett had expected the JCS Chairman, but not the other man.

"Mr. President, this is General William Thon, Commander of the U.S. Special Operations Command," said Keeney. "General Scott asked that he attend this meeting and I agreed, with your concurrence, of course."

"By all means," replied Bennett, shaking Thon's hand firmly. "General, nice to see you again. If I'd been thinking a little more clearly, I'd have invited you here myself." The President's warm reception of Thon was both courteous and calculating. The SOCOM Commander had a reputation as a solid, no-nonsense professional, and since he was present for the meeting, Bennett wanted the full benefit of his judgment and candor. "Gentlemen, let's take a seat and get started."

A military aide slipped in with a tray of cups and a thermos pitcher, while Bennett himself pulled a chair from the corner for General Thon. After a quiet rustle of paper and snapping of briefcase locks, the six guests settled into the leather-padded, cane-backed office chairs neatly circling the large and ornate desk. It was an impressive structure with the presidential seal chiseled into the front panel. Keeney noticed that the top of the large desk was clear except for a leather blotter and the low bank of four clocks that tracked the local time in Tokyo, Beijing, Moscow, and Bonn. The National Security Advisor had learned to gauge the temperament of the President by the condition of his desk. The absence of clutter indicated that he was in a decisive mood.

"Okay, Morton," the President began, "where are we on this thing?"

Keeney frowned and folded his hands on the thigh of his crossed leg. "Im afraid there's nothing new to report concerning our efforts to contact MUSTANG. Armand and his people are doing their best, but the current limited access to the Kola and the secluded nature of the Lumbovskiy site have made this very difficult. We're not optimistic about any contact with this agent by conventional intelligence means in the near future, although he could surface on his own. And that leaves us with the military option, or more specifically, the clandestine insertion of a special team to contact MUSTANG. General Thon's people at the Special Operations Command have developed a workable plan to track down our man, and I've briefed you in general terms on the proposal, along with the success and compromise probability estimates." Keeney paused to retrieve his cup and saucer, taking a quick, measured sip. "However, the information that the Russians will begin their initial shipments of nuclear weapons sometime after the first of the year is a new wrinkle. Since we talked on Friday, I've asked General Scott to see if his preparations to put a team into the Kola can be accelerated to possibly head off these alleged shipments. General Scott?"

"Mr. President, gentlemen." Scott's rich baritone rumble was a sharp contrast to Keeney's nasal, New England clip. "The answer is yes, we can deliver a team earlier, but no sooner than December twenty-sixth without a serious degradation in the probability of mission success. Even moving the timetable this much is not without some additional risk. Since this operation is being planned and directed by SOCOM, I've asked that General Thon be allowed to speak about the preparations underway, and the impact of moving the operation forward."

"I think that's an excellent idea, General." Bennett leaned back in his padded swivel chair and motioned for Thon to speak.

Thon pushed himself to his feet and jerked the front of his jacket straight. A Silver Star and Purple Heart, the latter tagged with two stars indicating he had been wounded three times, topped his seven rows of campaign ribbons. Thon and Scott were the last of their generation in uniform, men who fought as young second lieutenants in Vietnam. Bennett himself had been an enlisted G.I. in Korea, an infantryman, and had fought to the Yalu River on the Chinese border, survived the retreat to the U.N. perimeter at Pusan, and then back north to the cease-fire line at the 38th Parallel. For this and other reasons, Bennett listened very closely to his military advisers, and had been known to call in junior field-grade commanders for consultation. Thon clasped his hands behind him and began.

"Mr. President, on the first of December, I was given this tasking, and we commenced the planning process. A Navy SEAL element was selected for the mission because the best means for extracting the team is by submarine. This action element was put in isolation six days later and briefed into the operation on December 8, just four days ago. They are in workup and rehearsal training as we speak. A detachment from the 8th Special Operations Squadron has been positioned at Ramstein Air Force Base in Germany and is preparing for the insertion. The USS *Archerfish,* our only operational conventional submarine, is based in Karlskrona on the southeast coast of Sweden. She's busy making ready for sea to support the team's extraction.

"We had initially been given a month's time for preparation and rehearsal, and I fully understand why that time frame has been shortened. This presents no problems with the insertion aircraft. The SEALs understandably would like more time, but since the mission profile, with the exception of the extraction, is within the scope of their readiness training, they'll be able to schedule ninety percent of their planned workup in the remaining twelve days. If they're to be dropped on the twenty-sixth, they'll have to be flown to Ramstein on Christmas Day.

"Our only problem is with the submarine. They have a twenty-two-hundred-mile transit ahead of them. The *Archerfish* can cruise at fifteen knots, but once past the North Cape, she'll have to slow down to deal with the Russian hydrophone arrays and any chance encounter with a Russian attack boat. The sub's captain, Commander Griffin, estimates it will take him a good ten days to make the transit. He also says he'll need at least eight more days to prepare his vessel for the voyage. I spoke with him late yesterday by secure voice-link in an effort to determine if there was some way for him to make an earlier departure." Thon tugged at his ear and shifted his weight. "Commander Griffin is a brutally frank man, and he informed me that if I want him in the Barents Sea with a mission-capable submarine, I should get off his ass and let him do his job. Admiral Lawver, Commander of the Atlantic Submarine Fleet, tells me that Griffin is as competent as he is hard-boiled. I thought it best not to push him on the matter. So the *Archerfish* can't be on station until the thirtieth of December at the earliest.

"We've estimated that it may take as much as a week to make contact with the agent, transmit the required information, and move the team to the extraction point—perhaps it can be done in four or five days, or it could take as long as ten days. The mission concept calls for the submarine to be on-station prior to inserting the team. If we make the drop on the twenty-sixth, they'll be in there with no way out for about five days. This cuts our margins slightly and it's something we wanted to avoid, but at this time we don't view it as mission critical. Sir, we're prepared to move ahead with the mission and insert our team on the twenty-sixth with every expectation of achieving results by the third of January. This is not an operation without risk, as the probability figures indicate. But I can guarantee you that a group of very highly trained and professional young men and women in my command will do their best not to let you down." Thon shot a quick glance at Scott before again meeting Bennett's eye. "Mr. President, that concludes my report."

"Thank you," said Bennett. He was silent for a moment, then continued. "Tell me, General Thon, what do you think the odds are for success?"

"Well, sir, our calculations indicate that—"

"Screw the calculations, General," he interrupted gently. "Tell me how you feel about sending your people in there. What do *you* think are the chances that we can put those boys in there and then get them back safely?" Bennett held Thon's eyes with a penetrating stare, trying to fully absorb the innermost thoughts of the other man.

"Thank you for asking that question, sir," Thon replied with a trace of a smile, indicating that he understood the President was asking about the safe return of the men rather than the success of the mission. "This is a dangerous operation and there're no guarantees. If they have problems on the ground, there'll be precious little we can do for them, and that really bothers me. If I were a young special operator, I'd be chomping at the bit to lead this mission, but sometimes it's harder to command than to lead. I like their chances, sir, but I won't rest easy until they get back."

Bennett was again silent for a moment. "Who's the team leader?"

"It's a Lieutenant John Moody, from SEAL Team Two in Little Creek. He's comes from Wyoming and is a highly capable winter- warfare specialist."

"I see," replied Bennett. "Now tell me about your mission planner and controller, this lady named Brisco."

Thon hid his surprise. The President would only know about Major

Brisco if he had read the OPLAN. The operations plan was a thick document that described the operations scenario and covered each phase of the mission—support requirements, communications plan, rules of engagement, action on target, etc.—in exacting detail. It had been prepared, and largely authored, by Major Brisco. There were only five copies of the classified OPLAN in existence, and only one in Washington—the one signed for by General Winston Scott. *I wonder why Scotty didn't tell me that the President had seen the OPLAN.*

"Major Brisco is an operations officer in our special plans section. Her immediate superior recommended her for the job, and after I reviewed some of her work, I accepted that recommendation. She's the best *man* for the job."

"How does she feel about the mission?"

Thon hesitated, but just for an instant. "I believe she would breathe a great sigh of relief if the mission were scrubbed. She'd also be disappointed, because she's developed a solid mission concept and built a fine operational plan around it. But I know she'd welcome the opportunity not to put these men at risk."

"General Thon, thank you for your information. General Scott?"

"I support General Thon's mission concept and his plan of execution, Mr. President, as well as his assessment for the success of the operation."

"Questions?" Keeney, Grummell, Noffsinger, and Garza all shook their heads. "Very well, then." Bennett pushed himself to his feet and offered his hand first to Scott, then to Thon. "Thank you for your time, gentlemen, and for your professional handling of this matter. Secretary Garza will let you know of my decision."

Bennett walked the two Army men to the door and returned to the desk. He waved the others to their seats and stood behind his chair with his forearms resting on the chair back. "Okay, gentlemen, time to get your oars in the water. What are we going to do about this?" There was a reluctant silence, so the President looked inquiringly at his Secretary of Defense. "Jim?"

Garza rubbed a hand across his face and pursed his lips. He was clearly not comfortable. "Mr. President, Winston Scott and Billie Thon are two of the finest men in uniform, and I wouldn't second-guess their opinion or integrity for a second. Militarily, I believe they've given you the facts, and God knows we'll do our best to make this undertaking a success, if that's your decision. But somehow, putting American soldiers on Russian soil in peacetime just seems all wrong to me. I'd like to be more supportive, but that's how I feel—sorry, sir."

"Don't be. I can hire yes-men when I need them, and this is not one of those times. Armand?"

"Well, this is a policy question, and as you know—"

"Hell, I *know* it's a policy question, Armand, and I know you CIA guys avoid policy issues like the Pope avoids pussy. This is a secure room and there are no active microphones. Pretend that you're the President and *you* have to make a policy call."

Grummell smiled. It was not that he did not privately like to speculate on policy issues, but as an intelligence professional for the past thirty-odd years, he had been drilled to render fact without opinion and estimates bathed in caveats.

"Mr. President, I don't think we have enough to go on to take this kind of drastic action, and I think the insertion of military personnel into Russia is courting disaster. Remember KAL 007 that was shot down over Sakhalin Island in 1983? The Russians were genuinely puzzled by the West's outrage, because the airliner was clearly in Soviet airspace. The average Russian is quite skeptical about his government, but he is zealously loyal and protective of his homeland. I can think of no single reason the average Russian would accept as valid for a foreign soldier to be on their soil. As for the nuclear weapons, they may or may not already be on ships heading out of Murmansk. We have no way of validating Dr. Bunting's information. And anyway, I think we all know that in the not-too-distant future, there are going to be nuclear weapons in the hands of every Third World military power, foe and ally alike—it's just a matter of time." Grummell pulled the wire-rimmed spectacles from his face. "At this juncture, Mr. President, I think a military response, even a small one like this, is too large a risk for too little gain."

"Would you be more comfortable if this were a paramilitary response, with, say, a team of Ukrainian nationals making the jump into the Kola?"

Grummell considered this—it was his kind of question. "Not really. This is a pretty sophisticated undertaking, with success depending on the skill of the team; and only this country, the Israelis, and the Brits could pull it off, or train someone to do it for them. It would still have our fingerprints all over it, and we could lose more than we stand to gain in the process of denial."

"Fair enough. Dick, what do you think about all this?"

"I have to agree with Armand. I'd like more than anything to get this genie back into the bottle, but the ramifications of those boys' getting caught is a political and diplomatic nightmare. Think how we'd react if a SPETSNAZ team were found sneaking around Los Alamos or Lawrence Livermore trying to contact one of our top scientists. In addition to the points Armand raised, there are two things that really bother me if this thing goes sour. First of all, Stozharov's position within his government is not all that firm. I'd just as soon not give the conservative, hard-line factions a rallying point, and a public trial of our men, if they're caught, could do just that. Secondly, it could be another replay of the Francis Gary Powers affair, and I can just see Ambassador Kirkland up there in the U.N. trying to explain this one. And speaking of the U.N., the Russians have been pretty cooperative with us on that score, and I'd hate to jeopardize that. I think we either go public with what we have, or we keep trying to contact this agent by clandestine means."

"Morton?"

"I think we have to take action. We have an understanding within the SALT agreements not to allow this kind of thing to happen. They've violated the accord. During Dick's offical meeting with Stozharov, he made it pretty clear that we think his military was selling nuclear weapons, and Stozharov flatly denied it. I don't believe we can allow this to stand without doing something."

The President nodded slowly, and his eyes had a faraway look to them. Then, he took notice of Keeney as if he had just become aware of him. "Thanks, Mort," he replied, and again assumed a distant expression. After some time, he slowly reached for the intercom. "Would you please ask Colonel Williams and the recorder to come in here." Seconds later, Colonel Buck Williams, USMC, the President's senior military aide, and a male clerk armed with a steno pad stepped into the room. The recorder slipped behind a small stenographer's desk by the door while Williams stood at parade rest nearby. Bennett rose and began a slow, measured tour of the office.

"Note the time and date," he said in a firm voice. "I have just concluded a meeting with the Secretary of State, the Secretary of Defense, the Director of Central Intelligence, and my National Security Advisor. The subject of this meeting is the potential and/or imminent sale of nuclear weapons by the Republic of Russia in the international arms market. At my request, a military special operation has been planned that will require U.S. military personnel to penetrate the Kola Peninsula in the Republic of Russia in an attempt to obtain evidence of these activities—activities which are in direct violation of the bilateral SALT accords, and which, in my judgment, constitute a serious threat to world peace.

"I have received excellent counsel both for and against such an action, but it is my decision, and mine alone, to authorize a military penetration of the Kola Peninsula for the purpose of obtaining proof of Russian intentions to traffic in nuclear weapons. The Vice President is aware of the situation regarding the potential sale of nuclear weapons by the Russians, but he has no knowledge of this meeting or my decision, nor will he be made privy to the action being taken until a future date of my choosing." Bennett stopped at the recorder's desk, his brow furrowed. He started to add something but stopped short. "That'll do, Buck. I'll want everyone here to sign it."

"Aye, aye, sir." The Marine held the door for the recorder and they both left. Bennett made another lap around the office and picked up the coffee thermos.

"Mort?"

"Just a touch, sir."

"Dick?"

"I'm fine, sir."

"How about you, Armand?"

"Thank you, sir."

He looked expectantly to Garza, who politely declined. Bennett returned to his seat and sipped pensively from a garish mug adorned with red-crayoned panda bears, a gift from his granddaughter. He drummed his fingers on the blotter before turning back to Noffsinger.

"Dick, how many points you gonna give me?"

"Points? With all respect, Mr. President, you can't be serious. Rypien's hurt and they're playing in St. Louis. I think you ought to give me a touchdown—at least!"

"Give *you* points. The Skins are eight and three, and the Cards are four and seven, and you want points! Give me a break."

Bennett and his Secretary of State began to negotiate the spread, while Keeney and Grummell, for whom a spirited game of bridge was mortal combat, exchanged patient glances. Garza quietly sipped his coffee and tried to keep scenes from the *World at War* series from his thoughts—scenes of the German Sixth Army at Stalingrad as they were being pummeled by Zhukov's artillery with lines of frozen corpses in the snow. Colonel Williams returned with a manila folder and handed it to the President.

"Thanks, Buck." He opened it and read the top sheet carefully, then signed it and each of the two photocopies. He took the three documents and spread them on the desk. "Okay, gentlemen, you know the drill." When they had all signed each of the three sheets, Bennett gave one to Keeney and another to Colonel Williams, who saluted and left the room. The third he placed in his desk safe, spinning the combination wheel and jerking the handle to ensure it was securely locked.

This ritual was enacted whenever an important or potentially embarrassing decision was made. President Bennett wanted there to be no question as to his role in the decision-making process, and he was purposefully ambiguous about the position taken by his advisers. Under the scrutiny of some future inquisition, he wanted no doubts about who was responsible, as well as who knew what and when. Bennett had said on more than one occasion that when he was retired to his farm in Missouri, the last thing he wanted was to turn on the TV and see members of his administration subpoenaed before some congressional committee. His vice president took the lead on many of the administration's domestic issues, and was often kept "out of the loop" at the early stages of a foreign-policy matter. The document that Colonel Williams carried from the room would be archived in a secure vault at the National Security Agency.

"I guess that concludes our business here this morning, Jim. I hope you'll convey my appreciation to Winston Scott and General Thon for their views, and that I'm counting on their skill and professionalism. Needless to say, if we get a break in this thing or some new information, I'll scrap the operation in a heartbeat." As they filed out, Bennett caught Secretary Noffsinger's eye. "Dick, could you stick around for a minute?" After the others had left, the President led him to a pair of wingback chairs across from the desk.

"If we go ahead with this thing," Bennett began, "and it does go badly, you're going to be on the front line—you and Ambassador Simpson." Noffsinger nodded, acknowledging the obvious. "So I'm going to tell you why I authorized this dangerous course of action, which I'll ask you to share only with Joe Simpson if you care to. The spread of nuclear weapons is inevitable—it's going to happen, whether we take action now or not. We may stick our finger in the dike in this instance, but there are dozens of other potential holes. I also know that the consequences of this incident of nuclear proliferation will probably not be felt while I'm in the White House. However, the next president or the one following him will surely have to deal with it, and may even have to square off with a regional nuclear power over oil or human rights, or to honor a treaty commitment. The thing I want to do, which is why I authorized this operation, is to let the world know that we are willing to take big risks to oppose the spread of nuclear weapons. I want no doubt in anyone's mind that wherever or whenever it happens, we'll take positive action to stop it." Bennett sat forward with his forearms on his knees, rubbing his palms together. He'd bucked hay in the summers through his junior year in college, before he enlisted in Army, and his hands were permanently callused.

"You see, nuclear weapons are like drugs to these power-hungry dictators. They want the same respect we gave the Soviet Union for four decades, and they feel it will make them immune from international conventions." Bennett paused, resting his elbows on the chair's arms, fingers laced together in a prayerlike fashion. "Remember how apprehensive we were when we thought Saddam Hussein might use chemical weapons? How will we handle the next showdown when we *know* the resident thug-in-power has nukes?" Bennett sat back and exhaled forcefully. "It's not a smart political move to take this action, but it's the right thing to do."

Bennett walked Noffsinger to the door and the two shook hands. "Thank you for sharing this with me, Mr. President. I'll see that Ambassador Simpson understands your reasoning. I'm sure he'll appreciate it, as I do. And perhaps, if this special team has to be sent in to get the information, they'll be successful and get out undetected."

"Perhaps," replied Bennett, "but neither one of us is paid to sit back and just hope that all goes well."

After Noffsinger left, Bennett stood by the window overlooking the Rose Garden for a very long time. The rain, interspersed with a few large white flakes, had just begun to fall.

Moments later, Morton Keeney caught Noffsinger in the hallway. "What'd he say?"

"Just like that old guy in the Quaker Oats commercials on TV," the Secretary of State replied, shaking his head. "He says it's the right thing to do."

"Now why," said Keeney, "would the President of the United States use that kind of reasoning for an important decision."

They both chuckled and continued down the hall.

It was just past 7:00 A.M., and the snowfields at the base of the Haffner Glacier glistened under a low three-quarter moon like a carpet of fine powdered diamonds. It was an oblique lighting, as the moon hung about fifteen degrees above the horizon. The portion of the sky abandoned by the low moon was so dense and bright with stars that it took on a synthetic appearance. The glacier was no more than forty miles from the coast. The seasonal snowfall, which amounted to just under twelve feet, still rested on two thousand feet of ice. There had been no new snow for several days, but each night the fierce wind that swept in from Baffin Bay had its way with the light, dry surface pack, pushing it around like desert sand. It was a cold, flat, terminally quiet world.

From the south there was a faint humming sound, barely discernible but growing louder, like a herd of bees trampling across the frozen waste. Two tiny specks appeared on the horizon, bobbing and weaving as they made their way across the snowpack and leaving white rooster tails in their wake. The pair stopped once for a few moments and the sound died to a low rumble, then they resumed their dash across the snow, desecrating the stillness with their howling.

The lead machine came to an abrupt stop and one of the riders dismounted. He placed a small, flat, canvas-covered pack on the surface of the snow and knelt beside it for a moment. He waved to the others and turned back to the box. The machines were turned off and the white land was reclaimed by a silence that now seemed unnatural. There were four of them, dressed in heavy arctic snowsuits that caused them to waddle when they moved. The helmets with full face shields gave them a Neil Armstrong look.

The first man, with his mittens dangling by strings attached to his sleeves, was now delicately working the dials on the front of the small receiver. He had removed his helmet, but retained what appeared to be a light wool aviator's cap with the flaps tied under his chin. Finally, he looked up at the others and a smile cut his handsome, black features.

"They should be about fifty to seventy meters in that direction, near that shallow berm."

"Let's go have a look," replied Master Chief Tolliver. He pulled off his helmet and replaced it with a black watch cap. He staggered back to the second snowmobile and took two pairs of snowshoes from the carrier on rear of the machine. Another rider toiled up behind him, struggling with the helmet. "Let me help you with that." He eased the helmet off as best he could, but still raked one of her ears.

"Ouch!"

"Sorry, ma'am. Here, put this on." He handed Major Brisco a watch cap like his, and began pulling at the zippers of his bulky overalls. "We can leave these with the snowmobiles. They're hard to walk in."

"Yeah, Master Chief, but I'm freezing."

"We all are," replied Tolliver, even though he wasn't, "but the only way to get warm is to move, and you can't move in that thing." Ligon and a SEAL named Deacon, already mounted in their snowshoes, shuffled over from their machine. They wore several light layers of polypropylene and Gortex covered by a loose white vinyl-like outer shell. They joined Tolliver to watch as Brisco thrashed about like a ten-year-old trying to fight her way out of her snowsuit. They watched her struggle for several minutes, then both Ligon and Tolliver stepped forward to give her a hand. When she was dressed like the three SEALs, they strapped her into the snowshoes.

"Ready?"

"Just a second—let me catch my breath," she replied, desperately wanting a cigarette. She took a tentative step and almost fell down. "I still don't see how those things can be that accurate," she said to Ligon, gesturing to the receiver that was now slung in a canvas pouch from his shoulder. "You sure they're out here?"

Ligon tapped the SATNAV receiver affectionately. "Major, I verified the coordinates they sent last night when they went to ground, remember?" Brisco nodded. She and Tolliver had arrived late yesterday. Moody and the rest of Echo Platoon were out on a three-day, two-night bivouac exercise, conducting movement and lay-up drills as well as communication exercises. The platoon was using their SATCOM transceiver as well as a satellite navigation system, or SATNAV. They had sent the coordinates of their location along with a status report using a burst transmission. Any station monitoring that frequency, if they heard anything, would have picked up only a high-pitched beep lasting just a few seconds. The beep was harvested by a very sensitive low-flying communications satellite and relayed on a different frequency to a ground station near Warrenton, Virginia. There it was decoded, reencoded and again relayed by satellite to Camp Melville. During the real operation, the signal would be sent to the SOCOM headquarters Crisis Action Center, which would be controlling the operation. The time delay in flashing these signals around the globe was measured in nanoseconds. Last evening, Ligon had received Moody's signal and acknowledged receipt. Early that morning they had set out with the exact coordinates to link up with the platoon.

"The book calls for an error factor of plus or minus fifty meters," Ligon continued. "But I personally calibrate all our gear and you can cut that down to twenty feet—we're that good. They're over by that swale, I guarantee it."

Tolliver set off at a casual pace in the direction indicated by Ligon, and Brisco flopped along behind him. A combination of moonlight and starlight bathed the snowfields, creating an eerie off-white world of semi-darkness. "Just shuffle along, Major," Tolliver called over his shoulder, "it's kind of a jog-trot."

Right! Brisco thought as she trudged along, trying to keep up. They covered seventy meters in about a minute. Brisco was no longer cold, and she was breathing hard. "So," she said, huffing clouds of steam into the dark morning, "where are they?"

"I'd say they did a damn fine job," said Tolliver, looking around.

"What . . . where?"

"Not bad," replied Ligon. "What do you think, Deak?"

"Pretty fair," said the third SEAL, squatting to sift some of the snow in his hand, "considering how fine the top cover is."

"What are you talking about? There's nothing here."

"Look around you," said Tolliver, "what do you see?"

"Snow," she replied, making a quarter-turn but unable to move farther, as she was standing on one of her snowshoes.

"But what else?" Brisco was becoming irritated and was about to say so when Tolliver motioned her to squat down. She managed to do so, but not without almost taking a tumble. "See how smooth the snow is out about twenty meters or so?" She nodded. "Well, notice the ripples in the area around us—see how uneven it is?"

"Okay." The low moon provided enough light to silhouette the rumpled snow.

"Here's where they went to ground. Yesterday evening, they dug an entry hole in the snow and began tunneling. This rippling around here is from their tailings as they scooped snow and ice from their burrow and scattered it about. Then the wind came up last night and did the rest."

"So they're . . . down there? That's amazing."

"Well," Tolliver said with a wink, "Ligon told them you'd be coming out with us, and I know they didn't want to disappoint you. Hey, Ron, you want to get 'em up here?"

Ligon flicked off one of his mittens and jammed his pinkie and index fingers to the corners of his mouth. A shrill whistle tore into the cold darkness. Seconds later, a four-by-four canvas-framed panel lifted from the ground not thirty feet from where they stood, and a head and shoulders emerged, like that of some mutant gopher. The man vaulted to the surface and waved to them. Tolliver led the group over to him.

Moody was dressed in baggy, dark wool-blend pants, a white Thinsolite undershirt and a watch cap. He stood nonchalantly by the entrance of his warren, holding a steaming cup of tea. He took his free hand from his trouser pocket and tugged the sleeve back from his watch. "You're late." He smiled easily through a three-day stubble that gave him a shadowy look. "Morning, Major, Master Chief. How's it goin', guys?"

"H'lo, sir," replied Deacon, who was now crouched by the trapdoor-like entrance, peering in with a professional interest.

"Sir," acknowledged Ligon, who was again kneeling over his SAT-NAV receiver. Two SEALs emerged from the lay-up complex, one of them with a receiver similar to the one Ligon carried and another with a pair of transmitters. The three of them fell into a quiet conversation about signal strengths, dead spaces, and battery life. Half of the failed or aborted special operations in the past were the result of communications problems. Equipment preparation and communication procedure were a significant portion of the team's premission workup. Another SEAL appeared at the lip of the hole and began handing out plastic mugs of sweet tea.

"How was the trip out?" Moody inquired.

"Not bad," Tolliver replied. "Good visibility once we broke out of the coastal fog. You know we got a green light?"

Moody nodded. "How's everything with the support elements?" he inquired, taking a mug and handing it to Brisco. There was something about Moody's manner—a kind of aloofness as if her presence were an intrusion. Brisco was all too familiar with male hostility, but this was subtly different. As close as she could recall, it was a smugness that she first noticed in her younger brother when she visited him at Boy Scout camp. Moody had tolerated her presence, even made her feel welcome during the planning sessions, but his manner now said that out here she was at best only a guest.

"You know the insertion has been moved up?" she countered.

"Yeah, I got the message yesterday. Then D-day's the day after Christmas?" She nodded. "Why the change in schedule?"

"New information indicates the Russians may not have shipped any warheads, but they will begin soon after the first of the year. They feel that if we can get the documentation out of there sooner, something can be done to stop it," said Brisco.

"I rogered up on the schedule change, since you were in the field," added Tolliver. "I figured we could cut one jump from the workup and do any additional comm drills from the camp, okay?" Moody was still the platoon commander, but since Tolliver would not be with the insertion team, he assumed the lead roll for the mission planning and workup. It was as if he now coached the team and Moody was the quarterback.

Moody shrugged. "I guess we can live with it. How does that affect our support elements?"

"That's the rub," Brisco said evenly. "The submarine can't be on station until about five days after you're inserted, so you can't be taken out until about the thirty-first."

Moody whistled softly and said what they all were thinking: "Or not at all if, for some reason, that sub doesn't get there." The original schedule called for the submarine to be on station before the drop. The mission would be delayed if the submarine was delayed. The mission would be canceled if for some reason the *Archerfish* was unable to take a position off the Kola coast to make the extraction.

"There's one person I know who'll be doing his damndest to have that boat on station. Lieutenant Commander Graham Smith is the executive officer on the *Archerfish.*"

"You mean Gorgeous Graham?" blurted Moody before he could check himself.

"The same." Tolliver smiled.

"Well, I'll be," said Moody, shaking his head. "Small world, ain't it?"

Brisco noted Moody's mixed reaction to the news that the executive officer was Smith and a SEAL. They were silent for a moment before she spoke. "The captain of the submarine wasn't too happy about this either. He knows he's committed to a time line, with little or no option to abort the rendezvous." There was another awkward silence. Brisco felt the risks and success probabilities were still within an acceptable range, but it was the first time she'd had to deal face-to-face with the men who would take the risk. For them it was not a numbers game—they faced certain imprisonment, possibly torture or death, if the probabilities generated by the SOCOM mission-analysis computers worked against them. "If we're cutting this too close, John, say the word, and I'll take it back up the line."

Again Moody shrugged. "Thanks, Major, but no. The Master Chief was right to roger up for a drop on the twenty-sixth. I'd sure as hell like to have that sub waiting on the other end before we make the jump, but there's nothing we can do about that. All we can do is concentrate on our workup." Most of the SEALs were aboveground now, pulling equipment bags from the hole and assembling the *akios.* The little sleds were constructed so the sides collapsed, making them easier to hide when the team went to ground. Moody motioned Tolliver and Brisco away from the group.

"Chief, can you take two more men back with you?" Tolliver nodded. "It'll be a little tight, but these are long machines. What do you have in mind?"

"The more I think about it, the more concerns I have about the extraction. Getting in and getting the job done will be a matter of doing what we know how to do—and a bit of luck. Getting the information from this agent flies or dies with Valclav, but I'm starting to think he can pull it off—he's a damn good man. But getting out bothers me. I'd like to spend as much time as possible rehearsing the extraction and escape scenarios. In order to get as much done as possible, we've got to make some cuts. Five SEALs plus Valclav will make the drop. I think we ought to train with five principles plus Valclav and two backups, with everyone else in a support role. What d'you think?"

Tolliver absentmindedly rubbed Chap Stick on his lips and nodded slowly. "It'll allow us to move faster, with fewer guys to train and more guys to help. Have you decided on the final team?"

"Snyder and Garniss for sure. Probably O'Keefe and Walker, but I'll make a final decision after we're into the water work. I'll also want McKnight and Beach in the training element." Moody had made his decision, but he watched Tolliver's reaction carefully.

"It's the way I'd play it, sir. You want me to tell them?"

"No, I think that's my job." Moody stepped over to where the SEALs and Sergeant Valclav were preparing their gear for travel. Everything was either in white bags or had white vinyl panels tied securely around it.

Major Brisco watched as Moody culled four SEALs from the group and took them aside. He talked to them in low tones, as if he were having to tell them of a death in the family. She could see that all four were bitterly disappointed. One became angry and Moody cut him off with a sharp word—another was clearly pleading with him. Moody placed a hand on his shoulder in a consoling manner. Brisco wasn't prepared for the emotion of this sorting process. The rejected SEALs were all devastated, and one of them still looked as if he were about to kill Moody, all because he told them they would not be allowed to challenge the computer's prediction that they could be dead before the end of the year. *Perhaps these men are more special than I thought,* she thought, *or just plain crazy.* The drama had almost made her forget about just how cold and uncomfortable she was.

* * *

The two crowded snowmobiles arrived back at Camp Melville two hours later. Brisco made the trip sandwiched between Tolliver and the angry SEAL. After they parked in the compound, the young man vaulted from the machine and stomped off to the barracks.

"That guy going to be all right, Master Chief?" she asked as she stomped her feet to try to warm them.

"He'll be okay—he's just a little disappointed." He was busy unstrapping equipment from the snowmobile.

"No kidding!" Brisco replied.

"Tell me, Major," Tolliver continued, "how long have you been in training for the opportunity to control an important mission like this one—not just in your current billet, but how long have you been preparing for this kind of responsibility?"

Brisco thought about it. "I don't know—eight, maybe ten years."

"And what are the odds that you'll get to do another live one like this?"

"Probably zero.

"Now," he said, turning to face her, "what if the Otter lands here today with a bird colonel who has orders to replace you—and there's not a damn thing you can do about it. Bang, you're out—just like that. How would y'all feel?"

Brisco grimaced and shook her head.

"See? Johnson there has been in the teams for six years, and he's just been told he can't do what he's worked all those years to be able to do. He'll settle down or he'll have me to deal with, but I don't expect him to like what's happened. Hell, I wouldn't care much for him if he did."

"Fair enough," said Brisco. "Now you tell me something. If you weren't needed to look after me and help with the planning, what would you do if Lieutenant Moody cut you from the action element?"

Tolliver weighed the question carefully and said without hesitation, "I like Mr. Moody, but it'd take everything I had to keep from punching him out."

"Then you should be thankful you've got me to look after." They both laughed.

Tolliver tossed her a small bag that contained her personal survival gear. "Guess I should also thank you for not mentioning my age as a disqualifier, since I'm as old as dirt."

"We don't call it age in this business, Master Chief, we call it experience." They laughed again. At first, Brisco had allowed Tolliver to participate in the support briefings only because she thought it was in her best interest as the operations controller to humor Moody's request. Now she found herself actually starting to like Tolliver—and to trust him. More and more she was coming to realize she would need him during the control phase of the operation.

"Well, thanks anyway. And speaking of Otters, will that welding equipment and flat stock I requested be on the flight today?"

"I'll check on it." She dug for her watch buried under the cuff of her suit. "The plane isn't due to leave Thule for another hour, but I'll let you know if it's not going to get here today."

Tolliver nodded. "See you later, Major. We got a lot of work to do before the rest of them get back here tomorrow." She smiled as he turned and headed for the equipment staging building.

Katrina Shebanin strolled casually through the laboratory, stopping periodically to watch a milling process or the handling of a component during a delicate assembly procedure. The construction of a nuclear weapon was a most exacting process. And while there were a few sensitive areas she felt she needed to monitor, she basically just wanted some contact with her fellow scientists. As she moved from one area to another in the lab, she tried to spend a moment or two with each member of her production team, at least those who were not involved in a critical procedure and could take a moment from their work. A few of them, those who had regular contact with her, had remarked how rested and fresh she looked since her short holiday in Murmansk.

Katrina would have agreed with them. The dinner and evening of passion with General Borzov had been a physical and emotional tonic for her. She had tried to analyze it, but could only conclude that she somehow felt more relaxed and at peace with herself after such a weekend.

The next morning he had taken her to a small café for breakfast, where they had fresh rolls and several cups of bitter, aromatic coffee. They talked about art, music, and the Russia each had known in their youths. By midmorning he was becoming restless, and she sensed he was beginning to feel the pressure of his duties. They walked back to the hotel, where he called for a car to take him to military headquarters. He thanked her, rather formally, for the evening and the companionship, and said that he hoped they could meet again for dinner, his duties and her work permitting.

It was the kind of a relationship with which she was comfortable. She'd had affairs with men who were more attentive and solicitous, but those men were also more demanding, wanting more of her time than she was prepared to give. Or they became frustrated or resentful when she could not or would not change her schedule and priorities to suit them. Her work was important to her and so was her personal time—time she required for reading or listening to music, or for the pursuit of an independent line of research. She did not need, nor particularly want, the daily attention of a lover. More specifically, she didn't want the intrusion or obligation created by that kind of a relationship. She'd had that before on more than one occasion, and it simply hadn't worked. She also sensed that Borzov, not unlike herself, was a man who lived with the daily pressure of his duties, and that an occasional rendezvous with a friend and lover added some equilibrium and sanity to his life as well. The fact that he wanted to see her again, but had been purposely vague as to when, was both reassuring and exciting.

There was only one thing that gnawed at Katrina. Her work was interesting and technically challenging, but she was still not convinced the sale of nuclear weapons was the right thing for her country to be doing. For years, she had helped with the production of nuclear weapons as the Soviet Union tried to keep pace with the United States. Like most scientists in the old regime, she had enjoyed a privileged and often isolated status—often segregated from the bland, sterile existence that was the lot of the average citizen. She had welcomed the new order, but with it came the realization of just how ruthless and usurious the old system had been. Now she was again fabricating nuclear weapons, not for strategic deterrence, but for food and foreign exchange. She understood General Borzov's reasoning, knowing just how desperate his situation had become, and that he had few options. *But is this right,* she asked herself on more than one occasion, *or is this work and my need to do it just an indulgence on my part so I can continue being a scientist? More important, is this another formula for national, or even world, disaster?* She was a confident and capable woman, but she also shared the same fears of many former Soviet bureaucrats and *intelligentsia* about life outside the government domain. More often than not, she came to the conclusion that there was no alternative to the course she had chosen. *Or is there, and again, I just don't want to face it?*

"Dr. Shebanin?"

"Yes, what is it?"

"The Director is in your office. I thought you might want to know."

"Thank you, Igor. I'll be right there." She quickly completed her circuit of the laboratory. She preferred to think of it as a lab, but in reality it was a factory—a very precise and sophisticated one, but a factory nonetheless. Five minutes later, she opened the door to her office to find Dr. Zhdanov pacing about the room. "Good morning, Leonid, what can I do for you?"

"Just thought I'd stop by," he said. He had removed the gown and cap, but still moved about the office in the booties. His hands were thrust into the pockets of his lab coat, but she could tell he was nervously clenching his fists. "Still no obstacles with the initial deliveries next month?"

"As I told you at the last production meeting yesterday, we'll have the first five devices ready for shipment on or before the tenth of the month, okay? Have a seat, Leonid—you look all worked up. Cigarette?" She shook one out on the desk blotter, and held a light for him before taking one for herself. Zhdanov was a sporadic smoker, yet he greedily pulled on the cigarette, coughing slightly as he exhaled. He was content for a moment, then got up and again began to pace.

"Katrina, I have a problem. Actually I may be in trouble—serious trouble. I need someone to talk to. You're the only one I can really trust—do you mind?"

Uh-oh, thought Katrina, *here it comes. And with Zhdanov, it could be anything from screwing his secretary to having been diagnosed with terminal cancer. I can certainly do without this.*

"Of course, Leonid, sit down and tell me about it."

Zhdanov again found the chair, but there was a chalky-gray cast to his complexion, and Katrina was becoming worried. "St. Petersburg has become an increasingly difficult and expensive place to live," he began, "and the private schools which Sasha and Nikolai attend seem to raise their fees monthly. Having a family and helping them to a decent life is not so easy these days. I've tried to do the best I can, but with the inflation and the shortages, it's impossible." He gave Katrina a crooked half-smile as if he had seemingly resigned himself to his fate, whatever that was.

"Leonid, just what are you trying to tell me?"

"We receive shipments of kerosene from Gremikha for the power turbines, and due to the high priority of our facility, they come without interruption at our request. I would venture to say we are one of the few installations that are not on some form of rationing program." He again bolted to his feet and began to pace. "I know I should never have listened to them, but the dispatcher at the fuel depot in Gremikha said it would be okay—that sufficient allocations were there and no one would ever miss it. I know it was wrong, but he said everyone did it and that no one would be the wiser."

"For God's sake, what are you talking about?" she said.

He stopped and stared at the floor, unable to meet her gaze. "Every month I have been signing for a truckload of fuel that we haven't received."

"And . . . ?"

"The dispatcher has been selling it into the black market and we've been splitting the proceeds. It's the only way I've been able to keep the boys in school and buy a few extra things for my Irina."

"Leonid, you must stop this," she replied, coming to her feet. "You know what can happen if you're caught." The Russian economy was largely a black-market economy, but this was much less the case in the

Northern Military District. Colonel General Borzov had made it a capital offense.

"Yes, I know," he said sadly, "but it may be too late. The driver of one of the shipments was apprehended by some of Colonel Makarov's men, and they are holding him for questioning."

PART FOUR

The Kola

The MC-130H Combat Talon II was about four hours out of Camp Melville. The Combat Talon had very long legs, but the nine-hour flight to southern Germany was at the very limit of its range without in-flight refueling. With the exception of Master Chief Tolliver and Petty Officer Ligon, who would meet them at their destination, all of Bravo Platoon was aboard. However, it was no longer a platoon, but two distinct and separate groups. One consisted of Moody, Garniss, Walker, Snyder, O'Keefe, and Valclav, who were in the action element, and the other of men who formed a separate and distinct cluster of SEALs. There was an attempt at kidding around and the camaraderie that had bound them together on the flight up to Greenland was now superficial and transparent. The danger of the mission had done nothing to dampen the disappointment, even open resentment, on the part of those being left behind. The very thing that made them good SEALs made them fierce competitors and very poor losers. A lanky man in a red sweatshirt came up and sat down next to Moody.

"Ho fucking ho, little boy. And what do *you* want for Christmas. Wait, I know—you want a blowjob, right? Well, ol' Santa will see if he can find you a cute little fräulein just as soon as we're on the ground." He had a spindly beard slung from his ears and a red stocking hat. Instead of a mustache, he had two cigarettes stuffed into his nostrils that sprouted at forty-five-degree angles, flanking his mouth.

"Do you honestly know just how ridiculous you look?"

"Hey, it's Christmas Eve, sir—lighten up." He pulled the red stocking from his head and shucked the beard. Then he put one of the cigarettes behind his left ear and lit the other one, inhaling thoughtfully. "Valclav says the Russians up there butt-fuck their reindeer. D'you think there's anything to it? More important, if we get caught, do you think they'll butt-fuck us?"

Moody smiled and sipped at his cold coffee. "You're not getting squirrely on me, are you, Garniss?"

"Nah, just trying to stay loose, that's all. Everybody's a little tight." He ducked his head through the sweatshirt and was again dressed in his BDU uniform. He sensed his platoon officer's mood was turning serious, so he sat quietly and finished his cigarette.

Petty Officer First Class Robert Garniss had been assigned to Bravo Platoon when he reported to SEAL Team Two just over a year ago. This was his first East Coast assignment, but he was something of a legend in the West Coast teams. Garniss was a fourteen-year veteran in the teams. He should have been promoted to chief petty officer several years ago, but making rate had never been that important to him. Physically, Garniss was the strongest man in the platoon, although Moody could usually stay with him on a run. Only one or two of the younger SEALs in Team Two could consistently beat him on the physical-readiness test and the monthly five-mile timed runs, but these young men trained hard, both at the Team and during their off-duty time, competing in marathons and triathlons. Garniss participated only in the platoon PT evolutions, and did no additional training. He just seemed to have some form of personal toughness that other men could achieve only by a hard physical-training program. Most weekends would find him at Awful Arthur's, one of the East Coast teams' hangouts in Virginia Beach. He could drink an incredible amount of beer, but it never appeared to have an effect on him. He could run forever and do endless push-ups, pull-ups, and flutter kicks.

Garniss didn't look like an athlete, or a SEAL for that matter. He was rather average in appearance, with sandy brown hair and a perpetual vacant look promoted by crooked front teeth that protruded far enough to rest on his lower lip. There was an easygoing manner about him that was very deceiving, but he had shrewd, dark eyes that were constantly on the move. Garniss was six three, but he slouched so no one thought of him as being particularly tall. His arms and legs were slightly long for his torso and, although he had smooth muscles with little definition, he was deceptively quick. In spite of this, he was embarrassingly awkward at team sports like volleyball and soccer. His SEAL warfare skills, however, were excellent, and he was a natural snap-shooter, both with a pistol and a rifle. The SEALs at Team Two had quickly learned not to bet with him at the firing ranges, or anywhere else for that matter. When it came to individual competition, he became deadly serious, but unlike many SEALs, he was a graceful loser. Moody concluded that he could do this because he always gave one hundred percent, and this allowed him to easily praise someone who, on a rare occasion, beat him. Garniss had another compelling qualification—he, along with Master Chief Tolliver, was a combat veteran.

Just before the Gulf War, Garniss had been with one of the assault elements tasked with boarding Iraqi tankers entering the Persian Gulf and turning them away. Thereafter his platoon had been assigned to the task unit at Ra's al Mishab, where they had conducted successful attacks on several offshore oil platforms. Then there was the terrorist incident in Seattle. Garniss had been with Echo Platoon of SEAL Team Three, the SEAL element that boarded the ferry *Spokane* in Puget Sound to retake the vessel from Arab terrorists. The details of the encounter were still classified, but several SEALs had been wounded and killed, and Garniss had been awarded the Silver Star for his role in the action.

Once Garniss was assigned to Bravo Platoon, it hadn't taken Moody long to realize that he was something special—a winner. For Garniss, everything was a game, but he always played to win. It was said that he was as cool under fire as he was in a card game, and he was very good at both.

"Bob, things are going to start to happen very quickly in a few hours," Moody began, "and I may not have a chance to bring this up with you before we jump, but . . ." Moody hesitated, framing his words carefully, "if something happens to me, I'm counting on you to get the job done, and more important, I'm counting on you to get the rest of the guys out of there. If somehow I get taken out, you shit-can me and take care of the rest of the guys, okay?"

Neither man spoke for several minutes, and Moody was about to repeat himself when Garniss shifted in his seat. "Mr. Moody, let me tell you something." Moody looked at him sharply. Garniss and the other men usually called him "Boss" or "El Tee." It was the first time he could recall that Garniss had addressed him as "mister." "On my last combat operation, I lost my platoon officer. He came up against a terrorist with an automatic weapon and he hesitated—just for a second—but it cost him his life. I watched him die, and it's something I never want to do again, so I'll make you a deal." He wetted his thumb and index finger and rolled the lighted butt between them to extinguish it. "If you go down and it's hot, I'll leave you where you drop. I'll take care of the troops and if the job's doable, I'll get it done. But you gotta promise me one thing. If it comes to a fight, you shoot first and think about it later. Now I know we're on a sneak-and-peek job, and the last thing we want is to make contact. I also know we're probably going to be given some fucked-up rules of engagement drafted by a staff puke or some politician—someone who has no fuckin' idea what it's like to be out there in the deep linguine. But promise me, sir, that if it comes to a fight, you won't hesitate—you'll just go full automatic and let the chips fall where they may—okay, sir?"

It was the closest thing to a speech he'd ever heard from Garniss, and there was no questioning his sincerity. Moody smiled and held out his hand. "Deal." They sat quietly for another moment and Moody again sipped his coffee, making a face. "Christ, this stuff tastes like weasel piss!"

"I saw the crew chief with a thermos up on the flight deck," said Garniss, glad to talk about something else. "I think the Zoomies are holding the good stuff back on us." He grabbed Moody's cup and furtively tossed the contents under the seat. "Let's see if we can do a little better."

Garniss returned in a short while with two cups of hot, fresh coffee and handed one to Moody.

The MC-130H landed at Ramstein AFB just before 3:00 A.M. on Christmas Day and taxied straight to the hangar reserved for the 8th SOS Detachment. It was snowing lightly as Moody stiffly stepped onto the tarmac. Garniss and the others stayed with the aircraft while Moody walked the short distance to where Major Brisco and Master Chief Tolliver waited to greet him. They were accompanied by a tall, square-shouldered man whose fur-lined parka hood was bisected by a magnificent mustache. Tolliver, along with Ligon, had left Camp Melville two days earlier to work with the rigging on the insertion aircraft. Major Brisco had arrived some four hours earlier from SOCOM headquarters in Tampa.

"Yo, Master Chief. Major, how are you?"

"Very well, Lieutenant," Brisco replied. "How about you—ready?"

Moody laughed. "As ready as we can be. The bird all set up?" he asked, turning to Tolliver.

"Yes, sir. By the way, this is Major Black. He'll be the command pilot for the insertion."

Moody stepped past Tolliver and extended his hand. "Pleased to meet you, Major. I'm John Moody."

"John," Black replied, "call me Dan. Been looking forward to working with you. We're all set, and we'll get you in there—right on the money."

"Dan, I'm counting on it." Moody had never met Black before, but he'd known several like him. The SEALS had nothing but respect for the SOS pilots.

Brisco approached them, looking at her watch. She tried not to show it, but she couldn't help but notice how quickly Black and Moody sized each other up with a handshake, each acknowledging the other man's military credentials. Almost instantly, the trust was there. *Men!* she thought. *For once I'd just like to be accepted as a professional without having to constantly prove it to them. They'll trust another man until he makes a mistake, but not a woman!*

"Lieutenant, you and your men are scheduled for a medical exam in a half hour. Then it's a meal, gear prep, and eight hours of scheduled sleep." For the past several days, the platoon had gradually adjusted their sleep patterns so they could sleep during normal working hours Murmansk time and be on the move, when they had to, in the late evening and at night. The SEAL's mission was to avoid detection, and surveillance was most active during the working day, even if there was very little daylight. The doctor would check them for any last-minute medical problems and provide a mild sedative to ensure that they slept well the night before the drop. "But," Brisco continued, "I thought you might want to take a few minutes to inspect your aircraft."

"Sounds good to me," Moody replied.

"You go ahead, sir," said Tolliver. "I'll help Garniss with the gear."

Moody followed Brisco and Black to the hangar and through a small exit door that was cut into one of the huge hangar-bay doors. Moody knew what to expect, but he still let out a low whistle at the magnitude of it. Inside the brightly lit hangar was an Air Force KC-10 tanker that looked nothing like an Air Force KC-10 tanker. Instead it was a sparkling, freshly painted and waxed KLM DC-10 airliner. The blue-on-white color scheme and the large, diagonal "KLM" on the tail of the aircraft made the military tanker look like a full-fledged member of the Royal Dutch Airline's fleet. As he inspected the aircraft more closely, he could see that the line of "windows" along the fuselage were outset about an inch from the skin of the plane. They wouldn't fool anyone who approached closer than the wingtip, but then, they didn't have to. These windows, which were lighted strips attached just a few days ago to each side of the fuselage, would look no different than the windows of a real KLM DC-10—just so long as the plane kept moving on the taxiway and the observer was kept at a distance.

"Well, what do you think?" There was a measure of pride in Black's voice.

"Great. How close does a MiG have to get to tell it from the real thing?"

"Closer than I'll let him get," Black replied with a wink. "We're still carrying a full suite of sensors and electric countermeasures. We'll be listening very carefully while we're in their airspace."

Moody again walked around the tail section of the plane to the boarding stairs. "This the champagne flight, Ron?" he said to the black man in overalls coming down the steps to greet him.

"It's a little rougher on the inside than the outside, but it'll get you there, and I'll make sure you get out of it clean. How's it going', sir?"

"Okay. We've done what we can—now it's just a matter of commuting to the job site and going to work."

"Hoo-yah." Ligon grinned. "C'mon inside and I'll show you how we've got her rigged." As he followed him up the stairs, Ligon continued in a low voice. "These Air Force guys and especially that Army captain you met up at Camp Melville *really* know their shit. I seen some good riggers in my day, but these guys are tops."

Moody was beginning to feel the fatigue from the trip, but he knew it was important for Ligon to show him the inside of the aircraft. "Screw the Zoomies and Doggies, Ron. We ain't jumping outta this crate unless you say it's right."

There were six of them, five SEALs and Sergeant Valclav, in the front row, seated in thickly padded captain's chairs. They all felt a little ridiculous, but the facility had been built in more affluent times to brief SAC and strategic reconnaissance crews, and Air Force pilots always seemed to require such trappings. Most of them relaxed quietly as they waited for the briefing to begin, while Garniss, wearing a pair of snow goggles, jockeyed a broom handle between his legs and talked into a clenched fist, saying things like "Roger, Blue Leader" and "Hold on, hotshot, here we go!" Behind the insertion element was Major Black and the members of his flight crew. By and large, they appreciated Garniss's performance, and they offered an occasional technical comment. Even the SOS crew was overwhelmed by the plushness of the briefing facility. Special Operations Squadron crews, like SEALs, were used to metal folding chairs and chalkboards in Quonset huts.

Major Brisco stood off to one side with Steve Carter and Master Chief Tolliver. Tolliver was still a SEAL and the Bravo Platoon Chief, but he was no longer a part of this group. Behind the aviators sat a lone SEAL. First Class Petty Officer John Beach was a communications specialist, and as capable as any of the SEALs selected for the mission. He would sit in on the briefing, and make the flight across Russia and the Arctic Ocean to Elmendorf Air Force Base in Alaska. He had to be prepared in all respects to make the drop, but he would only jump with the others if one of them fell ill or somehow became incapacitated between now and the time of the drop. As the supernumerary for the insertion element, he was not in the group of SEALs who sat in the front row, nor was he part of the remaining men in Bravo Platoon who were out in the hangar completing the final rigging checks on the pallet of equipment that would parachute into the Kola with the team. If all went according to plan, he would be the SEAL who didn't make the jump into Russia, and chances were, the mission would be so highly classified that he would probably never be able tell anyone what he had almost done.

Brisco glanced at her watch. In about three minutes, she would begin the final round of briefings and the countdown that, barring an order to abort, would place the first American fighting men on Russian soil since the U.S. invaded Russia in 1918 to protect White Russians in Vladivostok, Murmansk, and Archangel. That incident is a trivial historical footnote except for those few Americans who seriously study European history. It is an event well remembered by the Russians and has been taught to the last four generations of Russian schoolchildren.

She looked at Tolliver, who stood with his arms folded, rocking forward occasionally onto the balls of his feet. She knew him well enough by now to know that his heart was aching to be with Moody and the others. Rationally, Tolliver understood why he was being left behind, and the reason for him to remain with her to assist with controlling the operation. But as a young SEAL he had been where the others were now, and he longed—just one more time—for that curious rush of adrenaline that comes only when one willingly puts himself in jeopardy. It was more than just that. It was a singular feeling of camaraderie, spiced with danger, that somehow produced a peculiar form of intimacy—a unique kind of brotherhood, one reserved for men who risked their lives alongside other special men of their own kind. It was why they volunteered, and why those who had been excluded from the drop were so bitterly disappointed. Tolliver had been there. He knew that his maturity and experience were now needed elsewhere. For the younger SEALs left behind, it was a bitter experience that only another dangerous mission could exorcise.

"Gentlemen," said Brisco as she stepped to the podium, "it is now fourteen hundred hours in Murmansk and Gremikha. Petty Officer Garniss, I'd appreciate it if you'd land that thing and taxi over here to the briefing room—we're about to get started." She gave him a tolerant smile. Chief Tolliver had talked at length about Garniss and his value to the team, which included the clowning. He kept the others relaxed, but he was serious when it counted and they all knew it. "This will constitute your final briefings before you board the aircraft. We are now six hours and fifteen minutes from drop time. Mr. Carter will begin with the final intelligence overview. Steve?"

Carter spread his notes on the podium and looked up at the men in front of him. He could not help but notice that a few of the SEALs and airmen were not much older than his children. In all his years as an analyst, he'd never had to face the men who would risk their lives on the basis of his information. It was a sobering and humbling experience.

"Good afternoon. There has been no change in the last twenty-four hours regarding the mission requirements or information about your area of operation. To date, we have had no ELINT or COMINT that would suggest a heightened condition of awareness. Naturally, you will be advised should that change prior to your departure, and by secure data-link once you're airborne. The *Archerfish* is currently three hours ahead of its PIM and is now scheduled to be on station by zero three hundred hours on the thirty-first, or D plus five. Her ETA will be updated daily as she progresses into Arctic waters.

"Our agent is still out of contact. Should contact be established prior to the drop, the mission will be scrubbed. If communication is made by other means after the drop, but prior to Sergeant Valclav initiating contact, you will proceed to one of the assigned safe sectors and wait for the *Archerfish* to signal that she is on station and available for extraction operations." Carter adjusted his glasses and swallowed. "As you are aware, only Sergeant Valclav knows of the identity of the agent and is aware of the contact instructions. Should he not . . . ah, survive the jump or in some other way be incapacitated, the mission is to be aborted, and you are to proceed to a safe area and await extraction. In the unlikely circumstance that contact is authorized without Sergeant Valclav, instructions will be passed by secure SATCOM relay to you on the ground." Carter then covered the location and current movement of military units in the north central Kola area, and provided them with an updated weather forecast. "That concludes my portion of the briefing. Good luck to all of you." He stepped away from podium and was replaced by Brisco.

"Thank you, Steve," she replied. "Operationally, there are no changes from the mission as planned. In the time remaining, I will cover your rules of engagement. The rules have been approved and signed off by the Chairman of the Joint Chiefs." Brisco could feel the tension as the group seemed to lean forward in their seats. It was the real purpose of the final briefing.

"I will first cover the airborne rules of engagement. As a scheduled commercial air carrier en route to Tokyo with overflight clearances, you will observe all international flight conventions. You are scheduled to cross the Finnish border into Russian airspace approximately three hundred miles north of Helsinki. From there you will be approximately three hundred and fifty miles from the primary drop point. After the drop, you will continue as planned out over the Barents Sea toward Novaya Zemlya." At this point she turned to a small-scale map of the top of the world and armed herself with a pointer. "As you know, we've debated the merits of having you continue on a great-circle route to Japan and Yokoda Air Force Base south of Tokyo. This has been rejected due to potential complications with the Japanese government, and the fact that this route would require that you reenter Russian airspace here on the Taymyr Peninsula and fly another two thousand miles across Siberia. Therefore, when you reach a position seventy miles east of Novaya Zemlya, you will alter course to the north on a heading that will carry you between Franz Josef Land and Severnaya Zemlya, and on to Alaska and Elmendorf Air Force Base. We know that the Russians only loosely monitor Western commercial aircraft operating under existing overflight agreements. We anticipate little or no notice will be given to an amended flight plan that takes a commercial airliner away from Russia, especially a Dutch carrier." Brisco surrendered the pointer and returned to the podium. "You'll be in Russian airspace for about an hour over the Kola, and we don't expect any problems. We have the listeners concentrating on their military air control frequencies, and you will be advised of any unusual activity." Brisco did not make mention, for they had no need to know, that a low-flying ELINT satellite had been rerouted for that specific purpose. Additionally, a dreadfully seasick, two-man electronic surveillance team bravely monitored Russian radio signals from the deckhouse of a Norwegian trawler in the Barents Sea.

"In the unlikely event that you are challenged, you are to maintain the cover of an airliner on innocent passage. In this scenario, and if sufficiently threatened by interceptor aircraft, air-to-air missiles, or ground-to-air missiles, it will be at the discretion of Major Black to surrender the aircraft. The biggest threat is from interceptor aircraft. Major Schultz," she nodded to the aircraft communications officer who spoke Dutch and German, "can argue all he wants to on the voice circuits, but if your sensors indicate they've locked you up with a missile fire-control radar, you're to drop your gear and land as they direct. Your welfare and release will be sought after through diplomatic efforts and the Geneva accords. Once on the ground, you are to destroy all coded materials and comport yourselves as United States military personnel and prisoners of war. Are there any questions?" This was standard operating procedure for a special operations penetration, and there were none. "Very well, this concludes the airborne rules of engagement. The air crew is excused."

Black and his men rose and filed quietly from their seats, like the faithful leaving their pew to take communion. Moody and his men waited patiently.

As the airmen shuffled out, one of the sergeants paused to whisper something in Garniss's ear that caused both men to chuckle. Brisco lit a cigarette and waited for the last of them to leave. She then nodded to the Air Force security guard, who stepped back through the door, closing it behind him. She wasn't looking forward to this portion of the briefing, for she knew the engagement orders passed to her would not be entirely to the SEALs' liking. *These guys are going to be pissed, and I guess I can't blame them. But they have to take orders—same as me.* She took a folder with "Top Secret—Eyes Only" stamped across the front and pulled a padded folding chair from the wall over to where the six men were seated. This was not a matter to be presented from a podium. Again she looked at her watch. They were now on a time line that had to be religiously observed.

"There are about six pages of do's and don'ts in this document, but I'm going to give you the gist of it. Lieutenant Moody, I'll expect you to read and sign this before you leave here. Inasmuch as this is an agent-contact mission, and your function on the ground is to establish a covert base of operations for Sergeant Valclav and to conduct secure communications, these rules of engagement make sense. However, they leave you very little latitude in the use of force if you're discovered.

"During the past few weeks, we've talked about several scenarios, including masquerading as a Russian SPETSNAZ squad, or as smugglers, or even as a group of hunters. None of these ideas were seriously entertained, as it would classify you as spies and deny you privileges afforded to American military personnel. It has been determined that underneath your white camouflage shells you will do nothing to hide the fact that you are a U.S. military unit. Your orders are to evade contact and detection, but you are not, under any circumstances, to use deadly force to evade capture. In the event capture is imminent, you are to surrender and conduct yourselves as prisoners of war."

There was a spontaneous undercurrent of disapproval from the SEALs.

"That's enough," said Moody sharply, and the others fell silent. It was the first time Brisco had heard him speak to his men like that. "Please continue, Major."

"Again, if capture is imminent, you are to destroy your code chips and surrender without armed resistance. It is felt that nothing can be served by an armed engagement, and that your repatriation can only be made more difficult by dead Russian security forces or military personnel. However," she opened the folder to read from it, "it does say that 'if it is crucial to the success of the operation or to the continued secrecy of your presence *and* such action is of a singular nature and, within reason, nonattributable to your presence should you be captured, the use of deadly force is authorized.' Do you understand that?"

"I think so," replied Moody. "If you have to waste a guard or some polar-bear hunter we stumble across, we have to stash the body where nobody can find it."

"As we all know, there're no polar bears on the Kola, but that's the general idea. Any questions?"

"Just what are we to do if we're taken under fire, say by a platoon-sized unit, and we're not given the opportunity to surrender?" Moody continued.

"Wave a white flag."

"And if that doesn't work?"

"Wave a bigger white flag."

Moody was silent for a moment and shrugged. "Understood, Major. Can I assume that as American military personnel, we are still to be an armed force?"

"Correct, but just the standard military weapons which you have already prepared for the drop. The purpose of your arms is strictly defensive. If you are engaged by a Russian security force, it will allow you to establish a position from which to formally surrender." There was a long silence before Brisco continued. "Very well, if there are no further questions, you are hereby advised that all other conventions and standards of conduct remain in effect while you're on the ground. You're scheduled to board the aircraft in exactly fifty-three minutes. Good luck to you guys. Get the job done and get the hell out of there."

No one moved until Moody stood up. Valclav and the other SEALs filed out while he stayed behind. Brisco handed him the top-secret folder with the rules of engagement. He quickly flipped to the last page and signed it.

"You're not going to read it?"

"You're my controller—I trust you. Is there something else you haven't covered?"

"Well, no, but I thought you'd at least want to . . ."

Moody waved his hand. "Hell, Janet, half the time I can't understand the disclaimer on a pack of cigarettes. It's crunch time. If you say that's what the damn thing says—that's good enough for me." He smiled and held out his hand. She hesitated for a second and took it. "We have a saying in the Teams: it ain't over till the fat lady goes backstage and takes a shit. You've done a good job for us so far. Now you gotta stay tough in there and don't let them hang us out to dry." Moody was still smiling, but both of them knew he was deadly serious.

"Count on it, John."

Master Chief Tolliver followed Moody out of the room. Brisco gathered her briefing materials together while Steve Carter rolled up the maps and slid them into their storage tubes.

"You think he understands the engagement directions you've given him?" asked Carter with a measure of skepticism.

"Oh, he understands them, all right. Whether or not he'll play by those rules is another matter."

"It's not really my area," said Carter, "but it seems unusual to forbid them to take steps to protect themselves if someone's shooting at them."

"It just seems strange to you because you're not in the military and you're a rational individual." *Christ,* thought Brisco, *I'm starting to get cynical like Moody and the other SEALs. Or maybe I'm just afraid for what might happen if they do make contact. Get a grip on it,* she told herself, *you're their controller, not their mother.*

Moody took his eyes off the gleaming KLM KC-10 and glanced at his watch. He had about five minutes before he had to join the men in one of the equipment bays where they would gear up for the jump and then board the aircraft. He thought about a cup of coffee, but put it from his mind. Once he was dressed out for the jump, going to the bathroom was nearly impossible. So he wandered aimlessly about the hangar with his hands thrust in the pockets of his utilities. He smiled to himself. They called it the Big Chill—that brief time when the training and the workups and the briefings were finished and the team waited for the operation to begin. Idle time was now their enemy, for when there was nothing to do, their minds were free to expand and move ahead into the mission—and all the things that could possibly go wrong. Moody had carefully planned the final day at Ramstein so the Big Chill would be as short as possible. He looked at his watch again—maybe four more minutes.

"How's it going, sir?" Tolliver had suddenly materialized at his elbow.

Moody shrugged. "Just waiting it out, Master Chief. When do you and the Major leave for SOCOM?"

"In about fifteen minutes. That's our bird standing by out there." The patent whine of idling jet engines filtered through the hangar doors. "She wants to be on th' ground in Tampa before you're on th' ground in th' Kola. You okay, sir?"

"Yeah," Moody replied as he forced a grin. "Guess I got a little bit of the Chill."

"And you might even be a little nervous."

"Nervous? How about just plain scared."

"Hell, sir," said Tolliver, "you damn well should be. I'm scared, and I don't have to make the drop." They both laughed. "Mr. Moody, you been around long enough to know that we get paid for doin' scary stuff. If you ain't scared, you ain't doin' your job."

"Guess you're right." They continued on a slow circumnavigation of the aircraft. "You were in Vietnam right at the end, Master Chief. Ever have a really close one?"

Tolliver looked sharply at Moody. He didn't really like to talk about Vietnam. It dated him, and he considered it old business. "Really, just one time," he began. "We ran into a bunch of NVA one night—more'n we could handle, so we were trying to break contact. We made a couple of leapfrog moves, and finally we were just runnin' like hell and they were chasin' us. The squad leader stopped to set a claymore, and I was coverin' him. You know the green tracers the Chicoms use?" Moody nodded. "Well, I turned to shoot, an' I got bracketed by green tracers—couldn't have been more'n a foot off either hip. I just stood there an' sort of watched them go by.

Moody looked closely at Tolliver, noticing that he was a little flushed. "And?"

"That's it. I laid down a base of fire while the lieutenant rigged the claymore. It did the trick, too—after the claymore detonated, we broke contact."

"But you weren't scared?"

Tolliver gave him a sideways glance with one eyebrow cocked. "Sir, after we got back aboard the boat an' I thought about what happened, I shit my pants—I mean big time. It smelled so god-awful that the coxswain hove to so I could jump over the side and wash it out." They walked a bit before Tolliver continued. "An' I'll tell you something else. For a while I would wake up in the middle of the night and wonder about those other four rounds—I mean I was dead center between those two tracers. What happened to the rounds between the tracers?"

Moody thought a moment about what Tolliver had told him. "Master Chief, you didn't just concoct that to cheer me up, did you?" Tolliver caught the glint in Moody's eye, and they both chuckled.

"No, sir, I did *not* make that up, and if the platoon hears about me crapping my pants, I'll have your ass . . . sir."

"Hey, Boss," yelled Garniss from across the hangar. "This ain't a come-as-you-are party, sir. Time to gear up and do it!"

"Be right there!" Moody called back. He turned back to Tolliver and found a serious look on the older man's face. He put a hand on Moody's shoulder.

"Sir, this is a good mission and you guys are ready. Just stick to the plan. An' if Valclav can't find that agent in a reasonable time—don't wait around too long. Get up to the coast and get the hell out of there."

"I will, Master Chief."

"There's not a helluva lot we can do for you while you're in there, but let us know if there is. I'll do what I can, an' I know the Major will too. An' remember, if things start to break down or you don't like the look of it, haul butt up to the extraction point, okay?"

"Okay, Master Chief."

Tolliver shook his hand, then stepped back and saluted. "Good luck, sir."

"Thank you, Master Chief," Moody replied as he returned the salute. "See you in a couple of weeks."

He watched Tolliver as he made his way across the hangar bay to the exit door. The scene had been *déjà vu* for Moody. He recalled the day he left for college. His dad had found him out sitting on the corral fence. His father, like Tolliver, was a man not given to a lot of talk, but his words were much the same—*time for you to go, son, but come back safely.* And in much the same way, his dad had said it was okay to be afraid. *Strange,* thought Moody, *making a combat drop into the former Soviet Union is scary, but not a lot more scary than leaving home.* And with sudden clarity, Moody realized that his dad had known just how hard it was for him to leave the ranch. *I'll be damned!* He shook himself from his reverie and glanced at his watch. Then he broke into a trot as he headed for the equipment bay, relieved to finally be on the move.

The *Archerfish* plowed through the cold waters of the Norwegian Sea at a depth of two hundred feet. Johnny Mathis and "White Christmas" echoed quietly through the compartments and passageways. She was about a hundred miles northwest of Bodö, Norway, keeping to the deep water just off the Lofoten Bank. They had been able to maintain just over fourteen and a half knots since leaving Karlskrona, and with the Gulf Stream helping them along, Griffin felt he could maintain that speed until they reached the North Cape. About a third of the time they ran at snorkel depth on the main diesel and charged batteries, saving the air-independent Stirling engine to transit more dangerous waters completely submerged. Once the North Cape was behind them, they'd have to reduce speed to eight knots in deference to the Russian hydrophone arrays. Slowing to eight knots would cut their acoustic signature to one fourth of what it was at fifteen knots. Given the state of the Russian Navy, no one was sure just how effective their underwater listening capabilities were, but there was no sense inviting trouble. Griffin was quite sure they had slipped out of the Baltic Sea and through the North Sea undetected, and he'd just as soon keep it that way. The real work would begin when they entered the Barents Sea three days from now. Until then, they'd cover water as fast as they could.

The *Archerfish* herself was as ready for the mission as her crew and the support facilities at Karlskrona could make her. Three crewmen had been left behind to make additional space for the passengers they expected to have aboard on the return trip. There were also the additional provisions for such a long patrol. The boat had tremendous range for her size, but she was still a coastal submarine and this was a very long trip.

Griffin sat in the control room of the *Archerfish,* seemingly oblivious to everything around him. They were at a Condition Three steaming watch, and would not go to Condition Two until they were in Russian waters. Senior Chief Dawgs was the Officer of the Deck. Normally the watch was stood by a commissioned officer, but *Archerfish* was anything but a normal submarine. He occasionally rose from his stool by the periscope and prowled the control room, but there was little work for the OD and the other members of his watch team. The boat had been told where to go and at what depth and speed to run, and she pretty much took care of herself. Those on watch supervised the computers and system monitors that controlled their submarine, and periodically made entries in logs. Lieutenant Commander Smith had recommended that log entries be made on the boat's PC, but Griffin had overruled him, saying computers did enough of the work on his boat. So the sailors of the *Archerfish* made careful entries in lime-green, hardbound logs as they had for decades, while integrated circuits on microchips made dozens of life-support and ship-control decisions per second.

Griffin stared at a small-scale chart of the Barents Sea from the North Cape to the approaches to the White Sea. A shaded line had been drawn from the middle of Svyatonosskiy spit and continued west in a shallow arc to the White Sea. This was the edge of the pack ice, based on satellite intelligence that was scarcely eight hours old. For the hundredth time, Griffin traced their projected track down the Kola Peninsula and under the pack ice about eleven miles off the coast near Lumbovskiy. Their projected rendezvous was in eighty-five feet of water some five miles from shore. for a nuclear-trained, blue-water submariner, it was like a fat man crawling under a king-size bed. There was forty feet from the keel of the *Archerfish* to the tip of her sail.

"Y'know, Cob, I get claustrophobic every time I think about creeping up under that pack ice into shallow water."

"I hear you, Skipper. I wish we'd had a few more days to practice, but as long as we've got plenty of time to maneuver on the way in, it shouldn't be too bad."

"You served on the old boats, didn't you?" Griffin asked.

"Yes, sir." Dawgs leaned forward on the stool and pulled up a leg of his coveralls. A tattoo on the side of his calf proclaimed, 'Diesel Boats Forever.' "I put the old *Sea Lion* out of commission in 1972. Never thought I'd see anything but a nuke boat from then on."

"You ever take the *Sea Lion* into a hole as tight as where we're going?"

"No way, skipper, but then, she was pretty old and big for a diesel boat—not nearly so nimble as this little gal. We take it nice and slow and it'll be no problem."

"Hmmm," replied Griffin as he rubbed the stubble on his chin. He looked around the control room. The degree of miniaturization was incredible, and it never ceased to amaze him. The Germans had built the *Archerfish* as a prototype, with little heed for military conventions. They were also free of the cumbersome and inefficient construction procedures the Navy Bureau of Ships imposed on Electric Boat, the maker of U.S. submarines. *Sometimes,* Griffin thought as he turned back to the chart, *I wonder if I'm commanding a submarine or playing a video game.*

In the control room of another submarine in another navy, Captain First Rank Viktor Molev sat on a stool by the dead-reckoning tracer and reviewed his sailing orders. He was a harsh and taciturn man, but the prospect of going to sea, even for a short time, had put him in good spirits. The *S-592* was one of the few boats that had not been placed on restricted availability, but they were still lucky to get five days a month at sea. The sailing orders before him called for a generous ten days of sea trials and crew training. Molev was forced to admit that limited underway time and the rigorous schedule of pierside drills had kept the boat at near-peak efficiency, but it was not satisfying work. He longed for the days when the Soviet attack submarines ranged freely off the North

American coasts, sniffing along the international boundary near Kings Bay, Georgia, or the Strait of Juan de Fuca in Washington State for the elusive American ballistic-missile submarines. *Those were the days,* he thought. *Our technology had almost matched theirs, and the American boats were beginning to fear us.*

Molev was a gruff-looking man with dark eyes and a perpetually troubled expression. He had a compact, practical build with reliable shoulders, but his midsection had now expanded to a larger circumference than his hips. He was old for a seagoing submarine skipper, just over fifty, but that was now in his favor. Admiral Zaitsev had determined that since his captains could no longer be trained at sea, his few active submarines would be commanded by the most experienced officers. Zaitsev had also taken a liking to Molev when the Admiral commanded the Soviet Pacific Submarine Fleet. Against orders from Moscow, Molev had placed his submarine in the path of a hijacked American Trident missile sub. The Americans recaptured their boat, but Molev had not made it easy for them. The commander of the Pacific Red Banner Fleet had wanted him severely reprimanded, but Zaitsev had intervened and seen to his transfer when he himself had been assigned to the Northern Fleet. Now Molev was one of the few skippers who took Russian attack submarines to sea. Even if it was only for crew training in the Barents Sea, it was better than being tied to the pier in Severomorsk, and for that, Molev was profoundly grateful.

The *S-592* was one of the latest of the Akula nuclear-powered attack submarines, and she was a large one, displacing over ten thousand tons. She was fast and powerful, and for a Russian submarine, very quiet.

"I have the training schedule prepared for your review, *Kapitan.*" The *Starpom,* or Executive Officer, stood at attention.

"Thank you, Commander. Please, stand at ease." Molev took the folder and opened it, squinting as smoke from the cigarette in the corner of his mouth drifted across his eyes. The Captain was seldom without a cigarette. "I see you are concentrating a great deal of time on passive sonar drills—that is good. And what do you propose as targets?"

"The icebreaker *Vaygach* is scheduled to carve a shipping lane into Archangel the day after tomorrow to allow a number of merchantmen to transit the Barents Sea. We can track them after they leave the pack ice in the White Sea and make for the North Cape."

"Very well, and what do you propose for our exercise area?"

"In this vicinity," he replied, pointing to the chart of the Berents Sea on the DRT. "Just inside the Asian Coastal Buffer Zone off Ostrov Nokuyev."

"Hmmm," Molev replied as he studied the chart. "Perhaps, but I want you to see that we are cleared to operate outside the Buffer Zone in the Murmansk area."

"As you wish, Captain, but I should warn you that—"

"Understood, *Starpom*—warning given and duly noted, but I want the area cleared. Other than that, the schedule appears in good order. Thank you."

The executive officer came to attention and snapped his head forward in a Prussian-like acknowledgment. Molev waved his hand casually in dismissal.

"One more thing, Captain—do you plan to be aboard this evening?"

"I do."

"Then, sir, perhaps you wouldn't mind if I . . . well, what I mean to say is, it is Christmas . . ."

"Will I see to the engineering reports and reactor readings? Of course, Alex, and give my best to your lovely family."

"Thank you, sir." He turned and left the control room.

Molev was mildly irritated. Either the captain or the executive officer was required to be aboard the night before they left port to ensure that all preparations to get underway were properly made. Molev always remained aboard prior to going to sea, so it was no imposition for him to attend to the duties. Still, it bothered him that a senior submarine officer would want to spend his last night ashore before such a short cruise, Christmas day or not. *Ten days,* mused Molev. *In the old days we would spend over half of our time at sea, often sixty or even eighty days at a time. We'd all smell like goats by the time we returned! But,* he reminded himself, *the old days are gone forever. And, sadly, so are most of the old submariners.*

The *Starpom* had sought to remind him that Russian submarines had been advised to remain away from the approaches to Murmansk during training exercises. There was often an American attack boat patrolling the North Cape and the Rabachiy Peninsula. They usually stayed outside the Buffer Zone but not always. One of their Delta IIIs had collided with an American 637-class boat in the Barents Sea near Murmansk less than a year ago. The American boat was clearly in Russian waters, and Moscow had registered a strong complaint about the incident. But rather than further offend the Americans, who were now a prime source of investment capital, they had been ordered to take no chances of a repeat incident. *Fucking spineless politicians—afraid to allow us to patrol our own territorial waters.*

The crew of the *S-592* was pretty raw, but he did have a few experienced sonar operators. *It might be fun to see if we can acquire and track one of the American boats,* he thought as he smiled and sucked on the cigarette until it nearly burned his fingers, *just like in the old days.*

President Bennett walked into the Oval Office trailed by his National Security Advisor. The President was dressed in a tired brown cardigan with reindeers prancing across the back and under his armpits. His oldest daughter had knitted it for him when she was carrying his first grandchild. Each Christmas, Mrs. Bennett led a family contingent on a search-and-destroy mission to segregate the Chief Executive from the sweater, and each year, he managed to turn up for the annual family dinner wearing it. The Bennett family Christmas dinner was an informal, raucous affair with some fifty relatives that included four generations of Bennetts. Since the death of his wife five years ago, Morton Keeney had been included in the Bennett Christmas.

"How about a drink, Morton?"

"I'd enjoy that, sir."

Bennett gave him a wry smile. On several occasions, he had tried to encourage Keeney to call him by his first name when they were alone, but had been unsuccessful. "When the voters kick my ass out of here," he once told him, "you call me by anything but my Christian name, and I'll punch you in the mouth." To that Keeney had replied, "Very well, sir." Bennett went to the wet bar concealed in a wall panel and set up two glasses. For Keeney, he splashed a dollop of Crown Royal on the rocks and added a squirt of mineral water. Then he decanted three fingers of Wild Turkey for himself, neat. It was, after all, Christmas.

"Here y'go, Mort. Now, what'll we drink to?"

"What else, Mr. President—to peace on earth and glad tidings to men of good will."

Bennett nodded appreciatively and they touched glasses. Then he motioned them to a pair of comfortable armchairs across from the presidential desk. They sat in silence for several moments, sipping quietly. Finally, the President made a show of looking at his watch.

"They should be airborne by now," he said.

"I expect so," Keeney replied. "They entered Russian airspace about fifteen minutes ago, which means they'll be on the ground within the half hour. The communications plan called for the aircraft to break radio silence only if there's a problem with the insertion. We'll get positive confirmation when the plane files for an amended flight plan, in perhaps another ninety minutes."

"When do we hear from the team on the ground?"

"Not for another eight hours or so. Their first order of business is to gather their equipment, hide the parachutes, and hike out of the area as expeditiously as possible."

Bennett took another measured sip. "Are the contingency plans in place?"

"Yes, sir. If the team is compromised, then we—"

"You mean," interrupted Bennett, "if the Russians catch our boys and toss them in prison."

"Right, sir. If they're captured, we're prepared to call an immediate press conference and go public with the evidence we have concerning the Lumbovskiy facility, including their preparations of nuclear weapons for export. We also have some updated satellite coverage that documents the toxic effluent from the facility's plutonium-conversion process. The imaging is quite good. We showed it to an environmental guru over at Johns Hopkins, and he was moved to make a few stinging remarks about this deadly new source of Arctic pollution, which he was kind enough to allow us to tape. Our, ah, media consultants tell us that our allegations of the Russians' selling nuclear weapons will play well internationally, but it's the pollution issue that will carry the most weight domestically."

Bennett frowned. His distaste for the press was well known, and it even extended to the small, highly competent staff of media experts Keeney retained for advice. "You mean to tell me that Americans are more concerned about pollution than if Saddam Hussein or the Ayatollahs get nukes?"

"So it would seem. And Anne Bunting is of the same mind." Keeney thoughtfully swirled the ice in his drink with his ring finger. It was the kind of intellectual question he enjoyed. "You see, sir, we've become used to the forces of evil *having* nuclear weapons—they've had them for decades. So long as we have them too, it's assumed that no one will be stupid enough to use them." Keeney shrugged. "Write if off to complacency or fifty years of the Cold War, but it's a threat we've learned to live with."

"Until some lunatic decides to use one of them."

"True," continued Keeney, conceding the point, "but the American public, for some reason, has made little distinction between nuclear weapons possessed by factions of the former Soviet Union and nuclear weapons that might be acquired by the Third World. Perhaps it's that the Russians are now our friends. And possibly it's because we feel that Iraq or Syria, or even North Korea, if and when they do acquire a nuclear capability, won't use them against us."

"Now, pollution and concern for the environment—that's the popular topic these days. It's something people feel they can *do* something about—a problem that can be solved. They feel there is little they can do about the nuclear weapons that can kill large numbers of people, but they're always ready to fight for the environmental health of the planet."

"The Constitution says the federal government can provide for the common defense," said Bennett. "I sort of thought that applied to bombs and missiles, but stopped well short of penguins and sea otters."

"A constitutional crisis we can handle," replied Keeney as he cautiously sipped his drink. "It's good treatment in the press that I'm worried about."

Bennett smiled and shook his head—then a shadow seemed to move across his weathered features. "Tell you what I'm worried about, Mort.

I'm concerned for those young men that will soon be crawling around in the snow over there in Russia. If I have one wish this Christmas, it's for God to watch over them." Keeney inclined his head and raised his glass in acknowledgment.

The two men sat and drank in silence until the door to the office flew open and in charged two preschoolers. They were the emissaries of a sly First Lady telling the President that she didn't want him working on Christmas Day.

"Grandpa, my dolly's arm fell off—can you fix it for me? Grandma said you could."

"And the landing wheels on my airplane don't work right. They're supposed to fold up."

Bennett tossed off the last of his drink and smiled broadly. "Here, sweetheart, let me see your dolly. And, young man, you better let Uncle Morton take a look at that airplane—that's his department."

John Moody could barely move. The high-altitude-exposure suit made him feel like a fat little kid who had turned turtle in his snowsuit. The reserve chest-chute was bunched on top of the equipment bag that pressed on top of his knees, while his main parachute held him off the backrest of the low canvas seat. He was sitting on another equipment bag that was mounted just under the main chute. Smaller gear bags, ammunition pouches, and radios hung at various attachment points on his harness assembly. The equipment felt strange, for much of it was not standard team gear. They had been issued Czech-made parachutes, harnesses, and equipment bags, and much of their clothing was Finnish. It was first-rate equipment. If some of it was found after it was discarded following the jump, it might cause less of an alarm than U.S. gear. Only the German-made H&K MP-5A submachine gun pinned under his armpit felt right. He painfully shifted his weight from his left bun to the right one.

This was a part of the mission that all special operators hated—the ride in. It was like the Big Chill, only less comfortable. During the previous weeks of mission preparation, they had worked fifteen- and sixteen-hour days with very little time to themselves. The training was physically demanding, especially the diving. He was usually the first man in the water and the last one out. Whether on the glacier in a snow cave or in the barracks, he was the last man to turn in and the first one out the next day. Most of the training began with his saying, "Okay, guys, let's get at it," and setting the pace. They were either too busy or too tired to think about what it would be like to actually make the jump or to be on the ground in Russia. And there was always the possibility, a probability really, that the mission would be canceled at the last moment—it followed them like a cloud during the training exercises at Camp Melville. Now the training was behind them, and their drop point over the Kola Peninsula was just a few hundred miles ahead. The abort signal could come at any time, bringing frustration and relief, but Moody was sure the mission was a go.

He tried to recall just when he knew in his heart that the mission would not be scrubbed. It was well before Major Brisco had told them that the operation was sanctioned—that if no agent contact was made, they would be parachuted into Russia to make the contact. It was early on, when they were working on the glacier, and their SATNAV equipment was found to give faulty readings at the high latitudes. Moody reported the problem, and it was determined that a modified receiver would have to be sent from the factory in California. The new set was air-dropped to them the following morning, just ten hours later. *This isn't just some contingency or a response drill,* he had told himself. *They want us ready!* From then on, he bore down on the men, and soon they too began to understand it was for real. A cold fear suddenly went through him, and he physically shook himself to make it pass. *Just a few more minutes,* he told himself, *and we'll be playing for keeps.* He couldn't wait, for he knew the fear that periodically seized him could not be entirely banished until they were moving on the ground. The forced inactivity, not just the discomfort, was beginning to wear on him.

At first, Moody was relieved to finally be geared up and on the aircraft. The responsibilities for the men, the training, and the equipment had been consuming, but that was now behind them. The hardest thing he'd had to do was cut the team down to the four SEALs who were with him on the aircraft. Telling capable, highly motivated men they would not be making the drop was a painful chore, one that he had been unable to put behind him until he boarded the aircraft. But the relief of having the training over was quickly replaced by the responsibility of the mission.

What's it going to be like on the ground? he thought. *What if there's a SPETSNAZ element waiting for us?* It was the special operators' worst fear—that security had been compromised and their insertion would be met by a reception committee. *What will I do if Valclav can't find this agent, or worse yet, gets caught? If the alarm is sounded, will I be able to get the rest of the team out?* This feeling was not new to Moody. It was the same one he remembered from the rodeo circuit when he had drawn a particularly nasty bull and had had too much time to think about it before his turn in the ring. Once astride the bull, the fear vanished. *Will it be the same once we're on the ground?* He took a deep breath and squirmed in his seat, to the extent that his equipment load would allow.

The KLM KC-10 had left Ramstein AFB just after 10:00 P.M. and landed a half hour later at Rhineholm AFB, or Rhine Main as it was called, the American Air Force base that shared the runways with Frankfurt International. They taxied about for nearly a half hour while Major Black, with the help of a well-placed agent in the German air traffic control network, filed a KLM flight plan for Tokyo Narita. They left Rhine Main at 11:20 P.M.

The cabin had been depressurized twenty minutes earlier in preparation for the drop, and the oxygen, force-fed under pressure, had a metallic, manufactured taste. The newer, demand-type regulators had not been adapted to this aircraft, so he had to exhale forcibly to get another breath. The cabin temperature was down to zero, but he was still sweating. Some of the SEALs at Team Two lived for skydiving, but he had never particularly liked to jump—in fact, if he allowed himself to think about it, he could almost become terrified. For Moody, jumping was just a way to commute to the job site.

They had a saying in the teams: "Training's never over." It greeted new SEALs after they graduated from the rigorous basic training, and reminded them that their life as a SEAL was one of constant preparation. *Well,* Moody reflected, *training's sure as hell over for us—nothing to do but wait till the show begins.* Except for the normal stomach cramps that assaulted him on every training jump, he was now beginning to feel more calm than he had a right to be. But the calm was still punctuated with bursts of anxiety. *Christ, we should be there by now!*

The pilot's voice crackled in his earpiece: "This is Dan the Man up here in the cockpit. We're about ten minutes from the drop point. Near as we can tell, you'll be picking up a band of clouds about fifteen thousand feet, and it looks like they may go all the way to the deck. Zero winds are projected at the LZ. The AWADS system holds us well within acceptable tolerance. Good luck, gentlemen." *Acceptable tolerance,* Moody chuckled to himself, *which means you'll be well out over the Barents Sea and in international airspace by the time we're on the ground.*

The six jumpers, three on either side of the aircraft, waved feebly in acknowledgment. They were like fat, lumpy spacemen, bound to the mother craft by an oxygen and communication umbilical. *Ten more minutes,* thought Moody. *Ten minutes, then it begins.* Garniss was seated directly across the oxygen console from him, flanked by O'Keefe and Walker. The red night-vision lights in the ceiling of the aircraft reflected dully off their oxygen masks, goggles, and helmets, making them look like mutant insects from an old Japanese sci-fi movie. Garniss had jammed a bent, half-smoked, unlit cigarette in the nose of his oxygen mask, and it rode at a jaunty angle. He maintained that a cigarette always helped to calm his nerves before a jump. Occasionally he would take the butt from the crease in his mask, tap away an imaginary ash, and replace it. Now and then, a member of the flight crew, dressed in a fur-hooded parka and balaclava would step past and give him a thumbs-up. Moody again shifted his weight as best he could to keep his legs from going to sleep. *Dammit, let's go!*

"Get ready!" The jumpmaster stood in the center of the aircraft just aft of the oxygen console, facing forward, his arms extended in front of him, fists doubled. Moody fumbled for the cord to his earpiece and disconnected it. Then he jerked the toggle that activated his oxygen bottle and pulled the oxygen hose from his mask, separating himself from the on-board system. When he was finished, he held out his right fist, telling the jumpmaster he was ready. The bottled O_2 rushed through his mask, and he had to remind himself to breath evenly.

"Stand up!" The jumpmaster owned them now, like the conductor of an orchestra. He was bareheaded, wearing a small, clear plastic mask, so the jumpers cold see his face and he could make eye contact with them. His palms were turned up and he moved his arms in a lifting motion. Moody struggled to his feet, one hand just above his head on the support cable that was stretched tightly for that purpose along the side of the aircraft. His equipment load weighed just a little more than he did.

"Check e-quip-ment!" cried the jumpmaster. Moody put both hands over his head while the man in front of him ran his hands over him. He checked the harness attachment points, tugging here, pushing there. Then he traced the ripcord from Moody's front left riser back across his shoulder to the main chute to ensure that it was free of obstructions. He tapped him twice on the helmet, indicating he was finished, and Moody began to check him. All the while, a black SEAL in battle-dress utilities moved from one jumper to the other in a reassuring, professional manner. When he got to Moody, he shined a red penlight into his face, looking for signs of hypoxia.

"Just want to get a good look at you, sir, since it may be the last time," he yelled over the noise of the aircraft. "If you don't make it back, can I have your motorcycle?"

"Only if you promise not to ride it unless you're drunk," Moody shouted back. He extended a mittened hand, and the man shook it with both of his own.

"Give 'em hell, sir." He popped Moody on the rump and moved on to the next man. The aircraft began to mush about and yaw slightly as the pilot lowered the flaps to slow down.

"Stand by!" The two files of three waddled back to the cargo door. They assembled behind their equipment pallet, half standing and half hanging from the cables. They would follow it out the door as closely as possible. The jumpmaster and his assistants swarmed over them, making final equipment checks—a wink here, a smile there. The man with the clear goggles gave them a final thumbs-up, and they replied in kind.

Moody had been outwardly calm, since they had boarded the plane in Frankfurt, but it was a practiced indifference. From takeoff until they went out the door, there had been absolutely nothing for him to do but manage his thoughts. He was like the equipment pallet—just another piece of airborne baggage. That was about to change. A banshee howl invaded the plane as the hydraulic door crawled up to the ceiling of the aircraft, and the tranquil detachment he'd manufactured to insulate himself from the terror of the jump vanished. He and the others dropped to a slight crouch and stared at a point just under the red light at the side of the door where the green light should be.

"One minute! One minute!" screamed the jumpmaster, but they didn't hear him—they were hypnotized by the red light. Garniss made a show of dropping his cigarette to the deck and crushing it underfoot. After what seemed like an hour, Moody saw the red light wink out—then green. Seconds later he was in the violent, black emptiness over the Russian Republic.

Moody tumbled once before he stabilized and caught a fading glimpse of a light on the rudder of the aircraft. The roar of the wind, even with the insulated helmet, was deafening. The sweat that had collected inside his goggles now formed frozen BBs and danced around on the plexiglass. The temperature was minus forty degrees, and the windchill factor was well off the charts. He slowed to his thin-air drop speed of a hundred eighty knots and picked up the strobe on the equipment pallet. It was programmed to flash for ten seconds once out of the aircraft. Moody glanced at the altimeter perched on his reserve chute—passing thirty-eight thousand. He quickly picked up the lime-green Chemlites of the other jumpers as they, too, closed on the pallet. Carefully, he made a wide circle of the pallet and counted all five of them—so far, so good. The air was becoming noticeably denser now, more "solid," and he was softly buffeted as he screamed through the cold night. Then they went into the clouds.

Scientists and intellectuals, as well as people with great amounts of responsibility, often find themselves awake at unusual hours. The same can be said of those who are troubled. It was not surprising, then, that Dr. Leonid Zhdanov was in his office early Sunday morning. Except for the security personnel, the building was empty. Once again he'd slept poorly. Zhdanov had few interests other than his work and his family. He'd thought about trying to get to St. Petersburg or having his wife meet him again in Murmansk, but that would have been far too costly, even if time away from the facility were available to him. In Russia, as it had been in the Soviet Union, Christmas was not a time when workers took time off from their jobs as they did in the West. The holiday was now celebrated openly, and many of the Russian Orthodox churches were festively decorated. But an American, accustomed to the commercial and consumptive aspects of a Western Christmas, would notice few outward signs of celebration. In these terrible times, most Russians were not spending their rubles on frivolous things. Still, Zhdanov had been able to send a few small presents to his wife and sons. The flush of pride he felt when he thought of his boys was quickly replaced by a feeling of desperation. *How could I have been so stupid as to think this venture would be without risk!* On further reflection he conceded, *I was not stupid, I was greedy.*

Colonel Makarov had come to visit him exactly one week ago last Friday. There had been a certain amount of controlled delight about the man as he pushed his way unannounced into the office. Then he proceeded to prowl about the room as if he were inspecting it for his own purposes. He removed his overcoat and cavalierly draped it across the corner of Zhdanov's desk, placing his gloves in his hat and dropping them atop the coat. Makarov's appearance wasn't totally unexpected, but it filled Zhdanov with terror nonetheless.

"My dear Doctor, we have a serious incident of pilferage in Gremikha, and it involves the shipments of fuel oil to your facility."

Zhdanov had reacted with surprise and retreated behind his desk with a show of concern. Actually, he was thunderstruck and so sick with fear that he was afraid his legs would fail him if he didn't find a seat. "Are—are you sure?" he managed to reply.

"Oh, yes—quite sure. As you know, fuel stocks and diesel oil are brought in by tanker and stored at the fuel dock in Gremikha. From there it is trucked to the airfield at Kachalovka and to your facility, as well as to other installations in the central Kola. Well, it seems," he said with a certain smugness, "that about once a month, an additional truckload of fuel leaves the storage area for the facility here at Lumbovskiy. The vehicle returns to the fuel dock empty, but without ever having made a stop here to discharge its contents. What do you make of that, Doctor?" Zhdanov could only shrug and act puzzled. His mouth was so dry, he was unable to speak. "The documents authorizing the delivery were in order, signed by you or," Makarov smiled broadly, "by a clever forger."

"What are you going to do?" Zhdanov finally managed.

"Do? Well now, I haven't quite yet decided." The security man rose and began to pace triumphantly about the office. "We interrogated the driver, and he quickly gave us all the information he had. My people are quite experienced at that kind of thing, you know. We know quite a bit about the operation, but not everything. The driver was sent on his way with the excuse that the vehicle had broken down, and that he had made the repairs himself to account for the delay. He is a simple man, and is now taking direction from us. I believe we need to allow this pilferage of fuel to proceed for a time to allow for us to gather additional information.

But, Doctor . . ." Makarov again sat down and lit a cigarette, not bothering to offer Zhdanov one. He inhaled appreciatively and continued. "I am going to need your help."

"Of course, whatever I can do," Zhdanov said quickly. He was now plagued by visions of himself being led away in handcuffs while his staff watched.

Makarov reached inside his tunic and retrieved a sheaf of documents. "I have here a number of fuel-request authorizations that I would like you to sign for me. Your signature is all that is required; I will take care of the rest. We want to continue to, ah, shall we say, 'divert' a number of these shipments to see where the trail leads us. As you know, General Borzov treats those who deal in black-market activities quite harshly, especially those who have used their position for their own gain. Since it is such a serious crime, I want to proceed carefully with my investigation. So, Doctor, your signature, please."

Zhdanov quickly signed ten of the blank fuel-request authorizations while the Colonel watched. When he was finished, Makarov recovered the documents and placed them in his tunic. He was sure of himself now. He tossed the cigarette into the ashtray, not bothering to crush it, and rose, handing his overcoat to a shaken Zhdanov. He turned his back to him, allowing Zhdanov to help him on with it. The Director stood helplessly by the desk while Makarov donned his cap and carefully pulled on his gloves.

"And one other thing. I require your assistance with a small, trivial matter." Makarov told what he wanted while Zhdanov stared at him with the same terrified expression. "I'm sure, Doctor, that it should pose no serious problem for you. Are you with me, Doctor?"

"Yes . . . yes, of course—I'll do my best."

"Good! And your cooperation with these fuel shipments is appreciated, Doctor. With your help, I'm sure we will be able move against these criminals at a time of our own choosing. No, don't bother," he said to the man frozen by the side of the desk, "I'll show myself out."

For several days following the encounter, Zhdanov was in a daze. He expected to see an OMON detachment or a military security detail from Severomorsk storm into his office and take him into custody. It could have been worse, he told himself—Makarov could have arrested him on the spot. Finally, it had dawned on Zhdanov what had happened. It was a situation simply too good for Makarov to pass up. He had Zhdanov's signature on the authorization forms, and probably a signed confession from the driver of the truck that would implicate him. Now the good Colonel was free to steal fuel and sell it on the black market himself. In the unlikely event that the shipments were discovered, Makarov could arrest Zhdanov and hold him accountable for all the missing fuel. These suspicions had been confirmed only yesterday. When he compared the delivery slips to a copy of the shipping manifest from Gremikha, there was a shipment on the twenty-first that had not been received at the facility.

At first, Zhdanov thought Makarov might no longer be a threat, since he, too, was now on the take, but he concluded this was probably wishful thinking. He'd even thought of reporting the matter to the Director of Science and Technology in Murmansk, Zhdanov's civilian boss, but he knew that would not work. Makarov was far too clever not to have his bases covered if he were to take the matter over Makarov's head. He'd even thought of confronting Makarov, asking for a share of the proceeds, since it was his signature that made the fuel requisitions possible. But Makarov was a ruthless man, and he might find a way to dispose of Zhdanov in order to keep all of the money. *It appears he's content to take the profit from the fuel so long as he can blame me if anything goes wrong,* thought Zhdanov. *That's some comfort, but he's sure to make other demands. He already has.*

Zhdanov tried to light a cigarette and found he had to steady the match with both hands.

As soon as he went into the clouds, the equipment pallet vanished. Moody reacted slower than he should have, turning one hundred eighty degrees and pulling his arms slightly closer to his sides, which would allow him to track away from the pallet. One of the dangers in a group drop was a midair collision, or entanglement with other jumpers or the equipment pallet. Without visual reference they were forced to scatter, which complicated rallying the team once they were on the ground. The equipment pallet had a barometric sensor that would open its parachute at two thousand feet. The jumpers would pull at twenty-five hundred. On training jumps they opened much higher for safety reasons. The lower they and the equipment pallet opened, the less would be their chance for detection on radar, which was much greater under canopy than in freefall. The airfield at Kachalovka had an old, modified GS-13 air-search radar that dated back to the mid-sixties, but it now served primarily as a ground-controlled approach radar. The impact point had been planned so as to place the eleven-hundred-foot hill twenty miles southeast of the airfield between them and the radar installation. If they had a good spot, the operator at Kachalovka would have two or three sweeps on his scope to pick them up before they disappeared into the shadow of the hill. That was if he was carefully watching his scope, which was unlikely at 5:30 on a Sunday morning in winter.

After he had turned to move away from the pallet, Moody floated through the blackness, watching his altimeter slowly unwind. The fifty seconds it took him to fall from fourteen thousand feet to his pull altitude was an eternity. As he tore through three thousand feet, he extended his right hand and cocked his left arm to catch the rip-cord knob on his left breast with his mittened hand. Twenty-seven hundred . . . twenty-six hundred . . . He jerked the cord, extending both arms forward in a "hands up" motion. At first nothing happened, and a cold stab of panic shot through him. Then he automatically dipped one shoulder. The pilot chute, riding in the dead-air burble just above his shoulder blades, caught some air and quickly ran out on its tether to deploy his main chute. A good free-fall opening has none of the violence of a static-line jump. Moody swung gently under the canopy. He was breathing hard, which was normal for him following an opening. He had never been able to break himself of holding his breath during the last several thousand feet prior to the pull. While he gasped for breath, he immediately began to prepare for landing, fumbling for the straps that would release the equipment bags he carried under his reserve chute and on his rump just below where his main chute had been. Following a short, frantic struggle, the bundles fell away and dangled on their thirty-foot nylon lines. Twelve hundred feet . . . but how high above sea level was the land beneath him?

Now, he commanded himself, *get ready—good landing.* A parachute landing on a pitch-black night is a mental exercise. Since a jumper cannot see the ground, he has to force himself to relax, keep his feet together, and above all, keep his legs bent. To tense up or "reach" for the ground is to invite a broken ankle. Eight hundred, seven hundred. *Won't be long now . . . Toes pointed, legs bent, easy, easy . . .* When a marksman shoots properly, it's always a surprise when the weapon fires. In much the same way, a night parachute landing is a surprise. *Easy . . . anytime now, easy . . .* It was over before he knew it, and he was on his back in the snow. *Thank God,* he breathed out of habit, *cheated death once again.* A gentle tug on the risers told him he had to move. He came to his knees and shrugged off the harness and reserve chute. Without thinking, he began to work his way down the shroud lines until he reached silk and on to the apex of the main chute. Then he quickly coiled the parachute, working his way back to the harness assembly. He pulled the nylon sack from a pocket of his heavy jumpsuit and bagged both parachutes and his harness, along with his helmet and goggles.

It took Moody almost twenty minutes to retrieve his equipment bags, bury the parachutes and his jumpsuit, and prepare to move out. The adrenaline-driven euphoria that followed the jump had largely been expended by the effort. As he paused to rest a moment, he was almost overcome by the silence and isolation. In locating his equipment bags, he had surveyed the immediate area with a shielded, red-filtered penlight. It was almost pitch black, but the snow seemed to have a slight translucent quality about it, radiating a faint glow from the ground. He'd tried the night-observation-device goggles, but they were only partially effective. The NODs were a light-amplification instrument that required starlight or a sliver of a moon to be effective. Without the goggles he could make out large features in the amorphous terrain, but he had little or no depth perception. Two feet of loose snow blanketed the hardpack. An occasional shrub thrust a bony finger through the thick white carpet. The land was mostly flat, cut occasionally by a shallow ravine. He found a small grove of scraggly, tortured, birchlike trees that appeared to be having a difficult time of it. They were gnarly and looked terribly old, and Moody was glad he hadn't found them on the way down. *I might as well be on Mars,* he thought, *or a back-country ski area high in the Rockies, for that matter.* He was nearly overcome by an urge to find the others and be with them.

A low-powered direction-finding signal with a three-mile range was located with a transponder on the equipment pallet. Moody turned in thirty-degree arcs and interrogated the transponder with his own DF transceiver. The needle finally jumped, indicating the direction of the pallet. He took a compass bearing and set off toward the beacon. He was used to moving with a heavy pack on snowshoes, but he carefully picked his way across the loose snow, pausing periodically to check his bearing and study the cold, near-black terrain in front of him. He was about to recheck his bearing with the DF, when he cut another trail in the snow. With his penlight, he verified that it was a snowshoed traveler like himself, with alternating holes made on either side of the track by ski poles, just like his own. Knowing that he would soon be with other humans allowed him to enjoy a strange surge of gratitude. He jumped into the fluffy rut made by the preceding traveler and hurried after him.

Moody saw the Chemlite on the pallet before he picked up the movement off to his right. "Glad you could join us, Boss," said Garniss as he appeared at Moody's side. "Thought you might have stopped off for a beer." He sounded casual, but Moody saw that he had a silenced pistol in his hand.

"Who's here?" Penlights flicked like red fireflies as two lumps busied themselves over the equipment pallet.

"Everyone but Walker and O'Keefe." Garniss looked at his watch. "Wait another five minutes, and then give 'em a shout?"

"Sounds good," Moody replied. "The gear okay?"

"Near as we can tell. Snyder and Valclav are breaking it down now."

There was a commotion in the opposite direction from which Moody had come, and Garniss was instantly alert. He snapped on his NOD goggles and pointed a blunt cylinder in the direction of the noise. It was an infrared light, invisible to the human eye, but with the IR feature of his NOD he was able to see clearly for about thirty feet.

"It's the doc," he said, removing the NOD. A moment later, O'Keefe came toiling up to where the two SEALs worked unpacking equipment bundles.

"Christ on a crutch," he said, dumping his pack on the snow. "That was some scary shit. *Dosvaydanya,* comrades," he said as he leaned across the pallet to identify Snyder and Valclav.

"How many times do I have to tell you," growled Valclav, *"dosvaydanya* is good-bye—*zdrahst'voitye* is hello."

"Zdrahst'voitye, comrades," O'Keefe replied. Then he shuffled over to Moody and Garniss. "H'lo, sir. Garniss, you got that five bucks?"

"Five bucks?" asked Moody.

"That's right, sir. He bet me five bucks I'd get killed on the drop." He punched Garniss playfully on the shoulder. "Fooled ya, didn't I?"

Garniss sighed audibly in Moody's direction. "Figured he'd probably make it just to collect the bet."

O'Keefe was not a large man, barely five eight and a hundred forty pounds. He seemed smaller, though, because of his chalky complexion and straight brown hair that fell to a peak in the middle of his forehead. He wore glasses and had a pair of plastic athletic prescription goggles strapped to his head like an NBA basketball player. And he was a whiner. He was from New Hampshire and his voice had a clipped, nasal quality that would have bothered the other SEALs had they not quickly learned to ignore it. No matter how easy the task before them, O'Keefe found some reason to complain about it, or to surface some hardship that was personally unique. When things became difficult and uncomfortable, O'Keefe maintained a steady level of protest, but he always did it. When confronted with the impossible, O'Keefe would begin to whine and the platoon would proceed to get the job done.

"Where's Walker," he said. He pronounced it "wah-kah," but there was concern in his voice.

Again Garniss shrugged. "Don't know. He sure as hell should have beat you to the rally point. Sir?"

"Yeah, you better go ahead."

Garniss took a Motorola Saber from the Velcro carrier on his vest. The transceivers had limited, line-of-sight range, and an embedded crypto feature that scrambled the transmissions. The sets had also been tuned well away from any known Russian commercial or military frequencies, but it was still an electronic emission to be avoided if possible. "Walker, you there, over?" Silence. "Come in, Walker." Again no reply. "Roger, nothing heard, out." Garniss replaced the radio and looked at Moody.

"Better find him," Moody said. Garniss stepped over to the pallet, where Valclav and Snyder were busy unloading the gear and erecting the *akios.* After a brief exchange, he returned with a radio component that was similar to their personal DF units. It was a small transmitter that was programmed to activate a transponder each man carried. He clicked it to Walker's frequency and activated the set. This was yet another electronic emission they did not want to make, but it would carry no more than five miles.

"Got him, Boss. He's over there," said Garniss, pointing in the general direction from which O'Keefe had come.

"Okay, let's you and me go get him," Moody replied as he dropped his pack. "Snyder and Valclav can stay with the gear. Doc, you better get your kit and come with us." O'Keefe was the platoon corpsman.

While they waited for O'Keefe, Moody began to worry. *Shit! What if he's dead or seriously wounded—what if he can't be moved?* The mission planning had covered this. If a man was killed on the jump, they'd bury him and move on. A wounded man would be moved with the team if possible, but if the wound was critical, one of the SEALs would have to be left with the casualty while the others continued on to the objective. In this case, they would attempt to rendezvous for the extraction. Should more than one of them be wounded or incapacitated, it would be Moody's option to abort the mission. But what the mission planning did not take into account was that these men were his friends as well as his responsibility. Leaving a friend behind would be a tough call.

"How about it, Doc?" he said irritably.

"All set, boss. I got the litter, just in case." A portable litter had been strapped to the equipment pallet for just this eventuality. If it wasn't needed, they would discard it with the pallet before they moved on.

It took them just fifteen minutes to find Walker's parachute. He had landed on a shelf near a fifteen-foot rock face that rimmed a steep raving. The landing had gone well, but after his chute collapsed, his first step had taken him over the edge. He had fallen and slammed into a rock outcropping. The chute had caught on a stand of the dwarf birch trees behind the shelf, and Walker was hopelessly tangled in the parachute shroud lines.

"Walker, you down there?" Moody and the other two SEALs stood on the shelf looking at the twisted shroud lines that disappeared down into a mass of snow and rock.

"Right here, boss. Boy, am I glad to see you guys. I'm sorry, sir, but I don't think I can move." Walker sounded weak.

"Don't try to move, Don. I'll be right there." Moody was afraid of what he might find, but tried to keep it from his voice. "Garniss, you stay here and make sure that the chute doesn't break out of those trees. I'll go first—then, Doc, you follow me down." He didn't wait for a reply as he bunched the shroud lines at the skirt of the canopy and started down the short rock face. A few seconds later he called back up. "C'mon down, Doc."

While O'Keefe eased himself down the face, Moody worked to brush the snow away from Walker's face and cut the shroud lines tangled about his feet that held him upside down.

"Christ, I'm sorry, sir. Wouldn't you know I'd be the one to fuck up. I tried to cut the lines, but I cain't move my left arm. Heard you callin'—couldn't get to my radio. Gawd almighty, I'm sorry as hell about this."

"You apologize again, Don, and I'll kick you right in the crotch. Now, where does it hurt?" Moody was now straddling the fallen SEAL, bracing his legs against a large rock to ease Walker to a horizontal position.

"It's my left shoulder. I almost had myself upright once, but it hurt so bad I think I passed out."

While Moody held him steady with the help of a boulder, O'Keefe was busy cutting through his free-fall exposure suit and the layers of undergarments. He held a penlight in his mouth as he sliced through the last undershirt.

"Can't see anything. Take a real deep breath—that hurt?"

"No more'n normal."

O'Keefe put a bare hand over Walker's mouth. "Spit."

"What?"

"Just do it, Don. Give me a hawker." Walker complied, and O'Keefe inspected it carefully. He wiped his hand on his trousers and shined the light in Walker's eyes and nose. "Turn your head to the left . . . okay, now right—good. Now tilt it left and right—that's great. Okay, I'm going to start poking you a little. Sing out if it hurts." O'Keefe put the light back into his mouth and gently began to exert pressure with his thumbs on his collarbone and out across the top of his shoulder. Moody watched and said nothing as the little corpsman very professionally moved his hands across Walker.

"Hmmm?"

"No."

"Huh?"

"No."

"Hmmm?"

"No—OUCH!"

"Easy, big guy," said Moody as he clamped his hand over Walker's mouth, "unless you want a border guard for a doctor."

O'Keefe pulled a flap of clothing over Walker's chest and stood back, hanging on to the shroud lines. He snapped off his light and slid it into the pocket on his sleeve.

"Well?" said Moody, moving close to O'Keefe but still supporting Walker.

"Dislocated shoulder—I'm pretty sure of it."

"Can you fix it?"

"Maybe. It's not going to be easy or painless, but I might be able to pop it back into place with some help. We got to get him out of here to do anything. Let's try and reconnect his parachute harness. There's still enough shrouds attached to his risers to lift him."

"What's the story, Doc? Am I gonna be okay?"

"I don't know, Don. I wanted to shoot you, but Mr. Moody won't let me. Now, I want you to hold your left arm across your chest with your good arm while we lift you out of here."

Garniss and Moody pulled Walker back up the face while O'Keefe climbed alongside to make sure his shoulder moved as little as possible. It was a torturous trip, and several times Walker yelped in pain. Once back on top of the face, O'Keefe quickly conferred with the other two before the three of them surrounded Walker.

"Okay, Don," O'Keefe began, "here's the deal. Your shoulder's out of joint, and Mr. Moody is going to help me pop it back into place. Garniss is going to hold your legs in case you try to get up and walk around. Now, it may hurt a little, so you're just going to have to tough it out, okay?" Walker nodded. "And just in case you feel like you want to holler for a second opinion, I'm going to put this bandage in your mouth, okay?"

Walker was now staring straight ahead. "Just do it, Doc, an' let's get it over with."

O'Keefe had Walker lie on his right side. Garniss held his legs steady while Moody steadied him with his head in his lap.

"Okay, Don, this is what we're going to do. Your shoulder is out of joint, and I'm going to put it back. Now, it sort of popped out and your shoulder muscles are holding it out of place, sort of forward toward your chest. I'm going to lift it up and back into place. It might hurt just a bit as the muscles are again stretched to allow it back into place, but I'll be as easy on you as I can." Moody noticed that O'Keefe's voice had none of its normal whiny or caustic quality. It had taken on a soothing, concerned tone, like that of a kindly old doctor treating a child. "But I'm going to need your help, okay? I need you to relax as much as you can." He began to gently move Walker's shoulder up and back. "Hey, you're doing great, buddy," O'Keefe cooed. "That's it, relax—think about sitting in a hot tub drinking beer."

"Or about cruising the beach in July on your bike," said Moody.

"Or about pussy," Garniss added.

"UMMPFF!"

When O'Keefe finally felt the joint snap back into place, he kept his hands on top of the shoulder and moved closer to Walker, settling him down. "All right—good show, my man! Lookin' real fine." He nodded to Moody, who took the scarf from Walker's mouth. Walker's face was chalky, but he managed a smile. "How's it feel, pal?" Walker shrugged his shoulder, and smiled again. O'Keefe eased him onto his back, motioning Garniss to keep his feet elevated. Shock was now as much of a concern as the shoulder. "You know, Don, if you'd had that done on the outside, some orthopod would have wanted a couple grand. I'm only going to charge you half your next month's pay."

Walker continued to grin, and his color was coming back. "Jeez, it does feel better, Doc—a whole lot better."

"They always do that," replied O'Keefe, seeming to appeal to Moody but not taking his eyes from Walker. "They never want to talk about my fee." Walker tried to get up, but O'Keefe held him down. "Okay, I'm going to let you sit up in a sec, and then I'm going to tie your left arm across your chest. It should feel a lot better, but I don't want you moving that arm, okay?" Walker nodded, and they helped him to a sitting position.

"Now what?" said Moody as he stood up, noticing that he was trembling a little from the ordeal. He'd once dislocated a shoulder after being tossed from a bronc, and he clearly remembered the pain, but it was even harder watching it happen to someone else.

O'Keefe thought for a moment. "He'll be able to walk, although he'll not be good for much else for several days, and he's going to be in pain."

"Can you give him something for it?"

"Not if you want him to walk."

Moody considered this. "Garniss, you hide his chute and pack up the rest of his gear. The doc and I will start walking back with him. We'll see you back at the rally point." He looked at the litter and breathed in a sigh of relief. "And you can get rid of this thing along with the chute." Garniss nodded and went to work. They moved at a steady, comfortable pace back to the equipment pallet, but Walker had no problem keeping up. Moody looked at his watch. They were an hour and a half behind schedule, but time would not become critical unless there were further delays. He was almost giddy with relief that Walker did not have to be carried. Garniss arrived five minutes behind them.

"Okay, Kurt, let's see where we are."

A tall SEAL standing next to one of the *akios* opened a map case and spread it on top of one of the small, runnered equipment sleds. He snapped on a red penlight and pointed to a small *X* made with a grease pencil on the map's laminated surface.

"We're right here, Boss. I got a good cut from two satellites." He laid a plastic scale alongside the *X*. Then he placed a compass on top of the map and rotated the map and compass until it was aligned with magnetic north. "It's hard work for a compass up here, but that's close. The big hill between us and the airport is about seven miles in that direction. There's a road almost five miles due west. I'd say the spot was pretty fair—we're about a half mile from where they said they'd put us."

"You ready to move?"

"Yessir. The *akios* are packed and ready to move. We can split Walker's load between the two of them so he can travel light."

"Shoes or skis?"

"I'd rather use shoes for now, at least until I get the feel of the terrain. Satellite photos are one thing, but walking it is another. I judge we're about eight hundred feet here, and the ground's probably a little rough for skis. We'll need to get down to the flatlands before we can put away the shoes."

"How far to the first lay-up?"

"I'd say nine klicks—a little under six miles."

Moody thought about it for a moment. "Okay, let's have a quick huddle—then I want you to take us there."

In the jungle, they called him the point man. He was responsible for the safe movement of the patrol. In the snow, he was the trailbreaker or just "the breaker," but his function was the same. Find the best and safest route to their destination, and see any bad guys before the bad guys saw them. Snyder was one of the best, and Moody trusted him completely.

Kurt Snyder had been in the Teams for twelve years, all of it with Team Two. He was one of the SEALs who skied across Greenland in the summer of 1983. When it came to winter warfare or cold-weather survival, there were few better than Snyder. He was a solidly built man at six feet and just under two hundred pounds, and had narrowly missed two Winter Olympic biathlon teams. He couldn't run with Garniss or Moody, but he could ski or snowshoe circles around them.

"Okay, gang, here's the deal." Moody laid the map on the ground and painted it with his penlight. "Here we are. We're still going to try to make it to the first lay-up, here. We're a few hours behind schedule, but that's no big deal. Snyder, you and Valclav make sure the area is cleaned up. Garniss and I will take the first shift with the *akios.* Walker and the Doc will follow the second sled. Walker started to protest—his job was to pull one of the *akios*—but Moody waved him off. "Maybe tomorrow night. It's early in the game, and your job is to take care of that shoulder." He turned to Snyder and Valclav. "Kurt will break trail and the Sarge will bring up the rear. Any questions?" Moody flashed his light around the group. "Okay, guys, lets go earn our pay."

Katrina Shebanin had finished dinner, and sat at one of the tables in the cafeteria over tea. That morning, she'd attended to some paperwork and then taken advantage of the midday twilight for some cross-country skiing. There was an excellent trail along the main road that ran past the facility. Most of the afternoon she spent reading. She hadn't read Chekhov in years, and was enjoying a collection of his short stories immensely. The food quality at the facility was not that good, but there was usually plenty of it. Years ago, an important facility such as this would have catered far better to its staff or there would have been a storm of protests. The men and women of the elite Russian scientific community had been a pampered lot, but that had changed. Everyone there knew just how difficult things now were in the Republic, and there were few complaints. Most of the scientific and production staff, like Dr. Zhdanov, lived at the facility and sent their meager salaries home to their families elsewhere in the Republic.

Katrina reflected on her life before Lumbovskiy and what might lie ahead. Both of her parents were dead. She had a brother, but she had heard nothing from him since he left for Novosibirsk right after the fall of the Union. They had never been particularly close. Her work had been the focal point in her life, but the prospects of a nuclear physicist were not all that great in the new order. *After I finish this project, then what?* she often asked herself. With the exception of a few brief affairs, her experience with men had not been all that rewarding. Her liaison with General Borzov could be one of those exceptions. Sometimes she had a hard time believing that it had really happened. *What am I doing having an affair with a colonel general of the Soviet Army, a man who reminds me of my father?*

"Mind if I join you?"

"Not at all, Leonid, sit down."

He set his tea on the table as he pulled out a chair. She offered him a cigarette, but he declined, so she lit one for herself. "I saw that you were working this morning," he began, blowing across the top of his cup. "I thought of coming over, but I didn't want to bother you."

She gave him a sideways glance. "Just cleaning up some paperwork so I won't have to do it tomorrow. The bus in yet?" A small gale had blown across from the White Sea along with some scattered snow showers. Not a major storm, but Katrina liked to have all of her people back safely at the facility Sunday evening for a timely start on the production week.

"Just arrived. The driver said there was a little drifting snow over the road, but driving was not yet a problem. Going to Gremikha next weekend?"

"Perhaps," she replied. "The walls in my room are closing in on me again." In reality, she had been waiting to hear from General Borzov. He had called the weekend following their meeting in Murmansk, and had been most cordial in his stiff, formal way, but there had been nothing since then. She knew he was busy, but still, *I wonder if he'll call again.* She also wondered if anyone knew about their meeting. If they did, few would talk openly about the extracurricular affairs of the District Commander.

"You've had no more contact with Makarov, then," Zhdanov offered.

"No, thank God." She leaned forward. "And thank you again for telling General Borzov about it. Because of that, I believe I've been placed off limits to him." She shuddered. "The man still scares me, though. He should be let go, but if he wasn't in the OMON, he'd probably join the thugs and outlaws that are taking over the Republic."

He doesn't have to leave the service of the Republic to be a criminal, thought Zhdanov sadly, *but then, neither did I.* "Katrina," he said carefully, "I know the man is a nuisance, but would it hurt you just to be civil to him?"

"Civil!" she exploded. "The bastard assaulted me. Christ, you were there. Why in the hell would I want anything to do with that pig?"

"Well, he is the senior area security officer," he said defensively. "I just thought it wouldn't hurt to treat him in, well, a normal fashion."

"Normal fashion! Leonid, the man's an animal. There's nothing normal about him—he's a complete . . . Wait a minute." She had not forgotten about Zhdanov's problem with the fuel shipments, but he hadn't brought it up in well over a week, and she wasn't about to. "Makarov," she said quietly. "He's found out about the missing fuel, hasn't he?" Zhdanov just sat staring into his teacup. "For God's sake, Leonid, what's going on?"

"The good Colonel has 'appropriated' the operation for himself. And," Zhdanov continued in a barely audible voice, "he can do this because he has my name on a number of fuel-requisition vouchers. It . . . it looks as if I'm in a difficult position."

Katrina was furious, and her anger almost overshadowed her pity for Zhdanov—almost. "Just what did he ask of you, or more to the point, what is expected of me?"

"Not that much, really," he said hurriedly. "If he speaks to you or offers to buy you a drink, just be nice to him, or at least polite—that's all. It would be a favor to me if you would."

She took a long, steady pull on her cigarette and inhaled deeply, holding the smoke for several seconds before slowly exhaling. "Now, you listen to me carefully, Leonid Alexandrovich," she said coldly. "I will be polite to the man, and will speak to him if spoken to. But if he touches me or does anything to indicate that he has any claim to me, or that he is entitled to special favors, I'll go straight to the General." Zhdanov, much relieved, started to speak, but she held up her hand. "But you've got to resolve this thing. Go to the military police or the District Inspector General, or go directly to General Borzov yourself. If you cooperate, I'm sure it will be taken into account. Makarov will bleed you to death. You can't allow him to do that!" But even as she spoke, she saw him draw inward at the thought of it, and knew he hand't the stomach for it—Makarov had probably counted on that. "At any rate, I can't help you anymore. If that bastard lays a hand on me, I'll go straight to the General myself."

Zhdanov gave her a look of total despair. She felt sorry for him, but there was nothing she could do. She'd thought of telling him about her affair with Borzov. That would surely keep Makarov away, but how else would the Colonel use that knowledge against her or the General himself? *No, there's nothing I can do for Zhdanov. He'll have to find his own way out, if there is one.*

"Take care of yourself, Leonid," she said as she ground out her cigarette. After she left, he sat quietly by himself at the table for a very long time.

It was close to 10:30 A.M. when Moody called another halt to their march. They had come almost six miles from their drop point and were now some twenty-three miles south of Gremikha. In summer, the ground was a rolling blend of rock and tundra, mostly covered by shrubs and cut by ravines. In midwinter it had become a rumpled patchwork of ice and snow. A light snow fell intermittently and reduced their visibility somewhat, so the team never got a true feel for the land they were crossing. Only Snyder, who sometimes zigzagged in front of them, had some feel for the terrain. They were more like scuba divers paddling across a dark lake bed than men moving on land.

Out front, Snyder tried to keep them at a steady pace, occasionally moving away from the line of march to inspect an obstacle or to determine the best way around the occasional stand of trees. He had sharp eyes and extremely well-developed night vision, but occasionally he had to use his NOD and the IR flashlight to guide them. Chemlites were tied to their packs and to the rear of the *akios,* so others in line had only to follow the light on the clump in front of them. The terrain flattened occasionally, but never long enough to make it practical to shift to cross-country skis. During the trek, Moody called a halt about every forty minutes, and they took a break. The men didn't really need the rest, but since their compasses weren't terribly accurate, he wanted to be sure they were moving in the right direction. The SATNAV receiver was deadly accurate here, just as it had been during their training in Greenland, but there was an important difference. The SATNAV was more accurate than their maps of the Kola. Moody wouldn't be totally satisfied until he could sight a known object and calibrate the receiver to their maps. He could, however, track their progress across their large-scale area map and ensure they weren't following a false compass reading. He plotted each new position on the map, and their line of march looked like the wake of ship with a shoddy helmsman, but they were moving in the proper direction.

"We can't be too far off, Kurt." Snyder had worked his way back from the van, while Moody had again removed the TremblePac SATNAV receiver from its case on the side of the *akio.* He tuned the set and read off the latitude and longitude as Snyder noted them on his pad and marked their location on the map by a dot with a circle around it, noting the time.

"This is it, Boss, the first lay-up. We go to ground here?"

"If it looks good to you," Moody replied.

"Let me take a look around and see if there's a spot for it." He motioned to Garniss, and they set off to explore the immediate area.

Moody walked over to where Walker was resting while O'Keefe adjusted the sling that held his arm to his side. "Well, what do you think, Don? This place look good for a campsite, or you want to head down the road apiece and look for a Travelodge?" The activity and their finally achieving their first lay-up point, even if they were a few hours late, had boosted Moody's spirits immensely. It had been a textbook insertion. The only problem was Walker's shoulder. His prognosis was good, but they would know more after he'd had a night's rest. O'Keefe had been reluctant to give him any medication while they were on the move, and Moody could see he was in a lot of pain.

"A motel? Only if they have a swimmin' pool, an' a bar where I can get a brewski. Or why don't we just stop right here an' have a wienie roast?"

"Well, hang on a minute. Snyder and Garniss are out looking for a good spot to camp. How's the shoulder?"

"Well, it don't hurt like it did when I landed, but I got to admit that it's been smartin' a little for the last hour or so. I reckon it'll be a lot better in the mornin', though." O'Keefe handed him a canteen, insisting that he take a drink. It was easy to get dehydrated in extremely cold weather. "Goddammit, Doc, I ain't thirsty!"

"Drink it, Don," said Moody.

"Aye, aye, sir," and he took several long swallows.

Moody's attention was taken by Snyder and Garniss, who came shuffling up out of the darkness. "Sir, there's a shallow ravine about thirty meters over there," said Snyder. "We can kick snow down and have a snow cave dug in less than an hour."

"Okay, Kurt. What about the *akios?"*

"Easy deal," he replied. "Nestle them in the ravine just down from us and push snow over them."

"Sounds like a winner—let's do it."

Snyder pulled two portable shovels from one of the *akios* and a short fiberglass pole that he fitted to a flat piece of aluminum so he had a tool that looked something like a squeegee. With it, he and Garniss would push and pull the snow from the sides of the ravine and mound it up in the center for about fifteen feet along the bottom. They would then trample it with their snowshoes, compressing the outer layers of snow. After about a half hour the snow would "cure," allowing them to dig a tunnel along the bottom of the ravine from either end of their mound to create two snow caves. Whenever possible, they looked for ravines for a lay-up. Since they were below the flat of the land to either side, any blowing snow would only make their burrows more snug and less visible, not that they expected any company. When they were closer to the objective, lay-ups would be carefully chosen and prepared to avoid detection, but for now, they were well back in an uninhabited area, and were only looking for protection from the elements.

Moody and O'Keefe jockeyed the *akios* over to where Garniss and Snyder worked. Valclav followed, working over the area where they had stopped with an implement that resembled a light landscape rake with flexible tines. It was the same tool he had dragged behind them on the march. It didn't entirely obscure their tracks or the ruts of the *akios,* but it had the effect of leveling the snow where they had been so it was more easily covered by blowing snow or additional snowfall. Again, they didn't think there was much chance of someone cutting their trail this far out, but they were taking no chances.

Once at the lay-up site, Moody and O'Keefe guided their sleds into the ravine and began to unload the provisions they would need. When they had finished, they draped light tarps over the sleds and began to cover them with snow. Since Walker couldn't work, O'Keefe had him stand off to one side and stamp his feet, just as he had at previous stops. The temperature was fifteen below, and no matter how warmly they were dressed, they had to move or risk frostbite. None of them could remain idle until they were in the snow caves. Staying active in extreme cold was a cardinal rule, and Walker shuffled about while the others worked. Soon Valclav joined them in the ravine, and jumped in to help Snyder and Garniss finish the caves. The wind had come up and it was snowing harder. Moody smiled—he'd sleep much better knowing there would be little trace of where they were or from which direction they had come.

"The cave's ready, sir. Do you want to eat first or talk?"

Moody surveyed his men. They'd certainly had longer and much harder days in training, but there was something about doing it for real on the enemy's turf that made it all different. They looked beat, and he could feel himself beginning to drag.

"Let's eat. We'll call home after dinner. The folks'll wait up for us."

"Cheery aye aye," replied Garniss, "but you know Mom an' Dad will be fretting." Garniss now referred to Brisco and Tolliver as their parents back home.

"So they will, but they'll just have to be patient."

O'Keefe helped Walker into one of the caves that the two of them would share with Valclav, while Moody, Garniss, and Snyder wormed their way into the other. He also started the injured man on a heavy dosage of cortisone. The interior of the snow caves was tall enough for them to sit cross-legged and upright if they ducked their heads forward, and long enough for three sleeping bags to be laid out. Garniss handed in their sleeping and personal-gear bags, which were stowed around the walls of the warren. Then he fired up the small alcohol stove and began to heat water for rations. They had been eating along the trail, since they had to continually replace the calories lost during a cold-weather march. But there was something very appealing about a hot meal in arctic conditions that warmed the spirit as well as the body. Normally, only one stove would be used to heat rations for the entire team, but firing a stove in each snow cave would cure the interior of the cave and bring the temperature up to thirty-two degrees. Moody and Snyder watched as Garniss dropped the food pouches into the water. The small stove was like an altar, and he a trusted layperson, preparing communion. After the meal and a cup of cocoa, they used the rest of the hot water to wash. Of the three of them, only Snyder shaved.

"I guess we better get with the program," said Moody, who was feeling very warm and cozy. "How's our satellite time?"

Snyder checked his watch and thought for a moment. "We're good for another hour and then we're blacked out for about three."

"I'll set up the antenna," Garniss said as he shrugged on his parka. "One eight zero at thirty degrees?"

"You got it," Snyder replied.

Garniss wriggled out through the cave opening, dragging the small antenna case, and trudged up the short ravine slope. There he assembled the small mesh dish and affixed it to a folding tripod. Then he sighted on his compass to aim the assembly due south and cocked the dish back to elevate it thirty degrees from the horizon. Satisfied with the placement, he trailed the antenna lead back to the cave.

Inside, Moody sat over a computer keyboard tapping a message into the Gridset, a ruggedized, laptop-type computer with an LED screen that weighed less than ten pounds, including the battery. The Gridset was a fully functional personal computer that had to be "logged on" with a security code. The little PC would take message text and store it on its hard drive for reference and future transmission. It also had a function that allowed it to compress text so the message could be sent in a burst transmission. The computer was married by a connecting cable to an LST-B SATCOM transceiver, a black box that was two-thirds the size and about the same weight as the Gridset. The LST-B could send and receive coded voice and text messages using orbiting communications satellites. The team carried a complete set of backup components as well as several additional sets of batteries. Battery life would be monitored more closely than food, and as with the rations, the load would be lightened as they were used.

Moody didn't really have to compose a message. He merely pulled a standard Situation Report, or SITREP, from the hard drive. It was a miniprogram that prompted him through a series of questions concerning their location, personnel status, logistic status, current weather, and enemy sightings. What tens of thousands of office workers did at their data-processing stations across the nation, Moody was doing in a snow cave in the Russian wilderness. When he was finished with the standard prompts, he added some remarks that detailed Walker's injury, condition, and prognosis, including medications given. The medical officer who examined them prior to the mission would be available with a copy of Walker's medical record, and would provide advice and long-distance consultation as needed.

"Well, let's take a look," Moody said as he shifted the set so Garniss could see the screen with the finished text. This was standard procedure. Garniss was read into all communication in case something happened to Moody. Moody also shared much of the decision-making with Garniss so he would be able to assume leadership of the team at any time. He also wanted Snyder aware of decisions and communications that affected the team's mission. Their ability to move and remain undetected was his primary responsibility.

"Looks good to me, Boss. Could you ask them for the score of the Skins game? They played Dallas today."

Moody considered this a moment, and scrolled to the remarks section. "Did the Redskins beat Dallas?" he tapped into the text.

"Perfect," replied Garniss.

"You ready, Kurt?"

Snyder monitored a needle on the SATCOM indicating they were tracking their communications satellite. "I got a lock, sir. Anytime you're ready."

Moody hit the XMIT key. The Gridset could achieve a compression of about forty-eight to one, or about two percent, so the formatted data and three paragraphs of text were compressed to a four-second burst. After the transmission, it stored the text on the hard drive for future reference. The three SEALs waited patiently for the reply. Seven minutes later the LST-B chirped and fed its message to the computer screen:

MESSAGE RECEIVED//BRAVO ZULU—SLEEP WELL//NEXT CONTACT 2000(L)//REDSKINS 27-COWBOYS 13//

On the third deck of the SOCOM headquarters building, there were three Crisis Management Centers, or CMCs, that were identically equipped with their own communications terminals, status boards, and information-management systems. The CMCs were more than just communications centers. They were equipped for computer modeling and mission simulation to assist with decision-making, and had an immense data-retrieval capability as well. It seemed as if one of the rooms was always in use—sometimes two of them. There were numerous exercises around the world, usually involving allied forces in Asia or Europe. Some of them were dedicated to special operations, and some were large conventional force exercises with only limited special operations play.

The rooms were manned by three-section watch teams called Crisis Action Teams, or CAT teams. Brisco and her three CAT teams manned CMC Number Two. The tempo of exercise play was almost continuous, and reserve personnel were brought to SOCOM headquarters on their two-week annual training duty to augment active duty personnel on the CAT teams. At first, Major Brisco was reluctant to have reservists standing watch for a real operation until she learned that they had been utilized for exercise play to such an extent they were better trained than the active duty personnel. That was why RM1 Ken Isles, USNR, was on duty when the first transmission from Moody finally came in.

"I've got a carrier on the special dedicated frequency," he calmly told the Senior Watch Officer, or SWO. A moment later, "I have burst—looks like a clear copy." By this time the SWO, an Army light colonel, and Major Brisco were standing behind him. The ANDVT terminal simultaneously received and decoded the transmission, which had been relayed through the SOCOM communications center, and extended the compressed text as it printed it on an HP Laserjet. Isles reached for the message, but Brisco beat him to it.

"Okay," she said as she scanned the paper, "they're on the ground and have made it to the first lay-up point—no sign of Russian security forces. Equipment landed safely with no damage—uh-oh!" She came to the portion of the message that detailed the injury to Walker.

"Problem?" Master Chief Tolliver asked from behind Brisco and the Senior Watch Officer. Isles keyed the printer to deliver additional copies and handed one to Tolliver.

"Walker separated his shoulder when he landed," said Brisco. "They say they put it back in place, but he's lost the use of his left arm for several days. How do you reset a dislocated shoulder in the field?"

"It's not easy," said the SWO. He was a Special Forces officer, and like all SF men, well-trained in field medicine. "Usually somebody sits on the guy while another man pops it back into place. I'll get this information, along with the drugs they've used, down to staff medical." He said a few words to the MP stationed by the door. Another MP, armed with a .45, arrived and put a copy of the message in a clasped hardbound folder marked "Top Secret," and quickly departed.

Brisco winced as she thought about resetting Walker's shoulder without benefit of a painkiller. "We have anything for them?" The SWO shook his head.

"Let's put 'em to bed," suggested Tolliver. "They've got another big day ahead of them, especially if Walker's shoulder gets worse."

Brisco nodded, scribbling a single quick line on a message blank, showing it to Tolliver and then to the SWO for his initials—messages could be released only by his authority. Both men agreed. Isles put the message slip on his console and began to input the text, which would automatically be encoded, compressed, and sent out. A few moments later, the printer issued a copy of the message, indicating it was sent and that receipt had been acknowledged. Brisco scanned the copy and snapped her head around to Isles.

"That's not quite what I said, sailor!"

"I know, ma'am, but what's the harm." Isles was not a special operator, and his time in the field had been limited to camping with his son's scout troop. But he knew those men out there in the frozen darkness would be made a little warmer knowing-the Redskins had upset the Cowboys.

Brisco relaxed and smiled. "You're right. I should have thought of that myself."

Over by the entrance to the CMC, there was a shuffling of chairs that caught Brisco's attention. General Thon had just entered the room. The CMC under operational conditions was about the only occasion when the Commander's arrival would not be greeted by a call to attention. Thon hastily returned the SWO's salute and strode directly over to Brisco.

"Major, Master Chief," he began, "I understand we have contact with the team."

"Yessir." She handed a copy of both messages and quickly outlined their current situation.

Thon smiled grimly. "Things never quite go as you want them to, but it could be a lot worse. Sounds like they have things under control, though. Carry on, Major, and as your controller duties permit, notify me immediately of any further contact. I'll be in the building through their next scheduled reporting period."

After General Thon left the CMC, he went straight to the communications center and the dedicated secure line that rang into Morton Keeney's office.

Moody awoke just after 7:30 P.M. He shined the red penlight at a small alarm clock resting on a shelf punched into the side of the snow cave. The SEAL teams had almost unlimited access to expensive, high-tech electronic equipment, but he had found nothing superior to a ten-dollar Wal-Mart digital travel alarm. Swinging the light around, he saw that Garniss and Snyder were still sleeping, rolled in their bags like mutant larva offspring of some giant insect. Not wanting to endure its metallic bleeping in the cave, he reached over and pushed in the alarm button and stuffed the little clock into a pocket of his gear bag.

"Garniss, Snyder—reveille, guys. We got some traffic to pass and some ground to cover."

Garniss rolled over first. "Gooood mornin', U.S.S.RRRRR!" he called in a Robin Williams imitation. "Drop your cocks and grab your socks." Garniss was a morning person, even in a cold winter lay-up.

"Which could be difficult in your case," Snyder mumbled, "since your hand is probably frozen to your cock. What time is it, Boss?"

"Nineteen forty," said Moody. "Let's move it, guys. I'll check on Walker, and then we have a SITREP to get off."

"We're movin', Boss. Oh, Kurtie, would you get me a cup of coffee," said Garniss, "and if that silly paperboy has tossed the morning edition on the roof again, I'm going to file a complaint."

"How about you set up the antenna and I'll heat some rations."

"I can live with that," Garniss replied.

They had strung a cord across the ceiling of the cave to dry out their socks and gloves. An occasional hand reached up and pulled one from the line as the three thrashed about dressing in their bags. It was a relatively mild thirty degrees in the cave, but they always put on at least one layer in the bag. Moody was first out. He pulled on his parka, boots, and gloves before he pushed through the flap opening of the cave. He was greeted by three inches of new powder. They expected no problems, so they had not posted a guard. Nonetheless, he carefully watched and listened a moment before fully emerging from the burrow. Suddenly the moon broke from behind the clouds and he had his first good look at Russia. He scrambled to the top of the ravine for a better look.

The moon was low, but bright enough to cast long shadows over the rumpled landscape, creating a patchwork of black on dull gray. Periodically, a grove of the little gnarled trees blotched the pale landscape. *Must be what Neil Armstrong saw,* thought Moody, *only without the sharp edges.*

He glissaded back into the ravine and made his way to the other snow cave. Pushing the door flap back, he flicked his penlight around the interior. Moody grinned. There was a symphony of snoring and the sweet smell of farts. Their rations were designed for maximum calories, with very little waste and lots of gas.

"Walker, O'Keefe, Sergeant Valclav!" he whispered. "Let's get at it, guys."

O'Keefe moved first, coming up quickly and pushing his bag down to his waist. A moment later a light was in his hand, and he was hovering over Walker.

"Don . . . c'mon, wake up, Don."

"Huh, what . . . ouch!"

"Whoa, easy there, cowboy—no sudden movements. Now, real easy like, I want you to push your left arm out in front of you—good, good." Walker was hardly awake, but did as he was told. "Now, rotate your wrist—that's it, good. How's it feel?"

"Sore. My arm feels all bruised, like someone pounded the shit out of me."

"That's okay, Don, that's the way it's supposed to feel. Here, let me help you sit up." O'Keefe put Walker through a range-of-motion drills while Moody watched. In the third bag, Valclav wrestled with his clothes. Finally O'Keefe turned to Moody.

"I think he's moving in the right direction, but it's going to be sore as hell for a while. I still want the arm strapped down, and I want him moving without a load."

"Hell, Doc, I can carry a pack. Jesus, y'all think I was a . . ."

"He wasn't talking to you, Don—he was talking to me. How about medication?"

"I gave him a serette of morphine last night so he'd get some sleep. As you can see, it's already worn off. I plan to continue with the cortisone in decreasing doses unless the medical officer comes back with something different. He should start to feel a lot better, but the muscles that hold the shoulder in place need time to heal. That's why I don't want him carrying a load—not even a light pack."

"Aw, for Christ's sake, I can pack my own—"

"Look, dumb shit," said O'Keefe, beating Moody to the punch, "you'll do exactly as I say. That shoulder comes out again and we'll be carrying your dead ass all the way to the Barents Sea. For now, your only job is to *very* carefully dress yourself, feed yourself, and get ready to move. Do *nothing* that puts any weight or leverage on your left arm—you got that?"

Walker scowled and looked at Moody.

"You got that?" Moody echoed.

"Yes, sir," Walker replied, looking like a whipped dog.

"Good. Doc, we're going to fire off another SITREP in a few minutes and probably copy some traffic. I want you there in case they have some questions about Don's shoulder."

"Be right there, sir."

Moody started backing out of the cave, but hesitated at the door. "Hey." Walker looked up dejectedly. "Don, this could have happened to any one of us, but it happened to you. This is a long mission, and most of the work is three or four days ahead of us at the objective area. You're on this team because there are things you can do better than any of us. But for now, and until the doc says differently, your job is to heal up, and that means avoiding further injury. I need you back a hundred percent, okay?"

"Aye, aye, sir."

"Not good enough, Don." Moody grinned at him, forcing Walker to smile.

"Okay, Boss. I'll do what I'm told and get well as quick as I can."

Moody nodded and slipped out under the flap. Valclav followed him.

"I'm a light sleeper, sir, and I know he was in a lot of pain after we bedded down. He didn't quiet down until the doc gave him the morphine."

"Thanks, Sarge. Hopefully, he'll do better at the next lay-up. Keep me and the doc posted."

When Moody poked his head in the other snow cave, Snyder handed him an aluminum cup with a hot ration that looked like health-store oatmeal. He passed it on to Valclav and took another. Garniss had rolled up the bedding and was busy connecting up the communications modules. Snyder was their primary communications technician, but all of them were capable of using the SATCOM as well as the SATNAV equipment.

"You want me to work it up, Boss?"

"Sure. O'Keefe will be along in a few minutes with the latest on Walker."

"How's he doin'?"

"He's awful tender, but a lot better. He's still going to have to travel light. We'll split his gear again between the two *akios.*" Garniss nodded and started to peck at the computer. They were soon joined by Walker and O'Keefe. "Better hurry, guys," Moody said. "Chez Snyder is serving."

An hour later they were ready to move on. The SOCOM medical officer had little to add to O'Keefe's treatment of Walker, but reaffirmed the need to keep the arm immobilized to hold it in place while the muscles healed. Snyder replotted their position on their map with the SATNAV, and laid out a bearing to the next lay-up. After the strain of the jump and stumbling through the near-blackout overcast, the team moved across the moonlit snowfields like schoolkids across a tropical beach.

PART FIVE

Mustang

The village of Iokanga was about six miles southeast of Gremikha along the road to Lumbovskiy, straddling the junction of what the locals called the Coast Road and a spur road that ran south to the airfield at Kachalovka. The village itself was little more than a cluster of huts and a few former state-owned stores that were now scratching out an existence under private ownership. Only the tavern, which always seemed to have an ample supply of low-quality vodka, seemed to be thriving. In addition to being an intersection in an area with few roads, there was a small military complex and barracks facility on the outskirts of the village. The small base had served various purposes in the torturous history of the Soviet Union, from an interrogation center during Stalin's military purges to a training center for KGB border guards. For the past three years it had been the central Kola staging area and headquarters for the OMON security forces—the dreaded Black Berets.

OMON was a Russian acronym that roughly translated as "Special Assignment Militia Detachment." The Black Berets were organized as a special unit under the Soviet Interior Minister in the late eighties to crack down on organized crime. In reality, there was nothing terribly special about these troops, nor were they highly trained or respected as crime fighters. In fact, many of their officers were little more than thugs with histories of operating outside the law. In the final days of the Union, they were stationed throughout the Baltics to suppress popular and regional independence movements. Here they fought a rearguard action against democracy, using terror and random violence against unarmed populations. Their commander, Interior Minister Boris Pugo, committed suicide following the failed coup. After the breakup of the Union, they were repatriated to Russia, often under the protection of Russian troops to shield them from ethnic reprisals. For the most part they were disbanded, but some of the military districts accepted a few of them into their security forces.

One of General Borzov's predecessors repatriated two battalions of OMON and stationed one of them at Iokanga. Their charter was to guard high-security facilities, and to attack the pockets of organized crime that threatened to cripple the already strained commerce and distribution systems of the new republic. The idea was that it often takes a thief to catch a thief, and the terror of the Black Berets was often enough to dissuade criminals. They had, in fact, broken several smuggling rings in Gremikha, which usually resulted in violent confrontations and summary justice for the smugglers. General Borzov, like many military commanders, was all too aware that anarchy was just below the surface, and the last thing he wanted was to have to use his regular troops to restore order. Like all military commanders, especially after the aborted coup attempt to unseat Gorbachev, he feared any confrontation between the people and the Russian Army. That's why he tolerated the presence of the Black Beret garrisons. They were like junkyard dogs. They very seldom had to attack anyone because their viciousness was so well-known that their presence was often enough to keep order, especially in remote areas. Borzov had no illusions about their loyalty or their morality; nor did they command any of the respect he held for his regular forces. When civil and judicial authorities were sufficiently capable, the OMON would be disbanded. For now, their usefulness outweighed their liability.

It was another cold, winter Monday morning—the last one this year. Colonel Victor Makarov sat in his small office and sipped a glass of vodka. The vodka was quite good, a gift from the local tavern owner who feared Makarov would make good his threat to raise his "fee" for not placing the establishment off limits to his troops. He tossed a smoldering cigarette on the pile in his ashtray and lit another. "What a sewer this miserable place is," he said aloud. He took another sip of vodka and thought of the plush office he had commandeered for himself in Vilnius, where his OMON forces had terrorized Lithuania until the end finally came. *I served the State well back then,* he reflected, *and look at what they have done to me. I'm stranded in the middle of this frozen wilderness while others enjoy comfortable billets in Severomorsk. Well, at least I can conduct my affairs without their constant scrutiny.* There was a sharp knock at the door. "Come!" shouted Makarov.

"Good morning, Colonel. I have the weekly status report ready for your signature." Major Belyaev stood at attention in front of the desk. His Black Beret was tipped rakishly across his right eye, the OMON medallion centered and the red pennant riding high over his left ear. Belyaev had ten years' experience in the regular army, and knew something of soldiering. Makarov had found him to be an invaluable administrator, and much harder to corrupt than his other officers.

"Only five BTRs in operable condition? I thought I made it clear that the armored vehicles were to be a priority. That's less than half of our entire complement!"

"That is correct, Colonel. I personally checked with our maintenance officer, but we can do nothing without spare parts. He has been in weekly contact with the depot in Severomorsk, and all available spares are being sent to the motor-rifle divisions. That is by the direct order of Colonel General Borzov," Belyaev added.

"I don't give a damn what Borzov has ordered!" Makarov stormed from behind the desk and began to pace about the office. "I want at least eight BTRs in full readiness, is that clear?"

"Yes, Colonel."

"Now I don't care if you have to personally go to Murmansk to arrange for those spares, but I want them. Do what you have to, but get those BTRs fully operational. Is that understood?"

"Yes, Colonel." Belyaev was a reasonably competent officer, and he did understand. Makarov was telling him to bribe someone in the supply system for the spare parts or to get them on the black market. He was also smart enough to know that his Colonel would quickly abandon him if he was caught, and claim that he was acting on his own without orders. That was the way things worked in the OMON, and it had led to an officer corps that were either skillful criminals or prisoners in the dreaded Russian military stockades.

"Dismissed," Makarov said with a wave of his hand.

After Belyaev left, he slumped back into his chair, scratching his private parts while he poured himself another glass of vodka. Makarov knew full well why the BTR spares were going to the line operational units and why none were available for his own vehicles. There was absolutely no requirement, nor were there any duties assigned to the OMON, for armored vehicles. Nonetheless, he relished the feeling it gave him when he drove through the streets of a town mounted on one of the big eight-wheeled armored cars. When he looked down from the turret, earphones clamped down across his Black Beret, there was genuine fear in people's faces and it made him feel like a soldier. *Perhaps,* he thought, *I should take a BTR instead of the LAZ on my next visit to Lumbovskiy.*

Makarov would do nothing of the sort, for word would quickly get back to General Borzov, but the thought of it, along with the vodka, gave him a great deal of pleasure.

Twenty-three miles southeast of Iokanga, Dr. Katrina Shebanin had just finished meeting with her department heads to review the weekly production goals and discuss any problems that might impede the achievement of those goals. *Production goals,* she thought as she poured herself a mug of bitter tea from the pot on her desk. *All we need is a midmorning speech from a Party member and some posters of Lenin glaring down at us, and we could all pretend it was 1986 again.* For the most part, she was satisfied and more than a little proud of the work they had been doing. There had been several technical and engineering problems to overcome along the way, but they had solved them and remained on schedule. The members of her scientific and production staff were all glad to have work, but a few of them had let her know it was not work that should be done. Nonetheless, they worked hard—often brilliantly—and at times it was almost like the old days when they felt Russian science and Russian scientists would lead the people to a better world. She finished her tea just as the phone rang.

"Yes?"

"Dr. Shebanin, I have a call for you from Severomorsk. Can you take it now?"

"Of course, put it through."

After a series of clicking punctuated by static, General Borzov came on the line. "Dr. Shebanin, are you there?"

"General Borzov. It's nice to hear your voice. How are things in Murmansk?"

"Cold and dark, but otherwise in good order. How is everything at your facility?"

"Challenging," she replied, "but we've pledged ourselves to the service of the Republic." She held her breath, thinking she might have gone too far, but she was rewarded by a chuckle.

"I never doubted it," he said. "Doctor, I have a busy schedule this week and through the weekend, but I was wondering if you could join me for lunch in Gremikha this Saturday."

"Lunch?"

He chuckled again, as if understanding her unspoken question. "I have to be back at headquarters Sunday morning, so it will have to be just lunch—as opposed to dinner. Perhaps another time."

"I understand, General—another time. Lunch will be fine."

"Wonderful. My aircraft is scheduled into Kachalovka late Saturday morning. Shall we say noon at the Neva Club?"

The Neva was a private club and at best a two-star establishment, but it was Gremikha's best. She was sure they would arrange something special for the District Commander. "Noon will be fine. I'll be looking forward to it."

Charles Grey III sat in his office scowling at the editorial page of *The New York Times. Bloody liberals!* he thought as he tossed the paper on the desk. *The whole damn country is being taken over by minorities and gays, and the only Communists left are teaching at Harvard and Berkeley, and, God help me, Amherst!* His eyes came to rest on a picture of himself and

Richard Helms in front of the building, taken just before he had become the Director back in 1966. Helms was the first Agency professional to be appointed Director of Central Intelligence, and in Grey's opinion, the best DCI ever.

"Dick, we need you back," he said aloud. "With you and someone like Hoover at the Bureau, maybe we could take back our country." He sat there for some time, reliving past Cold War victories, until he was jarred back to the present by the intercom.

"Sir, Mr. Carter is here to see you."

"Send him in—no, wait, I'll be right out." Grey stepped around the desk and burst into the outer office to greet him. He pumped his hand furiously and threw an arm around his shoulder. "Welcome back, stranger! We were wondering if you had jumped ship and decided to become a field operative permanently. How is everything?" Without waiting for a reply, he took Carter by the elbow and guided him through the door to his office.

Grey had seen very little of Carter since he was detailed as a liaison to the Joint Chiefs. He was also aware that Carter had been requested by name for consultation by the President's National Security Advisor. A few days ago, he had met with the Deputy Director for Intelligence, who told him that "his man," referring to Carter, was doing some "damn fine work." Other than that, Grey knew nothing. In the secret world of the CIA, being in the "know" was not only a measure of trust, but one of importance and acceptance. As Grey closed in on the end of his career, he again wanted to be in the know.

Grey was also genuinely happy for Steve Carter. Like most Agency staffers of his generation, he had cut his teeth on operations, and had conducted his share of agent meetings in shadowy cafés in Paris and Beirut. And men like Grey, no matter how much grade or responsibility they acquired in the important technical or analytical side of the intelligence business, still longed to be in operations. This longing was no small source of frustration with the Charles Greys of the CIA. Unlike the generals and the admirals, who decorated their uniforms with campaign ribbons to proclaim their importance, all he could do is reminisce and occasionally swap stories with an old crony. And occasionally, one of his subordinates, like Carter, became involved in something. Grey was like an old gentleman who had been a frat-rat in college, pressing his son for news of the the old fraternity house.

"Coffee, Steve?"

"No, thanks, Charles. I'm afraid I've been drinking too much of it lately."

"Well," Grey said casually, "are you back with us for good, or is this just a visit?"

"Well, for good, I hope, but that all depends. As you know, there's an ongoing operation, and I'm back here to set up a small working group to grade the product when it comes in. We have some people cleared for this project at Los Alamos, so there's a chance I may have to go out there for a few days. If my wife has anything to say about it, I'm here to stay."

"I know what you mean. The womenfolk never get used to us leaving town on short notice, and never being able to tell them where we've been."

Carter gave him a puzzled look. He always told his wife where he'd been. "What I came to see you about, Charles," he continued, leaning forward in the chair, "is I have a need for secure space with some military-compatible, real-time secure communications equipment. And beginning this weekend, I'm going to have to man a twenty-four-hour watch. We've inserted a team into a denied area that will be sending back data. This information will have to be processed and graded, and may even generate follow-up requirements which have to be sent back to the men on the ground as soon as possible."

"No problem, Steve. I've been directed to provide whatever you require in the way of watchstanders and communications technicians. Don't forget," he said with a wink, "I've done this kind of thing a time or two. Now, I want you to give me a thorough briefing on what you're doing, and then we can get you properly set up."

Carter hesitated a second, then shrugged, and told Grey about the mission to contact agent MUSTANG in the Kola.

Moody had halted the team again, and sent Snyder and Garniss ahead to scout the area. This had become a frequent occurrence as they approached their final lay-up. It was Wednesday, D + 3, and this would be their fourth camp—the one from which they would try to make contact with MUSTANG. It had been a long and brutal night with a number of stops, including an especially long one as Snyder and Garniss searched for a place to cross the unimproved road that ran south from Iokanga and the airfield at Kachalovka to the village of Kanevka some seventy miles farther into the interior of the Kola. The worst of it was endured by those who had to wait, doing their best to stay warm until the others returned to the main element. Now, once again, Moody and the other three waited. After what seemed like an eternity, the two-man scouting party returned to the *akios*.

"What do you think?" Moody asked as the two SEALs dropped to one knee beside him, huffing clouds of steam into the moonlight.

"The frozen lake begins about two hundred meters ahead of us as this shelf we've been crossing for the last twenty minutes starts to fall off." The satellite imagery had indicated there was a narrow lake three miles long, formed by an earthen dam on the eastern end that also supported the road to Kanevka. "I make it that we're about two miles from the end of the lake on the western end. We think the best route is to turn west here and stay to the high ground until we clear it. No problem with cover—there's lots of trees along the shore." They were finding more wooded areas as they approached the coast. Picking their way through the woods added a measure of safety, as their tracks were better hidden, but it cut their speed dramatically. Moody dug through his mitten cuff to find his watch—3:30 P.M. His next communications window was 6:00 to 7:00, and he wanted to be at least partially settled in the lay-up before he had to set up the comm gear. It would be tight, but they could do it. *And if I don't call home exactly on time, what are they going to do—restrict me to my room?*

"Okay, Kurt, get us there. Bob, I want you back on drag to help Valclav. Since we're going to ground for a while when we get there, I don't want anyone following us." They both nodded and shuffled off. Soon the team was picking its way through the soft, shallow moonlight. A low moon was perfect for movement at night, affording them just enough light to see without the NODs, but with ample shadows for cover. In the "daytime," there was no light except for the 10:30 A.M.–1:30 P.M. twilight, unless there were stars out.

It took them only an hour and a half to get around the lake to the general area for their base camp, but it took Snyder and Garniss another hour to locate a suitable area to go to ground. They found a berm area at the summit of a shallow rise, bordered by a long stand of trees. The snow had drifted across the berm, allowing them to dig laterally as well as down to make a large snow cave. The nearby trees allowed them to come and go in the cover of the woods. The trees had become taller and more robust-looking as they approached the warming influence of the Barents Sea. Moody set the others to preparing the snow cave while he and Garniss set up the SATCOM.

"They'll want to know where we are, Bob, so get us a good fix."

"No problem, Boss." He turned on the SATNAV and began to look for a communications satellite. It took him less than five minutes. "Okay, sir—I'm ready to plot." The *akios* had been unloaded and flattened for storage, so Moody laid the map flat on the snow.

"Let's have it," Moody replied.

"Sixty-seven degrees, forty-six minutes, thirty-nine seconds north." He paused while Moody plotted a latitude line. "Thirty-nine degrees, thirty-one minutes, seven seconds east."

"Perfect," Moody said as he X'ed in their position. He knew they were about a quarter mile from the south end of the frozen lake, and that was validated by the coordinates Garniss had given him. He sat back on his heels and panned the map with his penlight. The outskirts of Gremikha were six miles away almost due north, while Iokanga and Kachalovka were just over six miles to the east. Twenty-five miles to the east and south was the weapons facility at Lumbovskiy.

"We there, Boss?"

"We're there. Have the guys dig 'em deep and build 'em for comfort, 'cause we're going to be here a while." *In place and on schedule,* Moody reflected with a measure of pride, *but we knew this was the easy part. I hope to God the rest of the mission goes this smooth.* He knew he should get right to the preparation of his SITREP, but decided instead to help with the digging of the snow cave. It was only a few degrees below freezing, almost a heat wave, but they had covered just over seven miles last night, making them tired and a little more susceptible to the cold. A few minutes of exertion would warm him up a bit so he could get back to the radio.

Senior Chief Cornelius Dawgs had just relieved Lieutenant Commander Smith on the 0800-to-1200 watch in the control room of the *Archerfish.* He completed his relief just after 0715 to allow Smith to make breakfast before the galley closed. Sometimes the enlisted watchstanders had a hard time telling just who the Officer of the Deck really was. Commander Griffin seemed to spend about twenty hours a day there, sitting in the padded captain's chair reserved for the command officer and chewing cigars. As often as not, Lieutenant Commander Smith and the operations officer were nearby. Only the engineering officer stayed clear of the crowded control room. Since the functioning of the Stirling engines and air-independent propulsion system was so critical to the success of the mission, he spent most of his time aft in the machinery spaces.

This morning, both the Captain and Smith were having breakfast in the galley, just a deck below the control room. There was a small wardroom for the officers, but they chose to take their meals in the galley with the rest of the crew. Dawgs had just completed his rounds, checking the *Archerfish*'s position, speed, and depth. Their track held them due north of the village of Vardo on the frozen, windswept Varangerhalvoya Peninsula, which marked the easternmost point of Norway. Technically, they were not yet in Russian waters, but they were very close, having made the North Cape some two hours ago. They really expected no problems getting across the Barents Sea undetected, but everyone would be a little more comfortable when the approaches to Murmansk and Severomorsk were behind them. Griffin had driven the boat hard up the long western coast of Norway, and the *Archerfish* was a little ahead of schedule. Everyone aboard was grateful when they had settled down to a comfortable, quiet eight knots. The last reported contact was a merchantman that had closed to about ten miles on the port beam, but that was several hours ago.

"Hey, Cob, I got screw noises."

Dawgs was instantly alert but not terribly concerned. While running submerged, the passive hydrophones were to the submarine like radar was to a surface ship, and these contacts were carefully tracked by *Archerfish*'s watch team. For the most part, it was an exercise that helped keep the sonarmen alert and pass the time on long transits. But they were especially alert since passing the North Cape.

"Merchantman?"

Sonarman Jim Magee stared intently at his scope while his hands automatically found the knobs and dials to clarify the shadows that filtered across his screen. Suddenly, he brought both hands to his headset, pressing the earpiece closer to the sides of his head, eyes closed in concentration.

"It's another sub, Cob!" Magee said, looking up at Dawgs, pulling one earpiece away to talk. "A Soviet nuke, and she's close—I'd say five thousand yards on the port bow, range closing."

Normally, Dawgs would have called Commander Griffin to the control room—American submarines *never* allowed Russian boats that close unless they were stalking them. It suddenly occurred to him that they could be the object of a Russian stalker, and he didn't really have the time to call the Captain.

"Right standard rudder—come right to course one-eight-zero. Make turns for four knots." The watch team, sensing there was danger, quietly repeated the orders as they quickly executed them, turning the *Archerfish* south and cutting her speed. Dawgs stared at the compass repeater and speed indicator. She quickly came to the new course, but it would take a few minutes for her to slow down. He snatched the microphone hanging from the intercom box on the ceiling.

"Captain to the control room—now, Captain to the control room."

Seconds later, Griffin stormed in. There was a wet coffee stain on the front of his blue coveralls. "What th' hell's going on, Cob?"

"It's Ivan, Skipper. He was waiting for us."

On the *S-592,* another sonar operator sat at his console, listening for the sound of propellers. Had he not been looking only for surface noise, he might well have heard the *Archerfish* sooner, but not a lot sooner, for she was a very quiet boat. At first it was a whisper with a steady beat count, yet no more than a phantom on the scope—then it vanished. Alexei Yashkin had been in the Soviet—now Russian—Navy for fifteen years, and was a highly experienced sonar technician. Captain Molev happened to be in the control room of the *S-592* when Yashkin signaled that he had a submerged contact, and in a few strides he was at Yashkin's side.

"I had it, Captain—it was moving southeast at close to ten knots, and then it was gone."

"I heard it too, sir, but Alexei found it first," said a junior rating on the next console, sensing this was something important.

"American?" said Molev to Yashkin, ignoring the younger man.

"I don't think so. In some ways it was like one of our Kilo-class boats, but different—much quieter." Yashkin listened for a moment longer, hoping for an additional audio clue. Again he shook his head. "I know this sounds strange, sir, but it sounded a lot like one of the German Type-206 boats. When we operated in the North Sea, occasionally we would catch one coming out of Bremerhaven." He shrugged. "That's the best I can do, sir."

"You did well," Molev replied, placing a hand on the man's shoulder, "but you still have nothing?" Yashkin again listened for a moment and shook his head.

Molev stood by the sonar console, considering options. *Do I look or listen,* he thought, *active or passive?*

"If you'd been able to hold his track, where would he be now?"

A sailor at the plotting table indicated a position thirty-five hundred meters from the *S-592* on her port bow. Molev grunted and turned to the Officer of the Deck.

"Come left to two-six-five and commence a standard long-range search on the projected track of the contact."

PING!

"Where is he?" said Griffin, hovering over Magee. The sonarman tried to ignore him, but the CO's stale, cigarette breath was almost overpowering. The Russian boat's active sonar could be heard unaided by everyone on the *Archerfish,* but for Magee on the sensitive passive array, it was deafening. He frantically adjusted the gain control on his equipment. *PING!*

"Well back on the port quarter, Captain—forty-five hundred yards." There was a long silence. *PING!* "And opening—range forty-seven hundred yards. He's shouting in the dark, sir." Magee listened through two more pings before dropping the headset around his neck. "He's behind us in the baffles now, sir, but the range is still opening. He's searching along our old track."

"What was it?"

"I only got a quick look at him, sir, but I'd say it was a Victor or an Akula—one of the newer ones. If I had to bet, I'd say it was an Akula."

Griffin nodded. "Good job, Magee. Keep an eye on him. Cob, bring it up to twelve knots and keep this heading. We might as well scoot off while he's making so much noise."

Dawgs gave the commands while Griffin heaved himself up into his chair and bit into a new cigar. *What in the hell was that boat doing out there? On patrol? Training? Or was he really waiting for us!*

"We're at twelve knots, Skipper, still on one-eight-zero. I'm still running at two hundred feet, and showing eight hundred fifty under the keel. This course will take us into Norwegian territorial waters in about an hour and a half."

Griffin said nothing, still lost in thought. Senior Chief Dawgs was used to his Captain's long silences, and waited patiently while his eyes darted around the control room to ensure his watch section were attending to their duties.

Griffin knew the Russians regarded the Barents Sea as something of a private lake, like the United States does the Gulf of Mexico. *In the old days, the barrier patrols seldom came this far west—what is this guy doing out here?*

"What's our range and bearing to Murmansk, Cob?"

Dawgs stepped over to the small chart table. The Quartermaster of the Watch had already laid a parallel rule from their current position to the mouth of the Kolskiy Inlet and was stepping off the distance with a pair of dividers.

"Hundred and forty miles at one-six-five, Cob."

Dawgs relayed the information to Griffin, who nodded and was again silent for a while.

"Where's Ivan?"

Dawgs was ready for him. "Seven thousand meters and opening. He's still active."

"Okay," Griffin concluded, "let's hold this course and speed for another half hour, then come left to one-six-five and drop to six knots. Their stationary hydrophones shouldn't pick us up at that speed. We'll just sneak quietly across the Kolskiy Inlet and then try to make up some time when we're past it. What d'you think?"

Dawgs raised his eyebrows and looked at the Captain. Lieutenant Commander Smith, who had been at the chart table, came over to join them.

"But that will take us down the Kola coast inside the Asian Coastal Buffer Zone," said Smith.

"And within twenty miles of the Rybachiy Peninsula, well within their territorial waters," added Dawgs. Their original track held them well in international waters while they made their way down the Kola Peninsula, closing the Russian coast only when they were near the Lumbovskiy Inlet.

"I know," replied Griffin, "but that Russian skipper had time to get a course and speed on us, or he wouldn't be running an active search on our old projected track. If he's worth his salt, before too long he's going to figure out that we went inside of him. When he comes back to look for us, he'll probably figure we'll stay outside the Buffer Zone." Griffin pulled the cigar from his mouth. "Besides, we'll be well inside territorial waters before this thing's over."

"But, Captain, isn't this a little chancy this far west?"

"Sure, XO, but I want to lose this guy before we have to duck under the pack ice. If he thinks we're here to play games with the fleet as they come in and out of Severomorsk, that's fine by me. You got a better idea?"

There was no sarcasm in Griffin's voice, as Smith would have expected if this were a training exercise. The younger man ran a hand through his thick hair, which dropped neatly back into place.

"No, sir, I guess not."

"Cob?"

Dawgs shrugged and smiled. "Why not?"

Smith stepped back to the chart table. As navigator, he wanted to immediately lay down their new track. Dawgs took a seat in the OD's chair.

"By the way, Cob," Griffin said around the cigar that stretched the side of his mouth, "that turn was a helluva fine call. Another five minutes and that sonovabitch would have been ringing our bell with his active sonar." He sent the messenger of the watch to the galley for some coffee and the dish of the dessert he had been called away from. *Perhaps,* he admitted to himself, *crawling up under that pack ice won't be so bad after all. If there's a Russian nuke out there looking for us, he sure as hell isn't going to come in there after us.*

Moody was late with his SITREP, getting it off a few minutes before 7:00 A.M. The message was relayed by a communications satellite to a ground station in Greenland, back to another COMSAT, and on to the U.S. Special Operations Command, a distance of some eighty-five hundred miles. However, it took almost ten minutes for the information to be received and digested by the SATCOM dish on the roof of the SOCOM headquarters building, find its way through the communications center, and be decoded in Crisis Management Center Number Two. By then, accounting for the seven-hour time difference, it was about eight minutes after midnight on the twenty-ninth when the text slid out of the printer into Major Brisco's hands.

She scanned it quickly, looking for a problem or something out of place. It wasn't until she found the section titled: STATUS SUMMARY, and read, ALL PERSONNEL IN LAY-UP #4//WALKER 90 PERCENT MISSION CAPABLE//TEAM GONE TO GROUND// that she realized she had been holding her breath. After inhaling deeply a few times, she looked around self-consciously and caught Master Chief Tolliver watching her.

He smiled. "Yes, ma'am, I was a little anxious myself. Now we know where they are, and where they'll be for a while, at least most of them."

She joined him at the plotting table, where an Air Force tech sergeant had taken the coordinates and was plotting their position on an enlarged map of the Gremikha-Lumbovskiy area. Tolliver then took a large pair of dividers and began to check distances to the town and to the airfield.

"They're exactly where they're supposed to be—on the west end of the lake about six miles from Gremikha," Tolliver said proudly. "You saw they were asking for a green light?"

"I sure did, Master Chief, but that call has to come from the Commander. I better get on the horn to him. He wanted to know the minute they reported in."

The operation had been divided into three phases—the insertion, the agent contact, and the extraction. Moody and his team had just completed the first phase by safely going to ground in the target area. If MUSTANG had been surfaced by other means, or the political situation changed such that an attempt to contact the agent was now considered too risky, the team could move on to the extraction point and wait for the *Archerfish.*

Brisco went to a green telephone on the Senior Watch Officer's desk and punched in a four-digit number.

"Good morning, General, this is Major Brisco calling . . . Just fine, sir. General, the team has reached their fourth lay-up and has safely gone to ground. They've asked for a green light . . . understood . . . understood . . . Yes, sir, we'll be standing by."

Two floors above the CMC, General Billie Thon sat on the edge of the mattress with his bare feet on the soft carpet, rubbing the sleep from his eyes. The times he'd been called from sleep with his butt on a canvas cot and his feet on a cold linoleum floor had been too numerous for him to remember. Dressed in olive-drab skivvy shorts and T-shirt, he started for the door to his office, then turned and walked into the bathroom. *First things first,* he thought as he relieved himself. Back in the office, he clipped on the lights and pulled a slip of paper with a phone number on it from the top drawer of his desk. There was a series of clicks while the STU-III engaged the scrambler, then an answer after the first ring.

"Seven eight six zero, Colonel Anderson speaking."

"Colonel, this is General Thon at SOCOM. Please inform Mr. Keeney that phase one is complete, and we are awaiting his direction."

Anderson repeated the message and rang off. Next, Thon called the JCS staff duty officer with the same message. Winston Scott would be notified immediately by Keeney's office, but it was good business to keep your immediate superior advised, even if you had been directed to go over his head. Then he called Brisco and told her once again to call him immediately if there were any further developments. After that, he crawled back into bed and was instantly asleep.

Polly Bennett had never really *disliked* Morton Keeney, but he was not one of her favorite people. She was warm and outgoing, and had always prided herself on being able to read people. In that regard, she had been a valuable and trusted asset to her husband, for he always consulted her on key appointments in his administration. But Keeney had remained an enigma to her. She sensed he knew this, for while he was always polite and displayed impeccably good manners, he remained slightly aloof and inscrutable. She was, therefore, a little unnerved when he called before breakfast and asked for her husband.

"He's in the shower, Morton. If it's urgent I can get him, or would you like to join us for coffee?"

Keeney declined, offering his thanks, saying that both he and the matter in question would wait for the President in his office. She became even more alarmed when she told her husband of the call halfway through breakfast. He stood up as he gulped his coffee and left the table without a word, munching on a slice of raisin toast on the way out.

"What's up, Mort?"

Keeney rose from the wingback chair by the door where he always sat when he waited for the President.

"Everything is going according to plan. The team just called in and has established their base of operations near the weapons facility. Thus far, we've detected no unusual radio activity or electronic emissions in the area, so I believe it is safe to assume they have reached their position undetected. Do we proceed?"

"Any reason why not?"

"None that I can see. I notified the senior staff duty officer at Langley about an hour ago. We have about twenty-four hours before the former Estonian national is scheduled to go undercover. Should something break before then, either at CIA or at State, we'll abort this portion of the operation and move the team to the extraction point."

"What's his name, Morton? The guy's got a name."

"The Estonian? It's Valclav, sir. Sergeant Sergei Valclav."

"So how do you want to handle it?"

"The operational people at SOCOM want to give them a UNODIR—that's a message which tells them 'unless otherwise directed' they are to proceed with their mission. I support that request. It allows the team to continue to prepare for their duties. We can always rescind the authorization if MUSTANG surfaces on his own in the next twenty-four hours."

The President remained silent for several moments. "Okay, give 'em the go-ahead. If the agent turns up, we'll recall them."

"Yes, sir." Keeney turned to leave, but Bennett stopped him.

"Call it in from here if you like. I didn't get my ration of coffee this morning—care to join me?"

"Thank you, sir, I'd enjoy that." Keeney used the secure phone on the President's credenza to call one of his assistants. Instructions would be passed to General Thon at SOCOM. Bennett punched the intercom and ordered a pot of coffee. They had just settled themselves at the coffee table, and the President was rattling the cups when Colonel Buck Williams rapped sharply at the door and strode into the room.

"Excuse me, sir, but I have a top-secret, flash-precedence message. It was sent to JCS via COMSUBLANT and readdressed to the White House. It's from the *Archerfish,* sir."

Both Keeney and Bennett rose. "Thanks, Buck," Bennett said as he took the cable. "Stand by." Williams stepped to one side and went to a rigid parade rest, eyes straight ahead. Bennett read the message twice and handed it to Keeney.

"How in the hell could they have just bumped into a Russian submarine? I thought the *Archerfish* was one of the quietest boats we have." Bennett slumped back into his chair and pulled off his reading glasses. Keeney also sat down, laying the message on the table.

"I don't know, unless it was just a coincidence." But Bennett knew Keeney was a man who didn't believe in coincidences. "At any rate," he continued, "they say that they've slipped past the Russian sub and are continuing on to the location where they are to meet the special operations team."

"Recommendation?"

Keeney carefully framed his words. "At this stage of the game, I think we have no option but to go ahead as planned. If for some reason they've been alerted to our presence, we should learn of it by an increase in radio and electronic emissions. The *Archerfish* says she will enter the pack ice and be on station in about two days. That's sometime in the afternoon on New Year's Day, but still only twelve hours behind the original schedule. I understand this is a complication, but if we're going to do anything about these weapons, we're going to have to make contact with MUSTANG."

The President slipped into one of his brooding silences while Keeney and Colonel Williams waited patiently. This was something they had talked about and wanted to avoid at all costs. A small reconnaissance team compromised on Russian soil would be a policy disaster, but the United States could bring countercharges, citing the Russians with violations of nuclear-arms agreements and by claiming ecological self-defense. But a confrontation between ships—men-of-war—was something far more serious. They fired torpedoes, not bullets, and a confrontation could result in the loss of dozens, maybe hundreds, of lives. The Russians had suffered their share of embarrassment over their submarines' being caught in the territorial waters of NATO countries, and they were still smarting over the collision of the Delta III with a U.S. fast-attack boat last year. That American submarine was clearly in Russian waters. If it happened again, knowledgeable sources in the U.S. Navy felt the Russians would use whatever means at their disposal to bring the trespasser to the surface.

"I suppose you're right for now. Let's get General Scott and his best submariner over here this afternoon to discuss options. And let's not forget that the *Archerfish* represents those boys' only way out of there."

Charles Grey had just struggled into his overcoat and was seated at his desk slipping a pair of flimsy, loafer-type galoshes over his thick-soled wing tips. The temperature was well above freezing outside, but it had been spitting snow for most of the afternoon. The Agency maintenance crews were most conscientious about keeping the walkways free from snow and ice, but they often neglected the parking lots. Grey anticipated there would be no accumulations, but he was a belt-and-suspenders man, and always wanted to be prepared. It was a short walk to the car, a new Buick that had an understated elegance he found appealing. Since he was a G-16 and a branch chief, he had a reserved space in the lot near the rear entrance. It mildly irked him that he had to walk past several rows of spaces reserved for carpoolers, but that was unavoidable. CIA branch chiefs did not carpool.

Driving west on the Dolly Madison Parkway, he chuckled as he thought about the operation going on in Russia. In years past, this type of operation would have been planned and carried out by the Deputy Director for Operations, and those in the Intelligence Directorate, like himself, would have been kept out of the loop, even if the operation concerned an area for which they had responsibility. Back then, the DDO had the resources to mount such an operation and its own special operations organization to carry it out. All they needed was executive authority, and often that was given by NSA to shield the President from any direct involvement. Now, special operations were the exclusive charter of the military, and the DDO could do nothing but sit back and wait like the rest of them. *Well,* thought Grey as he chuckled again, *not quite like the rest of us.*

The Central Intelligence Agency was a highly compartmentalized organization, and the Deputy Director for Operations had just learned of the Kola penetration earlier that afternoon. Soon after that, he had found out that a man from the DDI was serving as the Agency focal-point officer to SOCOM, not one of his own operations officers. This had generated a heated meeting between Deputy Directors for Intelligence and Operations, which included Grey and his boss, the Soviet Division chief. Just being in the room with three of the most powerful men in the Agency had been heady stuff for Grey. The meeting had threatened to become a full-blown turf war until the DDI said, "Look, Grey's man surfaced this thing and assembled most of the background work on it. The DCI asked for him by name. If you have a beef, don't tell me about it—tell Armand Grummell." The operations chief glared at the DDI and then at Charles Grey III, claiming he would do just that, and stomped out of the room. Before Grey left, the DDI had complimented him and "that Carter fellow" for their fine work. It wasn't like the old days when they were tunneling under the embassy of a Communist-bloc nation or destabilizing some Third World government, but it was still exciting.

The Thursday-afternoon traffic was lighter than usual. Grey drove west on the Dolly Madison Parkway for ten minutes before turning south. After negotiating a few cross streets, he wheeled into the parking lot of the McLean Inn. Several times a week, he stopped there for a drink on the way home. It was an old establishment with a quiet, dimly lit bar attached to the rear. The bar was appropriately stuffy and had a private entrance. Over the years, it had become a haunt for the old-line Agency staffers, and was commonly referred to in private as "The Safehouse." Grey paused a few steps into the bar to allow his eyes to adjust to the light, and to remove his coat and scarf. He laid them over the back of a chair, along with another badge of his generation of spies, a brown, felt, snap-brim hat. He bobbed his head in acknowledgment as several men around the bar greeted him. A solemn, elderly black man wearing a white apron, white shirt, and armbands approached from the other side of the bar. He wiped the spotless mahogany surface in front of Grey with a clean towel.

"Afternoon, Mr. Charles. The usual?"

"Thank you, William." A moment later he placed a tall whiskey and soda in front of Grey.

"Well, Charles," said a dapper gentleman who appeared at Grey's elbow. He was a short man in a dark three-piece suit, with watery blue eyes and magnificent gray hair. "I hear the elephants on the fourth floor were trumpeting at each other this afternoon. What's more, I understand that you were the white hunter who provoked them. Really, Charles, you know a lowly branch chief can get squashed doing that."

"It was a beef between the Deputies. I was just there as an observer."

"Well, that's not the way I heard it," said another well-tended man who had joined them. The three of them had the look of a trio of stockbrokers discussing a particularly active trading session.

"Just what *did* you hear, James?" said Grey, turning to the newcomer.

"That you fellows in the DDI were straying a bit—crossing into the sacred realm of operations."

"That's a fact, Charles," said the first man, "and we all know how much the gods of operations resent someone stomping around in their rice bowl, especially in these uncertain times."

There was something compelling, almost mystical, about the Operations Directorate at CIA. Although it commanded only about fifteen percent of the Agency's budget and a correspondingly fewer number of personnel, they were still the spies and the spymasters, and they carried on the legacy of William Stephenson, Stewart Menzies, and Bill Donovan—shadowy men of action who opposed the forces of evil during their careers, and still lived in the pages of spy fiction. During the past few decades, overt sources and technical collection capabilities had relegated the DDO to a far less significant role in the generation of the national intelligence product. Nonetheless, the aura of the Operations Directorate remained, perpetuated in part by the old guard like Charles Grey III, who had spent their younger days in operations and now served in senior staffing positions throughout the Agency.

"Well, I think you both have been highly misinformed," Grey replied, smugly sipping his drink. He surveyed them both coyly, then lowered his voice. "I can tell you this much, Ivan's been misbehaving, and somebody finally found the guts to do something about it."

"They're sending troops to Serbia?"

"They've moved more troops into the Crimea?"

"I'm afraid it's a lot more serious than that," Grey replied solemnly, clearly relishing the attention. "It appears they have resorted to selling nukes to the Third World." His companions raised their eyebrows in surprise and slowly nodded their heads in a knowing manner. All three sipped their drinks to recognize the gravity of this new development.

"Should have guessed."

"We knew it was just a matter of time. You say we have an operation in progress?"

"Not us, I'm afraid. My shop found and documented the problem, and we've been tasked with liaison responsibility and technical support. No, gentlemen, this one's been handed off to the cavalry."

"You mean . . . the military?"

"That's exactly what I mean." Again there was a round of raised eyebrows and knowing looks. These were men who would rather have their daughter date Charles Manson than have the U.S. military become involved in intelligence operations. Each took a long swallow to acknowledge this sad turn of events. "We have an agent in place," Grey continued, "but he's gone silent. A team's been sent in to resurrect him."

"Another round, gentlemen?"

All three tapped their glasses, and William busied himself behind the bar.

William had been there for as long as most of the regulars at The Safehouse could remember. He had become a fixture because he was capable and reliable, and he poured tall shots. His presence behind the bar endowed The Safehouse with a calm dignity, and he showed a deference to the patrons that reminded them of a different era in time or a different part of the world—times and places where men of color served and waited on white gentlemen, becoming almost invisible with their quiet efficiency.

The Russian Intelligence Service, or RIS, the successor to the KGB First Chief Directorate, had abandoned most of their operations in North America. This included its highly successful illegal-aliens program as well as most of its industrial espionage—activities that had done so much to keep Soviet military technology on a par with the Western armed forces. Those intelligence operations that survived the changes at Lubyanka were those that had produced spectacular results, and did not require large amounts of money to keep in place. So each month, William continued to meet for a quiet beer at a tavern on Q Street in the District with a man who called himself Frank.

Frank, like his predecessors before him, spoke with an accent and stood out as much at the tavern on Q Street as William would have on the other side of the bar at The Safehouse. At these monthly meetings, William received several thousand dollars in cash, and told the man about the casual conversations he had heard across the bar. In addition to his stoic expression and even temperament, William had a photographic memory, and could repeat conversations nearly verbatim. He had closed the bar on Thursday at midnight as usual, washed and cleaned the glasses, and carefully totaled out his till. It was 1:30 Friday morning by the time he stopped at a pay phone on the way back into the District and called a number he had committed to memory a long time ago, but seldom used. The conversation he had heard that afternoon might not wait until his next scheduled meeting with Frank.

The team had been settled into their base camp for almost two days, and the extra time to rest, with successive hot meals, had made everyone noticeably sharper. They had lost a measure of that haggard look of men on the move. After their first day's sleep, they set out to expand the snow-cave complex, building compartments for sleeping as well as one for cooking and nonsleeping activity. The SATCOM antenna was hidden just below the berm and covered with white camouflaged netting. Moody had the equipment tested, both the primary system and his backup transceiver, for voice, text, and facsimile transmission. The *akios* had been broken down and cached in the woods nearby. Some of their gear and food bundles had been brought into the cave and stored around the walls, while others were hidden with the *akios.* They all took a strange delight in fashioning little niches in the cave that would make some routine task a little easier or life more comfortable. O'Keefe had a laminated picture of his girlfriend that he attached to the ice wall with toothpicks. Garniss broke out a pair of fleece-lined slippers with a little bunny head on each toe. They rested at the foot of his sleeping bag. Though they had done this many times before in training, and this time for real, there was still the boy in each of them, and they were still camping out. Moody allowed this, even encouraged it to some degree, for it kept them active and their spirits up.

They were very careful about their movements outside. Each journey away from the camp made some kind of a trail that could lead an unwanted visitor back to them. They were still miles away from any known civilian or military activity, but they were taking no chances. Garniss and Snyder carefully scouted the area, and the day before had meticulously worked back along their line of march to cover the tracks. Whenever they were moving about, they wore cloth covers on their snowshoes that left less of an impression in the snow. Finally, about 10:00 P.M. last night, a strong wind had come up with four inches of new snow, and all traces of their movement were obliterated. A message from SOCOM had warned them that a front was moving through, so the storm was no surprise but nonetheless welcome. The team huddled in their warren, drinking hot chocolate and playing cards while the wind howled above them.

Walker's arm continued to improve. At the second lay-up, O'Keefe had been able to get him to sleep with Demerol instead of morphine, and he had been able to rest without medication during the last stop. He continued the cortisone, but in decreasing doses. He still had to move with extra care, since living in snow caves involved a great deal of stooping and crawling. On O'Keefe's advice, Moody assigned him a number of light-duty tasks and responsibilities, which kept him busy and, more important, made him feel like he was no longer a burden to the others.

It was 4:00 A.M. Friday morning when Valclav came worming his way into the main cave from the sleeping area. Moody flicked his light across him from head to foot. He was dressed in a baggy pair of green woolen trousers, hooded sweatshirt, pea coat, and workman's cap. Each article had been made in Russia or one of the other republics.

"Ready?"

"Da."

"Got all your papers and identification?"

Valclav patted the inside of his jacket. "Yes, sir. I've been over the checklist twice. I'm wearing it or it's in my bag."

"I don't know, Boss," Garniss said. "I don't think this guy's smart enough to be a sailor." Valclav's papers said that he was a merchant seaman and that he hadn't worked in over a year. His reason for being in Gremikha was to look for something on one of the fishing boats, or a chance berth on one of the coastal freighters.

"Okay, let's do it."

Outside the cave, Moody, Snyder, and Valclav all donned their white shells and prepared to travel. Each man carried a light pack and their snowshoes. At least to begin with, they would move on cross-country skis.

"Okay, Bob, we'll see you in about eight hours. Listen up on the Motorola on the half hour, but you won't hear from us unless there's a problem."

"Don't be gone too long," Garniss replied, "you know what a worrywart I am. And, Sarge, I don't want you to try an' sneak off back to the old country—you owe me too much money."

Valclav smiled and held out his hand. "That's a deal, Navy."

They worked their way down the tree line for several hundred yards before Snyder took a cut with his hand compass and led them north toward Gremikha. The storm had blown itself out, and the low quarter-moon was obscured only occasionally by clouds. They moved quickly over the new snow, followed by the accusing tracks from their skis. The last half mile they shifted to snowshoes and moved very carefully, staying among the trees whenever possible. Three and a half hours after they left the base camp they were on a rise overlooking Gremikha. It wasn't like an American town, with a festive white glow from well-lit houses and streetlamps. The lights of Gremikha were muffled and yellow, and it had a lonely and frightened look. There was an unimproved road about a hundred yards from their position. Small cottages, shades pulled and wreathed in wood smoke, clung to either side of the road.

"This'll do, sir." Moody nodded and they carefully hid Valclav's skis, snowshoes, and pack. He had changed from his Sorrell boots to a worn but serviceable pair of work boots.

"You sure you don't want to take a small radio?"

"No, sir. Leave it with the other gear—I'll come back if I need it. I don't want anything on me going in." He shouldered a small tote bag and pulled the cap low on his forehead. "Well, how do I look?"

"Like a guy who's down on his luck and needs a job. I know this is your part of the mission, but how do you plan to go about finding this guy?"

"Nose around and ask a few questions. Places like this always have a low-rent bar where they serve cheap vodka. There's nothing for a lot of these people to do but sit around, and drink and talk."

"But our man's at the weapons facility, right?"

"Yes, sir, but if they come to town, they come here. And I'm sure many of the day workers live here. It's just a matter of steering the conversation in the right direction and then listening carefully." Valclav pulled a pint of vodka from the pocket of his coat and twisted off the cork stopper, offering it to Moody.

"Little early for me," he said questioningly.

"I look like a Russian—now I gotta smell like one." He took a drink and swished it around like mouthwash before swallowing. Then he carefully splashed some on the front of his jacket before returning the stoppered bottle to his pocket. He drew an old pocket watch from his trousers. "Sunday noon here?"

"Sunday noon unless we hear from you. I'll put the Motorola with your gear. Good luck to you, Sergeant—be careful."

He and Snyder both shook Valclav's hand. He took a few steps down the hill and turned back.

"Sir?"

"Yeah?"

"Happy New Year."

Moody smiled. "Happy New Year, Sergeant."

Moody and Snyder watched as he toiled his way between two cottages and began walking down the road toward the center of town. Sergeant Sergei Valclav had been a most interesting addition to Bravo Platoon. In the beginning, Moody and the others had felt he was just a language specialist in uniform who could jump and dive. As the long days of training and preparation unfolded, they learned there was a great deal more to this man. First, he was a professional soldier and highly capable winter-warfare operator. Secondly, concerning his adopted country, he was a superpatriot. The President of the United States was God as far as he was concerned, and he always referred to him as the Commander in Chief. Anyone, including Moody, who poked fun at the President of the United States did so at their own peril if Valclav was within earshot. He was a lot like Garniss—competent and reliable—but he was almost humorless. Nonetheless, he seemed to blend well with the SEALs who were always full of gags and jokes. Valclav had come to the United States when he was thirteen. He had a bachelor's degree in history from CCNY, conferred with honors. Moody had asked him why he didn't apply to become an officer. Valclav explained that he would have had to wait six months to be admitted to Army officers training due to the additional security checks because of his background. That was too long—he wanted to serve immediately.

When he was out of sight, Moody turned to Snyder.

"Let's get back, Kurt."

"Go ahead, sir. I'll clean up behind us."

The moon was down but there were a few stars about. Moody put on his NOD goggles and began picking his way along the trail they had made on the way in.

Thirty-three miles east and slightly north of where Moody watched his sergeant walk down into the outskirts of Gremikha, the *Archerfish* carefully felt its way toward the pack ice and the Lumbovskiy Inlet. Their station was an exact set of coordinates six miles north of the tip of Obornyy Spit that formed the western side of the inlet. The crowded control room was heavy with stale body odor and apprehension.

"How far?" Griffin asked for the third time in the last five minutes.

"I still make it about a mile, Skipper," replied a patient Jim Magee. "We're not moving that fast, and the exact edge of the pack is hard to pinpoint—too much background noise." The passive array that had allowed them to hear the Russian sub before she heard them was now their eyes as they crept toward the pack ice and the Russian coast.

"Depth?"

"Hundred and seventy-five feet, sir. Ninety feet under the keel."

"Position?"

"Twenty-four thousand, three hundred yards from station—twenty miles from the nearest point of land. I hold us fifty yards left of track."

"Very well. Graham, bring her up to periscope depth. Nav and comm teams, stand by."

"Aye, aye, Captain."

There was a flurry of activity as the submarine slowly ascended to a depth where her sail ran a mere ten feet below the surface, making just under two knots for steerageway. The first mast to break the surface was a periscope. Griffin made two full turns, one with normal optics and one with the IR sensor—nothing.

"All clear," he barked. "Okay, people, let's move."

The periscope was replaced with the communications mast, which quickly found its COMSAT and burst a brief, terse message to the heavens:

ALPHA FOXTROT NOW LESS THAN ONE MILE FROM PACK ICE//UNODIR WILL ENTER PACK//ETA STATION 1000L//

Its message sent, the communications mast began to search on predetermined frequencies for the same navigation satellites that had guided the SEALs on their trek. Aboard the *Archerfish,* the coordinates were not only flashed on a screen to the Quartermaster of the Watch, they were plotted on the boat's automated surface display plot and relayed to the ship's inertial navigation system.

"Message sent and receipt acknowledged, sir—good fix received. SINs has it locked in."

"Very well."

Griffin looked at the stopwatch hanging from the overhead that had been punched when the first mast broke the surface. A second stopwatch had been started when acknowledgment for their message had been received. They would listen for three minutes—no more. At periscope depth with a mast up in Russian waters, Griffin felt like he was walking through a shopping mall nude.

"Two-thirty, sir."

"Very well."

"Sonar reports pack ice fifteen hundred yards on the port bow, sir."

"Very well. Radio?"

"Negative, sir, two forty-five."

"Very well."

"Three minutes, sir, nothing received."

"Very well, bring it down. Graham, take us to a hundred feet. Make turns for three knots to station." Again there was a flurry of activity in the control room. Griffin watched impassively as Lieutenant Commander Smith smartly brought the boat to the ordered depth and speed. The quartermaster punched in the coordinates of the station into the computer, which instantly flashed the course to station and brought the boat to the proper heading.

"Steady on course two-zero-five, sir. Speed three knots, depth one hundred feet with seventy feet under the keel. Time to station at this course and speed, six hours and ten minutes."

"Very well." Griffin sat motionless for the next five minutes, listening. Then he heard it. He glanced around the control room. Magee, with his headphones around his neck, heard it too. Then Senior Chief Dawgs cocked his head and grimaced—he also heard it. It was a soft, persistent grinding noise—the unmistakable sound of pack ice. Griffin looked at Graham Smith, busily laying down a track from their last fix to station on a large-scale hydrographic chart. *It'll be another five minutes before he hears it,* mused Griffin. But Smith suddenly raised his head from the chart, listened a moment, and smiled.

The message was received at the headquarters, Commander Submarine Force Atlantic, in Norfolk and relayed simultaneously to the Crisis Management Center at the Special Operation Command, the JCS Communications Center at the Pentagon, and to the White House. At all three locations, a number of serious-faced men and one woman read it with care and grimly went about the business of waiting patiently.

* * *

Katrina Shebanin arrived at the Neva Club precisely at noon on Saturday. It was a small, private club whose members included former party officials, senior bureaucrats, and the local management of the Murmansk Shipping Company. More recently, though few in number, were the members from the new merchant class. They were the owners of a fish processor or a small fleet of fishing boats—entrepreneurs and the nouveau riche. They were few in number, but prone to flaunt their new wealth. They were despised by most Russians.

The manager approached. "I'm sorry, madam, but this is a private club, and you must be escorted by a member."

Which means, Katrina recalled, *the Neva is a men's club and women are only allowed in the company of a male member.* "I see. Well, then, could you please . . ."

"You're from the military facility at Lumbovskiy, are you not?" he asked harshly.

"Why yes, but I . . ."

"Then you should know this is a members-only club. What are you doing here unescorted—answer me that?"

She stared at him coolly. Evidently General Borzov had not told them that his luncheon companion was a woman.

"May I have your name, please?" she asked.

"Why—what for?"

"When Colonel General Borzov asks why I stood him up for our luncheon date, I want to give him the name of the man who insulted me and then turned me away."

The man blanched. "Oh my God, I had no idea, madam—please forgive me. I . . . I just . . ."

"Stop it," she commanded. "Show me to the General's table without another word. And next time an *unescorted* woman arrives at your silly little club, try not to act so boorish."

The manager was still white, but there were flashes of color coming to his cheeks. He led her to General Borzov's table and graciously held her chair for her.

"Thank you for coming," Borzov said when they were alone. "You look wonderful."

"It's good to see you again, General." The table was very private, but in uniform, it was hard to address him other than by his title.

His eyes narrowed and he lifted his head slightly. "Do we have to go through this again? I have no intention of calling you Doctor over lunch."

"Okay, Dmitri." She laughed. "It's just that in your uniform you look so . . . so military."

They both laughed. He signaled the waiter and called for soup. Since his time was limited, he ordered for both of them. They fell into a comfortable conversation while the nervous manager supervised the luncheon service, waiting to be summarily dismissed from his position. The halibut steaks were excellent, but the boiled potatoes were not. They both had sherbet and moved on to tea.

"Are you in town for the weekend?"

"I planned to stay over, even though most things are closed for the holiday," she replied. New Year's Day was observed in Gremikha but not really celebrated. "I'll probably have dinner with Dr. Zhdanov—unless there is another option."

He looked at her wistfully. "I wish there were. I've been on an inspection tour of the military installations in Archangel for the past four days, and there's a stack of work on my desk. The work I could put off, but there's been an incident of thievery on the part of two senior officers at a supply depot near Murmansk."

"And that won't wait?"

He offered her a cigarette and then took one for himself. "There is one thing which I insist upon within my command, and there are no exceptions. There can be no fraud, no embezzlement of money or supplies, and no stealing. The people will never believe in their government or the new order if this is allowed to continue. The Communist system allowed this corruption, even condoned it, and used the secret police to keep order. We had order, but the system hemorrhaged from within and finally collapsed. We are a democracy now, and until we develop a legal system to provide order, it is my job."

"Is it really that bad?"

"It's like a cancer, and it is sucking the life from us. It is," he shook his head sadly and tapped the ash from his cigarette, "perhaps the most damaging legacy of the Communists. Our people have been taught for generations that success is finding a position within the system from which you can steal—a vantage point where the goods and supplies are so numerous, the portion you take will not be missed. Unfortunately, too many are still doing that. Those of us in a position of trust must be held to a higher standard. The bureaucracy must serve the people—not steal from them. We are a nation with rich natural resources and we have farms that produce enough food, but we cannot get those commodities to market."

"But surely we are just moving through a difficult period of transition. Things will improve."

"Perhaps," he said quietly, "but time is not on the side of those who favor reform. I am afraid, Katya—afraid for our nation and for our democracy."

"But, Dmitri, you can't do it all."

"No, I can't, but in matters of corruption within the civilian and military bureaucracy, at least in my command, I will send a very strong message. Those who steal and feed off the system will be treated with the same harshness as spies. Both are traitors and both threaten our security—our very lives." His eyes became sad, and she could feel his frustration. "You see, Katya, all my life I've been a soldier, trained to fight the enemies of the state. And now I'm finding the most dangerous enemies are within the borders of our Republic."

"It's a new year and we are in a new era," she said hopefully, trying to steer him onto safer ground. "Perhaps these market forces we've come to place so much hope in will finally arrive and save us from ourselves."

"It's possible," he conceded. "Personally, I hope the new year will allow for an occasional evening so we can again enjoy an unhurried dinner."

"So do I."

He reached across the table and squeezed her hand, and for a moment, the fire blazed in his eyes. Then he reluctantly released her and looked at his watch. "My pilot tells me the weather will deteriorate, and we should not chance a late departure. May I drop you at your quarters?"

"Imagine what a tragedy it would be if you were forced to remain overnight. Yes, I would appreciate a lift to the apartment."

The manager was waiting for them at the door to help the General on with his greatcoat and hand him his hat and scarf. He brought Katrina her coat but could not meet her eyes. "It has been an honor to have you as a guest at the Neva, General. I hope everything was satisfactory."

"Thank you. The lady was just commenting that the excellent fare was exceeded only by the polite and courteous service."

The manager swallowed hard and forced a smile, bowing slightly as he held the door for them. Outside, they waited in front of the club while the General's driver brought the car around.

"You knew?"

"It was written on both your faces. That ass represents yet another problem with our country." Borzov glanced over his shoulder to their host, who watched cautiously from the window. "He will defer to me because of my rank and position, but he will go to great lengths to avoid serving those he feels are beneath him. And you, my good woman, have paid dearly for your lunch by having to listen to my anti-Socialist ravings. The next time, we talk of nothing but art and music."

"Next time."

The sedan screeched to a halt, and the driver raced around to hold the door for them.

Later that evening, she sat at yet another eating establishment waiting for Dr. Zhdanov. It was a small café that catered to the local fishermen. The food was simple but well prepared, and the vodka was good and reasonably priced. While she waited, she thought of General Borzov's strong feelings about those who held positions of responsibility and used that position for their own benefit. If Zhdanov could not somehow get free of Colonel Makarov and distance himself from this business with the fuel appropriations, he would surely wind up in prison, or worse. She felt some obligation to Zhdanov. It was he who requested her by name for her current assignment when there were literally dozens of others who were qualified and wanted the job. *But what can I do? It was foolish for him to take such a chance in the first place. Now he has Makarov to deal with. And when he's caught, what will Borzov think when he finds out I knew about it?* That, she felt, she could manage, for Borzov was a military man and surely he would understand loyalty to one's immediate superior—or would he? *Strange,* she reflected, *I have a lover who detests corruption and who happens to be the most powerful man in Northern Russia, and my boss is involved with a crooked head of security and they're both on the take. How do I do it?*

"Good evening, Katrina. I hope you haven't been waiting long?"

"Not at all, Leonid—I just arrived a few moments ago."

They took a moment to order and Zhdanov continued, "I understand that our District Commander was in town and that you had lunch with him?"

"That's correct," she said sharply, "and now I'm having dinner with my Facility Manager."

"Now, calm down—it was just an observation. And if it's not too much to ask, what brings him to Gremikha? I had no official notice that he would be in the area."

"He's on a return trip from Archangel, and he just stopped to have lunch—nothing more."

"He, ah . . . didn't happen to mention anything about, well, you know . . . missing fuel?"

"No, he did not, and I think that's a topic about which we should have no further discussion. You know how I feel about it. I can tell you that General Borzov has absolutely no tolerance for what you've done, and I think . . ." She froze, staring at a man who had just entered the restaurant. "What's he doing here?"

Before Zhdanov could explain, Colonel Makarov walked straight to the table and took an empty chair.

"Good evening. How nice to see you both again." A large elderly woman with her head wrapped in a *babushka* and a sour look on her face approached with a steaming plate in each hand. "Please, go ahead and serve them—I'll just have vodka."

Katrina, with a great deal of effort, managed not to flee, and was even able to eat a portion of her dinner. Makarov also commented on her lunch with General Borzov, which may have accounted for his restrained behavior. But after his second vodka, he had begun to leer at her. As the old woman set a third drink in front of him, she took the opportunity to bolt from her chair.

"Leonid, thank you for the fine dinner. I'm sure you men have much to discuss. . . . Please, don't bother to get up. Good evening, Colonel," and she slipped quickly out the door.

Her apartment was just a few blocks away, and she hurried in that direction. The stench of the man was still in her nostrils, and only partially purged by the cold night air. She was still furious with Zhdanov for having arranged for Makarov to join them, but a part of her was thrilled at having made good her escape. She managed a swift glance as she fled out the door, and the image of the two men sitting there, mouths open in bewilderment, caused her to smile. Then she saw the man following her.

The apartment was now only a block away. She increased her pace, only to find that he was closing the gap between them. *That drunken bastard—do I run or do I scream!* She did neither. Instead, she swung to meet her pursuer, clutching her handbag to use as a weapon if it came to that. She was terrified, but she was also livid. *I can't go on like this—we'll settle it now!* He kept coming, out from the shadows, but something was different—he was too short.

"Good evening, Doctor Shebanin. I hope you're not going to strike me."

"Who are you?"

"I'm a friend of Bill's in Moscow. And weren't we in the same psychology class back at the university?"

"W-what?"

"You heard me, Doctor. I said, weren't we in the same psychology class at the university."

"I never took psychology," she replied numbly.

"Really. I swore you sat right next to me."

She was stunned. *How can this be happening!* She quickly looked around, but they were alone. "What do you want?"

He motioned her to the alleyway that bordered the apartments. "We need your help, Doctor. It has to do with the work at the Lumbovskiy facility."

"How did you find me?"

"That's not important. I'm with American intelligence, and we need information about the work being done at Lumbovskiy."

"I . . . I can't do this. I helped you in the past when we were a part of the Soviet Union. Not now—things are different."

"Are they? You know that my country cannot allow nuclear weapons to get into the hands of Third World dictators."

They know—the Americans know! "If you know, then why do you need me—what can I do?"

"If there's somewhere we could talk, perhaps I can explain. I know this is quite a shock for you," he said with a measure of compassion. "Your apartment, perhaps."

Her mind raced. *Why this—why now! I have to do something—Makarov could come along any moment!*

"All right, come to my apartment in a half hour or so, and be very careful. There's a chance I may be under surveillance by the local military security. I'm in apartment number—"

"I know which apartment, Doctor. I also understand this is very hard for you. I'll come by later and only if it's safe." With that, Valclav turned and walked up the alley.

It was an hour and a half before he slipped down the hall and quietly rapped on her door. Her revelation that she might be under surveillance caused him to wait an extra hour, carefully observing the building for any sign that someone was watching her. Valclav wasn't a trained intelligence operative, but he was street smart, which was often just as good and sometimes better. Once inside, she made tea and they sat across from each other at the small kitchen table while he delivered his prepared briefing as instructed. When he finished, she rose and began to pace the room, her arms folded across her stomach as if she were hugging herself.

"Why are you doing this—you're not an American?"

"I was born in St. Petersburg and raised in Tallinn, but I'm an American by my own choosing. I am a sergeant in the United States Army."

"How did you get here, and how will you leave?"

"That is no concern of yours, Doctor Shebanin. Do you understand what we need in the way of information?"

"Yes."

"Then you'll help us?"

Again she began to pace. Valclav sipped his tea and waited patiently. He had no love for Russia, but it was not the bitter hatred he held for the old Soviet Union. He also understood something of the love that a Russian could feel for the *Rodina.* Being a traitor to one's country is never an easy thing, even if one knows his country is wrong. Finally she turned to him.

"I'll need some time to myself. Will you come back in the morning?" He looked at her skeptically. "No tricks—it will be either yes or no, but I need time to think."

Valclav could see she was not the kind of woman who could be pushed. He got to his feet and pulled on his cap. "Thank you for the tea and for considering to help us. What time?"

"Seven o'clock."

He nodded and slipped out the door. Once clear of the building, he made his way back to the waterfront. For the better part of the past two days he had been drinking at one of the taverns that overlooked Svyatonosskiy Inlet. By midafternoon on the previous day, he had bought a few drinks for some of the regulars and was quickly accepted as one of them. They liked him because he bought drinks, but also because he was a good listener.

General Igor Rakipov was lying on his back snoring when the telephone jolted him from sleep. A pain from the previous night's vodka jabbed at him somewhere from behind his eyes. Actually, it wasn't the phone that brought him fully awake, but a sharp elbow from his wife. He overturned the nightstand and its contents as he groped for the receiver.

"Yes, what is it?"

"Sorry to disturb you, General. This is the duty officer, and I have a priority cable from our office in Washington."

"What time is it?"

"It's four-thirty, sir."

Rakipov considered this. *What could be so important that one of our party-boys in Washington would take time from the cocktail circuit to send off a priority cable.* Rakipov struggled with the mental calculation as he looked at the clock. *If it's 4:30 A.M. on Sunday here, then it's 9:30 P.M. on a Saturday in the American capital.* He had a low opinion of the general work habits of some of his officers stationed in Washington. In reality, they were overstaffed, and the current political climate precluded an aggressive agenda of intelligence operations.

"Are you there, General?"

"I am," he snapped. "Can you tell me something about this message."

"It is from the SABLE, General."

"Understood. Does Colonel Gurtovoi know about this?"

"Yes, sir. He was notified a few moments ago, and is on his way here."

"I see." Rakipov thought about going back to sleep and allowing Gurtovoi, the head of the Russian Intelligence Service, to handle it. Rakipov was now half awake and more than a little curious, and Gurtovoi was a brash and very ambitious man. "I will be there in a short while. Ask the Colonel to take no action until I arrive."

"Very good, General."

Rakipov sat on the edge of the bed with his cold feet on the floor while he lit a cigarette. The thought of driving himself to Dzerzhinsky on a cold Sunday morning was not a pleasant one. He frowned as he recalled the old days when a heated Zil limousine would be sent to collect him. *Vodka,* he thought as he stumbled toward the shower, *too much vodka.*

General Rakipov pushed his way into his office and was gratified to find a fresh pot of tea on his sideboard. The duty officer trailed him and laid the current message folder on his desk. The offices were still housed in the building at Dzerzhinsky Square, but the organization was now called the *Ministerstvo Bezopasnosti,* or MB for short. Under Stozharov, the MB was responsible for domestic and military counterintelligence, internal security, the espionage activities of the RIS, as well as all electronic intelligence and communications. Only the presidential security detail was segregated from what had been the old KGB organization.

"Thank you, Major. Have Colonel Gurtovoi wait in the outer office—and close the door."

After the duty officer left, Rakipov poured himself a cup of tea and unlocked the lower drawer to his desk. He removed a small flask and decanted a measure of the clear liquid into his cup. Then he turned to the folder.

The message was indeed from the Washington Station, and contained a meeting report from agent SABLE. SABLE had been one of the KGB's most productive agents in America for a number of years. The station contact, Lieutenant Colonel Averin, was an experienced intelligence professional—one of the few like himself who had escaped the reorganization, a purge really, following the breakup of the Union. *It takes both,* Rakipov thought, *an agent with good access and a contact officer to encourage him, to push him—but not too far.*

He sipped his tea and carefully read the cable for the second time. SABLE reported overhearing a conversation among senior CIA officers about Russia selling nuclear weapons to the Third World. He also said there was some sort of a military operation underway to contact an agent in place who had information about the sale of these weapons. The implication was made that this operation was intended to stop the sale of the weapons. Normally, this information would have been sanitized and routed to the military district commanders for precautionary action, unless there was corroborating information to support stronger action. In this case, that corroboration had been provided by President Stozharov himself.

Rakipov winced as he recalled being summoned by the President in late November. Stozharov had demanded to know why the Americans seemed to know more about the possible construction and sale of nuclear weapons in the Northern Military District than the MB did. Rakipov could only promise to look into the matter, and cited the strong regional control exercised by the District Commander. He had carefully explained that Colonel General Borzov may have better information than himself. "I'm not asking Borzov," Stozharov stormed, "I'm asking you!"

Could this information from SABLE and the problem in the Northern District be related? Probably so. But military intervention? Surely the Americans would not be so bold or so stupid.

"Please ask Colonel Gurtovoi to step in here."

"At once, General."

Rakipov added more tea to his cup and waited. A moment later, Gurtovoi arrived.

"You've had time to digest this information, Andrei. What do you make of it?"

"We've been alerted to watch for the transfer of nuclear arms and technology in the Northern District. If this information is accurate and relates to that military district, then the Americans seem to be taking an active role." Gurtovoi was young for a colonel in the MB—or the RIS, for that matter. He was well-educated and from a good family. He reminded Rakipov of an American.

"Do you really believe they would attempt a military penetration of the Kola Peninsula, even with a small group?"

"Have they hesitated to use their forces in other parts of the world? Perhaps since they now fancy themselves as the only superpower, they feel they have the authority to take this kind of action."

In reality, they are the only superpower, thought Rakipov, *whether we choose to admit it or not.* "So what do you recommend?"

"That we notify our district office in Murmansk immediately, as well as Colonel General Borzov." Gurtovoi smiled. "It will give those donkeys in the GRU something to stew about."

Rakipov again remembered Stozharov's reaction when he suggested going directly to General Borzov on the matter of nuclear weapons. Gurtovoi's recommendation was the correct course of action from an operational perspective, but Rakipov had not become head of the MB by ignoring political considerations.

"Where is the President now?"

"He is at his dacha in Pirogovskiy. He is scheduled back tomorrow morning." While the President was no longer guarded by an MB detachment, his whereabouts and movements were still carefully monitored.

"Cable Washington to see if they have any additional information that may relate to this information from SABLE. I will present this to President Stozharov in the morning."

"So we are not going to disseminate this to Murmansk?"

"Correct, we are not."

"But, General, on the chance that there is an ongoing military operation—an incursion—we must . . ."

"Are you questioning my judgment, Colonel?"

"Of course not, General. I will cable Washington Station at once." Gurtovoi snapped to attention and left immediately. Rakipov reread the message and again reached into his lower drawer.

Katrina Shebanin continued to pace the floor like a caged animal. Sleep had been impossible, and for the past few hours she had been unable to sit in one place for more than a few minutes. It seemed as if the disillusionment that came with the end of the Soviet Union, the disappointments of the new order, and the poor choices she herself had made all descended upon her at once. As a member of the intelligentsia, she had never wanted for material things and intellectual challenges. But as a member of that privileged class, she bore a responsibility. Millions of Russians lived in poverty so that she and people like her could study at the university, become scientists, defend the fatherland, and lead the people to new prosperity. *Prosperity! The long-suffering Russian people still struggle with little hope for the future, and their lot is no better than when Lenin seized power in the streets of Moscow when my grandmother was a girl. We should have known it was all wrong decades later when Stalin brutalized our land. And I've been such a fool. I've used my talents as a physicist to make bombs for the Soviet Union and once again for the Republic. I betrayed the Union, thinking if the West knew of the huge atomic arsenal we possessed, they would find a way to halt the arms race—to deescalate. Now they want me to betray Russia.*

She paused and sat at the dressing table looking at herself in the mirror, pulling the lapels of her robe close around her chin. Her eyes were hollow and tired, accented by the streaked makeup. She was certainly getting no younger. She had no real friends and no real family. *Thank God I have no children I have to explain this to, or to tell them why their future is so dismal.* She did have a lover—a man perhaps like no one she had met before—but his true mistress was his obligation as a Russian general officer. If he learned of her contact with the Americans, or even of her knowledge of the diverted fuel shipments to the facility, any feeling he may have for her would be swept aside by his duty. *He's made that clear enough.*

What do I do about this Russian-born Estonian-American who has appeared and wants information on the work we are doing at Lumbovskiy? He has the same look of purpose and determination as Dimitri Borzov. She had no love for the West. The blame for the destruction of her Russia rested with the Communists and the corruption within the bureaucracy. The West, led by the United States, had forced the staggering diversion of resources to the Soviet military, and in doing so had hastened the collapse. Now there was precious little help coming from those in the West who had so strongly opposed communism for most of her lifetime.

She studied the woman in the mirror, looking for some answer—some way out of her dilemma. But she was a scientist, and she knew answers did not come from wishes or regrets, or from idle hopes that future events would somehow treat her favorably—or from some shining prince who would sweep her into his arms and carry her to safety. Carefully and analytically, she reviewed her options and each course of action available to her.

"I guess I really have no choice," she told the woman in the mirror, who seemed to understand.

She rose and walked into the small bath, dropped the robe to the floor, and stepped into the shower. After she had dressed and combed her wet hair back from her forehead, she sat at the kitchen table with her notebook. It was almost six o'clock when she finished the first page and began the second. She had a calligrapher's hand, and the prose was punctuated with engineering symbology and scientific notations. An hour later she was finished, and sat smoking a cigarette when the soft rapping came at the door.

"Come in—it's open," she said.

First his head, then the rest of him quickly slipped inside. He closed the door and carefully looked around before he stepped fully into the room.

"Well, you're prompt, I'll say that much for you. Sit down—would you like a cup of tea?"

"No, thank you." He stuffed the cap in his pocket and sat across the table from her. This was a different woman from the one he had met last evening. That one was hesitant and afraid, glancing furtively from side to side as if looking for a way out. This Dr. Shebanin was cool and measured, with a deliberate look to her. "I probably shouldn't stay any longer than necessary, Doctor. Have you decided to help us?"

"Perhaps. I've prepared this for you." She pushed the pile of notes across the table. He looked at her sharply and then began to scan the papers. "I sense that you are neither a scientist nor an engineer, Sergeant, so let me tell you what is there. I have briefly described the conversion process by which my section at the Northern Military District Munitions Disposal Site Number Three, or what we call the Lumbovskiy facility, converts old Soviet tactical nuclear warheads into relatively simple nuclear devices for use by Third World armies. Most of them are being configured as air-dropped weapons or for air-launched cruise missiles—primarily for the AS-6, though they can be adapted to a number of cruise missiles in our inventory. As you're probably aware, all our cruise missiles, as well as most of our military hardware systems, are for sale. A number of these nuclear devices are to be modified for Scud III missiles, and some of the smaller ones for the 152mm artillery shells. The production schedule calls for me to deliver a hundred weapons. Then I would expect we'll sit back and see how many buyers there are. I assume you wouldn't be here if sales weren't expected to be brisk. We plan to begin shipping the first weapons in about two weeks. My instructions were to meet a January tenth delivery for ten air-dropped weapons, and I will make that deadline. The last few pages briefly describe the type of construction—they're all U239 devices—the arming sequences, and the expected yields. They're nice little bombs—very clean and nothing over sixty kilotons."

Valclav tapped the papers endwise on the table and laid them in a flat, neat stack between the woman and himself. He was mildly surprised that she had signed and dated the papers, and affixed her title—Special Projects Director, Lumbovskiy Site Number Three. "I believe you, Dr. Shebanin. This is helpful and I'm sure of great interest to our people. But I think you know that we need more—we need the official documentation from the Lumbovskiy facility that can actually prove this is all taking place."

"I understand perfectly, and I will get it for you. This is just, as they say in America, a down payment."

Valclav was being led down the garden path and he knew it. He reached across the table and took one of her cigarettes without asking. She pushed the lighter across the table to him. He blew a cloud of smoke over her head and made a face. "How do you stand these things?" he asked, looking critically at the cigarette.

"Like most things in Russia—you make do with what is available, or you do without."

"Dr. Shebanin," he said, shifting his attention from the cigarette to her, "how and when will you get the documentation?"

She leaned forward, resting her elbows on the table. "I will be leaving for the facility in about five hours. What you require is in the files in my office, and will easily fit in an attaché case. I will bring it to you, but only on the condition that you take me with you when you leave. Unless you can agree to this, our business is finished."

Valclav stared at her a long minute. A number of thoughts sprung to his mind—*I don't have the authority to bring you out; give us the information and we'll plan for your defection at a later time; I can't take you because I'm leaving on a merchant ship.* But he could see from the determined look on her face that this was not negotiable. He could threaten that the CIA would expose her if she didn't produce the documents, but he sensed this kind of heavy-handedness would not work either. He settled on a version of the truth.

"Dr. Shebanin, I was parachuted into the backcountry some forty miles inland, and I will leave by an equally difficult and dangerous means. I cannot say that it is totally impossible for us to get you out of here, but I will have to place your life at risk, along with my own, to accomplish it. If you insist on this, I will look into the matter and let you know. Please understand, it is not a decision that I can make here and now."

Katrina considered this. "Then you are in contact with the outside."

"Yes."

"Then understand this, Sergeant. I am in an impossible situation, and it is dangerous for me to stay here. Because of this," she tapped the notes on the table, "and a number of other reasons, I must leave here—now, with or without your help."

Valclav nodded slowly. "I will see what I can do. How will I contact you?"

"Just call me." She handed him a piece of paper with a telephone number and a name. "That number rings directly into the switchboard at Lumbovskiy. Sergei Shebanin is the name of my brother. I have not seen or spoken with him in several years. I think he's in Novosibirsk, or he was. Say that you have seen him recently and have news from him."

"That should be easy to remember. My name is also Sergei."

"Are you able to get to the facility at Lumbovskiy as soon as tomorrow—Monday afternoon?"

"It can be done."

"Each day, usually for an hour or so after lunch, I cross-country ski. There's a ski trail alongside the road that goes past the facility. The trail runs east from the turnoff to the site. It's well-marked, but not a lot of people from the facility use it. We can easily meet along the route. If I were to leave permanently during one of these outings, there's a good chance I'd not be missed until the following day."

"I guess there's not much more to say," he replied, stuffing the slip of paper into his shirt pocket. He rose, taking her notes and folding them lengthwise so they would fit into the inside pocket of his pea coat. "I will call you tomorrow to confirm our arrangement."

"And I will be prepared to leave with the documentation you require. If for some reason this is not possible, don't even bother to call. What you have in your coat is both an indictment and my death warrant, but I will do no more unless you agree to get me out of Russia." A look of sadness passed across her face, but it was quickly replaced by one of determination. "My life is in your hands, Sergei. Do what you must."

"I understand." With that, he slipped back out the door.

Once in the hall, he glanced quickly at his watch. He had a lot to do before he left town.

Moody and Snyder lay not far from where they had bid good-bye to Valclav over two days ago. They had approached the rally point from a slightly different direction so as to mask their movements. Snow was expected, but there had been neither snow nor wind for several days, and Moody was beginning to worry about traffic patterns around the base camp. It was 12:20 P.M., and Moody was becoming concerned. It wasn't like Valclav to be late.

"I got him."

"Where?"

"Over there near that first cross street—wait, he's hidden behind a house—there." The NODs were ineffective if there were lights nearby, and the dim windows of the houses exploded like supernovas through the goggles. The noonday twilight also made them less effective. Snyder had spotted him using a small pair of Zeiss field glasses.

"Okay, I see him now." They waited until Valclav was almost on top of them before showing themselves. Moody watched Valclav for any unnatural movement and Snyder searched along his route to make sure no one was following him. "Over here, Sergeant." Valclav altered his course and slogged over to where they waited behind a fallen tree.

"Sorry to keep you waiting, sir. I've had a busy two days."

"Did you find MUSTANG?"

"Yes, sir, I did. I also got part of the information, but our mission won't be complete until she comes up with the rest of it."

"Did you say *she?*"

"Yes, sir." He dropped to one knee. "She provided me with information regarding the number, type, and construction of the weapons they're building at Lumbovskiy. The technical details and engineering specifications, the real proof of what's being done there, won't be available until tomorrow at Lumbovskiy. And there's a problem, sir—the information comes with a price." Valclav quickly summarized his meeting with Shebanin.

"Is she serious—do you believe her?"

"Absolutely. She's a tough one. Not American tough—Russian tough."

"Can we work around her, or get her to deliver the data without really trying to take her with us?"

"I don't think we have a choice, sir. We have to *tell* her we're going to get her out of here. The only question is whether we kill her immediately or take her out on the pack ice and kill her. But if we say we can't get her out, I'll bet a month's pay we get no more information from her."

Moody was silent for a moment as he digested this. "How long do we have?"

"Not long. This lady is very impatient. She'll be ready to go as soon as tomorrow, and I recommend that we don't wait too long. I've made a few contacts around Gremikha that may be helpful."

Again Moody thought for a moment, then turned to Valclav. "Okay, I want you back at the camp tonight. I've got a feeling we're going to call home more than once this evening, and I'll need you to help me develop a workable plan. Kurt, get the Sarge's gear from the cache, and let's get out of here."

Once clear of the immediate vicinity of Gremikha, Snyder pushed hard for the base camp while Moody and Sergeant Valclav struggled to keep up. This time, Moody ordered Valclav to move ahead of him while he pulled the small drogue rake to help cover their tracks. It was close to

2:30 P.M. and beginning to snow when they arrived at the base of the small valley that lay before the bermed tree line where their camp was hidden. They paused a moment, and Moody noticed with satisfaction that their tracks were already being covered by the snow and an icy wind that was now blowing in from the Barents Sea.

"We're gettin' close, sir," said Snyder as he halted them for a short rest. "We should be within a klick or so of the camp. Let's keep to the high ground and work our way across the side of the ridge. The blowing snow will cover our tracks." Moody knew they should be seen by one of their team well before they got near the camp. Whenever there was an element out of camp, a sentry was posted before their time of arrival for security and to guide them in. After traveling another five minutes, Snyder took out his penlight and flashed "alpha-alpha" in thirty-degree arcs. Ahead and to their left he saw a "november-november," and they moved toward it. Walker came toiling down to meet them.

"Boss, we got company."

Moody automatically reached for his weapon. "How many!"

"Just one—a border guard. He must have crossed our tracks and started following them. He stumbled into the camp about an hour after you left."

"Has he said anything—are there others?"

"Y'all better come an' see for yourself." Walker led them to the main snow cave. They had worked on the cave daily, and now it was a small room with a four-foot ceiling. They had also worked on concealing their presence, and their burrow in the snowbank was all but invisible unless you were on top of it. Moody parted the white canvas flap that served as a door and ducked into the warm, dimly lit interior.

"Afternoon, sir," said Garniss loudly. "Zee-dra-sto-vita, an' all that shit. Meet my buddy, Boris."

"Zdrahst'voitye, Leytenant," said a squat, dirty man in a tattered, green border-guard uniform. Garniss and the Russian sat spread-legged on the frozen, snow-covered floor leaning against a wall of the cave. There was a bottle of vodka between them and they were both very drunk.

Katrina Shebanin sat looking straight ahead as the bus worked its way through the driving snow. The wind, which now came in unpredictable gusts, indiscriminately mixed the falling snow with that already on the ground and swirled it before the headlights. Occasionally, it swept across the road in great clouds as if from a white dust storm, forcing the driver to slow to a crawl, but he knew the road well and patiently waited until the visibility cleared before pressing on. It would take another hour to reach Lumbovskiy.

A strange sense of calm purpose had overtaken her after Valclav left.

The thought of going to live in the West filled her with anxiety and resignation. Leaving Russia would be bittersweet at best. She had no family to speak of and no real career prospects. She had a lover and a few acquaintances, but strangely, neither was foremost in her thoughts. *What is it about this tired, cold, harsh land that makes us love it so? And why do I feel such kinship to those millions of Russians who must work and suffer within her vast borders? I have nothing here, and yet a part of me will always be Russian—curiously bound to this cruel land. Can I ever learn to live in a milder, kinder place?* Her thoughts were disrupted by the man squirming in the seat next to her.

"Katya, I know you are upset and disappointed with me, but it is very hard for me now. This Makarov is a madman. I even told him I would not cooperate with him if he persisted in this unreasonable behavior toward you."

"And what did he say?"

Zhdanov lowered his head. "He said I would do as I was told or suffer the consequences. But I cannot go on allowing him to treat you like this!"

"Does he know that I am aware of the fuel shipments?"

"I think so. Katya, I am so sorry to have you involved in this, but I didn't know where to turn. Perhaps when we finish the current weapons-production run, they will close the facility and we will be reassigned to Murmansk or even St. Petersburg."

"Perhaps."

"Katya, don't be too angry with me. I'm really doing the best I can."

"I know, Leonid, I know. And I'm not angry—just tired. We'll get through this." She gave him a tolerant look.

He's a tragic person. He will do what he can to shield me, but he'll protect his family at all costs, and he'll deliver me to that animal, Makarov, if he has to. Katrina smiled sadly and shook her head. *And this weak, well-meaning little man is probably the closest thing I have to a friend.*

Katrina swayed with the other passengers as the driver dodged a pothole on the road and plunged into another white cloud.

Moody crouched on one knee and looked from Garniss to the drunken border guard. He glanced behind him to Valclav, whose face showed nothing.

"Zdrahst'voitye," Moody said as he carefully seated himself on the floor of the snow cave. The border guard wore a tattered canvas army coat that was unbuttoned, revealing a soiled green uniform shirt. He had strong, unwashed smell to him and a dense stubble of growth on his face. The man didn't look well.

"Sir, why don' you have a drink with me an' ole Boris here." Garniss winked and made a show of splashing some vodka in a cup, handing it to him. "You too, you old Communist, you," and he handed Valclav a cup. Valclav slipped the bottle from his coat pocket and said something in Russian that made their guest flash his yellow teeth and nod. Then he made a show of pouring a measure in each of their cups.

"To friendship," he said with a forced smile.

"Friendship," Moody echoed.

"Fuckin' A," said Garniss while the Russian slurred something in his native tongue. They touched cups and drank.

"Sergeant, why don't you have a chat with our friend here, while Garniss and I slip outside for a minute." Valclav nodded but didn't take his eyes off the Russian. Moody set his cup down and slid through the cave opening. Garniss made a pantomime of saying that he had to urinate, which caused the visitor to laugh and clap his hands in appreciation.

"What the hell gives, Bob?"

Suddenly, Garniss was no longer the drunken clown. "The guy just showed up, Boss. Walker and O'Keefe were coming from the sleeping cave and he found the guy standing right here, shivering. I think he was hunting, since he had an old shotgun with him."

"Give you any trouble?"

"None. By the time they called me he was starting to jabber in Russian, but he was shaking so badly he could hardly talk. It was either shoot him or feed him. We fed him—boy, did we feed him. He ate a whole day's rations. I tell you, sir, he's just like an old skinny dog who shows up at your back door."

"How'd he get here?"

"While O'Keefe fed him, I checked back up the trail you and Snyder took to town. Found a set of tracks that came into your trail about a mile out. His boot marks are pretty distinctive. He just found your route and followed it to camp." It was beginning to snow harder, and the wind was now strong enough to reach them behind the berm.

"We'll not have to worry about tracks now. He speak any English?"

"Just a word or two, but I think he understands a little more than that."

"Shit, I really don't need this right now."

"How'd Valclav make out?"

"We found the agent, and we may be out of here tomorrow. Let's get back inside."

Valclav and the Russian were deep in conversation, and it was obvious that Valclav was interrogating him. Occasionally his voice became loud and guttural, and the man seemed to shrink from him. Moody and Garniss sat and watched. O'Keefe was pinned against the wall behind them in the crowded space, while Snyder and Walker waited in the sleeping cave. A single candle flickered shadows around the dull-white walls, while the gruff Russian-phrases and steamy clouds of breath seemed to transform the proceedings in the cramped space into some kind of a pagan rite.

Finally, Valclav turned to Moody. "Our friend says he was out hunting. There are a few arctic fox and hare on the Kola. He says he was working his way around the lake and got lost, then found our trail and followed it in."

"Do you believe him?"

Valclav shrugged, indicating he wished to talk about it in private. "The food and the booze have made him pretty sleepy. I suggest we bed him down in the other cave while we sort this out."

"Do it. Have Walker keep an eye on him."

Valclav and the Russian had a quick exchange. He cast a furtive, worried look at Moody and followed Valclav to the sleeping cave. The Sergeant returned in a few minutes with Snyder. O'Keefe, who had been tending a small alcohol stove, began handing out cups of hot chocolate. Garniss declined, saying he had a buzz going and didn't want to ruin it.

"What's the deal, Sarge?"

"Near as I can tell, he really was out trying to shoot some game and just stumbled in here. The border guards are little more than conscripts. They're kind of outcasts, looked down upon by the regular army and resented by the local authorities. I told him I was SPETSNAZ, and that the rest of you were part of a special, English-speaking training cadre. I said we were part of a secret training exercise, and that there were other SPETSNAZ units out looking for us."

"You think he bought it?"

"He's not too smart, but I wouldn't count on it. He also said he had to muster at his barracks outside Gremikha tomorrow morning. They could start looking for him, although it's probably not too unusual for these guys to get drunk on a holiday weekend and not show up for duty on Monday morning. Depends on how tough his sergeant is."

Moody frowned, turning to Snyder. "Kurt, what's our comm window?"

Snyder pulled a laminated card from his shirt pocket. "About another hour and fifteen minutes, then we're blacked out for three hours."

"Okay, guys, we have some serious planning to do." He laid out a large-scale map of the Gremikha-Lumbovskiy area. "We'll figure out what to do with Boris later."

"His name is Felix," said Valclav.

"Whatever. Okay, guys, listen up."

For the next forty minutes, Moody laid out their exfiltration plan. There were frequent comments and an occasional disagreement, but all agreed it could work—with a little luck.

"Anything I've overlooked?" Moody asked.

"Looks good to me, Boss," said Snyder.

"It has to work," concluded Valclav. "It's risky, but what other choice do we have?"

"No balls, no blue chips," said Garniss. "Let's do it."

"Are you kidding me?" said a whiny, New England voice. "This is crazy—I'm gonna die—we're all gonna die."

"Well, that settles it," said Moody with a grin. "Let's get to work."

For the next half hour, Moody typed furiously on the Gridset. Snyder connected the scanner, a portable fax machine that looked like a small hair dryer, to the computer. When Moody finished, he methodically scanned each page of MUSTANG's report. The facsimile as well as the text were compressed into a twelve-second burst and sent skyward just before their comm window closed.

Six miles from the Russian coast on a bearing of zero-two-seven from the tip of Obornyy Spit, the USS *Archerfish* lay quietly on the bottom in eighty-seven feet of water with a five-degree port list. There was sixty-two feet of water and two feet of pack ice between her main deck and the surface, which meant there was only forty-seven feet of water between the top of her sail and the bottom of the pack ice. They had been in position for almost forty-eight hours, and the crew had settled into a quiet routine while they awaited the arrival of the special operations team. The control room and engineering watchstanders made routine tests and calibration checks of their systems, but there was little for them to do. The sonarmen kept a listening watch, but there was little to hear, or a lot to hear, depending on your point of view. The grinding and groaning of the pack ice could be heard throughout the submarine. The sound was not of the intensity it had been during their passage under the edge of the pack, where the ice was unstable and constantly shifting. Now, some five and a half miles from the edge, it had become an eerie, persistent moaning that at times seemed almost human. The sonarmen could electronically filter some of the noise, but their acoustic capability was severely limited.

The crew, freed from their underway routine, had time on their hands. When they weren't on watch, they were reading or watching movies on the boat's VCR. Many of them took to sleeping eight hours at a time, something they could never do while underway. Cribbage boards and coffee cups had begun to sprout in the working spaces. They were prepared to wait for up to ten days, although the team was expected within the next five. If required, they could remain on the bottom for three weeks, and push it to a month if they had to. *Archerfish* was a small coastal submarine, designed for short patrols. There were few of the creature comforts found on American fast-attack or missile-firing submarines. No one relished the thought of having to remain bottomed for another ten days.

As boring as their routine now was, few of them would trade it for the tense and dangerous journey they had just made to arrive at their assigned station. Graham Smith was the general-quarters Officer of the Deck, but it was Commander Griffin who took the con and guided the boat to station. No American or NATO submarien had ever maneuvered in such close quarters. Once they were in less than one hundred feet of water, one sonarman called out the depth under the keel while another the clearance of the sail to the pack ice above. Senior Chief Dawgs supervised the buoyancy control, which was no small task as the salinity of the water, and therefore its density, changed constantly under the pack at these shallow depths. Graham Smith monitored their position on the automatic plotter, calling bearing and ranges to station, and distance to the left or right of track. Griffin gave course, speed, and depth commands, which were repeated by the helmsman, the lee helmsman, and the plansman. At one point, the *Archerfish* had less than fifteen feet clearance under the keel *and* the top of her sail.

The on-board computers could do all manner of routine maneuvering, but they had not been programmed for this, nor were the sensors integrated to a degree that would allow the computers to do something as crazy as drive the submarine under the ice in seventy feet of water. So Griffin had done it by the seat of his pants. He had not only brought the boat to the exact station coordinates, he had driven past it, executed a Williamson turn, and brought her back to station, bow pointing back to the edge of the pack ice and freedom.

"How's it going, Cob?" Smith was taking his turn on the four-section control-room watch.

"Okay, XO. How about yourself—wish you were up there mushing through the snow instead of down here sweating it out?"

"Sometimes. I sure thought about it a time or two when we were creeping in here."

"The Skipper's really somethin', ain't he? I've seen him do that before. He kind of goes into a trance, and it's like he becomes a part of the boat. Most of the time he storms around like a rutting bull, but when the money's down, he's an ice man."

Smith recalled Griffin's cool performance and shook his head. He saw a little of it during the brush with the Russian sub, but during the run under the ice, he was calm—almost relaxed. *He became,* Smith reflected, *the thing he says he detests: a computer—receiving sensor data and input from the control-room watch, processing the information, and giving the proper commands. Except that no computer that I know of could do what he just did.*

"I understand you put the DF mast up?"

"Yes, sir. It's all rigged out and tests satisfactory."

"ELF?"

"Received the test pulse about an hour ago, right on schedule. Hey, relax, XO—we could be here for another week or so."

Major Brisco and Master Chief Tolliver each pored over their copy of the SITREP from the team in the Kola. The Russian text was being processed in the bowels of CIA headquarters in Langley, Virginia, and would be sent to them by secure fax as soon as it was translated. It was a long message that detailed Valclav's contact with MUSTANG and the capture of the border guard. What held both of their attention was the final portion of the message headed PLANNED ACTION FOR NEXT 24 HR:

> UNODIR WILL DISPOSE OF BORDER GUARD AND PROCEED TO EXTRACTION POINT WITH ADDITIONAL DOCUMENTATION AND/OR AGENT MUSTANG//WILL XMIT DATA PRIOR TO EXTRACTION IF FEASIBLE//REQUEST ARCHERFISH BE READY FOR GUESTS 1200–2400(L) D PLUS EIGHT//REGARDS MOODY//

"Well, Master Chief?"

"D plus eight—that's tomorrow. They're on a short leash, and I think they know it. The border guard will be missed and that will probably generate a search. It also seems that MUSTANG is at the end of his rope."

"What's Moody thinking, Master Chief—what's he going to do? And dammit, why didn't he tell us exactly what he was going to do?"

"Major, I think they have a plan, and if they put it in message format, we'd probably think they're crazy—or worse, try to second-guess them. They're requesting the only help we can give them now, and that's to have that sub where it's supposed to be at the right time and ready to receive them."

Brisco lit a cigarette and angrily sucked the smoke deep into her lungs. It was a no-smoking area, and several of the officers on watch in the CMC glared at her. "Okay, what do *you* think they're going to do?"

Tolliver paused and rubbed his chin. "I think they're going to kill the guard and hightail it for Lumbovskiy. When they get there, they'll contact MUSTANG and say what they have to in order to get the information they need. Then they'll probably kill him, and move out onto the pack ice for the extraction."

"Will they have to kill MUSTANG? Once they get the information from him, can't they just let him go?"

"Only Mr. Moody can make that call. There's no way they can take him out, so the Lieutenant will have to decide whether allowing him to live is a threat to the rest of them. If there's any doubt in his mind at all, he'll kill MUSTANG—or at least he should."

Brisco ordered an enlisted man from his computer terminal and took his place. While the cigarette dangled from the side of her mouth, her fingers flew over keyboard.

FROM: SOCOM
TO: JCS
CLASSIFICATION BEARCAT//SENSITIVE HANDLING REQUIRED
ENDORSEMENT TO SPECOPS SITREP NBR SEVEN DTG 021523ZJAN94

UNLESS INFORMATION PROVIDED BY MUSTANG THIS SITREP SUFFICIENT TO SATISFY MISSION OBJECTIVES, REQUEST TEAM BE ALLOWED TO PROCEED WITH PLANNED ACTION. BRISCO SENDS/COMSOCOM CONCURS.

Tolliver read the screen over her shoulder and nodded approvingly. His hand was resting on her shoulder, just as it would have been if one of his teammates had been typing the endorsement. When he realized this, he jerked it away.

"Uh, you think General Thon will buy it?" Tolliver asked.

"He will or I'll jump right in his shit!"

Tolliver smiled broadly. He took the tin of snuff from his back pocket and almost offered her a pinch before he took one for himself.

The President was seated behind the big desk dressed reading the *Washington Post* when Morton Keeney entered carrying a file labeled "Top Secret." Bennett was dressed like Mr. Rogers, while Keeney wore his typical weekend ensemble consisting of a dark-blue blazer, striped school tie, and slacks.

"You've read the latest traffic, sir?"

"I have. What do Armand's people say?"

"MUSTANG's report, or letter if you will, confirms what we suspected, but really doesn't provide us with anything new. We still need supporting technical data to make a good case."

"That what your people say?"

"Well, they all agree we need additional information to make a compelling argument on the proliferation issue at the U.N. or to swing the European allies behind us. If possible, Anne Bunting wants any data that can be obtained on pollution from the fuel-conversion process."

"And Geist?"

"He'd prefer you to authorize an air strike on the facility, but I think he approves of the action we're taking. He also cautions that we shouldn't expect too much. The Russians, like the Soviets, are very good at denial."

"I see. So what does General Scott have to say? Seems to me our Lieutenant Moody is telling us he's coming out, and he's asking our permission to kill a few Russian nationals along the way. Do we want to do this?"

"I would like to think there's another option, but I'm not sure there is. We could go back to him with something like 'don't kill anyone unless it's necessary,' but he knows that. I think we have to let him do his job, and trust in his judgment."

"So do I, Mort. I just wanted to hear you say it. Make sure that's made clear to him, and keep me posted. Looks like it's going to be a long night."

"You'll be here the rest of the afternoon?"

"I will. The Skins are on TV against Seattle. Probably won't be much of a game, but we have to stick to normal routine during potential periods of crisis, right?"

"You're quite correct, Mr. President."

Moody stood on the berm near the snow cave and checked his watch—it was 3:30 Monday morning. Following their comm check just after midnight, they began to assemble their gear and prepared to leave the base camp. The message from SOCOM was brief but supportive, even encouraging:

> PROCEED WITH PLAN AND EXTRACTION//ARCHERFISH STANDING BY TO RECEIVE YOU//NCA ACTUAL SENDS BEST WISHES//GOOD LUCK//

Moody knew that NCA was National Command Authority, which meant presidential authority, but NCA ACTUAL was the President himself. *Could that have really come from the President?* Moody wondered. *Nah, probably just Brisco or Tolliver fooling around with them.* They had been able to consolidate the remaining equipment onto a single *akio,* buried the other one near the camp.

"We're ready to move, Boss," said Garniss. "Valclav isn't too fond of Russians, as we all know. He says he'll do it. But, to be honest, it should be one of us, so why don't I take care of it."

"He still sleeping?"

"Yeah, and I'd just as soon do it while he is—better for him that way."

None of them, including Garniss, was too excited about killing Boris, or Felix as he called himself, but there didn't seem to be an alternative. They all knew he was a simple man from a peasant background, and that there was an even chance he would be too worried about being AWOL to report them. But given what was ahead of them, they needed a better-than-even chance of remaining undetected. Moody frowned and nodded.

"You going to shoot him, Bob?"

"No, sir, I'll just take a rifle butt to his head. We need the uniform, and I don't want to chance splattering it with blood." Garniss reluctantly started for the sleeping cave with his rifle.

"Sir, I got an idea." Both Garniss and Moody turned to O'Keefe. "If you want, I can give him a double load of morphine, and that should knock him out for eight, maybe ten hours. Leave him some heat tabs and a few meals. The first thing he's going to do when he wakes up is puke his guts out—then he's going to be hungry, and it takes a long time to heat chow with heat tabs. I figure he'll be lucky to be out walking in twelve hours."

"An' if we take the laces from his boots," Garniss added, "he'll not be able to move too quickly."

"We've got plenty of cash," Moody thought aloud. "If we leave him a wad of rubles, he may be tempted to forget the whole thing."

"And if he does report us, he'll take time to hide the money first. By that time we'll be long gone."

"I can't believe you Navy guys," said Valclav, who had just joined them. "This guy's a Russian border guard—an ex–KGB border guard. He may not be the brightest guy in the world, but he took an oath to protect the fatherland. Don't count on his sense of fair play, or his recognizing what a swell bunch of guys you are. He's not an American—he's Russian. Shoot him and let's get the hell out of here."

While Valclav was speaking, Felix staggered from the sleeping cave, cautiously moving about in the moonlight. Valclav saw him and spun around with his MP-5A trained on his midsection. The Russian's hands shot up and the whites of his eyes could be seen in the dim light.

"Okay, Sarge, easy does it." Moody looked to Garniss, who gave him a thumbs-up. "Tell him that we're leaving, and that he is to stay here for twenty-four hours. We'll leave him food and some money, but we're going to give him some drugs that will make him sleep."

Valclav rattled off several sentences in Russian. Felix took a step backward and held his hands out in a pleading motion.

"No no, pleeze, not so, pleeze!"

Valclav pulled the bolt of the submachine gun back, and the clattering action of the weapon plainly told Felix of the alternative. He dropped to his knees and sat back on his ankles, head down. He was shaking so badly, his teeth rattled.

"All right, Bob, Doc—get it done."

Garniss threw the Russian on his stomach and sat on him while Valclav pulled his pants down. O'Keefe plunged a serette of morphine into one hairy cheek and a second in the other. Felix soon began to smile and babble incoherently. They quickly stripped off his uniform, stuffed him into a sleeping bag, and dragged him back into the sleeping cave.

O'Keefe made him as comfortable as he could and lit a six-hour candle. There was a chance he could lose a few toes, but the heat from the flame and the bag would keep him alive. Then he laid a penlight, matches, rations, heat tabs, and a wad of rubles nearby, and joined the others outside.

"After all that," observed Walker, "he'll probably git eaten by a bear."

"Let's hope so," said Valclav. "We're ready to move, Lieutenant."

"Okay, Kurt, take us out of here. Bob, you want the first shift on the *akio?*"

"Got it, boss. Don, you gonna be my pusher?"

"You bet—that okay, Doc?"

"I guess so, Walker, but be careful."

The team was mounted on skis and took to the route that would lead them to Gremikha. Inside the cave, Felix somehow knew they were leaving him behind, but he was so warm and relaxed, he really didn't care.

President Stozharov made it a point to arrive at his office at least an hour early when he'd been away for the weekend. The early start was a small price to pay for the weekend at his dacha outside Moscow. It was not a grand place by Western standards, but it was quiet and private, and he could insulate himself to some degree from the pressures of his office. He had just settled behind his desk and a larger-than-usual stack of official correspondence, when the intercom summoned him.

"Yes, Tanya Pavelovna, what is it?"

"General Rakipov is here to see you, sir."

What could Rakipov want this early on a Monday morning? Stozharov thought. *It can't be anything good.* "Send him in." Rakipov projected an urbane, businesslike appearance that he had cultivated in trying to change the image of his ministry. MB officers now dressed like midlevel managers at IBM, but the organization was still staffed and run by KGB-trained personnel, and Stozharov never forgot that for a moment. Rakipov and his type were still needed in the Republic as a counter to the reactionary forces waiting in the wings, but they were never to be trusted. They served much the same function in the Republic as they had in the Union, but their continued existence required that they be much less visible.

"Igor Igorovich, this is indeed a surprise. Please sit down." Rakipov took a chair while Stozharov retreated behind the desk. "A visit by the head of the Ministry of Security at such an hour could only be on a matter of some importance. What is it?"

"Perhaps nothing, but the subject possibly relates to accusations by the Americans that our Northern Military District is selling atomic weapons. I felt you would want to be briefed on it personally and as soon as possible." Stozharov sat back and motioned for Rakipov to continue. "Our agent SABLE, perhaps our most reliable operative in Washington, has reported that the Americans are taking some rather bold steps on our soil—possibly in the Kola." Rakipov repeated the conversation between Charles Grey III and his cronies at The Safehouse.

Stozharov leaned forward, elbows on the desk. "Have you anything that can substantiate this information or verify it?"

"No, Mr. President, we do not. SABLE's past reporting has been highly reliable, but we have no corroborating information." Rakipov was careful to keep any inflection from his voice. This could develop into a crisis, and his primary objective was to avoid any fallout or blame. But as MB Director, he also commanded the two-hundred-and-forty-thousand-man army of border guards, so he was vulnerable if a group of Americans had somehow entered Russia undetected.

Stozharov pondered this development. "Do you have a written report on this?" Rakipov pulled a single sheet of paper, folded lengthwise, from his inside jacket pocket and laid it on the desk.

"I have the only other copy," he said, as if to imply "you can trust me—up to a point."

"Very well, General. I appreciate your bringing this personally to my attention." He rose, signaling an end to the meeting. "You will let me know at once if there are any further developments concerning this matter."

"At once, Mr. President."

After Rakipov left, Stozharov sat at his desk, slowly shaking his head. *It's inconceivable that William Bennett would do such a thing. If not Bennett, then maybe it was the work of that fox Morton Keeney—if the report was accurate!*

Stozharov pounded the intercom. "Get in touch with Minister Solovyov. Tell him I want to see him immediately."

"Yes, Mr. President."

Vladimir Solovyov understood Stozharov's Monday-morning habits, and unless he was traveling, was never far away. Five minutes later, the Foreign Minister rapped softly on the door and stepped inside.

"We may have more problems in the Kola, Vladimir," Stozharov said, handing him the single-page report left by Rakipov. Solovyov sat down and carefully read the document while Stozharov paced behind the desk. Finally, he pursed his lips as he laid the paper back on the desk.

"Well?" The President of Russia stood with his hands on the back of his chair, glowering down at his Foreign Minister.

"SABLE has been one of our most trusted agents for a number of years. His information is invariably accurate. If we are to believe this report, and assume it pertains to activity in the Kola, then this 'agent in place' would have to be an American agent at our production facility there. And as crazy as it sounds, the Americans have sent some sort of a team or military unit there to contact him."

"How would they do this?"

Solovyov shrugged. "Traditionally they would parachute them in or put them ashore by submarine. Perhaps they came by merchant ship or masquerading as fishermen, but midwinter in the Barents Sea is most inhospitable. The whole notion seems so unlikely, and yet, can we afford to ignore it? More to the point, do we call it to General Borzov's attention?"

"Warn him the Americans may have infiltrated the Kola to stop the sale of nuclear weapons, something he has told us is not taking place?"

"Exactly."

"You've met Borzov. What do you think of him?"

Solovyov frowned. "Competent, patriotic, a strong leader, and except for this business with the nuclear weapons—completely loyal."

"My impression exactly," said Stozharov, turning to the intercom. "Tanya, get me a secure line to Colonel General Borzov in Severomorsk, top priority."

Murmansk and Severomorsk were in the same time zone as Moscow, but the state of Russian communications was such that it took almost two hours for the connection to be made. Stozharov silently cursed Rakipov, whose ministry also controlled the Federal Agency for Communications and was responsible for secure government communications.

Colonel General Borzov was conducting an inspection of a motor-rifle regiment bivouacked near Guba. He smiled as he walked along a line of armored vehicles. The men and the equipment looked superb. Given the resources available and the harsh conditions, they had done an extraordinary job. He took time to commend each unit commander as well as to shake the hands of several of the first sergeants. *This is what it's all about,* he thought proudly as he moved on to inspect their defensive positions. *The sons and grandsons of those who fought the Great Patriotic War are still willing to endure hardship in defense of the fatherland.*

He had just sat down with some enlisted men at a makeshift field-mass table for a bowl of watery soup when his aide came running up.

"General, forgive me, but there is an urgent call for you on the radiophone. It is from Moscow."

Borzov rose, motioning the soldiers to remain seated. "As you were, men. It seems my duties have saved me from this wretched soup, but I thank you for the splendid company." They laughed and applauded him as he followed the aide at a brisk walk. The regiment had a communications tent better staffed with personnel than equipment. An officer extended him a handset.

"This is General Borzov."

"Please hold, sir." While he waited, he realized just how much he would rather be back with those young men drinking that tasteless, watery soup than waiting on a call from Moscow.

"General Borzov," President Stozharov shouted into the receiver. He glanced irritably at his watch—10:15 A.M.

There was burst of static on the line as the secure connections were made. "Yes, this is Colonel General Borzov speaking." The scrambler slightly altered his voice, but Stozharov recognized it.

"General, this is President Stozharov. I must speak to you quite plainly. Six weeks ago I sent Foreign Minister Solovyov to Severomorsk to speak with you about reports of the sale of certain weapons from the Northern Military District."

"Yes, Mr. President," Borzov replied carefully. His tone was respectful but not deferential.

"Well, we now have information that the Americans, in a response to what they believe to be happening there, have put military personnel into the Kola to try and stop it. General, I am going to tell you very candidly all that we know of this matter. Then I will ask that you do your duty as a Russian general officer and take the proper action."

"I am listening, Mr. President."

Five minutes later, Borzov handed the phone back to the communications officer. He stood there a moment, oblivious to the men standing at attention around him.

"Major," he said to his aide, "we must return to Severomorsk immediately. Have the car brought around." Then, to the communications officer, "I need a secure line to District Headquarters, personally to Admiral Zaitsev." The Admiral was on the line in less than five minutes.

"Yes, General. I was notified of the call for you from Moscow. Is there a problem?"

"I'm afraid so, Alexandr. It seems there may be an intruder or even a possible military penetration aimed at our special project in Lumbovskiy. I want you to place a tactical air squadron and an attack helicopter squadron on standby, and have two companies of SPETSNAZ prepared for rapid response. And if you have any naval units in the area, have them alerted."

"Understood, General. Anything else?"

"Not at this time. I'm leaving Guba immediately for headquarters."

Borzov strode from the communications tent to the staff car. Unlike many general officers, it was his practice to ride up with the driver while his aide rode in back. They were only thirty miles from Severomorsk, but it would take the better part of an hour to get there.

Sergei Valclav plodded through the streets of Gremikha in the direction of the waterfront, huffing clouds of steam into the dry air. The weather had cleared and turned colder. His cap was pulled low over his ears, and his hands thrust deep into the pockets of his pea coat. A seaman's bag was slung over his shoulder. They had arrived on the outskirts of town not far from their previous rendezvous point shortly before eight o'clock, and it had taken him another hour to change clothes and make his way across town. The rest of the team was well hidden, but not nearly as safe as they had been at the base camp. Something as trivial as an inquisitive, vocal dog could upset their timetable and put their plan in jeopardy. The storm of the previous afternoon had blown itself out and a fresh set of tracks now connected them with the base camp.

"Sergei—welcome back. What can I get you?" The tavernkeeper was always glad to see a paying customer, especially one that could become a regular if the past several days were any indication.

"A vodka, and one for yourself, my friend. Tell me, have you seen Eduard, the fellow with the truck? I was with a man last night who may have some work for him."

"He'll be glad to hear it. It's a little early for Eduard, but I can get word to him if you like. What kind of work?"

"Just the delivery of some building materials, but he needs to have it done before noon," Valclav said casually. He knocked back his drink and signaled for another one. The tavernkeeper called one of the other patrons to the bar, and after a few words, the man nodded and left. Then he hurried to refill Valclav's glass.

"Is there a telephone here I can use?" He placed two ten-thousand-ruble notes on the bar."

"Certainly—it's in the back room. Just come around behind the bar."

It took him nearly fifteen minutes to get through to Dr. Katrina Shebanin. Only his insistence that it concerned her brother and that it was very important finally moved the local operator to place the call into the Lumbovskiy facility. Then the operator who took the call at Lumbovskiy questioned Dr. Shebanin about the call before she was sternly directed by the Doctor to make the connection.

"Hello, this is Dr. Shebanin speaking."

"Doctor, my name is Yuri Simonovski, and I am a friend of your brother. I met him in Novosibirsk about six months ago and he made me promise to call if I was ever in the area?"

"I haven't seen Sergei in some time—is he well?"

"He's fine and sends his love."

"Will you see him again?

"Yes, most definitely. I will be seeing him in a few weeks, since I plan to leave Gremikha this afternoon. He wanted to know if you're keeping up with your cross-county skiing?"

"Tell him I am—fact, I'll be doing some skiing this very afternoon."

"Splendid—he'll be glad to hear it. Well, I don't want to keep you. Sergei will be happy to know we talked."

"Thank you for calling, Mr. Simonovski. Good-bye."

When Valclav returned to the bar, the man named Eduard was there waiting for him. The tavernkeeper had poured him a drink, which Valclav graciously paid for. While they negotiated terms for the lease of his truck, Eduard's eyes kept flickering to the ruble notes on the bar.

All calls to and from the Lumbovskiy facility came through a small exchange that was carefully monitored.

"That was a call for Dr. Shebanin from a man who had news about her brother," said one of the women at the switchboard. "It was a strange call—I guess she hasn't seen him in a while."

"If he's anything like my brother," said the woman next to her, "she probably never wants to hear from him again."

"You're sure COMSUBLANT has been told the team is coming out, and that they'll notify the *Archerfish?"*

"That's correct, Major."

"How do we know they've received the message?"

"We don't. The ELF channel is a one-way communication system. The transmitters are up in Michigan and Wisconsin. They send a strong pulse into the bedrock of the earth, and it resonates through the earth. Submarines with ELF receivers can pick up the signal, but they can't respond. The message is repeated several times, and we just have to assume they get it. It's a very reliable system. Slow but reliable."

The Senior Watch Officer on duty was a Navy Commander, an aviator attached to the J-5 Plans staff. He was very competent, and had been sent to SOCOM to get his joint-service ticket punched so he could be promoted to captain. Right now, he'd had his fill of Major Janet Brisco, and was on the verge of punching her.

"You sure about that, Commander?"

"Oh yes, Major. Just as sure as snot is slick and plebes piss in the shower." He was also an Academy man.

Brisco was about to go after him when Master Chief Tolliver intervened. "Major Brisco, could you give me a hand over here?" She gave the SWO a brutal look and stepped over to where Tolliver was marking off distances on a chart of the Gremikha-Lumbovskiy area.

"What is it, Master Chief?"

"How does the scale on these charts work—is it every second or every minute of latitude that equals a mile?"

"It's every minute—hey, wait a sec, you know that!"

"Yes, ma'am, I do, and the SWO knows how to get messages through the Navy communications system to the *Archerfish.* These people are good—let 'em do their job." She gave him a long, cool stare. "We're gettin' down to the short strokes, ma'am. Y'all have to be thinkin' about those guys on the ground. What are their alternatives if somethin' goes wrong? What can they do if they can't get to the sub? What if somebody gets hurt? Let the watch team do their job. Pretend you're Moody in Gremikha, and you're tryin' to get down the coast to the weapons facility and out to meet the sub."

Brisco smiled. "That bad, huh?"

"Yes, ma'am."

"You're awfully perceptive for an enlisted man, Master Chief."

"I used to be dumb as a box of rocks. But when you make chief in the Navy, you're suddenly blessed with infinite wisdom."

"Like a sergeant in the Air Force?"

"I wouldn't quite go that far, ma'am, but you got the idea."

She put her hand on his arm. "Thanks, Master Chief."

Brisco looked at the clocks above the large, backlit chart of the Barents Sea on the wall. They gave the local time in Tampa as well as the time in London, Bonn, and Gremikha, and seconds were crawling by in all four locations. She turned toward the commotion across the room at one of the communications consoles.

"Major, we have some trouble, maybe big-time trouble." The SWO handed her a message:

FROM: CIA LANGLEY
TO: SOCOM//JCS//NCR
SENSITIVE HANDLING//CLASSIFICATION BEARCAT

AFLOAT, AIRBORNE AND SPACEBORNE COMINT AND ELINT PLATFORMS ALL REPORTING A MAJOR SURGE IN RADIO/ELECTRONIC EMISSIONS. ACTIVITY PARTICULARLY STRONG AMONG C3 COMPONENTS MURMANSK AREA. TACAIR AND SELECTED ARMY UNITS HAVE BEEN PLACED ON STANDBY. CARTER SENDS.

"Damn! Do we have a comm window open!"

"Not for another hour and a half, Major."

"Double-damn! Notify the *Archerfish* we have a problem. Have them stand by to go active."

"Yes, ma'am!"

"Is that jammer in place?"

The Senior Watch Officer leaned over a console where an Army communications specialist was furiously pounding a keyboard. "He's on line and ready to go, but we need General Thon's authorization."

"Get it!"

The SWO snatched the green phone, not stopping to reflect that Air Force majors don't give orders to Navy commanders.

Eduard drove the one-ton, covered stake truck to a fuel depot owned by one of the local fishing companies, and with the money Valclav gave him, filled the tank. After a price was negotiated and the fueling complete, he climbed back up into the cab. He felt so smug at having arranged a good price on the fuel, with a healthy kickback to him, he failed to notice the change in Valclav's dress until they were a block from the depot. His trousers and pea coat were rolled into a ball on the floorboard, and he now wore the green uniform of an MB border guard.

"What's going on—I do not understand!" pleaded Eduard, fearing that he was the victim of a sting operation. "I am just a driver—I only acted on your direction."

"Correct, and you will continue to act on my orders, for your life as well as your profits now depend on it." He took a Sig Sauer 9mm automatic from under the roll of clothes and pushed it in Eduard's ribs. "Turn left on the main road and drive in the direction of Iokanga." Valclav then took a Motorola Saber from his pocket and extended the aerial. "Get ready—I'll be there in a few minutes." Eduard's eyes widened. He was no linguist, but he knew English when it was spoken. Valclav directed him to take a deserted side road as they reached the edge of the city, and they drove for nearly a half mile.

"Stop here. Good, now flash your lights twice and turn them off."

In a few minutes, five men—one of them pulling a small, square, heavily loaded sled, materialized out of the twilight. They were dressed in loose white coveralls and moved with purpose. Eduard's mind raced. At first he thought they were smugglers, but they seemed too disciplined. They could be soldiers, but why were they speaking English? *Perhaps they are both!* he concluded. The men in white loaded the sled and its contents into the truck and climbed aboard. One of them banged the back window of the cab twice to signal they were ready.

"Now listen closely, my friend. I can kill you here and now, or you can do exactly as I say, stay alive, and earn a bonus. Which will it be, eh?"

Moments later, Eduard was carefully picking his way east along the snow-packed road that led from Gremikha to Iokanga and Lumbovskiy.

A hundred miles north out over the Barents Sea, Major Frank Tipton sat in the left-hand seat of the RC-135 as it circled in a lazy orbit at thirty-five thousand feet. The modified Boeing 707 was on autopilot, allowing Tipton to leaf through the most recent *Far Side* edition.

"Gary Larson's got a handle on it," he remarked into the intercom to his copilot. "He should be elected to Congress along with the rest of the clowns." His copilot smiled and nodded as his eyes swept the instrument panel.

"Hey, Skipper." Tipton was instantly alert—it was his electronic warfare officer, or EWO. "We have a message directing us to radiate on the Russian HF and UHF military command frequencies."

Tipton put the cartoon book aside. "Do we have authentication?"

"Yes, sir. We're fully cleared for jamming operations."

Tipton and the other pilot made eye contact. "Okay, Johnny, it's your show now—light the fire." The EWO rogered up and went to work.

The RC-135 was a flying broadcasting station whose function was to selectively jam enemy command, control, and communication (C3) networks. The aircraft was crammed with electronic equipment, and was capable of radiating a great deal of power. Normal Russian military radio traffic was carried on HF bands, while their SATCOM was all UHF. Once the RC-135's jamming transmitters were turned on, the military radio receivers along the Kola coast began to hear nothing but static. Many of these radios were equipped with frequency-hopping capabilities, but the computers aboard the 135 followed these frequency shifts and made them unusable.

There was little more for Tipton and his copilot to do, but they were now both fully alert, scanning the dull glow above the land mass to the south. Even from their vantage almost seven miles high, the sun was still below the horizon. The RC-135s had been used with great success during the Panama invasion and in the Gulf War, but there was a big difference. Panama had no fighter aircraft, and over Persian Gulf, there was usually a section of F-15s parked on their wing. Jamming was a hostile act, and it wouldn't take the Russians long to figure out where it was coming from. Given the time it would take them to climb out they were about ten minutes away, as the MiG flies, from the fighter bases near Murmansk. And with the jammers radiating, they would be very easy to find. Tipton keyed his radio.

"Overlord, this is Popeye, over."

"Go ahead, Popeye."

"Overlord, we are hot, I say again, we are hot. Keep a sharp lookout, over."

"Roger, Popeye—we copy you hot. We'll keep you posted, over."

"Roger, Popeye out."

The E-3A Sentry was another 707 airframe, but this one was modified for airborne warning and control. It was orbiting another hundred miles to the northwest. Tipton calculated that if the AWACs caught the fighters coming off the ground, it would take them less than thirty minutes to run the RC-135 down in a stern chase. The planners back at the Pentagon figured the Russians wouldn't chance shooting down an American aircraft that was almost two hundred miles off their coast in international airspace. It was a rational assumption. But the planners didn't have to fly the mission, and if a Russian fighter jock proved to be irrational, Tipton knew they wouldn't stand a chance.

Ninety miles south and slightly east of the orbiting RC-135 jammer, the *Archerfish* waited patiently under the pack ice.

"Skipper, I have some traffic on the ELF." Griffin, Smith, and Dawgs all gathered around the radioman who sat at the small communications console. The ELF receiver laboriously printed the characters while the RM carefully typed them into his computer. The ELF system was like a huge bass drum that beat low-frequency pulses into the earth, and it was very slow—only a few characters per minute. The characters identified the particular submarine or submarines called and usually referred to predetermined commands or coded instructions carried aboard the sub in their code books. After a long fifteen minutes, the RM tapped in the final characters and the computer quickly spit out a finished translation:

> STAND BY FOR PICKUP 1200-2400(L)//BE PREPARED TO ACTIVATE DF ON COMMAND//COMPROMISE OF TEAM PROBABLE//TAKE ALL PRECAUTIONS//

"Skipper?" Griffin tugged on his ear as he reread the message.

"If they know they're there, we have to assume they know we're here." He handed the message to Smith, who read it along with Dawgs. "Get your DF mast ready to go, Graham, and tell the escape-trunk operators to stand by."

"Aye, aye, sir. Do we want to go to general quarters?"

Griffin considered it. "Not yet. Let's wait until they get here. If that Akula's waiting for us when we come out from under the pack ice, we may be at GQ for quite a while.

The stake truck reached Iokanga just before noon, passing the turnoff that led to the airfield at Kachalovka. The OMON encampment near the intersection was dimly lit, and the dark line of lumps formed by the row of barracks was just barely visible in the midday twilight. Valclav lit two cigarettes and handed one to Eduard. It was a fairly smooth ride in the cab, and the heater worked very well. Valclav smiled as he thought of the Navymen bouncing around on the drafty hardwood bed behind him.

"You've driven this road before?"

"Yes. I have delivered supplies to the facility at Lumbovskiy."

"Have you driven past Lumbovskiy?"

"No, it is a restricted road. You need a pass to continue on. There's a guardhouse alongside the road."

Valclav nodded. From Lumbovskiy, there was nothing for seventy-five miles until the road reached Ponoy, the largest town on the eastern half of the Kola. The road was restricted, not for military reasons, but to prevent its use by smugglers. And there were safety considerations. A breakdown along the way could prove to be fatal, so only military traffic and travelers with permits were allowed use of the road. *Well, my uniform will serve as my pass,* Valclav thought, *that or my pistol. One way or another, we will use the road.*

General Borzov reached his headquarters just after midday. Instead of going to his office, he went straight to the operations center, leaving instructions with the duty officer for Admiral Zaitsev to join him there. The Northern District HQ Operations Center was very similar to the Crisis Management Center at SOCOM except that it was bigger, with less sophisticated equipment and many more people. All the status boards, situational plots, and unit locations were updated by hand on the maps and display boards around the room. And unlike the CMC, there were no women present among the uniformed personnel.

"What's happening?" Borzov demanded as he returned the Operations Watch Officer's salute.

"Sir, the 92nd Fighter Squadron is prepared to scramble and on a ten-minute standby. The Third Battalion of the Seventh SPETSNAZ Brigade is at the ready. A squadron of Mi-8 transport helicopters are en route to the SPETSNAZ camp, and another squadron of Hind gunships are standing by awaiting further orders. We have no surface combatants at sea, but two Udeloy-class destroyers are now underway from Kolskiy Inlet for the Barents Sea. There is one attack submarine at sea on training exercises along the central Kola coast.

Borzov nodded and turned to Admiral Zaitsev, who had just entered. "Admiral?"

"Something is definitely happening. There is an airborne jammer well out in the Barents Sea that is smothering all our HF and UHF communications. Our electronic people tell us that only the American RC-135 has this capability and the range to reach an airborne station in the Barents. Our tactical communications are all but impossible unless we rely on microwave relay and line-of-sight transmissions."

"What do you recommend?"

"We have to neutralize that jammer. I suggest that we launch a flight of MiG interceptors. And since air control may be difficult, they should be instructed to take no offensive action if the jammer ceases operations or moves out of effective range."

"And if he doesn't?"

"The jamming is clearly a hostile act. If the aircraft continues to radiate, they should be warned off with cannon fire, and if they persist—shot down."

Borzov hesitated. KAL-007, the Korean 747 that was shot down over Sakhalin Island, was mistaken for an RC-135. *But what choice do I have?* "Very well, but make sure the section leader of that flight fully understands his rules of engagement. He is to first warn them before he shoots to kill."

Zaitsev said something to an Air Force major on duty in the Operations Center. The major saluted curtly and left. "And what of the site at Lumbovskiy, General?"

Borzov took him to one side. "Stozharov tells me that the Americans have an agent at Lumbovskiy—a very well-placed agent. We have to seal off the facility, but if possible, we have to do so without raising the alarm."

"Until the jammer is neutralized, we have to rely on land lines. Any call to Lumbovskiy will go through their switchboard and then through the Facility Director. You don't think it's Zhdanov?"

"I don't know," but a sad, cold feeling in his stomach told him it might not be. "Call the OMON detachment at Iokanga and have Colonel Makarov take control of the facility." Zaitsev frowned: "I know, but we have no choice. Then I want two companies of that SPETSNAZ battalion lifted to Kachalovka along with the attack helicopters. Have a helicopter pick me up here, and I will meet them there on the tarmac. You will remain here and in full control of District forces, and I will take charge of the tactical units at Kachalovka."

After Borzov left to change into a field uniform and trade his greatcoat for a parka, Zaitsev called over one of his naval aides.

"Get one of our naval air communications aircraft aloft at once. Direct them to order Captain Molev to make his way to Lumbovskiy at flank speed, and to be on the lookout for an intruder submarine—probably an American boat."

Valclav motioned for Eduard to slow down as the guard stepped from the guard shack and held up his hand. Just past the small shack, a well-traveled spur turned left into the Lumbovskiy site while the main road, which showed signs of far less traffic, continued on to Ponoy. The perimeter fence of the facility and a well-lighted guard post were visible where the spur road entered the compound some fifty meters from the main road. A glimpse of the buildings inside was just barely possible in the fading light.

Eduard stopped at the guard's direction. The man curiously approached the passenger's side of the cab. He was dressed exactly like Valclav, except for the Kalashnikov AKM slung over his shoulder.

"Good day to you," Valclav said, smiling broadly as he rolled down the window. He clutched the pistol at his side out of sight. He knew that a number of automatic weapons behind the canvas to his rear were also trained on the guard.

"May I see your pass?" He eyed Valclav closely, recognizing the uniform but not the face.

He gave the guard an incredulous look. "You weren't told?"

"Told what?"

"The man you relieved didn't tell you that we would be coming back?"

"What's going on?" The guard took a step back and looked at the canvas-covered bed.

"I guess he kept it all for himself." Valclav smiled and shook his head. "I was told you fellows at the garrison in Gremikha were a crafty bunch, and now I know why. I'm from the garrison at Ponoy. We had some, ah, special supplies to pick up in Gremikha. My explanation of this matter to the man on duty this morning was, ah, most generous. He said he would make it right with you."

"He said nothing to me," the guard said carefully.

"I guess that's my loss. Then perhaps I should show you my pass." Valclav handed him two ten-thousand-ruble notes—about forty dollars. The guard palmed them.

"Just what are these supplies for our brothers at the Ponoy garrison?"

"I was told that it would be of no concern to you." He handed him another note.

"Very well," said the guard as he touched a mittened hand to his fur-lined cap. "You are cleared to pass."

After they had cleared the guard shack, Valclav dropped the hammer on the automatic and pushed it into his belt. A rivulet of sweat ran from Eduard's hair down along his temple.

The cross-country ski trail from Lumbovskiy had joined the main road to Ponoy across from the guard shack, and ran parallel along the shoulder between the road and the coast. Valclav ordered Eduard to slow down. Five minutes later, the headlights picked up a lone skier gliding along the trail, moving away from Lumbovskiy. The skier wore a light pack and cast nervous backward glances.

"Flash your lights twice and pull over just ahead of the skier." Eduard did as he was told. "Good—now keep the motor running and your eyes straight ahead."

Valclav slipped from the cab and Garniss quickly took his place. He had a rifle on his lap and a smile on his face. Eduard stared straight ahead and said nothing.

"Doctor Shebanin, this is my officer, Lieutenant Moody. He is in charge of our group."

"It's a pleasure to meet you, Doctor," Moody said.

Katrina Shebanin had just stepped out of her ski bindings when the men began pouring from the back of the truck. It reminded her of stories her grandmother told about her youth in Vologda—about the *Cheka,* when soldiers came in the night to take people away. It made her shiver. She was relieved to see Valclav, even in the border-guard uniform. He had told her to travel light, so she was dressed in wool touring slacks and a heavy sweater under a vinyl parka. She pulled the ski cap from her head, shaking free her brown hair that was only partially controlled by a ponytail.

"Your skis, ma'am," said one of the men, who took her skis and poles and slid them into the bed of the truck.

"I appreciate what you're doing for us," Moody continued, "and I can understand how hard this must be for you." Valclav had told him that her English was good but that he should speak slowly. "Well, that is not entirely true, Doctor—I do not know. It must take a great deal of courage to leave your homeland."

"Thank you, *Leytenant."* The taillight of the truck gave them some illumination, and Katrina tried to read Moody's face in the dim red light. Valclav spoke highly of his officer, and she had no choice but to trust Valclav. *No,* Leytenant *Moody, you can't know how hard this is, but I appreciate your saying so.*

"The documents, Doctor Shebanin. You have them?"

She had wanted to hold on to them for a while—until they were out of the country, she hoped. *If I try to hold back, they will just take them from me. Again, I have no choice but to trust this man—this boy, really.* She pulled the pack from her shoulder and opened it, handing Moody a file. She said nothing, but her eyes told him that she was placing her life in his hands.

Moody received the folder solemnly, as if it were a sacred offering, and bowed his head in acknowledgment. "Thank you, Doctor. Now, if you will excuse me for just a moment." He walked across the road to where Snyder had the SATCOM antenna concealed in some brush and the components laid out on a piece of canvas.

"We up yet?"

"Not quite, sir." He checked his watch. "I should have the satellite in about five minutes."

"Great. That should give you enough time to scan these documents into the computer. Get them out with our final SITREP just as soon as you have an uplink. I want to be out of here as quickly as possible."

"Aye, sir."

Moody went back to Valclav and Shebanin. "We have to communicate with our headquarters," he said carefully. "Tell me, Dr. Shebanin, have you ever heard about scuba?"

"Sku-bah?" she replied.

"Yes. Underwater breathing apparatus—aqualung—Jacques Costeau."

"Oh—sku-bah. Yes, I know." Then her eyes widened with fear and understanding. "I know, but I do not do!"

"Doctor, I want you to listen to me carefully. You are a scientist—I want you to think like one. From where we stand here to where my friend is with our radio is about twenty-five meters, correct?"

"Well, yes."

"It is not far, but that is the distance you will have to travel underwater if you are to leave with us. We promised to take you with us, but this is what you must do. It will be difficult, but if you do exactly what we tell you, it will not be dangerous. We will guide you and help you along. You will never be alone. Do you understand?"

She swallowed hard, almost too shocked and afraid to speak. "Yes, I understand."

Atta girl, Moody thought, but it didn't seem like the right thing to say. "Excellent. This is Petty Officer Walker. He is our most experienced diver. He will explain what you are to do. He and one of the other men who will escort you on your short underwater swim to safety and freedom."

"Ma'am," said Walker, who waited at Moody's shoulder.

Another boy, thought Shebanin. *But I have no choice but to trust these children. I'm dead if I stay, but the thought of going underwater is as frightening as death itself.* "Just tell me what it is I have to do, and I will do it." Her voice was filled with equal measures of resolve and resignation.

"Hey! Mr. Moody!" It was Snyder. Moody trotted across the road. "They copied our traffic. Now the Major wants you on secure voice." He passed him the handset.

High over the Barents Sea, Major Tipton and the crew of his RC-135 sustained their orbit and their frequency-jamming offensive against the C3 networks of the Russian Northern Military District. The aircraft was more than vulnerable—it was an electronic beacon that shouted to enemy fighters, *Here I am, over here—huge radar picture, limited maneuverability, an easy SAM target!*

"Popeye, this is Overlord, over."

"This is Popeye, go."

"I have a flight of MiG-29Ks that are just climbing out and will cross the coast in less than a minute. Look's like it's Miller time, over."

"That's a roger, Overlord—keep us posted. Popeye out."

Even while he was talking, Tipton had pulled the 135 into a tight turn away from the coast and put the nose down for some additional speed. His copilot shoved the four throttles all the way forward. They would continue to radiate while they ran, but would shut down well before the MiGs came within missile range.

"Moody, where in the hell are you?"

"Just like the SITREP says, we're about four miles east of the bomb factory. What gives?" The voice was very clear. Except for a two-second delay for the scrambler to code and encode the transmission, it was like a Sprint commercial without Candice Bergen.

"You're hot, John! The Russians know something's up and there's a bunch of military units on the move. We were able to jam their C-three for a short while, but that's no longer the case. The tac frequencies are alive again. They're looking for someone, and we think it's you."

"We're headed for the boat now. Good copy on the fax?"

"Fuck the fax—get the hell out of there!"

"Roger, Moody out."

He tossed the handset to Snyder. "Pack it up and throw it on the truck. The Russians are right behind us." A minute later they were on the move again. Katrina sat between Valclav and Eduard, and was able to point out the road that turned off to Obornyy Spit and the coast. It was snow-blown but passable. They were five miles from the pack ice.

At SOCOM headquarters, Major Janet Brisco sat on a stool near one of the communications stations. The CMC was air-conditioned, but her light-blue uniform blouse was sweat-stained under the armpits. Master Chief Tolliver gave her a grin and a thumbs-up.

"What now, Major?" said the SWO.

"Get an ELF signal to the *Archerfish.* Have them go active with their DF. Those guys are going to be booking across that pack ice, and they aren't going to have time to stop for a SATNAV fix."

"Uh, I don't know quite how to say this, Major, but I've been ordered to keep the *Archerfish* passive and out of play for the time being."

"What in the hell are you talking about!" She was screaming, and every head in the CMC turned. Tolliver was right beside her.

"The *Archerfish* is not a player until further notice—I'm sorry."

"Says who!"

"The General. He called while you were talking to Lieutenant Moody."

"Goddammit, he can't do this!" Brisco grabbed the green phone and punched Thon's number, almost ramming the buttons into the set—busy signal. She threw the receiver at the cradle and missed badly. "I'll go see the sonovabitch myself," she said to no one in particular as she headed for the door.

"Mind if I tag along?"

"Suit yourself, Master Chief," and she was out the door.

"You better take along a leash and a muzzle, Chief," said the SWO.

"She's just looking out for her men, sir," Tolliver said defensively.

"I know she is, but tell her to go easy. I doubt this was Thon's idea."

"Good point—thanks, Commander," he said and hurried after her.

In the basement of the White House, a small group of very grim-faced men sat in padded chairs around a mahogany conference table in the Situation Room. A chart of the Barents Sea from the North Cape to the White Sea had been affixed to one of the sliding wall displays along with a large-scale map of the Gremikha-Lumbovskiy area. There was a bank of phones along the wall, and a communications suite manned by an Air Force colonel and an NSA communications technician. When the Russian forces had gone on alert, the President had called his advisers into executive session in the Situation Room. It was apparent that the special operations team must make good their escape very soon, or they were sure to be captured, bringing on a whole new set of problems. And there was the matter of the *Archerfish,* now well inside Russian territorial waters. General Winston Scott and Armand Grummell were both on the telephone, while the President sat at the table with Morton Keeney, Defense Secretary James Garza, and Secretary of State Richard Noffsinger. Visions of Dwight Eisenhower apologizing for the U-2 flight of Francis Gary Powers danced through Bennett's head. *I don't give a damn!* he thought. *It was still the right thing to do.*

It was ten minutes past six. There were cups and juice glasses strewn around the table, and a plate of breakfast rolls in the center that had hardly been touched. Most of them had been called from their beds shortly after Russian forces had been put on notice. Grummel finally hung up, and Scott put his party on hold to join them at the table.

"Okay, gentlemen," Bennett began, "where are we?" He looked first to Noffsinger on his left.

"We're getting nothing from Moscow. Ambassador Simpson has repeatedly tried to place a call to Foreign Minister Solovyov, but he has been 'unavailable.' "

"Armand?"

"The team has accomplished their mission," he replied with what seemed to be a touch of sadness, "and quite commendably, I might add. I just talked with my people, and they report we have a good document copy with plans, specifications, and production records of the nuclear weapons they were preparing for sale. Preliminary inspection of the data indicates they've prepared, or have in process, one hundred weapons for export."

"And the team?" He looked to James Garza, who deferred to General Scott.

"They're on their way to rendezvous with the submarine, but they could still be as much as two or three hours away."

"And the agent—our friend MUSTANG who has been so helpful?"

"She's with the team en route to the sub."

"She?" Bennett arched his eyebrows and looked at Grummell, who nodded grimly. The President sighed heavily. "What next? So, where do we go from here?"

"We get them out of there as soon as possible," said Garza. "The team leader says he will bring the agent with them if he can, but General Thon's people at SOCOM think this is all but impossible."

"I agree," said Noffsinger. "The quicker we get our people back and remove the potential for an incident, the better for all concerned. I have an ambassador in Moscow who's really sweating this one."

The President saw Grummell and Keeney exchange an uncomfortable glance. They both seemed reluctant. "Mort?"

Keeney shrugged slightly and looked at Bennett. "Mr. President, the objectives of this mission have been accomplished, and we now have six American military men in a position where they stand a good chance of being taken prisoner by the Russians no matter what we do. That was a risk we accepted when the mission was undertaken. Now we have the larger problem of the *Archerfish.* The possible capture of a U.S. man-of-war in Russian territorial waters is another and far more serious problem. And the longer she remains there, the higher the probability that she could be trapped there and forced to the surface—or worse if she's challenged and fails to surface."

"What are you suggesting, Mort?"

The National Security Advisor held the President's gaze, but it was not easy for him. "I'm suggesting only that a case can be made for sacrificing the team and MUSTANG. Let the Russians have them, and get the *Archerfish* out of there now."

"Por Dios! Are you out of your mind!" Garza was on his feet.

"You can't be serious!" added Noffsinger.

"Take it easy, gentlemen—please, sit down. You're all paid for your advice and your opinions, no matter how unpleasant they are. Go ahead, Morton."

"President Stozharov can't be comfortable with what his commander up there is doing. We have enough information to give the Russian Republic the kind of bad publicity they don't need right now. It could even abort the aid package now before Congress, not to mention support from the EC. There's a good chance the Russians will quietly return our people *and* stop the sale to keep us from taking this information to the international community."

"And there's a good chance they will cry foul," pleaded Noffsinger, "and drag *us* through the United Nations!"

"Oh, come on, Richard," said Armand Grummell in a gentle, Socratic tone. "You're not thinking like a Russian. What are their objectives here? What would they accomplish? Of course they'd like to embarrass us, but that would force us to reveal the reason for the team being there. We'd accuse them of unauthorized weapons development and demand international inspections. No," continued Grummell, shaking his head slowly, "the Russians don't want their dirty laundry aired at the UN any more than we do."

"There's too many people at SOCOM and SOCEUR who know about this operation," said Garza. "How do you think they'll react to having a special operations team deliberately compromised?"

"They don't have to know it's deliberate," said Grummell quietly. "This is a complex operation. The *Archerfish* could be ordered from its current position due to the imminent threat from a Russian fast-attack sub. They had a brush with one off Murmansk just a few days ago on the way to their current location."

"Well, I'd know it, you bastards!" Garza was again on his feet.

"All right, that's enough! Jim, sit down," ordered Bennett. Garza sat down, but continued to glare at Keeney and Grummell. "Let's remember, gentlemen, that you're paid to make recommendations, and I'm paid to make decisions. I don't like to think about this course of action any more than you do, but when there's this much on the table, I want all the options. Whatever happens, it will be my decision and mine alone."

Brisco charged into a well-appointed reception area belonging to the Commander, U.S. Special Operations Command, past a startled Army colonel who served as his executive assistant, and into General Thon's private office.

"General, what in the hell do you think you're doing!"

Thon covered one end of the receiver but kept the earpiece pressed to the side of his head. He raised a clenched fist, the infantryman's signal to halt, but it was the cold, deadly look in his eyes that arrested Brisco's assault at the edge of the desk.

"Stand fast right where you are and keep your mouth shut!" The blocky general spoke with the low growl of a big dog who meant business.

Master Chief Tolliver slipped into the office a moment later and stood by the door. Thon made a cutting motion with his hand, and Tolliver closed the door in the face of the openmouthed EA, who still couldn't believe a field-grade officer and a senior enlisted man had just bolted past him into the Commander's office. For several long minutes,

Brisco and Tolliver endured Thon's icy gaze while he sat there with the phone pasted to his ear.

"Yes, sir . . . yes, sir . . . right away, sir . . . I understand, Mr. Secretary . . . thank you, sir." Thon slammed the STU-III receiver down and picked up the green one. Brisco started to say something, but another murderous look from Thon stopped her. "This is the Commander—get me the Senior Watch Officer . . . Hello, listen up—I want you to contact the *Archerfish* and tell them they are cleared to extract the team. Following the extraction they are to leave station as quickly and as quietly as possible." Thon listened while the watch officer read it back to him. "Correct—now get on it."

"General, what's going on? First I'm told that—"

"Major, shut up and listen to what I have to say! I'm the Commander and I do my job in this office. You're the operational controller and your job's in the Crisis Management Center. Now you get your butt back down there and do *your* job!"

Brisco hesitated a moment, but no longer. "Yes, *sir!*" She saluted, spun on her heel, and strode out of the office.

Navymen don't salute uncovered, so Tolliver just came to attention. "General," he said, and turned to leave.

"Master Chief?"

"Sir?"

"She's doing a good job—hang in there with her."

"Aye, aye, sir." Tolliver followed Brisco out the door. "Mornin', Colonel," he said to the EA, who stood behind his desk with a puzzled look on his face.

Just outside the facility at Gremikha, the border guard again smiled at his unexpected good fortune. He permitted himself another small sip of vodka, the warm glow in his stomach complementing the lump from the wad of ruble notes in his shirt pocket. He was feeling so contented, he did not hear the rumble of the BTR-80s pressing down on his guard shack until they were less than a hundred yards away. There were five of them bobbing along the road, the huge rubber tires throwing snow into the air amidst the blue clouds of diesel exhaust. Colonel Makarov sat in the turret of the lead machine with his fur tanker cap pulled down around his goggles and muffler. He glared disdainfully at the guard as he led the small column off the main road, turning left into the facility.

Makarov stopped at the guardhouse and leaped down from the BTR. He had not been able to reach his security-force commander, Major Alksnis, until they were a short distance from the facility, but Alksnis still managed to meet him at the gate.

"You have sealed off the compound?"

"Yes, Colonel, per your instructions."

"And Dr. Zhdanov knows nothing."

"If he does, it did not come from any of our personnel. If anyone asked, I instructed our people to say it was a security drill, and that it would last no more than an hour."

"Excellent. Now, let's go and have a talk with our pampered and indulged scientists."

"One more thing, Colonel," said Alksnis. "My guard here at the gate reported that a civilian truck approached the MB guard shack across the road some forty minutes before you arrived. The vehicle then headed west along the road to Ponoy. He says they get few civilian vehicles this time of year. He also says that Dr. Shebanin, the Director of Special Projects, left the base well over an hour ago on cross-country skis. This is not unusual. She often leaves at midday to ski along the trail that follows the Ponoy Road, but she is the only senior scientist out of the facility."

Makarov considered this. His orders were very specific—seal off the Lumbovskiy Site and personally see that no one entered or left. *Is that insolent bitch up to something? Is it she they were looking for?*

"Major, take charge and deploy the additional men at strategic locations throughout the complex. Then notify the detachment at Ponoy to seal off the road at their end, and be on the lookout for a civilian truck. I will patrol along the road and look for both the truck and the good doctor."

Makarov remounted the BTR, which pulled off the road, did a pivot turn in the snow, and headed back for the main road. The other armored vehicles rumbled into the Lumbovskiy facility. Makarov paused just long enough to question the border guard. He claimed the truck had a valid pass. Makarov suspected he had been bribed, but that in itself was not unusual in Russia. He ordered his driver to continue east along the main road. A few of the eight heavily armed OMON soldiers in the bay of the BTR idly wondered why they had returned to the main road while the rest of the company and the other BTRs stayed at the weapons facility. Most of them just shrugged and assumed it was their bad luck for having been assigned to ride in the Colonel's vehicle.

When the ELF message came in from COMSUBLANT, the crew of the *Archerfish* was ready. Most of them were already at their stations when the word was passed to stand by to get underway. Underway was technically correct, but the *Archerfish* only planned to move about forty-seven feet—straight up.

"All set, Graham?"

"Yes, sir. All stations manned and ready. The DF mast tests satisfactory and is in place."

"Very well, blow negative. Cob, we may feel her lift off the bottom, but I want you to sing out the second you actually see her move."

"Aye, aye, sir." Dawgs and the Quartermaster of the Watch stared at the two depth sounders, one mounted on the keel and the other on the main deck. The one on the keel would not register until the boat was off the bottom, but the deck-mounted transducer pinging on the pack ice above would register the first indication they were moving. The boat shed her port list, but nothing happened. She was now buoyant, but the suction of the mud bottom to the hull held her in place.

"All ahead one third."

"All ahead one third, sir . . . maneuvering answers ahead one third, sir."

"Very well . . . All stop."

"All stop, sir . . . maneuvering answers all stop, sir."

"Very well."

Dawgs just saw the digital readout on the surface fathometer flash down a half foot, but Griffin had already felt the boat move.

"Be sharp, people—we're moving. Call 'em out, Cob."

"Aye, sir . . . sixty feet from the pack to the main deck . . . fifty-eight . . . fifty-five . . . fifty . . . forty-five . . . forty . . ."

"Flood negative!"

"Flood negative, aye."

". . . thirty five . . . thirty . . . twenty-five . . . twenty-one . . ." There was a slight jolt in the control room as the DF probe that projected six feet above the top of the sail rammed through the pack ice, pushed by the eighteen-hundred-ton submarine. The trick for Griffin was to bring the sub from its resting place on the bottom to a position under the pack ice *gently.* The *Archerfish* didn't have an armored sail, nor were the fair-water plains mounted on her sail capable of rotating to the vertical as they would have been if she had been designed to break through the ice. In fact, she could be seriously damaged if Griffin couldn't control her ascent and bring her up softly under the pack. He had done this by flooding her negative buoyancy tank to slow her ascent. Now that he had her there, he had to keep her there.

"Blow negative."

"Blow negative, aye."

They waited a long minute in silence. "How's she holding, Cob?"

"She's pinned there like a sailor under a fat whore, Skipper." There were smiles around the control, and even a grin from the Captain.

"Very well. Okay, Graham, fire up your DF."

Lieutenant Commander Smith had come up with the idea of rigging a hydraulically actuated steel mast to the side of the sail that would serve as a DF antenna. Since the sail of the *Archerfish* was not pressurized, it had been a simple matter to weld a sturdy pivot point to the sail and attach a piston actuator-arm to erect the mast from a horizontal position where it was stored while the boat was underway. While the sail of the

Archerfish hugged the underside of the pack ice, Smith's jury-rigged DF called to his brother SEALs across the windblown snow world above the pack.

The road ended at an abandoned lighthouse on the tip of Obornyy Spit. The truck's lights peered across the pack ice, which looked like a wrinkled white bedspread. Moody and Garniss came up to confer with Valclav, who climbed down from the cab.

"Can we drive on it?"

"Don't see why not. If we get stuck, we got plenty of guys to push, although it could get pretty rough farther out."

"What about the driver?"

"We better settle up with him now. I still have about two thousand dollars in rubles—that should cover it." Valclav walked around and jerked Eduard from cab, then handed him a fat roll of bills. "Better hide it in your boot—they might search you when they find you."

"Find me?"

"That's right, and they're probably not too far behind."

Eduard did as he was told and stuffed the bills into his boot. Valclav then took the pistol from his belt and whipped Eduard viciously across the face with it, sending him back onto the truck fender. He struck him twice more.

"What in the hell are you doing?" Moody said, grabbing his arm.

"He'll tell them that we forced him to help us. Now they'll believe him—maybe even let him go."

Moody looked down at the Russian. He was conscious, but he was bleeding from the nose and mouth. His face was already starting to swell.

"That's what I like about you, Sarge," said Garniss. "You're such a caring person."

"Hey, Boss! They're up!" The canvas tarp had been rolled back, and Snyder was standing in the bed of the truck, leaning over the cab with a DF receiver. He was pointing in a northerly direction out across the pack ice. "I got a good signal!"

"Let's get out of here," Moody said as he and Garniss leaped back on the truck bed. Valclav shed his parka, tossed it to the still-dazed Eduard, and jumped into the driver's seat. Dr. Shebanin sat erect in the cab, staring straight ahead and saying nothing. Valclav drove carefully down onto the pack and began picking his way across it, dodging the larger chunks of ice. Snyder manned the DF and called directions from the truck bed.

"Stop here!" Makarov shouted to his driver, who was seated forward and just below him in the BTR. From the turret, he trained a mounted searchlight down onto the fresh tracks that left the road for Obornyy

Spit. As they made the swing from the main road, he could clearly see the ruts made by the single front tires and the dual rear ones—it had to be the truck.

"Turn here," he ordered. "Follow these tracks." The BTR charged down the side road, the eight tires biting easily into the fresh snow.

At the airfield at Kachalovka, the snow-covered apron was littered with recent arrivals. The Mi-24P Hind-F gunships and Mi-8 Hip-C troop carriers waited patiently while fuel bowsers passed among them. Colonel General Borzov, however, was not waiting patiently. The Lumbovskiy facility had no tactical HF capability, so he still had no radio communication. He stormed up to the control tower in search of a telephone, and after only a short delay, was put through.

"Major Alksnis speaking."

"Major, this is General Borzov. Where is Colonel Makarov?"

Alksnis briefed him on the situation and the reason for Makarov's absence.

"And the name of the scientist who left the facility, Major?"

"Dr. Shebanin, sir. I have instructed my men at the gate to notify me immediately when she returns, but so far I have heard nothing."

"Very well, Major. A detachment of SPETSNAZ will arrive within the hour by helicopter. Be prepared to receive them and to place yourself under the orders of their senior officer."

"Yes, General."

Borzov returned to the helicopters. He quickly briefed the troop commander and the air squadron leaders. One company would deploy to Lumbovskiy and another to Gremikha. Most of the gunships were to remain on call at Kachalovka.

"However, I will take a company of men with me, along with two gunships. We will search along the coastal road to the east from Lumbovskiy." The men saluted and scattered to their machines.

"Everybody okay?"

"Okay here, Boss."

"I'm fine."

"I think my ass is broke—I'm sure of it."

"You'll live, Doc. How're you two up front?"

Katrina gave Valclav a forced smile. "We're all right, sir," he called up to Moody, "but I think the truck's done."

They were high-centered on a three-foot drop-off, and the nose of the truck was buried into a large ice boulder. Steam from the broken radiator frosted the front windshield and obscured the hood. Valclav had seen the ledge but had been unable to stop in time. Garniss and Snyder were quickly out of the back of the truck and scouting ahead.

"The truck wouldn't do us any more good anyway, Boss," reported Snyder. "We got a rotten section of ice here. It'll probably hold us, but I doubt it'll support much more."

"How far?"

"Hard to say," said Snyder, returning to the truck. "The signal's getting strong—shouldn't be more than a half mile, if that far."

"Okay, we take everything. Get the *akio* down and let's get it loaded. Snyder, you and Garniss move on ahead and find the DF. The rest of us will follow your tracks. When you find it, show us a light and bring us in."

It took them less than five minutes to load the *akio* and leave the crippled truck. The pack was too rough for skis, so they shuffled on through the darkness on snowshoes. Katrina had none, so she stumbled along behind them in the tracks made by the others, helped by Walker, who remained at her side. Moody struggled as he pulled the little sled across the broken pack ice while Valclav pushed. Several times they had to lift it up or down a rift in the ice. Ten minutes later, he paused to catch his breath and saw a red dot flashing ahead and to his left.

"Almost there, guys," he called. "Let's hump!"

Garniss met them halfway and brought them in. All seven formed a silent circle about the steel shaft that protruded up through the ice. It was hard for any of them to believe that an American submarine rested just two feet below.

"Let's get it done," Moody said, moving them from their reverie. "There's hot coffee and Navy chow down there." The mast was tapered, like a fat airplane wing with the narrow end pointing to the stern of the sub—and to the escape trunk. Garniss paced off thirty feet in that direction and set his pack down.

"Got it marked, Bob?"

"Yes, sir."

Moody took his MP-5 from his shoulder and banged the barrel against the mast—*CLANG-CLANG-CLANG-CLANG.* A few minutes later, they felt a slight rumbling underfoot and the mast slid cleanly back through the ice. The *Archerfish* drifted back down and again rested on the floor of the Barents Sea. While the others unloaded the *akio,* Walker worked with Katrina, talking with her in a patient and reassuring voice.

Walker came from dry-farming people in southwest Arkansas, and had never laid eyes on salt water until he was a junior in high school. His aunt died, and the family had driven clear to Galveston for the funeral. The sparkling blue waters of the Gulf of Mexico changed him forever. He joined the Navy right after graduation, knowing he didn't want to just go to sea—he wanted to be in it. The only way he could get diver training out of boot camp was to put in for SEALs. Walker was Bravo Platoon's diving petty officer. He also had become a licensed NAUI and PADI civilian instructor, and regularly taught scuba classes at the Lynnhaven

Dive Shop in Virginia Beach. He had certified several hundred sport scuba divers. Now he had less than fifteen minutes to teach this terrified Russian woman what she would need to know to dive through a hole in the ice and into the escape trunk of a submarine. If she panicked or failed to do exactly as she was told, she would die clawing for air on the bottom of the pack ice, or if she was lucky, of a massive air embolism as she tried to fight her way back to the surface.

"What's your name, ma'am?" he said slowly.

"Shebanin."

"Your first name, ma'am."

"Katrina."

"Okay, from now on, you call me Don and I'll call you Katrina. When you're in America, everyone's going to call you Katie. Okay if I call you Katie?"

She nodded.

"Great. Katie, in a minute we're going to put on our cold-water suits. Here, let me show you one." He pulled one of the drysuits from a pile by the *akio.* It was a vinyl-covered pair of overalls with a waterproof zipper up the front and attached booties. There were soft neoprene skirts around the neck and wrist openings that would form watertight seals. Walker was speaking slowly and carefully, and he had all but lost his southern accent. "Now this will keep you warm and dry when you're in the water. Y'all can wear the clothes you have on, and just pull the suit over them, okay? Now, to keep your hands warm, we have these rubber mittens, and for your head, this hood. Water will come into the hood and mittens—that's okay. It'll be a little cold, but before it gets too cold, we'll have you inside."

O'Keefe was taking protective caps from the valve stems of a half-dozen small, steel, wire-wrapped bottles, and carefully fitting scuba regulators to the valves. "This is crazy," he muttered. "We're done for." He gauged each minitank to make sure it had a charge. "We're out of our fucking minds." The bottles were no bigger than a three-cup thermos, and would allow a diver eight to ten minutes underwater. The regulators were standard Navy two-stage, single-hose models. The first stage had been filled with glycol so they would function in the cold water.

"Katie, this is your air supply and mouthpiece. Here, put it in your mouth and try it . . . no, the whole thing . . . that's it. Great . . . now take another breath . . . in—out . . . you got it!"

Walker showed her how to wear the face mask, and ensured that she had a proper seal. Then he briefed her carefully on the procedure they would use to take her down to the sub. Her only job was to try to relax and breathe normally. They would guide her down and into the air lock. "It'll be strange and a little scary," he told her, "but you have to relax, remember to breathe normally, and most of all—you have to trust me.

"Now, one more thing before we get ready to go. If your ears start to hurt, like when you're getting ready to land in an airplane, you have to hold your nose and blow to pop them. Let's try it." With the mask and regulator in place, she was able to pinch her nose and pop her ears.

"Okay, frog-lady, y'all are ready to go." He glanced over her shoulder to Valclav and O'Keefe, who were slipping into their suits. Suddenly, a huge shudder ran through her and she began to weep softly.

"Hey—hey, what's the matter?"

"I'm so afraid. Maybe I should just stay here and let them capture me." She buried her face in her hands and continued to sob.

"Katie. Katie, look at me." He pulled her hands away from her face. "We got you this far, didn't we? Well, we're not about to let you go when we're this close. You're one of us now, and we don't leave teammates behind. I can't promise that you won't be afraid, but I will promise that if you do just what I've told you, we'll be laughing about this over a cup of hot tea in just a little while. Okay? Are y'all with me?"

"Just b-breathe," she managed.

"And?"

"And relax."

Some voice inside Walker told him this woman desperately needed a hug, and that's what he did. "Y'all gonna do just fine—I promise. Everything'll be just fine."

"I hate to break this up," said Moody, "but we have to get moving. Looks like we have some company."

Both Walker and Katrina looked up to see a set of headlights off to the south picking their way across the pack ice. They stopped about where the group had abandoned the truck twenty minutes earlier.

The BTR-80 had a night observation device, but it was a crude, first-generation optic. Makarov saw some movement, and he could tell the group had stopped, but little else. He could take them under fire from here with the heavy 14.5mm machine gun, but that would do little but keep their heads down. And if they were going after them, it would endanger his own men and slow their own pursuit. Besides, she might be with them, and he wanted her alive.

"Damn," he shouted to the driver. "Are you sure we can go no farther?"

"This vehicle weighs fourteen thousand kilos, Colonel. We were lucky to come this far without going through."

"Sergeant, get your men ready to move out. We're going after them. They should be easy enough to follow."

"We're ready to move when you are, Colonel. I talked with the truck driver. He says there's at least five of them and they're well armed. He also says there's a woman with them."

"I knew it!" Makarov shouted as he banged the side of the turret with his fist. *That arrogant, traitorous bitch! Before I turn her over to her friend the General, I'll have my way with her. Maybe when I'm finished, the whole squad will take their turn.* He leaped to the ground among the OMON troopers. They were armed with AKMs, grenades, and side arms. Makarov carried only a pistol. "They've broken a good trail for us. We'll move quickly in single file, and then approach on a skirmish line when we get closer. Sergeant, select a couple of men and take the point." *We have to move quickly, and there's always the danger of an ambush,* Makarov thought. *It will be better if I follow a short distance behind.*

After the BTR turned out his lights, Moody put away his binoculars and pulled on his NOD goggles. There was a file of men working their way along the path they had just made. The men following could move rapidly, for the snow was well trampled and they appeared to be traveling light.

"Anytime, Bob," he called over his shoulder. "They're moving our way, and fast."

Garniss was working his way back to where the mast had been, unreeling wires from a small spool. "Just a few minutes, boss. I screw this up, and we'll have to race them on foot out to the open water." He had just laid a three-foot circle-shaped charge on top of the pack ice directly over the escape trunk of the *Archerfish.* The total weight of the explosives was under ten pounds, but it was powerful enough to cut a hole in a two-inch sheet of steel plating. It would also cut a hole in a two-foot layer of ice. Garniss had set a blasting cap into the molded Semtex explosive before playing out the firing lead. He was now testing his firing circuit. Then he attached the wires to a small hellbox that would detonate the cap.

"Okay, Boss, here we go. Fire in the hole—fire in the hole!"

Everyone hugged the ice. Walker pushed Katrina down and covered her with his body. The blast was deafening, and the shock wave punched each of them like a blow to the stomach. Garniss and Moody were up and running amid the clumps of ice and snow that had been blown into the air. They both arrived to find a neat, clean circle had been carved into the ice. There was a layer of crushed ice floating on the water, like the surface of a giant frozen daiquiri.

"Gawd, ain't that purty," said Garniss.

"It's beautiful," replied Moody, "but we better get moving. They'll be on top of us in no time."

Aboard the *Archerfish,* the explosion sounded like a firecracker inside a metal corncrib. It was expected, but everyone jumped nonetheless. It also signaled that they would be taking personnel aboard very soon. Early on, during the planning, they had talked about taking the team members aboard while the sub was nestled up under the pack ice, but Griffin had overruled them, saying that buoyancy control would be too delicate while the escape trunk was flooded and cleared as the men were brought aboard. The boat had only so much compressed air in her flasks, and Griffin felt they could more quickly and efficiently cycle the team through the trunk if the boat stayed on the bottom.

"Skipper, just got another coded message off the ELF. They say Russian naval units are converging on our location."

"Charming," Griffin deadpanned. "Simply fucking charming. Graham, let's get those buddies of yours aboard and get the hell out of Dodge."

He wasn't needed in the control room, so Smith went back aft to supervise the operation of the escape trunk.

Snyder was again the point man. He pulled the neoprene hood over his head and slipped on his face mask. He was already seated on the ice with his flippers on and his feet dangling into the hole. O'Keefe handed him the bitter end of a nylon climbing rope and he popped through the hole. They had trained on this in Greenland, and the ice entry was nothing new, but they had never had a real submarine to work with. The water was dark and clear, and the visibility excellent. Lights had been rigged running aft along the deck from the sub's conning tower to the stern planes, with a lighted circle around the escape trunk. They looked like the lights that ran along the floor of a commercial airliner to guide passengers to the emergency exists. Snyder glided down onto the deck of the *Archerfish* like a *Star Trek* shuttle craft making a landing on the *Enterprise.* It took him less than a minute to make it to the escape trunk and half that time to secure the line to a pad-eye on the deck near the trunk. He gave two sharp pulls and felt the slack go out of the line.

On the pack ice, O'Keefe pulled the line taut and secured it to an auger by the side of the hole. "Line's secure, Don."

"Okay, Doc. We'll give him five minutes to clear the trunk, and then we go." While they waited, Valclav and O'Keefe threw the radios and anything else that would sink into the hole. Each man would deep-six his own weapon before he went down the line.

Snyder's job was done. He pulled open the hatch of the escape trunk and slipped inside. It was like loading the man in the cannon at the county fair. He spun the wheel to dog the hatch down on top of him. It was a tight fit, but the chamber was designed to hold a large man wearing a Stanke escape hood. Snyder quickly found the lever that cracked a valve, allowing high-pressure air into the top of the trunk, and forced the water out from a drain in the bottom. When the trunk was empty, he closed the air valve and banged on the side of the chamber with a wrench that was tied by a thong to the side of the chamber for that purpose. Inside, a crew member closed the drain and began depressurizing the trunk. A moment later, the hatch at the bottom of the trunk cylinder opened, and Snyder climbed down into the bright interior of the sub.

"Welcome aboard, Snyder."

"Hey, Mr. Smith—glad to be aboard."

"How're things topside?"

"Not good, sir. The Russians are a few hundred yards out, and there are seven of us."

"Seven!"

"Yes, sir, and that isn't the half of it."

About two hundred and fifty yards from their position, the OMON squad fanned out on a skirmish line. It was too dark for them to see exactly where their quarry was, but they had a vague idea. They began to move forward cautiously, firing periodically in the team's general direction. Makarov hoped for some return fire so he could pinpoint their location by the muzzle flashes, but there were none. He stayed about twenty yards behind the line, calling encouragement to either flank.

An occasional round whined over their heads, but they stayed low and watched. Moody, Garniss, and Valclav peered out at the oncoming Russians and readied their weapons. Moody and Valclav watched them with their NODs, while Garniss tracked them through a Litton M-485 night scope mounted on his M-14. They held their fire, but the soldiers were becoming bolder with the lack of resistance, sweeping toward them at a faster pace.

O'Keefe dropped into the hole at Walker's direction, with his elbows resting on the side. "Okay, Don, I'm ready." He slipped through the hole. Walker helped Katrina to the edge of the hole and sat her down with her feet in the water.

"You see," he said brightly, "your feet don't even get wet."

"D-Don?"

"What is it, Katie?" They had to move quickly now.

"I—I can't swim!"

Walker looked at her. *Oh, really! This is a helluva time to tell me!* "I know that," he said sincerely. "If you needed to know how to swim, do y'all think I would allow you to do this? Remember, relax and breathe." Carefully, he set the mask on her face and pushed the regulator into her mouth. He watched her take two breaths and lifted her gently into the water.

O'Keefe felt her slip through the ice. With one hand on her ankle, he began to gently pull her down the line. Walker came through the ice headfirst, right behind her. A second later he was facing her, face mask to face mask, as they descended. He had a waterproof penlight that he flicked occasionally in her face, but for the most part he shined it on his own face so she would have a visual reference.

Katrina was past being terrified. *I have no choice—I have to do this,* she told herself again and again. Dr. Shebanin, the scientist, rationally assured herself that it was a matter of self-control—that if she put her emotions on hold and did exactly as she was told, there would be little danger. These Americans were highly trained professionals who knew what they were doing. But the person inside—the woman—was almost paralyzed with fear. While she commanded herself to go through the motions and do as she was told, she was never far from absolute panic. *Oh, dear God, don't let me die in this cold, black place!*

Walker watched her closely. About twenty feet down, her eyes widened in fear, then she squinted as if she were in pain. He gripped the line to stop the decent. When she didn't react, he dropped the regulator from his mouth and replaced it with the penlight, shining it in her face. Then, with his legs wrapped around her, he slid his two index fingers under her mask and pinched her nose. Suddenly, she remembered and blew, popping her ears. The pain was instantly gone, and at that precise moment, she knew she could make it—that it would be all right. She nodded her head to Walker, who shined the light on himself and gave her a big smile before replacing his regulator. Once again, O'Keefe began to tow them to the escape trunk. They paused once more to clear her ears before they reached the deck of the sub.

O'Keefe slipped into the trunk first, found the air valve and wrench, and began to ease Katrina in with him. It was a tight fit, but O'Keefe was not a big man. He slid his bottle from the Velcro keeper on his chest and tucked it under his armpit to save a few inches. Walker kept the light on them, and she was able to help to wriggle herself into the trunk with O'Keefe. They were in a lovers' embrace and terribly cramped, but her head was below the hatch. Walker tossed the light inside and slammed the hatch. As fast as she was breathing, he knew she had to be very close to exhausting her air flask.

Inside the trunk, Katrina became only slightly less terrified than when she had entered the water. The water drained past her shoulders, but the noise of the high-pressure air was deafening, and there was a dense fog created by the expanding air.

"It's okay! You're gonna be just fine!" O'Keefe yelled over the metallic hiss of the expanding air.

Then she panicked. *I can't breathe—so close and I'm out of air!* Then O'Keefe managed to get a hand up to jerk the regulator from her mouth, and she greedily gulped the cold, moist air. Her ears popped on their own as they were depressurized. Then the floor dropped away, but O'Keefe held her while many hands from below eased her down out of the trunk.

In the bright light of the interior, an incredibly handsome officer gallantly helped her to a stool.

"Welcome aboard the USS *Archerfish,* miss," he said. *Are they all this good-looking,* she wondered vaguely, and then she fainted.

"Quit gawkin' and cycle that damn trunk," O'Keefe shouted as he pulled the hatch closed behind him. "There's a man up there very low on air."

On the deck of the submarine, Walker was concerned but not worried. He was an accomplished diver, and very comfortable in the water. Every fifteen seconds he exhaled, took a short breath, and held it. It took just a few minutes to fill the trunk. Water was allowed back in through the drain, while the air was bled into a storage tank. When the pressure in the trunk was equal to that of the seawater outside, Walker opened the hatch and slid inside.

The OMON troopers were about seventy yards from the team's position and coming fast when Valclav slipped through the hole.

"Last time I'm gonna ask, sir. After you?"

"And for the last time, Bob, not a chance."

"Aye, aye, sir. Just remember what we talked about on the flight down from Greenland. And here, you might need this." Garniss tossed him the M-14 with the night scope, and began to scramble into the last diving suit. "That little slotted lever on the trigger guard, sir—it's the safety."

"I know where the fuckin' safety is, Bob. Get the hell outta here!"

Makarov's men knew about where they were, and their rounds were digging into ice nearby and cracking close overhead. Moody could hear a *snap* from the sonic wave as the rounds zipped by. Garniss was now ready, and Moody knew he'd need covering fire if he were to safely reach the hole. *Wave a white flag,* he thought, *give me a break!*

A grenade exploded fifteen yards in front of them, and he knew he couldn't wait any longer. While Garniss slithered over and pulled himself headfirst through the hole, Moody calmly lined up one of the forms moving toward him in a crouch. The figure glowed in the scope behind the black crosshairs. The rifle jumped, and the form pitched forward facedown in the snow. He took one more of them down and the line of men ceased to move. Moody glanced at his watch, wanting to give Garniss a few more minutes to cycle through the trunk. He could hear a man yelling, trying to rally his troops. Through the night scope, Moody could see a large man in a tanker's hat on one knee with a pistol in his hand. He was slightly behind the others, urging them forward. Moody put the crosshairs on his chest and squeezed. An instant later, the 165-grain, 7.62 round tore through his heart and toppled him over on his back. Then everything changed.

The first helicopter gunship came in low across the ice, spitting flame from its chin turret. A split second after Moody heard the rotor beat, the ice and snow erupted around him. He sat there dazed but unhurt. A heavy-caliber round had struck the scope on the M-14 and all but severed it from the rifle. Then a flare burst overhead, turning night into day. A second helo lightly touched down no more than fifty yards away and began to disgorge men. There was nothing tentative about these soldiers. They cleared the helo and began running toward him, firing on the move. A second gunship was rolling in on him. The hole in the ice was fifteen feet away. He took two strides toward it and slid the last few feet on his face. There was a brief, burning pain in his leg as an AKM round tore through his calf, but it was quickly forgotten as the icy grip of the Barents Sea claimed his entire body.

Under the ice, Moody could see the blurred lights below. *It's not that far,* he told himself. *But if that trunk's not clear, the game's over.* He had managed to straddle the line and hook a leg around it, allowing him to slide headfirst down toward the sub. Each purchase was increasingly difficult as the feeling left his hands. *They say freezing's not a bad way to go,* he reflected as he searched for the next handful of line. *I'm close—here's the circle of lights around the trunk. Hey, the hatch's open—that shouldn't be.* The cold and the lack of oxygen were making it almost as hard to think as it was to move. Then a pair of hands grabbed him and stuffed him in the escape trunk. A regulator was jammed into his mouth, and basic diver training took over. He took two breaths and surrendered the regulator. The hatch banged closed over his head, and a glow inside the trunk led his hands to the air valve. A moment later he sucked the cold fog into his lungs, and he knew he would live. He even managed a smile as he saw Garniss's penlight tied to the air-valve lever. When they helped him down from the trunk, O'Keefe saw the blood from his leg and began shouting orders to anyone who would listen.

A few minutes later, Garniss dropped through the trunk into the submarine. "Hi, guys—yo, Mr. Smith. How y'doin', sir?"

Lieutenant Commander Smith quickly shook his hand and reached for the boat's intercom. "Last man aboard, Captain. Escape trunk secure."

"Very well." A moment later there was a shuddering underfoot as the *Archerfish* came off the bottom and began making her way back to the edge of the pack ice.

Moody lay on a padded table in the submarine's small sick bay. He had been stripped of the wet clothing and wrapped in warm blankets. O'Keefe and the boat's chief corpsman worked on his leg, dressing it and applying compression bandages. The chief was certified for independent duty and highly skilled. Nonetheless, a jurisdictional dispute raged between the chief and O'Keefe over whose patient he was. Then the door flew open and there stood Garniss, dripping water and wearing a big grin.

"Don't you ever follow orders?"

"Sometimes. Did you get a couple of them?"

Moody nodded. "Three of them."

"Aw-right, Boss!" He crouched and made a piston motion with his fist and forearm. "But wait a minute—I left you a twenty-round magazine."

"When the helicopters and the other troops arrived, I decided to call it quits." Moody held a cup of hot tea, but he was still shaking so badly, he spilled some as he tried to get it to his mouth.

Garniss stepped over and steadied it for him while he drank. "Hey, Chief," he said to the corpsman, "you got a few officers on this tub. How about sending down to the wardroom for a cup with a nipple on it."

Moody chuckled and looked over Garniss's shoulder to see the drawn, white face of Dr. Katrina Shebanin. She smiled weakly and mouthed "thank you." Then a sailor gently led her forward.

The *Archerfish* made her way under the pack ice on a course of zero-one-five at a speed of three knots.

"Range and bearing to the edge of the pack?"

"Estimated range three thousand yards, Captain. Estimated bearing zero-three-five."

"Very well."

Griffin sat in his chair and slowly shifted the unlit cigar stub from one side of his mouth to the other. There was two-day stubble on his chin, and his hair was matted and uncombed. Yet there was a strange calm about him. He was relaxed. The pack ice was now like their mother's apron. They were safe here because nothing could come after them as long as they stayed there. But the longer they waited to come out, the more Russian surface ships and hunter-killer subs would converge on the area. At this speed, they would clear the pack in thirty minutes.

"What do you think, Graham?"

Smith studied the plotting table and chewed his lip. "Our best chances are to make for international water as soon as possible. The odds are against us if we wait."

Griffin nodded.

"And we have to assume that our Akula or one of his friends is waiting for us out there, and that they know exactly where we were ninety minutes ago."

"And we're one hour or three hours from international waters, depending on whose definition you use. Still a long way, no matter how you cut it. How do we shake them?" Griffin was now the professor, challenging a bright pupil.

Smith looked up from the chart. "We launch a MOSS from under the pack ice and have it come out ahead of us." The MOSS, an acronym for mobile submarine simulator, was a torpedo with a noise-generating transducer that could be programmed to simulate another submarine.

"And?"

"We launch the MOSS well back in the pack so they can't hear the transient from the torpedo firing. Make it simulate a 637-class boat at four knots—very quiet. They might just believe that one of our Sturgeon boats could operate under the pack ice in this shallow water. Then, as we approach the edge of pack, we turn and run under the ice parallel to shore until we're clear. Then turn back north for the open water. We can follow the edge of the pack ice at pretty good speed, since they'll not be able to pick us up because of the background noise."

"Turn left or turn right?"

"They'd expect us to turn left and head back for the North Cape. I'd turn right. We're only about twenty-five miles from the shipping channels that lead into the White Sea. Maybe we can follow some merchant traffic out into deep water."

Griffin sat there without moving for several minutes. "All right, that's what we'll do. Have the torpedomen set the MOSS to run straight at four knots and radiate like a 637 boat. We'll follow it to the edge of the pack, come right to a westerly heading, and sprint for the mouth of the White Sea."

Smith gave a string of orders while the control-room watch went about their duties with a sense of purpose. Five minutes later, the torpedo room reported the MOSS had been programmed and they were ready to fire.

"Very well," Smith replied. He had laid down a track for the false target as well as for the *Archerfish.* "We're all set, Captain. Recommend we launch the MOSS in seven minutes, forty-five seconds and follow it for another two and a half minutes. Then come right to one-two-five. Once we're steady on course, recommend we come up to twelve knots and stay about two hundred yards inside the edge of the pack."

Griffin stepped over to the plotter and looked at the projected tracks of the MOSS and his boat. He looked at Smith and nodded curtly. Then he turned to the watch section.

"This is the Captain. The XO has the con."

"This is the XO—I have the con."

The watch section acknowledged the change of conning officers, calling out their present course, speed, and depth, while the *Archerfish* crept northward to the edge of the pack ice.

"Question, Captain?"

"Ask."

"Is this course of action what you had in mind?"

Griffin was again silent for a moment. "No, it isn't. I'd send the

MOSS out ahead of us, and then lie on the bottom outside the pack and listen. If there's a Russian fast-attack out there, he'll find out soon enough that we've sent him a decoy, and he'll probably run along the pack ice looking for us. Don't forget, he's got more than a two-to-one speed advantage, and he can run us down pretty quickly." Griffin slowly scratched the stubble under his chin. "No, I'd wait until Ivan left the area to look for us down the coast. Then I'd go quietly straight north to international waters."

Smith looked at him sideways. "Then why are we doing it my way?"

"Because if *I* were Ivan, I wouldn't take the bait. *I* wouldn't run the coast looking for us. I'd let the MOSS go by, and sit right there and wait for us to come to him. You see, that Russian skipper could be an old dog like me. Maybe he won't flush. Maybe he'll hold his position and wait for us. If that's the case, then you're making the right call."

"I see," said Smith slowly, but he was not sure he did.

"One minute to the launch, sir!"

"Very well," Smith replied. "Flood the tube and open outer doors. Stand by to shoot on my command."

The control room of the *S-592* was quiet as a tomb. Just a few hours ago she had been racing at flank speed from her training station off Murmansk to reach the pack ice just off the Lumbovskiy Inlet. She had made the two-hundred-mile transit in just under six hours. Once she had arrived, Fleet Headquarters in Severomorsk advised them there was definitely an American submarine under the pack ice in the vicinity of Lumbovskiy Inlet. Now the *S-592* patrolled an area ten miles out from the pack. Captain Molev would have liked to move closer, but he was leery of the shallow water. His Akula was a very large attack submarine. Also, by remaining farther offshore, he could sweep a larger section of coastline with his passive array. The *S-592* was steaming in a flat figure-eight pattern, making two knots when her bow was pointed toward the pack, and kicking it up to eight knots when it wasn't.

That American captain must be insane to take his boat into such tight quarters. That, or he must have had a very compelling reason to do so. Four sonarmen sat at their consoles, watching and listening. The control-room watch went about their duties like a group of professional mourners. There was little conversation. Molev stood behind his lead sonar operator, smoking quietly.

"Something . . ." Petty Officer Yashkin said, pressing his headphones against the side of his head. "Yes!" He began tuning his equipment. Soon there was a pattern to the faint shadows that worked across his screen, but he concentrated on the sound.

"So!" Molev said impatiently. Yashkin raised his hand for silence. Only a sonar operator could do that to the Captain.

"Yes! Bearing three-zero-five relative."

Molev looked to the OOD. "Come left sixty degree, slowly." The OOD nodded and relayed the command quietly to his helmsman. The seconds dragged by. Finally Yashkin pulled one earpiece away and looked up at his Captain.

"It's American. The shallow depth makes it difficult to tell, but it sounds like a 637-class boat. About twelve thousand yards and closing. He's moving north from under the pack ice at four knots."

"Very well," Molev replied, turning to his *Starpom.* "Plot a course to intercept."

"At once, Captain."

Molev returned to his seat and mentally calculated the time to intercept. *Unless he changes course and speed, we will have him in a little more than an hour. And he'll still be well inside our territorial waters!* But something told Molev it was all wrong. The American Sturgeon class was much smaller than the *S-592,* but it was still a blue-water nuclear submarine—well over four thousand tons. *What's a boat that size doing in there! It doesn't make sense.*

"This is the Captain, I have the con. Periscope depth—all ahead flank. Make turns for thirty knots. Let's take a closer look at this American." The control room became a flurry of activity.

At this speed, they would intercept the contact in twelve minutes. Molev took the boat to periscope depth as a precaution while sprinting in shallow water. The disadvantage of speed was that he could not listen while moving that quickly, and he clearly announced his presence to any enemy boat listening for him. Five minutes later, he brought the boat down to eight knots.

"Do you have him?"

"Yes, Captain. It's still an American 637 moving at four knots on a course of zero-one-zero. Range is five thousand yards. Wait a minute . . . something's wrong . . . Captain, I'm not getting a proper frequency range for a 637."

Just as I thought. "Go active!"

"Yes, sir."

PING!

A moment later, Yashkin looked up. "Decoy, sir. We're tracking a simulator."

"Very well. Secure from active search."

So they've chosen to run along under or close to the pack ice before coming out—or have they? Molev took several slow, thoughtful laps around the control room. Then he turned to the OOD.

"Mr. Markin, you have the con. Rig for silent maneuvering and take us back to our original position at four knots. I don't think he's come out yet. We'll go back and listen for him."

* * *

Neither the Barents Sea nor the approaches to the White Sea are particularly deep, but the *Archerfish* had been designed for shallow-water operations. Nonetheless, it was almost two hours before the water consistently registered deeper than two hundred feet. A channel cut by the icebreaker *Vaygach* several days ago was still usable. They found a convenient tanker outbound from Archangel and followed it to open water. Early Monday evening, Griffin brought the boat to periscope depth and told the anxious listeners in Washington and Florida that they were in international waters with everyone safely aboard. It was later that night, well after they had turned west, before they felt safe enough to snorkel for an hour. It would take them the better part of two days to make Norway and the North Cape.

They were back to a three-section steaming watch, and Griffin again sat in his chair chewing a cigar. For the second time in less than an hour, the OOD had chased Garniss out of the control room.

"Contact! Sir, I have screw noises . . . three-three-zero relative. He's pretty close!"

Griffin was quickly behind him. "How close, Magee, how close?" *Crap! after all we've been through—they've found us out here.*

"Hold on, sir." Magee listened carefully, then a smile split his face. "It's one of ours, Captain—a 688 boat." Tension went out of the control room like a punctured air mattress. "And you're not gonna believe this, sir." He pulled the headphones around his neck and turned to Griffin. "It's the *Atlanta.*"

EPILOGUE

Moscow

Foreign Minister Vladimir Solovyov sat at the restaurant patiently waiting for Ambassador Joseph Simpson to arrive. Moscow was a far cry from Paris or London, but there were now a few establishments that were serious candidates for a four-star rating. Solovyov had spent enough time grazing in foreign capitals to appreciate fine dining. He and Simpson fenced spiritedly about the time and place of the meeting in preparation for who would control the agenda. Since the Ambassador was making him wait, he countered by ordering a wine without consultation.

Simpson arrived, with appropriate apologies. He made a neutral comment about the wine and they ordered dinner. Over the meal, they casually picked at the Balkans and the Mideast. By convention, the subject of their meeting would be reserved for coffee and cognac. Solovyov and Simpson had become close friends over the years, but it was a friendship based on a clear understanding of their respective duties and responsibilities. Both appreciated that the tone and substance of their conversation would form the basis of future policy between their two nations.

"Joseph, this business up in the Kola almost got out of hand. President Stozharov was most upset that a small invasion force was placed on Russian soil."

"I can understand that. President Bennett clearly felt that something had to be done. He's most adamant about halting the spread of nuclear weapons to the Third World."

"I see," replied Solovyov. "So what has this venture gained you? It has cost us the death of three Russian soldiers, one of them a senior officer."

"We now have conclusive proof of the allegations Secretary of State

Noffsinger made during his visit in early December." Simpson laid a folder on the table. "This is a synopsis of the weapons specifications and production statistics from the Lumbovskiy facility. It amply documents the manufacture of nuclear weapons specifically for export."

Solovyov ignored the folder. "If all this is true, where does that leave us? It still doesn't excuse a direct military incursion."

"Vladimir, this is an issue that President Bennett is prepared to pursue. He wants a full hearing before the U.N. Security Council. The Europeans will be outraged that you were preparing to sell nuclear weapons."

"So will a number of sovereign nations around the world—outraged that the United States has again put its troops on foreign soil."

Simpson smiled. "So what are you saying, Vladimir?"

"I'm saying that President Stozharov is prepared to overlook this small invasion, and to give your Mr. Bennett assurances that no nuclear weapons will be shipped from the Northern Military District."

"Only the Northern District?"

"Specifically the Northern District. It is the stated policy of the Russian Republic to oppose nuclear proliferation in any form, but these are difficult times in Russia. Can the President of the United States guarantee that the poor in some of your large cities are not going to take to the streets and riot this summer? We can only do so much."

"If I understand this, you are telling me that Russia will ship no nuclear weapons, and any violation of Russian sovereignty is a closed matter. It never happened."

"Correct."

Simpson sipped his cognac. "I will convey that proposal to my government. There may well be some basis for an agreement."

"Excellent," Solovyov replied as he signaled the waiter. "And since it is your turn to pay, I believe I'll inspect the dessert cart."

SEVEROMORSK

Colonel General Borzov sat at his desk and tried to concentrate on the operational training summaries and logistic status reports that detailed the health and capability of his forces. Since the incident at Lumbovskiy, things had become strangely quiet. Communication with Moscow was routine. At direction from the Central Military Command, the three dead soldiers had been reported as killed in a training accident. All units that had responded were back in garrison or in port, and ordered to treat the events in and around Lumbovskiy as classified information. Borzov himself expected to be summoned to Moscow and relieved of his duties—or worse. But so far, it had not happened.

He pulled open his top left-hand drawer and removed a letter. It was addressed to him personally, and posted several days earlier. He again took it from the envelope and read it slowly.

Dear General Borzov:

It is proper that I address you by your title, since as you read this I will be either out of Russia or dead, and in any case, no longer deserving of addressing you except by you title. Years ago I betrayed the Soviet Union to the West. I did so believing that I had a duty to try to stop the expensive and dangerous buildup of nuclear weapons. I believe what I did was right. I have again betrayed Russia, and you, by telling the West of my work at Lumbovskiy. Russia is not the Soviet Union, and I am not certain that what I have just done is a good thing. However, I had no choice.

My superior, Dr. Zhdanov, had no knowledge of my actions, nor did I give him any indication that I would attempt to defect. He is a loyal Russian, and a capable scientist and administrator. You should know that Dr. Zhdanov was being blackmailed by Colonel Makarov and forced to cooperate with him in a scheme to steal fuel shipments from the depot in Gremikha. Zhdanov was a pawn in the operation, and forced to sign for the fuel that Makarov has been selling for his own profit.

Thank you for your friendship, and deepest apologies for the pain my actions may cause you. Russia has become a struggle between men like yourself and the Colonel Makarovs. I hope you win. I also wish I could have done more.

Katya.

WASHINGTON

Major Brisco, Lieutenant Moody, and Sergeant Valclav were paraded at attention when the President and Morton Keeney entered the small but formal reception room in the basement of the White House. Each was an impressive representative from their branch of the armed forces. Bennett had insisted on the meeting, and Keeney had suggested something less conspicuous than the Oval Office.

"Please, stand at ease." Moody and Brisco relaxed a bit. Sergeant Valclav remained rigid in the presence of the Commander-in-Chief. To do otherwise would be like slouching in the presence of God. "Hey,"

Bennett said, putting a hand on his shoulder, "since we're the only two sergeants in the room, I can't relax unless you do, okay?"

"Sir, thank you, sir!" Valclav snapped to parade rest.

Bennett smiled and shook his head slightly. "Sergeant, I'm told that this operation was successful because you were able to contact Dr. Shebanin and convince her to help us."

"Sir, I only did my duty. Lieutenant Moody and the Major planned the mission. I was just proud to do my part."

"I see. Well, Sergeant, you're a fine soldier and a fine American. I'm proud to be your President, and I sincerely mean that."

Valclav snatched a look at the President, and saw that he was very earnest. "Sir, thank you, sir."

Bennett squeezed his shoulder and turned to Moody. "How's the leg, Lieutenant?"

"Healing well, thank you, sir."

"You did a fine job getting yourself and your team out of there. Tell me, do you always go swimming in cold water without your diving suit?"

"No, sir. Only when it's absolutely necessary."

"I understand it was. You Navy SEALs have a saying—something about yesterday."

"Yes, sir. The only easy day was yesterday."

"Well, let's hope the yesterdays don't get any more difficult. Major Brisco?"

"Yes, Mr. President."

"Congratulations on a job well done. General Thon tells me you are a highly capable and—now, how did he put it?—a most persistent officer. Even an old foot soldier like myself knows a good mission begins with a good plan. Thank you, and again, well done."

"Mr. President?"

"Yes, Major."

"I understand that after the information on the weapons was sent back by facsimile transmission, there was some talk of deliberately abandoning the team. Is that correct, sir?"

Moody stole a glance at Valclav, and they both rolled their eyes. The President thrust his hands into his pants pockets and regarded Brisco carefully. Morton Keeney cleared his throat, indicating he wanted to speak, but Bennett did not allow it.

"Major, I think there's a few things you need to understand. First of all, I understand your concern for your team. I share that concern, and it bothered me even to contemplate giving such an order. In this particular situation, I could see no clear purpose in the sacrifice of these men."

Brisco stared at him for a long minute. "Begging the Commander in Chief's pardon, sir, but just when *do* you see a clear purpose in it?"

Bennett looked at her sharply, then began to pace the small room.

"During World War Two, Winston Churchill allowed the Germans to bomb the town of Coventry when he had the ability to warn the townspeople about the raid. You see, he knew of the raid because the British had broken the Germans' secret code. The bombing resulted in the death of hundreds of civilians, but preserved England's secret ability to listen to coded Nazi messages. It had to be a terrible decision for Churchill, but he had to choose between the lives of citizens of Coventry and the fate of England. History suggests he chose well." Bennett again faced Brisco. "I hope I never have to give such an order, Major, but if I do, I'll expect people like you to carry it out—without question." Then he softened. "You can be sure that if such an order comes, it'll be because other American lives are at risk, and that I have no better alternative—fair enough?" He was looking directly at her, but speaking to everyone there.

"Fair enough, Mr. President."

After they left, Keeney turned to Bennett. "Lieutenant Moody and Sergeant Valclav look like they can handle themselves, but they're not in her league."

"No kidding," replied Bennett. "If we have a *really* tough mission facing us, let's parachute her in."

Boston

Linda Lewis sat at a Howard Johnson's just off Interstate 93. She was a case officer for the Department of Justice witness-relocation program. She was also assigned an occasional case involving a defector relocation, but defectors had become rare with the end of the Cold War. The witness business, however, was booming. For the most part, the defectors were just witnesses with a language difficulty. All of them had problems—alcohol problems, drug problems, family problems, medical problems—you name it. The witnesses were usually members of organized crime who had rolled over on the mob, and the defectors were traitors. Linda had a master's degree in psychology, so she knew something of dysfunctional personalities. Basically, she was a highly paid social worker.

Dr. Katrina Shebanin, or Catherine Lepana as she was now called, was different. Linda had met her only twice, but she quickly learned this was an independent and fiercely determined woman. Part of the relocation and settlement process involved finding the participants work. More often than not, the government paid fees or augmented the salary of the witness or defector to keep them employed. An engineering position was found for Shebanin at a polymer design firm outside of Boston. It was a small firm, run by two brothers who had developed a specialty plastics business for limited-production, injection-mold applications. Two weeks ago, the managing brother had called to say they were raising her salary and that they would require no further supplements. She was now their permanent employee.

A tall blond woman walked into the restaurant and looked around. Linda smiled and waved her over. She slid into the booth and signaled for coffee.

"You're looking well," she began. "How is life in America?"

"Marvelous, simply marvelous. You only have to work eight hours a day, and you make more money than you can spend. And spending it is a full-time job. There's so much to buy!"

"My information is that you're doing very well at work. We were concerned that the plastics business would be a little out of your field."

"Not really. They had some production problems I was able to help with. I'm quite familiar with molding processes and precision millwork."

"I see. And the new apartment?"

"It's wonderful! I have a sauna and a view of the lake, and everyone's so friendly. The pool will be open in May. You'll have to come for a visit."

"Thanks, I might just do that. Now, I understand that you made a four-day trip to New London to visit a certain submarine captain who was home on leave."

"Is that not permitted?"

Linda smiled. "It's permitted. Because of his position, Commander Griffin is required to report all contact with foreign nationals, so we were notified. Do you like him?"

Katrina thought for a moment. "Yes, I like him. But do I *really* like him?" She shrugged. "I am comfortable with him. He is very busy, with little time in his life for romance, I think."

"Like you?"

"Perhaps. He is very similar to Dmitri Borzov—I told you about him?" Linda nodded. "Jim Griffin is a good man, but he's dedicated to his submarines. His time for love will have to be scheduled around his work. Perhaps that is how it has become with me."

"If that is truly the case, Catherine Lepana, then you're going to do well in America."

Fic HQAF 476800
COUCH Couch, Dick,
Silent descent /
Dick Couch.